T0145688

HELLIFAX

Also by Keith C. Blackmore

Mountain Man

Mountain Man
Safari
Hellifax
Well Fed
Make Me King
Mindless
Skull Road
Mountain Man Prequel
Mountain Man 2nd Prequel: Them Early Days
The Hospital: A Mountain Man Story
Mountain Man Omnibus: Books 1–3

131 Days

131 Days
House of Pain
Spikes and Edges
About the Blood
To Thunderous Applause
131 Days Omnibus: Books 1–3

Breeds

Breeds
Breeds 2
Breeds 3
Breeds: The Complete Trilogy

Isosceles Moon

Isosceles Moon
Isosceles Moon 2

The Bear That Fell from the Stars
Bones and Needles
Cauldron Gristle
Flight of the Cookie Dough Mansion
The Majestic 311
The Missing Boatman
Private Property
The Troll Hunter
White Sands, Red Steel

MOUNTAIN MAN

BOOK 3

HELLIFAX

KEITH C. BLACKMORE

Podium

A special thank you to Eric Burke, Brad Burry, Mark E. Crouse, Ewart King, Ken Maidment, Rod Redden, Robert Richter, Miguel Tonnies, and Alexis Winning.

Cover design by Podium Publishing

ISBN: 978-1-0394-4986-2

Published in 2023 by Podium Publishing, ULC
www.podiumaudio.com

HELLIFAX

Prologue

They came from the west.

Three great cargo vans crossed the Ontario-Quebec border, threading the wide Trans Canada Highway as if driven by drunkards and blazing through the summer heat shimmers over the road.

Men with bad intentions filled the vehicles loaded with guns and supplies for a lengthy journey. Body armor and sports padding covered their frames in a patchwork that didn't always fit properly, bulking them up and widening their shoulders. Some wore helmets with face cages, while others had only visors spray-painted black on the outside, hiding their features. The men were well-built and strong, battered and scarred. Tattoos covered exposed flesh in red and black ink: dragons and chains, sickles and skulls, executioners and axes. Fearsome images etched across entire arms, spreading over shoulders and up the sides of faces like some horrible disease. Most of the men did not shave or cut their hair, in honor of the conquering Norsemen who had prowled the Atlantic centuries ago. They looked hard and possessed the stares of instigators and shit disturbers. All were born killers, once unaware of their true potential, which had been unleashed after the fall of civilization. They joked and guffawed amongst themselves, shoving shoulders and slapping backs like hungry bears taking fleshy swipes out of each other's hides. Sometimes, when they stopped for the night, the jokes would go too far, and fights would start. When that happened, the others would pull back and form a ring, allowing whoever was at odds to go at each other's throats with all the enthusiasm of rabid Dobermans, pissed beyond pissed. Two men had already been killed in such a way, practically sliced into bleeding ribbons. No doubt one or two more would go the same way before they returned to the west.

"Boys will be boys" was a favorite saying of Fist. He was perhaps the biggest, the strongest, and hands down the most *psychotic* of them all, and he regarded all of his companions as nothing more than meat that talked back—easily managed with a yank and a cut, if need be. That they took orders from him made no difference, and he knew more than one of them slept at night with knives in their hands, as he himself did, just in case. He didn't trust those walking husks of carrion feeders, and when he slept, it was usually in the van or in an apartment that could be locked. He didn't worry about them stealing the vans. Fear kept his minions in check, and he made it painfully clear that if any of them decided to run off with one of the vehicles, he'd find them. No matter how long it took, he'd sniff them out like a bloodhound on a mission from the Devil, even if the trail took him across boiling oceans and hateful volcanoes. He'd *find* them.

And skull-fuck the offenders with his Bowie knife.

Fear was power, and he'd learned that from the best. Fear kept them wary of opportunities. None of them feared the dead that walked the earth. The dead were easy to fight, easy to kill. The dead were nothing more than dried-up shit under the boots of empire makers. Fist was the first of many to come east. The east was the last great frontier in the new world. The last unknown. Fist had been sent east to *see* . . . and to report.

And thus far, he'd seen utter shit.

The east was *weak*.

Unorganized.

Ill-prepared for the chains of agony that would follow Fist's initial expedition.

The land was much the same as the rest of the world. The dead ruled it. The remaining pockets of humanity had shrivelled up like old men's scrotums after a dip in arctic waters. Fallout from nuclear reactors melting down after the power grid failed had ruined much of the earth. The same fallout withered survivors near the installations with the irradiated kiss of death. Fist and his crew avoided those places and the greater cities. They headed east to look not only for safe havens, but pure, uncontaminated sustenance.

There was no Canada anymore. There were no States. There certainly was no North, Central, or South America. There was only land and warlords cutting out the new order from the bones of the old, stamping their sign on conquered territory, basking in anarchy, and lapping up lakes of blood.

There were only predators . . . and meat.

The three vans screamed over the crumbling grey of the highway, barreling down the strip like spray-painted missiles. The early fall sun glared at the travellers through the windshields. Fist sat in the passenger side of the first battle van, his dark eyes hooded and lazy. The long drives sometimes made him sleepy, and he resisted with a sharp shake of his head or a widening of his eyes. The asphalt stitch that was the Trans-Canada Highway shoved the forest back on both sides, splitting it wide. The tree line's red, brown, and gold held no beauty for him or his self-named Norsemen, and more than one of the warriors entertained thoughts of stopping and starting a fire.

Just for fun.

At first, Fist hadn't really wanted to go east. But he was chosen, and he wasn't ready to challenge the man who had given the order. Fist had gone along with it, keeping his true feelings to himself. Sending him east was probably just a way of getting rid of him, removing him from the power structure in favor of someone less intimidating, easier to control. Eventually, in the back of his mind, he realized the expedition just might give him the edge needed to take power over the Norsemen. It might provide him with useful weapons, perhaps even children to be raised as future raiders.

And over time, the more he thought about it, the more Fist's mind had changed about the journey.

The driver of one of the other vans honked a horn. The sound hooked Fist from his sleepy drifting, and he shook his head to clear it. He blinked his soot-blackened eyes and paused for a moment, hearing the horn once more.

"What is it?" he rumbled at the driver, leaning forward in his seat, his bass voice as sonorous and silky as a fine burning scotch. Some of the men believed Fist might only possess one lung or that he had suffered from some extreme upbringing where he had screamed incessantly. They were half right. After the Fall, when the wild things rose up, there was plenty to scream about, and every time Fist did, it shaved away a little more of his already frayed vocal chords until only bedrock remained.

"Don't know," Pell answered. He was a beast of a rig pig, once hailing from Red Deer. "My side window's gone, too."

Fist filled his lungs and sighed long and deep. "Pull over."

Pell decreased speed immediately. He wore no helmet while driving, and Fist wasn't above slamming his driver's head into the steering column.

Flexing his fingers, Fist studied the knuckles rippling underneath his skin as the seatbelt kept him in place. The van slowed to a stop. Releasing the belt, the Norseman leader took a breath and heaved himself out of the van. Doors opened all round as the rest of the pack jumped to the highway, stretching their legs and arms with guttural glee.

Heels clicking on the road, Fist sauntered past his dogs and glanced toward the trees once more. Something lay beyond the thin fence of autumn color. A golf course, perhaps?

Steam issued from the opened hood of one of their vans, and two bulky Norsemen stood to one side when their leader arrived.

"What is it?" Fist asked in Norse speak, which all of the clan strived to learn. The harsh-sounding syllables came out as the exposed motor tossed grey puffs into the air.

"Carburetor," Herman reported, his sooty features screwed up in distaste. He was the mechanic of the group.

"Then, fix it," Fist ordered, the words coming out as *Gur ee agh grum.*

"And try not to fuck it up any worse." That came from Murphy, a tall, almost skeletal jackal of a man. He grinned behind a face cage, yellow teeth set below grimy eyes and an anvil of a nose.

"Fuck off," Herman lipped back.

Murphy's darkened eyes went wide before a snarl twisted his mouth. He nodded, licked his lips, and shoved the mechanic. Herman shoved back.

Then they were swinging at each other amid undulating whoops and hollers.

Fist stood back and watched the two men punch and slam each other around for all of ten seconds. It wasn't a particularly entertaining fight as they both wore armor, but it was something to wake him up from the monotony of the long drive.

Murphy suddenly upended Herman and dumped him on his back. Murphy pounced, pinning the other man's arms to the road. A knife flashed up, the steel dull in the daylight.

A thought shot through Fist's mind. Herman is the only mechanic we have on this trip.

Just as Murphy stabbed downward, Fist stepped forward and batted a hand across the man's face, knocking him flat.

"Aren't too many mechs around," the Norseman leader growled. He pointed at both men on the ground. "Don't fuck around anymore, else I kick the shit outta both."

Fist focused entirely on Murphy. "Might not stop on you. You aren't a mech."

"Takin' that shit stain's side?" Murphy asked, sticking out his chin.

"Murph," Fist warned in a voice low enough to shake spines. "Shut up."

And like that, Murphy backed off like a dog snapped hard across the muzzle.

Fist directed his attention back to Herman, who climbed to his feet and got to work. The leader lingered for a moment, turning his hips in the direction of the golf course and scratching thoughtfully at his ribs. He'd never played, but he had beaten the brains out of several undead golfers with their own clubs almost a year ago. The memory made him smirk in an unpleasant way. He only wished he could've done the same thing back when the world was still the world.

Hands on his hips, Fist meandered back to the lead van. Men quieted as he passed, not daring to look him in the eye, only to resume talking once he was out of arm's reach. Beyond the vehicle, the TCH stretched out for perhaps another kilometer before being eclipsed by a hill. Fist struck a fearsome pose in his roughshod armor made from tire treads. He glared at the road and wished for something to kill. The urge was hard to control, and sometimes it just took him.

Movement caught his attention.

Not far away, on the other side of the highway, was a subdivision of houses with their backs to the road. Fist held his breath for a moment, staring at a series of fences that had crumpled over time. Things were moving over there.

"Shut the fuck up!" Fist barked without turning around, silencing the rest of the men.

There was no wind, and the sounds that reached them came from the line of houses. There, through a thin mesh of trees sad with dying leaves, he heard the unmistakable sound of moaning.

A second later, Fist zeroed in on a clump of figures laying siege to a two-story house. Fleshy slaps against the panel wood punctuated the crisp afternoon calm. A mob of undead ringed the walls, attempting to get inside. That only meant one thing.

There was someone alive inside.

"Cray!" Fist's voice boomed like arctic ice cracking. "Get ten lined up."

The man protected by a suit of riot gear starting shouting orders.

"Pell, you keep the others in line here. Protect the vans," Fist ordered his driver and went to the rear of his vehicle. He slapped at his armor and snapped his fingers until a hockey helmet with a face cage was handed to him. He strapped it on and snapped down the cage. Next came his maul, a frightening length of hickory with a hammer and blade head, chipped, scarred, and heavy. Fist took it with one hand from the Norseman inside the van, hefted it as if it weighed one pound instead of ten, and walked away while others mobbed the rear, searching for their own weapons. They possessed firearms of the brutish, short-range kind—sawed-off shotguns. They wore the weapons swinging in crude leather holsters on their thighs or slung over their backs.

Fist sniffed and wiggled a finger underneath his chinstrap, as the damn thing was a touch too snug. Placing the head of the maul down, he reached to his hip holster, pulled out his own sawed-off shotgun, and checked the load. He didn't want to fire the weapon unless absolutely necessary, as ammunition was limited. Besides, all one truly needed when fighting zombies was a line of men strong enough to hold formation and to keep on swinging once the reaping started. Across the highway, the undead clambered against the house, clawing at it as if exhausted, beating their limbs against windows which held, and wailing for whoever was inside to just open up so all the nasty business of feeding could be taken care of.

Weak, Fist thought.

The others gathered on either side of him, a wrecking line of brute force. Clubs, baseball bats, and axes rasped against the pavement. Tugging and checking of armor plates, padding, and leather bindings went on for a few seconds more. Fist allowed it, waiting for the mass of dead to smell them. He had to hand it to them; they could smell anything from a very long distance, and on a day like this, he was a little surprised they hadn't turned his way yet.

But then, they were quite stupid.

Not bothering to ask if his men were ready, Fist raked his maul across the asphalt and shouted, the sound frightening in the afternoon air. He did that twice more. Then he took a breath, sniffed, and tongued at an area in his mouth.

Some of the undead turned around and saw them, while others kept pawing at the house.

Fist marched forward, and his boys followed. Some of the men eyed their flanks, mindful of zombies coming at their sides, but the highway remained empty. More dead peeled away from the house, catching either scent or sound, and lurched toward the approaching meal. The fences stopped them, but then a section swung open and bodies flowed through. Fist gathered his maul two-handed, drawing a bead on the first walking corpse he would put down. He couldn't count how many were turning away from the house, and it didn't really matter. It wasn't an army, and it would take at least that to stop the Norsemen.

Fist stopped them at the edge of the pavement. The terrain favored them there, and he liked having solid ground underfoot. The line of undead stumbled down over an embankment and gathered like spilled dolls at the bottom. Almost comically, they tripped and fell over each other as they struggled to their feet.

"More this way," one of the Norsemen called. Fist and the others saw a thick group of walking carcasses, perhaps thirty or more, emerging from the backyard of another house and forcing their way through a veil of trees and clawing branches. They were nowhere near as close as the ones coming from the house.

Fist turned his attention to the first group. They had pulled themselves apart, stood up, and closed.

None of the living said a word. They stood with their leader and watched with readied weapons.

The tide of dead things was no more than ten feet away.

A power lineman in his yellow and red reflective vest grimaced as he walked unsteadily toward Fist. Its open mouth was a dark hole, pitted in the center of a bush of grey beard. Its thigh had been opened up to the bone. The creature beheld Fist in wide-eyed delight, and it took the Norseman a moment to realize that its lids had been chewed away.

Fist took its head off with one swing. His attack signaled for hell, and the ten other Norsemen swung and stabbed at the wall of undead. Zombies had their skulls staved in or removed from their shoulders. Some heads, rotten to the center, simply exploded in a shower of particles. An axe split a face to the neck while another drove a zombie to its knees. An accountant type had her arm removed at the shoulder and got kicked back into the advancing throng. Fist swung his maul in a steady rhythm, his great arms flexing as he bashed in faces and skulls, driving corpses to the ground with each powerful swing. The dead stumbled over the low wall of bodies forming at the line of men, then had their own bodies added to the barrier. The moaning grew, then broke into single voices.

Then nothing.

In less than two minutes, Fist and his men had chewed through a hundred of the dead things, give or take a dozen.

"More here," someone shouted. Fist shoved some of his men out of the way, not caring in the least what they thought about it. He took up a new position and waited for the zombies to arrive. His arms felt good, like after a hard, but not exhausting workout, and he was nowhere near out of breath. Around him, his boys formed a new line and faced the next group of attacking dead.

Behind his face cage, Fist took a deep breath, readying a lungful of air. After killing so many of the zombies over what seemed like years, he was desensitized to the horrors of the reanimated flesh.

An old woman dressed in a bathrobe sprinkled with embroidered daisies stumbled toward him. A black, visceral shawl of torn scalp hung over one side of her face.

Fist stared at the thing's destroyed features, at the terrible faces crowded around it, bobbing and weaving in that slow, stop-go motion that marked them as undead. There were sometimes runners as well, but none in this pack. At the least the runners made things interesting.

The shambling dead were nothing to the Norsemen.

With a grunt, Fist swung the maul when the granny was within reach.

The slaughter was over in less than a minute, and the corpses lay in a ragged mound that stopped at the wall of living men. Sounds of heavy breathing met Fist's ears. He shrugged, causing his shoulders to *crick*, while shaking out his burning arms. None of his boys had been taken down by the mob, which was both good and bad.

There was strength in numbers, but he knew he'd probably end up cutting a few of their throats, anyway.

The dead were piled up on top of one another, creating a squishy embankment that Fist and the others climbed over. They grunted and cursed in disgust, and one even stumbled and landed facedown amongst the bodies. Once clear of the unmoving flesh, Fist held his maul by the neck and led the others straight to the house. The gate in the fence hung open, and pieces of cloth caught and torn from the zombies hung from its top. Fist carefully edged through the opening, listening and focusing on the back door and steps. Painted green with white siding, the house might've been a picture for life in the suburbs. A pool, the above-ground kind with flimsy walls, lay flattened in one corner of the backyard. A small garden ringed with white-painted beach rocks and filled with bare soil lay just to the left of the pool.

Fist walked up to the backdoor, listened for a moment, and then rapped on the unbroken glass. He placed his maul against the siding.

"Hello?" he said in a strained tone, as if unaccustomed to such pleasantries. Another rap of knuckles. "Anyone home?"

In the dark of the kitchen, in an open doorway, a man came into sight. He looked haggard and old and held a double-barreled shotgun—what the boys referred to as a "fat ass."

"Who're you?" he demanded, appearing close to losing control. A woman peeked out from behind him. Both looked somewhere between frightened and hopeful.

"We took care of the dead," Fist said through the glass and smiled.

"What?" The man's expression lightened and became even more hopeful.

"The zombies. We killed them."

"You did? That's wonderful!"

"What did they do, Rick?" the woman asked, appearing just as frayed as Rick.

"They . . . they killed those bastards!"

Fist straightened on the lower step. Even then, his forehead was level with the upper frame of the door.

"They killed those things! Jesus H. Christ, that's the best news I've heard all day! All week!" He broke into French then, which Fist didn't understand in the least.

Rick came to the window, beaming, and propped his weapon against a counter.

Fist waited until the old man threw back the locks and pulled away the wooden braces reinforcing the door.

It opened with a yank, and Rick leaned out, smiling from ear to ear. He offered his hand. Fist took it and allowed his hand to be pumped as if he were an old-fashioned water well.

"There's a few of you," Rick said suddenly, his smile dimming at the fearsome collection of men standing outside his door, eerily quiet.

While the warriors captivated Rick's attention, Fist held out his free hand. Cray placed a cleaver in it. Fist hacked at Rick's wrist and took it half off. Rick's mouth puckered into shock. He tried jerking his hand away as if he'd been scalded with hot water, but Fist held on, the wound yawning and spilling blood. He swung the cleaver at Rick's head and sheared away a healthy flap of scalp in another burst of blood. The woman screamed. Fist forced his way through the door, slamming a bleeding Rick against the wall and letting him crumple to the floor. The older man stared at his fountaining wrist in both shock and awe. The Norsemen forced their way inside and pounced on the wounded homeowner.

"Non! Non!" the woman squealed, but she didn't have strength in her legs to run. Fist caught her by the throat and dug his fingers into her windpipe, turning her pleas into rusty squeaks. He rolled her into his embrace. She bucked and clawed at his face cage, then his shoulders. Fist bear-hugged her, feeling several ribs pop like bubble wrap. Her screams transformed into breathless grunts. With the fight gone from his victim, he tossed her over the kitchen island to let his men finish her.

Process her.

The warriors crowded in, holding the couple down only as long as was necessary— mere seconds, really. More cleavers and meat knives came into view. Clothes were torn open. White flesh was cut, sawed, and chopped. The smell of blood became thick.

Heavenly.

Fist stood on the threshold of the living room and stuck his head in, breathing stale air. No doubt the room had been boarded up for a lengthy period. Some stairs were at the edge of the room, and he'd check the second floor in a moment. He didn't feel rushed. Two full-grown people were more than enough fresh meat for his men for a day. If any children were upstairs, they wouldn't get far.

Sustenance. Pure and filling.

The Norsemen would eat anything they came across. Anything that couldn't be consumed right away would be taken: leftover packaged food, wild crops, animals, and people. People, in Fist's opinion, were the easiest to hunt because most of them, if they weren't already insane, were gutless, fearful, and initially, *stupidly* hailed Fist and his minions as if they were saviors.

Just as this pair had done.

The truth became painfully obvious, especially when the meat hooks came out and the cleavers fell and pleas of mercy were met with the cruel laughter of jackals.

Fist paused, half-tuned out to the quartering going on in the kitchen. If fortune smiled upon them, there might be a few more survivors in the neighboring area. It went like that sometimes. It was enough of a probability that they would hunker down here for the night and do a search in the morning, maybe even set up camp for a few days and see what the hunting was like in town.

He sized up the many cupboards in the kitchen, wondering if they might find some condiments.

There was nothing like a bit of garlic salt to go along with a roast.

TENNER

1

The SUV wormed deeper into the core of the melancholy city, avoiding the prowling dead where necessary. In the last hour, Tenner had seen more zombies walking about than he had in all of Nova Scotia combined. Thick and porous, crowds of dead seeped into the streets like a mindless, flesh-eating ooze. They didn't have any sense of the cold or the stormy elements about to descend upon them. They weren't concerned with taking shelter. All they were focused on was the next bite. Tenner wondered if they could actually relish the taste of still quivering, warm meat. He wondered a lot about that at times. It had to be good, somehow, for the Philistines to want it so badly. Tenner wasn't a cannibal, but he could see himself partaking, especially if it came to the point where food was a concern.

The black vehicle snaked through a lesser throng of walking corpses, bumping some out of the way and knocking others down. The vehicle would go over them with a *whump*. Some waved at Tenner as he passed, perhaps angry, maybe drawing the attention of the zombies ahead. Even though he was thankful for the virus or whatever it was that had brought the dead to life and established anarchy as the new order, he didn't have time for the corpses. He considered himself above *all* the remaining human race. Perhaps even the only "one." Not the creator, of course. He'd never have fucked up so badly, although he wished he'd been around for input when ideas were being tossed around. But destroyer . . . Yes, he was a destroyer—*the* destroyer. Before everything had changed, he'd tried willing bankers and CEOs to appear, but he'd had to settle for people of little consequence, the ones who wouldn't be missed too badly.

However, that had all changed. Now he was free to kill off every last living soul. But not the dead. The dead were utterly beneath him, a nuisance to be wary of, but Tenner had no doubt they would soon be long gone. Whatever had reanimated them and preserved their flesh had its limitations. It slowed decomposition, but by no means did it stop the process. It merely delayed the inevitable.

Ahead, a zombie pulled itself along, chest flat on the asphalt, crossing the white lines of a crosswalk. Ropes of entrails snaked out behind the thing like dull, sun-scorched ribbons, and Tenner saw how the soles of the thing's feet had been ground down to where they could no longer support its weight. The protruding bones reminded him of the bare wires of a shredded umbrella. Even as the zombie dragged itself onward, its chest rasping against the dull cheese grater of the pavement, Tenner glimpsed the gleam of a shattered ribcage, the jagged ends of worn bones clicking from the dead thing's forward motion, like old cards in bicycle spokes. This particular corpse had even rubbed away the flesh on its knees and upper thighs, and Tenner wondered how long before the muscle remaining on its bony arms would continue to function.

Then the SUV rolled over the creature. Tenner steered the vehicle so the right tire would crush the skull. The crunch of bone pulsed through the steering column and stretched a smirk over his features.

They were beneath him. The dead only caught the ill-prepared ones. The cattle.

Tenner was so much *more*.

The street he followed ran toward the bay, where he glimpsed war ships on their sides. Even the military had fallen to the dead. He didn't expect to find many, if any, survivors in the city. There were simply too many walking corpses. Some of them even wore the remnants of body armor and helmets, marking them as former soldiers. Tenner hunched over his steering wheel and looked up. The damage was only superficial on the outskirts of the city, mostly from fire, but craters from artillery shells and other explosives appeared deeper into the city. The houses in this area weren't burnt to the ground, but flattened, as if a hammer the size of a train had repeatedly smashed them. Debris blocked the narrower side streets in places, while in others, telephone poles had been blown off their bases, and they prevented both Tenner and the Philistines from passing.

Only big guns could have wrought such destruction.

The warships had to have opened fire on all sections of the city.

Tenner marvelled at the destruction. Some of the taller buildings had huge bites taken out of them, and bare girders like loose teeth dangled and moaned in the breeze. Half-flattened houses and trees that had been felled from artillery fire lined the streets. Cars and trucks were torn in half, ravaged by flame and flipped onto their roofs. He spotted one zombie writhing underneath a minivan. God only knew how long it had been there. Tenner shook his head. There had been a death party in Halifax at some point in time, and he wasn't too troubled by missing it.

He found a road that wasn't so damaged or filled with zombies and drove down it. The hope of finding any sort of munitions, supplies, or survivors in this particular mess was waning. Ahead, the water of the bay beckoned, black and cold looking, and he drove toward it. The streets opened, and Tenner was mildly puzzled to see the crowd of zombies thinning. He turned the wheel and drove on, approaching twin towers that seemingly rose up from the sea, perched at the very edge of concrete covered land.

Then he spotted a row of military-made iron barricades, silent and cold. A pedway lay behind them, and a second wall of metro buses came into view just beneath the elevated walkway, tipped over on their sides, the gaps between them plugged with sandbags. He pulled closer to the barricade, noting how hundreds, perhaps thousands of the Philistines lay stretched out before the wall, put down for the last time. Limbs, heads, and ripped torsos lay strewn over a horrific expanse. Razor wire sprung up in places like broken springs. Tenner braked and parked in front of a corridor leading through the wire, right up to the buses and pedway. The long, fluted snouts of machine guns pointed at the sky and the field of shredded corpses, likewise dead to the world.

Tenner got out and hauled on his winter coat. Once that was done, his hands went to his holstered guns and he tensed for a moment, waiting to bolt back into his ride if things got too dicey. Nothing moved, however, and he walked through the wire and the fields of decaying flesh, wrinkling his nose at the smell. He paused and kicked at one body, feeling the frozen husk rip as it came away from the pavement. The wind caused some loose clothing still clinging to the dead to flutter, the only movement and sound in the immediate area.

Curious, Tenner thought.

He homed in on a ladder that went up one of the buses. He walked under the pedway and saw a gap between the underside of the construction and the tops of the overturned buses. The Army had put the buses behind and as tight to the pedway as they could manage, while still leaving a gap for soldiers to climb through. Tenner took a hold of the ladder and climbed. He stood on metal sheets on top of the bus and studied the nearest machine gun emplacement. He jumped up to the pedway and walked over to the weapon, only to discover it bone dry. Metal ammunition boxes were nearby, emptied completely. The soldiers had fired every shell they had.

Into that.

Looking down upon the scene, Tenner was impressed with the level of destruction inflicted upon the dead. The wall he stood upon gave him a great vantage point to take in the scope of the fortifications the Army had built. He scanned the area behind the defenses, seeing it mostly bare of dead things. That in itself was a puzzle. Something caught his attention then; no dead lurked beyond the wall of buses and rusted, military fabricated metal barricades. Tenner wondered for a moment just how far the defenses went.

And if there was anyone alive.

It didn't matter much if there wasn't anyone alive. The place had possibilities. Countless possibilities, and Tenner saw them all, considered each. He saw a place that might attract whoever was left in the city, searching for sanctuary. He saw a place that might attract anyone coming into the city, seeking out supplies.

Eventually, they would find this place. They would find him.

That thought made his face split into a creepy smile. Tenner envisioned a new game to play, one of deception instead of outright murder.

He quickly walked along the red carpeted pedway to a distant door, which lead to the first of the two towers. There was no time to waste.

He had work to do . . . and potential guests to prepare for.

Then, just ahead of him, the steel and glass door abruptly opened.

A man pointed a shotgun in his face.

2

Bowman had been around.

He'd traveled through Cape Breton, and had wandered as far as Yarmouth, walking the highways, but keeping within the treeline. Since the world went tits up, he found it was better to keep moving, check in on relatives—all gone—and friends—all gone as well—before making his way back to the capitol. He'd thought there would be a control center of some kind, a main base to take in survivors.

By electing to find friends and relatives, he had probably saved himself from what had gone down in Halifax. One of his favorite sayings was "shit the bed," and as far as he could tell, someone had unloaded a massive dump in the city. In all of his adult years, he had been something of a recluse, an oddity. Never had his driver's license and had lived off the beaten track in a small bungalow outside of rural Truro. Never owned a smartphone—he was dismayed and disgusted by how the devices turned intelligent people into dumbasses. At fifty-one, his wife had died of cancer two years prior to the outbreak, and he was eternally thankful that his precious Becky never saw their undead neighbors come up the long driveway one morning in August, lumbering through an early morning haze like hungry phantoms unearthed from a mass grave.

He'd stayed at his home as long as he could, fending off zombies until his ammunition ran out. His father had left him a small monetary inheritance as well as an impressive illegal weapons cache, the foremost being a vintage Kalashnikov assault rifle, more commonly known as an AK-47. There had been a polished Desert Eagle in the collection as well, but only two magazines for the hand cannon, and honestly, Bowman didn't like firing the monster, as it numbed his arm after every shot. The rifle was the most useful because his dad had stored hundreds, perhaps thousands of rounds for the weapon. In fact, when the shit had truly hit the fan, and Joe and

Francis Pardy, along with twenty or so strangers, decided to shamble over to see if Bowman was ready to be a spread and snack, the Kalashnikov was the beast that he took from the cabinet. Damn thing was a marvel of design, and it had rattled against his shoulder when he started firing at the corpses pounding on his door as if it had come right off the assembly line instead of being seventy years old. He wasn't even sure if the ammunition would be any good, but it was. He supposed his father might've had a hand in that. No point in keeping a monster like that around if you didn't have anything to feed it.

All the rounds were stored in the basement. Bowman never thought he'd use it all. Never in a hundred years.

Well, he'd used it all mighty fast. He even ran out of bullets for the Desert Eagle and his Winchester .30-30, both of which he tossed because finding spare ammunition for the weapons would be next to impossible. In his travels, he'd used a mountain bike hitched up to a two-wheeled storage cart to carry his gear. When the tires had blown out, he carried what he could.

In Antigonish, he'd come across a twelve gauge shotgun three days after leaving the Kalashnikov in a ditch. Ammunition seemed to be plentiful, but Bowman had learned his lesson with the assault rifle—conservation.

And he'd practiced that during his search for family and friends throughout the province. There were other survivors. Good people. Scared, but good. At one point in time, he'd been part of a band of about thirty survivors.

All gone now. Ravaged by the hunting dead.

Leaving him with only Halifax.

And the tall bastard he had just stopped from entering what Bowman considered to be his fortress.

"You scared me, man!" the taller newcomer burst out, holding his hands above his head.

"Back up," Bowman said. It wasn't like him to be forceful, but he could see the guns on the guy's hips. Better safe than dead.

The man, who looked like a biker dressed for winter, blinked and didn't move.

Bowman didn't like that. "Got shit in your ears or something? I said back *up*."

This time the stranger did as he was told, but there was a glimpse, a quick flicker around the eyes that Bowman almost missed, that indicated he didn't like being caught so flatfooted. The tall biker with the black eyes sized him up, noting Bowman's blue-black body armor—what he taken from a dead soldier in a nearby store. But what really had the lad's attention was the shotgun, its mouth not five inches from his face.

"Stop right there," Bowman said.

"Right here?"

"You trying to be smart or something?"

"Just asking is all."

"Shut the fuck up," Bowman said quietly.

The other man complied. Bowman had the drop on him and tried to look mean enough to pull the trigger. He'd grown a rusty-looking beard that had reached the base of his throat during his time on the road, and he wore a black toque decorated with skulls. One shot from this range would shred the newcomer's parka and chest, and no doubt blow him through one of the pedway's windows.

"Any more of you?" Bowman demanded.

"No."

"What are you doing here?"

"Looking for supplies," the other said, concerned.

"Supplies?" Bowman chuckled and quieted. He took a quick peek at the streets below. "Figured as much."

"You got anything to eat?" he asked, black eyes suddenly hopeful.

"I'll ask the fuckin' questions. You got that?"

"Got it."

Bowman exhaled. "Anyone else with you?" he repeated.

"No."

"You sure?"

"Yeah."

"Where'd you get those guns?" He dipped his chin at the other's waist.

"Father's collection."

"Hm. We got one thing in common."

"Huh? Why? That shotgun your dad's?"

Bowman let that one go unanswered. "Just you, eh?"

The other man appeared flustered. "You keep askin' me that. Take a look around, man. There ain't no one else around here but me. I could ask you the same thing."

That furrowed Bowman's hairy face. "Yeah . . . you could."

"Well?"

"Well what?"

"You going to shoot me or let me in?"

"Haven't decided yet," Bowman admitted. "Been . . . been a while since I've talked to anyone."

"I can see why."

Smart ass, Bowman thought. He gnawed on the inside of his cheek, his whiskers going one way and then the other, mulling things over.

"Take them guns out," he eventually said. "One at a time. Two fingers. Slow. You put them on the ground and kick them toward me. I got a twitchy finger, so you be careful doing that, else the neighbors get a wake-up call and dinner bell all in one."

The newcomer did as ordered, kicking one Glock toward Bowman, then the other. Neither man so much as blinked, nor did the shotgun waver. Bowman kicked the guns behind him.

"Now then," he asked. "What's in that truck of yours?"

"Some supplies. Food. Water. A rifle."

"And you got in here all by yourself?"

"Yessir."

That's better, Bowman thought, and he relaxed his posture just a bit. "I ain't no sir, so you can cut that shit out."

"That armor you're wear—"

"Not mine," Bowman interrupted. "Pulled it off a soldier in here a day ago. Plenty around, but this one was the only one that fit. Lucky me I found it inside, down in the lobby. I wouldn't worry about that. What I'd be worried about is what happens next. Like the elephant that caught the mouse by the tail and said, 'Now that I got you, what the hell am I going to do with you?'"

The other man shrugged. It was a good question.

"Shit," Bowman muttered. "Back up a bit."

The newcomer backed up three steps.

Attention divided, Red Beard stooped and picked up the guns, stuffing each down a boot. If he was going to be jumped, now would be the time.

But the man made no move to stop him.

"What's your name?"

"Tenner."

"I'm Bowman."

Tenner nodded, uncomfortable with the shotgun introductions.

"Can't be too careful around here these days," Bowman went on. "With dead folks about."

"Lots of that going around."

"That's right. The way I figure it, being introverted is probably the best way to be, know what I mean?"

"Yeah."

A breeze rose up, chilling and mournful sounding, and the big bastard before him seemed to realize he was either going to die here or not. It had been a long time since he'd had company. That part he didn't lie about. A long time on the march, looking for places to hole up for a while. Looking for others, until he gave up. He suddenly realized someone had found him and he was hesitating, and he wasn't sure why. Bowman sighed. It was probably from being on his own for so long.

"Get in here," Bowman said, lowering the shotgun.

Tenner took a deep breath. "Oh man, you ain't gonna rape me, are you?"

"Huh?"

"Please don't. I mean, fuckin' shoot me if you have to."

"The fuck's wrong with you? I ain't no *poof*," Bowman protested.

"Just what a rapist would say. To, you know, lure me in."

"The fuck he would," Bowman exclaimed. "Get your ass in here before something gets wind of you."

"You ain't gonna rape me?"

"The *fuck? No*, but I'll sure as hell stomp your ass if you don't get inside *now*." With that, Bowman backed up, kept the door opened, and glared.

Hesitating, Tenner made a wary entry. He was much taller than Bowman, well over six feet. The door closed behind both of them.

"This way," Bowman growled. "But keep your distance, all right? Let's get to know each other first."

Tenner stopped in his tracks. "What do you mean by that?"

Bowman winced. "Grow up, will ya? At least I don't have the gun in your face anymore. Christ, you're jumpy. Thought I was jumpy. You're fuckin' tweaked."

"Keeps me alive."

"Yeah, well, I sure as Wild Bill's shit stain got the jump on you."

"You did," Tenner said, puzzling over the odd expletive. "You did that."

"Where you from?"

"Ontario."

"Uh-huh. Things bad out there?"

"As bad as here," Tenner stated. Bowman led him though a corridor of glass, metal railing, and beige carpet. "This is indicative of most cities, I imagine."

"I only came into the city a few days ago," Bowman informed him, stopping at a black door. "Had to be careful on the way in. Packs of zombies all over the place, but they move around, eh. Like tides. Plenty of things lying around the city, though. Just have to find them is all. *Risk* finding them. Plenty of zombies around, too, if that needs to be said."

Bowman pushed the door open and went inside, mindful of where Tenner was behind him. An open walkway overlooked a main foyer with dark green fountains of people and animals, while sheets of iron could be seen barricading the outer windows at ground level, creating a fortress of sorts. They walked to a stairwell and went up a floor. This level had more empty corridors and offices with worn beige carpet and brown wood panelling. Paper debris and empty food wrappers gathered along the walls and corners, and a fresh breath of air whistled throughout. The area appeared more than a little secure.

"Jesus," Tenner said softly. "Somebody have a banquet up here?"

"You smell that?" Bowman asked, ignoring the question.

The other man inhaled. "Yeah, I do. Is that . . . is that *curry*?"

Bowman had to smile at the longing in that question. "It is."

"You have curry here?" His black eyes gleamed, ravenous.

"I found it here, amongst other things. MREs."

"You found MREs?" Tenner was amazed.

Bowman's smile widened. It was good to make another person feel some semblance of hope.

"Whole pile. Water, too, if you're interested."

"I'm interested."

"I can tell. Come on this way."

They finally entered the reception area of an office unit on the third floor, the interior dreary and cold. A desk had been upturned and a leather sofa rested against the right wall. A huge potted plant in the corner lay on its side, dirt spread across the carpet. Grey blankets covered the couch, folded neatly, a stark contrast to the remainder of the room.

"Have a seat there," Bowman said, indicating an office chair with a high, leather back. Tenner sat down behind the desk. An open doorway behind him allowed some light into the room, but otherwise, the place was a void. If either man didn't know any better, this place could have been located in someplace as desolate as the shores of the Arctic Circle or the South Pole.

The leather of the chair creaked softly as Tenner leaned back, his arms on the rests.

Bowman remained standing and, for a long time, contemplated his visitor.

"You know something," he finally said, "I've been on my own now for a bit. Had some friends at the onset of all of this, but the last one got bit and died a year ago. Been living 'n scrounging all along the South Shore, making my way here. Haven't seen too many others alive. Why do you figure that is?"

"Most have died," Tenner pointed out.

"Course most have died, I'm no igit. The way I see it, whoever's lived this long knows what they're doing. You probably know what you're doing, right? If you got all that shit aboard your rig out there."

Tenner's jaw slackened.

"Don't worry, I'm not about to take anything," Bowman went on, understanding the look. "But I'm getting on in years. Coming into the city was a mistake. Got this far and, well, made some good finds, but damned if I can't get it all back out."

"Uh . . . how did you get here?" Tenner asked, genuinely curious.

"Walked."

"You walked."

"Never drove a day in my life. Wasn't going to start after the apocalypse. Was a time I could walk or run ten, twelve kilometers in a day. Not hard to do. However, be that as it may, I'm faced with a problem here."

"Oh shit," Tenner looked to his feet.

"Why 'oh shit'?"

"You're gonna shoot me."

Bowman scrunched up his hairy face. "You seem awfully sure I'm about to do you harm. Didn't you hear what I just said? Them parts about being on my own for a while, but there's strength in numbers, right? Chances are, neither one of us is going to get out of the city before full winter hits. Not with all them dead people out there. What say you and I team up? Watch each other's backs?"

Bowman sat on the couch, placing his shotgun across his knees.

"Well . . . sure, why not?" Tenner said slowly, uncertain. "Until we get out of the city, then. You might turn out to be an asshole."

"Just might." Bowman smirked. "You never know these days. We team up, and you can have half of whatever's around."

"What is around?" Tenner asked.

"Food and water." Bowman paused. "Curry. Beef and chicken, from what I remember." He smiled again at Tenner's obvious dismay. The man was practically salivating. "Place was occupied by the military as far as I can see. Until they got overrun."

"This was an Army base?"

"Temporary one, at least. From what I can see, they barricaded the streets with buses and these iron walls, set up machine gun nests, and cut loose. What you saw coming in ain't got nothing on the mess on the other end."

"The zombies got everyone?"

"Looks that way. I've been here in this place for two days now, scouting the area, and haven't seen anything really. A few zombies wander through, but nothing like what hit this place before. You'll see. It's goddamn shocking is what it is. Especially on the other end. Dead piled up from one end of the street to the other, looking like . . . like . . . a great big fleshy U. Spooky, too."

"And you managed to live this long."

"Not the only one." Bowman nodded slyly at Tenner.

"Did you check out the armories?"

Bowman blinked as if remembering something. "That's right. There's a national one around here."

"You haven't been there?"

"Not my town," Bowman answered. "And you just got here."

"We'll have to check it out. They got weapons there. Ammo."

"Might be something to do. I'm running low, actually. You seem to be doing all right." Bowman reached down to his boot, pulled out one of Tenner's sidearms, and studied it.

"Be careful with the triggers," Tenner warned.

"Touchy, are they?"

"Very."

"Hm." Bowman inspected it for a bit before leaning forward and handing the weapon back to Tenner, butt first.

Tentatively, the tall man reached out and took it back. He smiled then, a shark's smile, and for a moment Bowman thought he'd made a mistake.

But Tenner disarmed him with a shake of the weapon and a genuine sigh of relief. "My baby. It was my dad's."

He holstered the gun.

"Wait," Bowman said after a few seconds. He stretched for the other in his boot, but Tenner waved him off.

"Keep it. That's a Glock you have there. Extended magazine. Seventeen shots in it. Much more than that blunderbuss you got. If you check the sides, you'll see a selector switch. It can go full automatic if you need it. I don't recommend it since you can burn through a mag pretty quick."

"Hm." Bowman grunted and returned it to his boot. "I'll keep that in mind. Thanks for that."

"Don't thank me," Tenner said eagerly. "Just break out the curry."

They talked into the evening, eating MREs that Bowman took from a supply room filled with boxes of the instant meals. Tenner explained his reasons for coming into the city as he dug into his curry chicken, eating noisily. He figured that with the two of them, they could take his truck and see what they could find at the armory. Bowman told him there wasn't much in the way of weapons in the building, and whatever was outside had been ruined by the elements. Except for the food and water.

When the room darkened, Bowman rose and closed the doors to the office before taking out a pair of self-generating flashlights and illuminating the place with wide beams of white light. The wind outside chilled the corridors and periodically rattled the windows, and the two men wrapped themselves in grey blankets. Bowman and Tenner told tales of their survival in the new world. Bowman wasn't surprised to hear Tenner's own group had eventually been decimated by the dead. It was a sad, but common story in the new world.

"Where do we sleep?" Tenner eventually asked.

"You can take any of the other offices. Sleep with the curry for all I care," Bowman said.

"No watches?"

"The barricades downstairs hold off the dead. And I haven't come across one yet that could use a ladder. We're okay. Just be mindful of flashing that light of yours around windows. The light might attract them."

"Just like fishing." Tenner smiled in the grey light.

"Yeah, like that," Bowman said.

"Well, how about we check out the armory tomorrow?"

"Nothing better to do."

Tenner paused, then stood up. He took in the office before resting his gaze on Bowman's huddled form on the sofa.

"Ah," the tall man began, "just want to say . . . thanks for feeding me and all. And thanks for not shooting me. Appreciated."

Bowman held up a hand. "Not a problem. Glad you're here."

Tenner seemed to think about something, but the big man shrugged and pointed at the door before Bowman could ask what was on his mind.

"In the morning, then," he said.

"In the morning," Bowman agreed.

Nodding once more, Tenner left the office, and Bowman listened to him fumbling about in the corridor. The sound of his steps receded to a pause, then there was a shrill squeal of hinges, and a door closed.

Bowman could understand that. He slept with the doors closed and barricaded himself. He got up and did just that, taking out a long piece of two-by-four, which he braced against the door knob. Just a precaution.

25

Despite a couple of moments where Tenner had seemed to study Bowman with a strange look in his eye, Bowman was pretty sure he was okay. The looks he could attribute to him being on his own for a while. If life on the run didn't change a person just a little, Bowman didn't know what could. The man even gave him a fully loaded gun. That made Bowman feel better about Tenner.

It was good to have someone to talk to after such a long time.

They ate breakfast under a heavy great canopy of a cloud that, as Bowman put it, looked as if it was deciding on whether to shit snow or piss rain. Once they ate, Bowman took Tenner on a short tour of the building, first showing him where the stacked cardboard boxes of MREs and wooden pallets of bottled water—enough to feed a small army—had been stashed on the second and third floors.

"They used this place as a command center, I figure," Bowman observed, standing outside one of the offices turned storage rooms. "There's an office with a couple of desks pushed together with an old downtown map on it all marked up."

"What's upstairs?" Tenner asked.

"Not much," Bowman replied. "Just a view of the city."

"How many stories?"

"About twenty? Maybe twenty one? It's a long hike. Too bad the elevator's out."

"Yeah, too bad," Tenner trailed off, thinking.

"What?" Bowman asked.

"Just wondering when we should be getting on looking for an armory. Figure it's about eight in the morning now. Let's head on up to one of the upper levels and see if we can't spot something to use as a reference point or a place to start looking."

"Well, there are naval shipyards around here somewhere."

"You know where?"

Bowman shook his head.

"Let's head on upstairs, then. We need our guns?"

"Nah. Nothing up there. Take one of your pistols there if you really need it."

"Already got it. Better to have it than yadda yadda." They had both heard the line before. Tenner started walking toward one of the stairwells, and Bowman followed. They opened a door, and Tenner noted for the first time the sparse light from above.

"Wedged some of the doors open," Bowman explained. "Not all. Not much light, but it's something. Otherwise, it'd be too damn dark in there. Spooky."

"Didn't you tell me yesterday you walked all over Nova Scotia?" Tenner asked with a smile.

"Did."

"That's some spooky shit to me."

"Never thought of it at the time. Too busy looking out for zombies," Bowman said.

"I've been on the road myself," Tenner said, pausing on the doorway's threshold. "Some side roads and whatnot. Easy to bypass the Philistines. The dead, I mean. But every now and again I'd meet up with folks like yourself. People looking for help, hoping I was with the government or the military, y'know. Good people. I'd stay with them for a while when I found them, but none wanted to leave their property. They all figured it was best to stay indoors. Befuddled the hell outta me at the time, but now I understand they were terrified. *Terrified* of what might be coming up the road. Dead or living. There are crazies out there."

"Crazies?"

"People gone insane. Or people who were insane before the Fall and are now just having the time of their lives. One guy lured me into his house, right? Had his girlfriend hide in a closet behind me and when I sat down, she came out and tried to take my head off with an axe. A fucking axe!"

"Christ. What did you do?"

"Did the only thing I could," Tenner said with a shrug. "Defended myself. I got out of there, too, and had them shoot the rear windshield outta my pickup."

Bowman blinked. "Your pickup?"

"Had it before the SUV," Tenner explained. "Anyway, those two scared the shit out of me. Chased me down their country road until I got back to the highway and got away. Close one, and there were others. But there's worse out there than just fucking bug-nut freaks. Much worse. Did you know that, of the whole population of the world—fifteen billion, right?—of that, I heard that experts once said that one percent were probably sociopaths. Folks who have no concept of good or bad and no inhibitions of any kind. Evil cocksuckers with no regard for those living around them, who wouldn't blink if they jammed a knife into someone's windpipe."

"You're freaking me out here," Bowman said earnestly.

"I know, right?" An excited Tenner went on. "Just think. *One percent*. Why, that's what, fifteen million of these psychos living amongst us with these basic . . . *urges* held in check just because they knew if they did anything, the law would find out and lock them away. Or worse. In theory, anyway. Something, eh?"

"It's a hundred and fifty million."

"Huh?"

"One percent of fifteen billion is a hundred and fifty million."

"So it's even more!"

"Yeah," Bowman said, no longer smiling.

"And I can tell you, I met a few while on the road. That's what I meant about traveling being scary. Now, the world as it is, this is . . . a fucking playground for people like that."

Bowman looked uncomfortably pensive, and Tenner frowned.

"Sorry, man. You look upset. You meet anyone like that? Sorry if I dredged up anything unpleasant. Like a bad memory."

"No," Bowman scoffed. "No, I'm fine."

"Well, let's get moving. Unless you think you can't keep up," Tenner challenged.

Bowman snorted, glad for the change of topic. "Lead on. We'll see who's puffing hard around the tenth floor."

They started climbing. Tenner took the lead, his black winter coat rendering him almost invisible in the stairwell. Bowman brought up the rear, glancing back every so often, more out of habit than caution.

As predicted, around the sixth floor, Tenner started breathing hard.

"Christ, this is harder than I thought." The tall man stopped three stairs ahead of Bowman, hunched over and gazing upward into the concrete dark.

"You've been driving around in that rig of yours for too long," Bowman said stoically, coming up and standing beside him.

"How many floors you say there were?"

"About twenty."

"Jesus."

They stood in the dark, the only sound Tenner gasping for breath.

"You know something," Bowman said. "Even though they're all gone, I expect . . . I expect someone to just appear out of the dark. And just at the same time, all the lights would come on. Maybe even a hum of electricity. Two years on, and I get like that sometimes."

Tenner said nothing to that.

"You ever think that way?"

"No. Never."

"You live in the now better than me, I guess," Bowman said. "You ever miss things? The way they were?"

Probably it was because he was tired from climbing the stairs, or perhaps he didn't hear the question right, or maybe he simply zoned out at that exact time. Bowman didn't know. But he did know that Tenner's answer was one that he didn't expect.

"Not once," the man replied with a chuckle.

"What?" Bowman asked, astonished.

His face partially concealed in shadow, Tenner met the other's gaze, and Bowman saw that the man's eyes gleamed like the tips of knives.

"Had too many unpaid parking tickets back then." Tenner smiled.

The burst of relief Bowman felt was wonderful. A joke. All it was. The man just had a sense of humor.

"Let's get moving," Tenner said, changing the subject again. "I want to see this top floor."

"Yeah. Well, it's a great view," Bowman confessed, still puzzling over his companion's odd reply, despite the joke—which really only felt like a clump of dirt tossed over a potential fire. "On a sunny day, you could see for miles. Even got a gym up there."

"Last thing I need is a gym," Tenner said, still breathing hard. "Man. This might put a damper on my plans today."

"Change your mind on going up?" Bowman asked.

Tenner nodded, his profile scowling in the gloom. "Yeah. That, and a few other things."

The spinning elbow caught Bowman on the cheek, shattering it, and knocked him back into the wall. His head rebounded off the concrete with a meaty bounce. Tenner grabbed him by the shoulders, righted him, and cracked two more fists into his jaw and right eye. There wasn't any need for those punches, as the first one had tilted Bowman's senses enough.

He didn't even feel it when Tenner's last blow, a devastating uppercut, sent him rattling back down the steps.

Into oblivion.

3

A cold winter wind licked Bowman's cheek, stirring him back to reality. His first thought was the wind wasn't right. There wasn't anywhere in the whole building to get such a breeze. He slowly came to. His head rang enough to make him grimace in agony, and he cracked opened his eyes.

Holy shit, he thought.

While he was unconscious, the treacherous bastard must have dragged him back down over the steps and taken him outside. Probably to his truck. Tenner had then transported him to a frosty street in some part of the city that Bowman didn't recognize. He tried to shout, but Tenner had duct-taped his mouth shut. Bowman's chest heaved. His panic flared. Mucus burst from his nostrils with each breath as his head whipped from side to side. He tried to move his arms, but they were outstretched and tied to a fallen utility pole in such a way that his lower body hung at a painful angle, as if he were exercising his obliques. His feet kicked air, dangling a good three feet from the pavement. *Jesus!* The sick bastard had removed his boots and socks. He could move his head enough to see that he was bound in place by extension cords and duct tape tied around his arms and upper torso. Through sheer strength, he curled his knees up into his chest, but he soon dropped them. He wasn't going anywhere.

Holy Christ, Bowman thought, and became still despite the agony of hanging at such an angle.

He looked around. A transport truck had rammed into the utility pole's base, bending the whole thing over the roof of a car. His feet were no more than three feet off the ground.

"Hey, you're awake?" Tenner's cheerful voice rang out. After a frantic search, Bowman spotted the man across the street in a narrow alleyway. He was leaning against the wall of a green house, almost as if he'd stepped outside for a quick smoke.

"Excellent," Tenner said, looking quite pleased.

Bowman's heart hammered in his ears. It seemed as if every one of his senses suddenly had their dials set at the highest level.

"Sorry, man," Tenner went on, focusing on Bowman's bulging, pleading eyes. "It wouldn't have worked out, y'know? I work better alone. I don't think you'd be interested in what I have going on, anyway."

Bowman erupted in a fit of muffled curses and kicks. He strained against his bonds while Tenner stood and watched from the alley.

"Yeah," Tenner drew out. "I taped and tied you down pretty good. Made sure of that. Got my gun back, too, by the way. Shit, I was worried there for a moment or two. Thought maybe you might have gotten the itch. All in here, after all." He tapped one temple with a wistful expression on his face.

"Just wanted to say thanks for showing me around, eh. And not blowing my head off when you had the chance there. Appreciated. And thanks again for the food. Hard to come by these days, but you certainly did secure the mother lode. There're guns out there, too, somewheres. I'll find 'em."

Tenner leaned out around the corner and peered, unconcerned, up one street and then the other.

"You're probably wondering why I'm doing this," he said.

Bowman's suppressed scream spoke of rage and terror.

"Yeah, I know," Tenner said sweetly. "Most people figure that. Funny thing is, they figure that part out only *after* I have them alone and trussed up. You didn't suspect a thing, which tells me my acting's getting better. No biggie, really. Easy to act freaked out these days. Anyways, you're probably wondering why I strung you up instead of quietly putting a hammer to your skull in your sleep. Thought of it, by the way. Last night, maybe just after midnight, I was outside your door there and actually had thought of just coming on in and putting a quick knife in you. But I couldn't, you see. Had to make sure the grub and water was all there."

Another outpouring of emotion came from Bowman.

"Careful, man. You might rupture something. Or worse."

Tenner leaned out and looked around again. Then his lighthearted expression slowly morphed into a blazing smile.

"Ah." He pointed.

Bowman felt his balls rise up and his heart freeze at the same time.

A small mob of zombies, attracted to Tenner's voice and his own thrashings.

"Oh, look!" Tenner nodded in the opposite direction. Another pack of zombies, mewling and closing in on him. Bowman gasped as if his lower parts had just been dunked into the North Atlantic.

"You know, as often as I've done this to people, it still amazes me how fucking *fast* they zero in on a free meal."

Tenner retreated back into the alley, out of the undeads' sight.

"Gotta pull back here, man. I got a place already scoped out to watch. I won't leave you. Think of you as a buddy now, actually. But I am interested in just . . . how they eat you. I'm big into games, y'know, but today, I think I'm not going to bother playing. No, today, I'm . . . I'm just going to watch. Save some ammunition. But I tell you what. If you really want to, I mean, if you *really* feel the need, you can pray to me. Okay? When the time is right. Pray to me. And if I hear you, and if I feel merciful," Tenner said in a lower, doubtful voice, "I might change my mind. Might come to your rescue. Not promising anything, though. Got that?"

Bowman thrashed against his bonds.

Having nothing more to say, Tenner slunk back into the alleyway. He leaned against a wall, grinned, and stared.

Perhaps two minutes later, they arrived.

The zombies came in from either side of Bowman like a tide of molasses. Their pitiful voices gouged the air and made him struggle against his bonds all the more. He couldn't budge them. He kicked and swung his legs from side to side, hoping to work himself loose somehow, but Tenner had done him up good and proper.

Bowman looked across the street and met the maniacal eyes of his killer.

Mr. One Percent. Standing right over there.

He scolded himself. Swore. Should've been more careful, should've even shot him first instead of being so goddamn *accommodating*. But he couldn't have known, and he wouldn't have done anything to someone he'd just met. Not another survivor like himself. That just wasn't him.

A mistake, he now knew. A terrible mistake.

That thought made him thrash once more, the pounding of his heart giving him all the energy he needed as the zombies, the *zombies* . . .

No more than twenty feet on either side.

Tenner had backed away into the shadows of the alley, eagerly waiting for the action to begin, for the *feeding* to begin. *Oh, Christ*, Bowman thought and writhed. Squirmed. The tape pulled painfully against his whiskers, but he kept struggling. He was about to be fucking *eaten alive*. His grunts and muffled whistles became drawn-out whines of hopeless terror. The undead had him. He'd had nightmares of this very instance, horrible sequences broken only when the teeth bit into his flesh.

There would be no waking from this one. Nothing at all.

Ten feet. Soldiers, police officers, office workers, and children comprised the creatures creeping up on him, no doubt wondering who had delivered them such a lively gift. They smelled horrible enough to almost make him vomit. The stench of putrid rot was so rank, Bowman was reminded of someone taking a shit in a basement—*twice.*

Bowman rammed his head against the pole, trying to knock himself unconscious, but he only managed to split the flesh covering his head. Blood streamed down his face. *Sauce for the goose!* His mind squealed. He glanced up and saw Tenner across the way, still watching, eternally jovial.

A zombie in a pair of workman's overalls reached him first. A long arm slunk out, and meaty fingers like fat sausages touched Bowman's denim covered knee.

That gentle contact sent him over the edge, and a fresh torrent of stifled screams burst from his lips. He booted the thing away with enough force to put it on its ass. His foot ached from the contact, and Bowman looked down, terror spiking.

Jesus Christ!

More zombies crowded around him. He kicked another walking corpse away, then broke his toes when he nailed yet another right under the jaw. He barely felt the pain. He pushed others back with his feet, keeping them at bay, but a few slunk in on his vulnerable side, the side not blocked by the car, and they laid their grey-blue hands upon his winter coat.

And ripped.

The seams gave away as more hands clenched material and pulled. One zombie wrapped its arms around one of his legs. Bowman struggled, trying to free himself even as he watched the thing attempting to sink an impossibly white set of teeth into his knee. The two groups of undead converged upon his dangling form, and the zombies in the rear pushed the ones at the front into him, bunching his legs up until he could no longer kick. He felt his knees pop under the increasing pressure of bodies and screamed into the duct tape. The corpses pressed up against his feet, his thighs, his pelvis. He heard more seams rip, felt the cold air on his exposed belly, distended from a few days of self-indulgent living.

Then he saw it.

The one about to take that first, terrible bite. A man in a white shirt splashed with black. A dead blonde stood next to him, along with a couple of child zombies. One great big hungry family. The zombies rippled against him like one great, voracious wave.

Bowman wailed behind his duct tape gag. He screeched for Tenner to do something. In that black second before excruciating pain, Bowman prayed, and the words came out as gibberish.

The family man bit into the flesh covering Bowman's lower left ribs. The pain from a dull rack of teeth gnawing into his body made him buck and shriek like a muffled whistle. Others chomped down. Something enveloped a foot and bit off a toe, then the rest of his lower digits were nipped off one by one. He felt his jeans slough off. Mouths fastened onto his calves and lower thighs. A long red sheet of flesh stretched out right before his watering eyes, and Bowman yowled hideously. More fingers crawled over him, softly at first, then with increasing urgency. The dead mewed at him, sizing him up with their lifeless eyes, mouths wide and starving. Hands pawed at his belly.

And became claws.

Bowman felt the hands and teeth rip him wide open, felt an abrupt *sinking* sensation, a *voiding*.

Then pulling.

That sensation stayed with him for what seemed like a very long time before his perception went mercifully red.

Across the way, Tenner watched the farmers' market crowd of Philistines feast on the lower half of Bowman. He saw the blood spurt. Saw the old man go into an electric frenzy. Some zombies, pushed onto the hood of the car by those behind them, got up and pulled themselves toward Bowman's upper body. Two of them started in on his arm, working their way up to his shoulder and face.

Tenner stayed back, enraptured, checking over his shoulder at times to ensure nothing was creeping up on him.

Unfazed, he went on watching the feast to the gritty end, when bones were worked free of moist sockets.

There were other things to do, but he could let them wait.

It was his world, after all.

And right now, some curry would hit the spot.

SCOTT

4

Halifax called.

Scott was going to see what it wanted.

The Durango SUV cut sluggishly through the mounting, swirling winds that lashed the tinted windshield and the highway beyond in a snarl of white. The ferocity of the storm made him scowl, depressing the brake and slowing his speed further. His breath came out in a quiet hiss, drowned almost immediately by the gale pummelling the glass, and he held on tighter to the steering wheel. The gust fought for control over the SUV, and Scott thought it would only take a little more power to whisk it off the road. The wipers streaked back and forth fast enough to potentially grind the rubber away, or even inflict mortal wounds if they could be used as a weapon, and he had to force himself not to look at the damn things whipping across his vision. The clock showed 9:16 in the morning, but the way the snow was attacking the vehicle and darkening the sky, it could have been almost sundown. The sun and sky were up there somewhere, smothered by monstrous war clouds seemingly intent on burying Scott alive. He sighed again, wishing he had something to plug into the stereo: music, an audio book, anything to alleviate the boredom brought on by his fight against the storm. Any second he expected a frozen cow, blown out of its pasture by this titan of a blizzard, to crash against his vehicle.

Why the hell had he taken to the road this morning, anyway?

Scott thought about it, shifting in his leather seat enough to make it creak. Windsor. He just wanted to be away from Windsor. The town had lured him into stopping, but after a couple of days exploring its historic streets and fighting gimps, he'd come up with nothing. The houses he searched held a few meager supplies, which he ate, saving the stores piled in the back of the Durango, but there wasn't anything to justify that initial feeling, that tractor pull, he'd had for the place. The only thing he did find was an aluminum bat tucked away behind the door of a bedroom that had, he suspected, belonged to a teenager. Could that have been the thing mysteriously dragging him to stop in the town? He had to admit, the bat was a useful weapon against deadheads. A little unwieldy, but nowhere near as bad as the war hammer he'd once had. It wasn't as unbalanced as an axe, and it didn't run the risk of catching in a gimp's skull like a sword. If the ammunition Gus had so generously given him ran out and he didn't find any to replace it, the bat would come in handy. It was the only thing Scott took away from Windsor, before climbing back in his vehicle and getting the H-E two sticks out of town. Anxious to get back to the hunt.

The hunt for Tenner.

That's what got him on the road, in a blizzard lathering up the countryside in freezing white. His anxiousness was rewarded with diminished visibility, which forced him to slow down to a crawl on the one, barely seen lane of a suspected four, split by a continuous wedge of waist-high concrete. He drove down the 101 heading into Halifax, straining to see anything on either side of him. The closer he got to the city, the mightier the storm became.

Scott stopped the SUV, listening to the brakes shriek. He leaned forward onto the steering wheel, as if about to gnaw on his own knuckles. *Jeeeeeesus.* If snow were shit, then the Lord had downed a case of fibre supplement and was voiding in spectacular fashion. Beyond the frenetic *one-two, one-two, one-two* of the wipers, he could barely make out the road anymore. The Durango wore all-season tires, but the first hill he came to would probably halt the vehicle in its tracks, spinning its wheels in place, four-wheel drive or no. On impulse, he turned off the wipers. It only took seconds for thick chunks of snow to blot the windshield, draping the already dark interior in deeper gloom. Perhaps the snow was really volcanic ash from Krakatoa, and the end of the world had started this very day. That made him shake his head. Only a couple of days since he'd left Gus and already he was thinking of dire shit. *Tsk*ing, he reached behind his seat, groping at the floor. His hand wrapped around the neck of a bottle, and Scott brought up a forty ouncer of Jack Daniels Sour Mash whiskey. The black label greeted him, and he twisted off the stopper. A sniff cleared his thoughts and distracted him from the weather. Not normally one to drink, and especially never when driving, Scott took a sip of the whiskey and grimaced. It didn't go down like water for him, unlike Gus, but he couldn't deny that in a world like this, on a day about to be buried in snow, the whiskey had a grounding effect.

He took one more sip from the bottle before replacing the cap and tossing the whiskey into the passenger seat. The last sign he had spotted declared Halifax was only thirty kilometers away. Only thirty, but at current speed, he wasn't going to get there anytime soon. A blast of wind slammed into the windshield, coating it with even more snow and darkening the interior to the point where the dashboard lights gleamed brightly. Well, he figured, he wasn't doing anything by staying here. Time to get a move on. The clock read 9:47. The faster he could get into the city, the better chance he had of finding some place to wait out the storm.

He flicked on the wipers, and the first swish revealed a face coated in snow and ice. Torn cheek flesh, meaty enough to have slivers of frost formed on it, exposed a ferocious sneer of yellow and black teeth, all the way back to the last molars and the thing's dirty alabaster hinge of a jaw. Inky sores and skin tags blotted the parts of its face not ripped away. Dead eyes peered into the interior of the SUV, the corpse's horrid smirk unflinching.

The fright of suddenly seeing the thing subsided, and Scott let out his breath. The undead outside couldn't see him. Certainly couldn't smell him. But it was there because . . . Why? Was it just wandering through the blizzard, searching for something to feast on? *Jesus Christ.* What were the chances of running into Frosty the fucking Flesh Eater on the highway?

Then another, more gruesome chill flooded his person, penetrating even his ass, which had the benefit of having a heater built into the seat under it.

What if Frosty wasn't alone?

The beat of the wipers matched the pounding in his chest. He put the machine into drive and edged past the dead thing in the road. The side mirror bumped the corpse and pushed it off-balance enough for it to fall. Just like that it was gone, and there was enough swirling around the SUV and in his mirrors to make the gimp disappear from sight. The truck pushed forward, reaching twenty kilometers an hour, but only a few seconds later, two more figures appeared in the road, hunched over and frozen-looking and wearing only summer clothing. Then three more—stood off on the shoulders of the highway, pitiful in the cold, but eyeing the moving truck with famished curiosity. Their blood-drained flesh repulsed Scott enough to speed up to thirty, and he kept his eyes open for others. Cars and trucks dotted the road, slowly being swallowed in white drifts, and the snow snaked around the remains like steam from fresh kills.

Why are there so many gimps around? Scott didn't understand it, unless there was a small town on the outskirts of the city. Something he'd passed without noticing the sign. Some of the signs were nothing more than broken wooden posts, appearing like jagged ankles and shins in the snow. Or maybe there were simply so *many* of the things about, and that notion did nothing for his nerves. He kept easing the SUV forward, craning his neck to see anything resembling a sign, but finding nothing except a thickening of cars and trucks. The wind subsided for a moment and, off to the right and through the passenger window, he thought the forest fell away into a valley. He stopped and lowered the window to see. The blizzard howled once more and spat snow into the interior. After a few moments of seeing nothing through the bleached veil, the window went back up.

He rubbed his face, feeling the growing carpet of stubble on his chin and knowing he needed a shave. Maybe he'd let the beard grow and become Gus's twin. The man would probably chuckle at that. The Durango's GPS still functioned, and Scott saw that he had reached Sackville. The SUV climbed a hill, and he slowed down to allow greater traction. After levelling out, the road ahead disappeared in a sheet of flying white that whipped across the highway. Ghostly buildings, their shapes barely recognizable, stood behind tattered fences of trees and brush on either side. He couldn't see anything that might provide shelter from the storm. Scott grimly drove on, pushing through wild streamers that screamed from the heights of rising drifts.

Another hour and the highways would be buried.

He suddenly wanted another shot of booze. Something to take the edge off.

More gimps, staring and partially bowed by the blizzard, came into view and vanished as the SUV squeezed by, not even moving on the vehicle.

But they were there.

Worse, they were there in numbers.

Scott remembered Saint John in his native New Brunswick, and how the city had become a teeming nest for the undead. Halifax was an even bigger city, due to an influx of shipyard construction contracts it had won some twenty-five years ago. The city had ballooned from a modest population of perhaps four hundred thousand to at least one and a half million. That number burned in Scott's mind and furrowed his brow. One point five million people. At least eighty percent probably turned into roaming flesh feeders, which made an army of well over a million. Perhaps some had been destroyed by Army efforts or law enforcement agencies. Maybe a few had been put down by folks like Gus. But in the end, a *population* waited for him. For anyone wanting to visit the city.

Scott sighed. Finding Tenner in the concrete guts of Halifax wasn't going to be easy, if he was even there. The only thing he had on his side was the weather and the freezing temperatures. The cold slowed the zombies down, and the elements certainly ravaged the pasty flesh and musculature covering their bones, but for some reason unknown, they never fully rotted away. At least, not after more than two years. Whatever was keeping the undead animated apparently kept them from decomposing, or at least slowed the process to a crawl. Somewhere, there were scientists in bunkers studying the deadheads, trying to better understand them . . . or so he liked to think.

Regardless, the season and everything that came with it were on his side. After that, he couldn't think of anything else. He could spend months, *years* searching the city for Tenner, but a central hub was perhaps the best place to start a major hunt.

The need for a secure base came to his mind. Something that was easily defendable against the masses, like Gus had with his estate on the mountain. Perhaps even one of the high-rises in the city, once the lower doors had been sealed off. It merited more thought and investigation. He would need a place to stay while hunting—hell, he needed a place *now* to get out of the storm.

Shops, restaurants, and gas bars on either side of the road passed by in the hoary gloom, filing into sight and rolling behind as if on a massive conveyor belt. An unmistakable golden M against a background of red loomed up on a dented post, appearing like a giant fly swatter poised to smash something. A shopping plaza formed at the absolute edge of his vision, its storefronts frosted and hunkered down in the gathering snow like forgotten bunkers. Fangs of ice hung from power lines and swung in the wind. Some houses appeared on the right, cresting a small rise, which Scott spotted the turn-off for. He slowed for a moment, considering the road ahead and the GPS, still functioning two years after the collapse of everything. *Closer*, he told himself. *Need to get closer.*

Trouble was, getting closer might become a problem. Abandoned vehicles littered the highway in growing numbers, appearing out of the heart of the storm and forcing him to slow down and weave amongst them. Driving in a straight line became more difficult. Ice coated several burnt-out wrecks, crystalizing metallic bones that rose up like clasping fingers.

A bleached wall rose up out of the raging blizzard. Scott stopped the Durango and stared at the barrier for a moment before finally realizing what it was—an overturned transport truck, its top facing him. The crashed carrier had smashed through the concrete barrier dividing the lanes and barred all travellers from proceeding any further. Snow rasped the outer shell of the Durango, sounding cold to Scott and daring him to step outside.

Fuck that, he thought. Looking around, he put the Durango into reverse. The GPS display built into the dash disappeared, replaced by a white speckled image of what was behind the SUV. Scott scowled and almost swore. Snow covered the lens of the rear camera, which showed only a partial image. He placed his arm behind the passenger seat and twisted in his seat to look out the rear window, not liking having to back up the old-fashioned way. All he could see was a blank, tinted canvass bordered by lumps that were car wrecks.

"Five feet." A calm female voice spiked the air, emanating from the speakers. It was the only voice he'd heard in days. "Four feet. Caution. Three feet. Caution. Two feet. Cau—"

Scott stopped.

He shifted into drive and turned around without having to engage the onboard sensors.

The wipers worked hard to clear the windshield, but he knew the blizzard was actually getting stronger. Some parts of the Maritimes experienced upward of one hundred and fifty kilometer winds, strong enough to rip a person off their feet or tear the tops off houses.

Snaking his way ahead, he turned off the road and drove through a gap of cars, heading south on the side of the blanketed roadway. The tires handled things beautifully, keeping him moving forward without getting stuck. The overturned transport came into view, then he was past it. More cars rose out of the white gloom, frozen in place, and he maneuvered around them, getting back onto the 101.

The clock said 10:12. That bothered Scott. The blowing snow, reduced visibility, and abandoned cars were all playing with him. He wanted nothing better than to get a little closer to the city before finding a place to hunker down and wait things out. Another gust of wind splashed his windshield, hard enough to startle him and sending a clear message to stop thinking *shit*. Best to get off the road *now*, while he possessed the control to do so.

Grimacing, Scott elected to do just that.

The Durango crawled through the storm, passing under overpasses that didn't offer much shelter from the weather pelting the SUV's metal hide. He soon realized that his opportunity to get out of the storm quickly had already passed, and he was committed to riding down the deep throat of highway. One of the overpasses had a sign that said Halifax, with an arrow pointing to the right. An almost ethereal exit materialized out of the storm, marking the way.

Beside it and swaying with the wind stood a skeletal figure, draped in rags that blew furiously about its person. Hair and cloth flapped around its head, masking its face, but Scott got close enough to see a frosty, lipless smile leering at him before it drifted past the passenger window and slipped out of view. He glanced over his shoulder, expecting the thing to reach out and smash the side of the vehicle, but it did not.

Then it was gone, swallowed up by the storm.

And he was on the exit for Halifax.

5

The Durango crept down the 102 and headed deeper into the storm. Scott thought he saw the tips of roofs to his left, through searing sheets of blowing snow, but there was no clear way to get the vehicle over galvanized steel guardrails, so he continued driving. The trees vanished at points and the snow ripped across the highway so fiercely that he simply stopped and gawked at the blizzard's fury. *Like a carwash*, Scott thought, peering out at it. He lowered the window on his side and stuck his head out, squinting against the blast of air and sting of ice and not seeing any farther than five feet in front of him. There was no way to get his bearings.

Then he saw it on his left—a grey, waist-high wall separating the opposing lane from the one he was in. Keeping his window down, Scott eased the Durango over until he could have touched the wall if he stuck out his arm, creeping along it as if it were a safety rope guiding him forward. Cars and other motor vehicles still littered the highway, and these he drove by as best as he could, leaving the guidance of the wall when he had to. The outline of a large building rose up on the left, and he realized it was a hotel.

A hotel!

It was close, and certainly tempting, but it wouldn't do. Large buildings like hotels could potentially hold a nest of deadheads, and cleaning it out would be long and dangerous. The smaller houses were his best bet.

He drove on.

By 11:34, a row of houses appeared on his right with their backs against the wind. A low wire fence was the only thing barring him from them, so he drove the Durango through it, cringing upon the contact and bouncing in his seat. The tires spun in the deepening snow, but he smashed through it. The Durango struggled as it pulled around cars half-buried in drifts. The GPS informed him that he was on School Avenue.

Hunched over the steering wheel, Scott slowly drove by houses, knowing full well that if the snow got too deep, he would spin his tires and become trapped. Worse, he was driving up an incline, and he knew he risked hearing the whine of tires losing traction. Even as he thought it, a red two-story house rose up out of the blizzard. With a gasp, Scott aimed the Durango at the closed garage attached to the house's side. He pulled into the driveway, stopped, and popped open the driver's door. Getting out, he put on his helmet with the lightning bolts decorating it. The wind whipped around him, spearing him through the layer of black and yellow Nomex and the extra layer of sweaters underneath. Bracing himself against the wind, he moved to the rear door of the SUV, opened it, and pulled out the aluminum bat. The sound-suppressed Ruger was already in his right boot, but he didn't want to use that unless absolutely necessary. Ammunition for the weapon was limited. Hefting the bat with one hand, he struggled to close the Durango's door with the other. *Cold.* It was so cold that his hands, protected by Nomex gloves, already began to feel chilled.

Pointing himself in the direction of the house, he strained forward into the strength of the wind. Snow rose to just below his knees the closer he got to the front door. The door was locked, but Scott put the bat through one corner of its window. A moment later, he unlocked the door, pushed it open, and shambled inside. Once out of the cold, he closed the door with a gasp.

Outside, the blizzard howled at his escape.

Scott lifted the visor and took a firmer grip on his bat. The front door led to a short hallway that opened up into a carpeted living room, while a stairway leading up to the second floor lay to his left. Pictures of tropical destinations and warm beaches speckled eggshell-white walls. Old, but comfortable furniture filled the living room, and one cozy-looking sofa tempted him to collapse onto it.

Scott hated the next part, but it was the fastest way to clear a house. He rapped the bat on the banister of the stairs, the sound of metal rattling on wood momentarily blotting out the raging blizzard outside.

"Hey," he called out. "Anyone home? Anyone there? Hey?"

Snow rasped against the window and door, and a blast of wind blew in through the hole he'd smashed in the glass pane. He'd have to fix it later.

"I said *hey!* Anyone in here? Mind if I stay for a while? Huh?"

Nothing.

He slipped through the living room, bat at the ready, into the adjoining dining room area, where a tall glass cabinet displayed fine china. The kitchen was full, complete with a single square table tucked into one corner, which struck Scott as very homey. Another door led to the backyard, buried in snow. A short hall led to a small washroom and shower and another door that opened up to a respectable garage, filled with all manner of tools. Fixing the front door's broken window pane once again entered his mind.

The wind made the house creak, as if it were trying to swallow it whole. Scott considered the upstairs. He closed the door to the garage and returned to the steps. There didn't seem to be a basement, and that suited him fine. Resting one gloved hand on the railing, he climbed the stairs to the second level. The steps groaned under his weight, but Scott didn't slow down until he reached the top.

"Hey. Not going to hurt anyone, okay?"

He didn't know why that came out of him, but it just did. He looked into the red and white bedroom that had likely belonged to a teenage girl. Boy-band posters tacked to the wall and stuffed animals lay everywhere, the largest a brown teddy bear that sat just inside the doorway. Scott stroked the animal's head once.

He left the bedroom and went into the main bathroom. The air, while not as frigid as it was outside, was still cold to breathe. He took his time inspecting the blue bathtub and shower, the matching tiles, and a countertop littered with curling irons, half-squished rolls of ancient toothpaste, and other toiletries. The sight of a toilet with a full roll of pink toilet paper fixed on a wall dispenser made him smile. He ignored the two mirrors, not wanting to see himself. Another door lay at the end of the bathroom, next to the toilet, and Scott opened it.

The master bedroom.

Whoever he was, he had placed a pillow over his wife's head where she lay in bed, just before he had shot her. He'd covered the shredded foam stuffing, black matter, and bone fragments with a much too thin white towel. Scott guessed the husband had probably planted the pillow over his wife's face so he didn't have to look at her as he pulled the trigger.

Then the guy had gone to the foot of the bed and sat down in an easy chair that matched the blue bed blankets. He'd apparently tucked the end of a long-barreled shotgun under his chin and squeezed the trigger, taking the top of his head off like a spent firecracker—the cheap kind with ribbons in it. Unfortunately for Scott, whoever the dead man was hadn't felt the need to cover himself with a towel, and a gruesome black pattern stained the wall above the corpse's ruined head. Scott let his breath out in a hiss that was both sad and relieved. He stared at the body for a bit, noting the withered flesh of the hands and the melancholy grimace left by the shotgun's blast.

"Sorry," he let out and sighed again. He didn't blame either one of the people in the room. Many times he felt like taking the very same flight out. Still might, but not until he finished what he set out to do.

"I hope you don't mind," he said, in a low, respectful voice. "Storm's pretty bad out there. I'd like to stay here for a while."

Neither corpse answered. The wind rocked the house once more, making its frame groan. He felt he should say a few words, but the need passed.

"Thank you," was all he said, closing both doors to the master bedroom as gently as he could. He didn't bother taking the weapon on the floor beside the dead man, feeling it wouldn't be right. Scott had his weapons and felt he was intruding enough by staying in the dead couple's well-kept home.

Deeming the house clear, he returned to the garage and rooted around until he found a hammer, nails, and a couple of wooden planks that he sawed short. He returned to the front door and nailed a thick blanket taken from a full linen closet over the broken glass. He nailed a few planks into place, reducing the wind coming into the house to an asthmatic wheeze. He pounded one last cut of thick wood into the floor, flush against the door and bracing it firmly.

Having done that, Scott went to the garage and opened its heavy outer door. Moments later, he squeezed the Durango inside and sealed the bay behind it. There were two oval windows in the outer door's surface, frosted over, but Scott didn't need to look outside. He'd already spent the morning staring at that white shit.

It was getting on into afternoon, and his stomach rumbled. Lunch lay in the back of the Durango and, feeling secure, he went and got it. Gus had given him a hodge-podge of canned and preserved food, all in three cardboard boxes. He opened up the one box he'd already started on and studied the gleaming grey tops. There was a little bit of everything in there, and while he'd been in Windsor, Scott found he liked reaching in and taking out a can without looking at the label.

This time, it was Irish stew. He sighed in relief. He knew there was soup in there as well, but he didn't want any. He needed something with a little more sustenance. A feeling of weariness hit him, and he pinched the bridge of his nose as if that one gesture could fight off exhaustion. *Sleep would be very good right now,* he thought, but not until he refilled his stomach. He gathered up the can opener—just in case there wasn't one inside—a four liter jug of water, a paperback copy of Jason E. Thummel's *The Spear of Destiny*, and trudged back inside.

The second upstairs bedroom became his kitchen and dining room because it faced the road and the livid might of the storm. He sat at a desk opposite the bed and ate the stew, listening to his own chewing and the wind intensifying outside. Time drifted. The sound of the spoon scraping against the empty can brought him back, and he felt the lump of cold lunch in his stomach. Ice rasped against the window, and Scott blinked bleary-eyed at the world outside. Only the dead would be out in such a blizzard. There might have been a joke in there somewhere, but he was too tired to extract it. The bed beckoned.

But he didn't want to relax just yet.

He made one last round of the house, checking the doors and windows on the ground level and weighing the idea of boarding them up. He decided to leave them for another time and climbed the stairway back to the bedroom. After placing his bat against the bed and the Ruger on the nightstand, he allowed himself the pleasure of taking off his boots and flexing his sock-covered toes. The Nomex coat followed, then the pants and the padded hockey vest. He kept his blue jeans and sweaters on. A nearby linen closet had a number of thick blankets, and they all went on top of the bed.

Crawling underneath the lot, Scott shifted about until he was comfortable on his back. He turned his head and saw the big brown teddy bear studying him with black crystal eyes.

"You're on guard now," he whispered, feeling the tension of the morning slip away. "Lemme know if anything . . . if anything goes on, 'kay?"

The bear didn't answer.

"All right, be that way," Scott muttered, closing his eyes.

And that was that.

6

The blizzard stayed overhead for two days, straining to take the roof off the house at times and beating the windows as if they were taut drum skins. It swallowed up the road outside in blustery huffs, buried the cars, and prevented Scott from seeing anything beyond the lane out front, worrying him that the end had finally come, a perfect storm heralding in a late Ice Age. Stranded as he was, he made the best of the time with what he had: finishing the paperback and starting *Dark Passage* by Griffin Hayes, playing Texas Hold 'Em with the teddy bear—who cheated, as far as he could tell—sleeping, and keeping guard at the upstairs window. At the end of the first day, he didn't have any fear of the dead coming inside, because the winter storm continued to pummel everything outside. The house allowed him to lower his guard, and if he didn't think about the two corpses in the master bedroom, things weren't that bad.

For being trapped in a house in the middle of a killer blizzard, that was.

Every now and again, he'd sip on the Jack Daniels, appreciating the warmth and the fact that no more of the stuff would ever be made. He supposed that increased the value of every bottle Gus had given him.

During one shift at the window, a figure had staggered along the road outside. Black limbs could be seen through the milky veil, and Scott tracked it only as long as it stayed in sight. It was a dead fucker, he had no doubt of that. No human would simply walk along the road in such piss-poor weather, not while there were so many houses along the way in which to take shelter. It disappeared into the blowing snow after a few minutes, but Scott remained vigilant until nightfall.

The next morning, the sun appeared as a yellow ball burning through a sky of cotton. The storm had broken, yet fat snowflakes sashayed to the ground like feathers. Scott finished eating a can of cold tomato soup while guessing at which way the weather would go. He estimated the time to be around eight thirty in the morning.

Then came the more difficult question. Should he venture out into the world? The only other option he had was staying at the house for the rest of the winter.

"No thanks," he said to the bear. "It'd be too dangerous for you."

Feeling the cold through the house, he suited up. He found a blue backpack in the garage and lengthened the shoulder straps to accommodate the bulk of the Nomex. He didn't put it on just yet, however, as he wanted to see what it was like outside. He had the strap for the shotgun and could sling the weapon over his shoulder, but he wished he had something for the bat like Gus did. He'd have to keep an eye out for sporting goods shops that specialized in golf clubs. He elected to stuff the bat into the already full backpack, moving things around until it stuck straight up like some fat antennae. Then he closed the zippers as far as they could go, right to the bat's grip.

That worked. He put on the backpack, then decided to take out the bat, figuring it better to have one weapon in hand. Once he put his helmet in place, he walked over to the garage door, bent over, and lifted with a grunt, opening it to knee-height.

A snow-packed wall stood in front the length of the door. Scott stepped back in awe. He should have expected it. Muttering about Nova Scotian winters, he stepped forward and pulled the door up to his waist, exerting a great deal of strength.

More snow. For a moment, Scott believed an avalanche had parked right over him. There was a wide-bladed snow shovel in the garage, but he didn't want to have to dig his way out onto the front street. He lowered the garage door and went to the kitchen, where the door led into the backyard. The door opened with a blast of frigid air, and a waist-high drift stopped him in his tracks.

Shit. He reached out and pushed the snow away. Whorls of white whipped past his head, blown into the kitchen by a stiff wind. The snow wasn't heavy, but it still took effort to clean enough of it away so that he could step out, his legs sinking in up to the knee.

Closing the door behind him with one hand, bat in the other, Scott stood on the deck and surveyed the buried backyard, which was tinted dark by his visor. A shed stood in the back, half buried, no doubt full of gardening supplies for a spring that seemed a long way off. He stepped awkwardly to the railing and poked his bat into the snow, testing for depth. The snow was deep, but he took a cautious step off the deck anyway.

Whomf. He sunk through the top layer and ended up submerged to his crotch. He stood there for a moment, flabbergasted at the memory of actually *enjoying* this shit when he was a kid. There were no fences in any of the nearby backyards that he could see, and any digging might attract attention, but there was no other way to get loose from the snow. Placing the bat to one side, Scott started digging like a dog to free his legs. Once that was done, he took the bat and retreated back into the house. A few minutes later, he re-emerged with the wide shovel, telling himself that if he was having trouble in the conditions, so were the undead.

He got to slinging snow.

An hour into it and he felt as if he were melting underneath the Nomex. He got clear of the one drift leaning against the back of the house, but the snow filling the backyard still remained almost knee-high. When he finally reached the door of the shed, he felt exhausted enough to crawl back into the house and sleep for a week.

Scott dug out the green door to the shed only to find it padlocked. He smashed the lock with the bat and swiped the ruined metal away. The door opened and, as expected, shovels, gardening tools, a lawnmower, and other landscaping equipment filled the small area. Fishing rods lined the ceiling, up and away in the low hanging rafters, and hand nets of various sizes hung like saggy spider webs.

"Couldn't you've had . . . a goddamn snow blower?" Scott asked the shed.

He looked to the sky. He hated to think he had wasted most of the morning on getting to a shed with nothing useful in it. He returned his attention to the light and spotted garages in some of the other backyards, but huge, pearly dunes barred the way. Thoughts of what the road looked like after the snowstorm entered his head.

Shovel in hand, he struggled toward the next backyard.

By afternoon, he'd dug his way to three sheds and garages and found a pair of snow shoes. Unsure if the things actually worked, he spent the next ten minutes strapping them to his boots. Tentatively, he rose up on the tennis-racket-shaped footwear and took the first careful step in the backyard of a yellow bungalow. He walked in circles, stumbling several times and even falling over once, until he got the hang of walking in the shoes. One hour later, he returned to the house he'd made base in, left the snow shoes sticking upright in a snow drift near the door, and got something to eat from the truck. While he feasted on cold beans and wieners from a can, he wondered if there might be a snow machine in one of the garages or sheds. If he was fortunate, he might be able to find one. If he was really lucky, the thing would start. Scott didn't want to think about heading deeper into the city with such a thick mess on the ground. It almost made sense to wait until spring.

When the rest of the dead would be up and walking around as well.

Sighing over the no-win situation, Scott finished his meal.

"What are you doing?" Kelly smiled at him, twisting around on the bed where she sat cross-legged. The television blared out a story on congested traffic on the highway, but he wasn't paying any attention. He was more interested in tracing a finger along the waistband of Kelly's plaid pajama bottoms, and the little wedge of white flesh between the parting fabrics as she leaned forward.

"Leave it alone!"

Scott lay stretched out on the bed next to her and didn't say anything. He smiled instead and kept on reading his Kindle. Instead of stopping, his fingertips brushed her bare skin above the waistline of her pajamas. She had the sexiest back dimples. It was difficult to read at times like these, and just watching her toss her hair, a lovely shade of dirty beach blond, was a delight he still hadn't revealed to her, not even after three years of marriage. She probably knew it anyway.

"If you don't stop, we're gonna fight." She warned him with a cross look that was somewhat thrown off by her efforts to conceal a giggle.

"Can't help it. You're flashing me here."

Kelly reached around and felt her exposed skin. "There isn't even any butt crack showing," she grated.

"Still flashing me."

"It doesn't count."

"Does so count."

"Jesus, it's only my lower back! Get a hold of yourself." She pushed his hand away.

Scott sing-song grunted affirmation, indicating it was an idea. Not a great one, however. Kelly returned to watching television, leaning forward once again, her faded T-shirt rising up her back like the rising curtain of a peepshow Scott wouldn't mind seeing more of. A *lot* more. His fingers dabbled at her back again, daring, right on the line, eliciting a dramatic growl of exasperation from Kelly. She reached around and grabbed his fingers, lifted one butt cheek, and plopped it down on his entire hand, trapping it under warm, firm, cotton-covered flesh.

Scott considered the predicament for all of three seconds, before he started wiggling his fingers.

Kelly's head slumped between her shoulders. "I'm warning you, man . . ."

It was adorable when she warned him.

But then from the hallway, Suzy bawled out, long and startling. The cry ended on the swell of another nerve-grating howl, barely separated by an intake of breath. Kelly immediately got up off his hand and the bed in a flash, her pale profile wrinkling with concern, and went for the door.

"Wait," Scott heard himself saying, while another part of him wanted to grab her by the arms and stop her from leaving the room. *Needed* to stop her from leaving, because he knew what lay beyond their warm bedroom. He knew what their only child was becoming. Right then his consciousness floated above the scene, as if secretly jettisoned from the figure still on the bed.

Suzy cried out again, but her little baby voice was morphing into the moan of something else. Something hungry.

"Don't go," he called in a pleading voice, reaching for his wife, who was well out of range.

Kelly wasn't even listening to him. The doorway became a dark portal then, where once there was light.

"Kelly—"

Again in that laid back voice while his inner thoughts wanted to shout *stop!*

"Don't. Come out," Scott heard himself saying, feeling the scene teeter and slip away, feeling the dream coming to an end, its reality being pinched away from him at the very center, like someone picking up a tissue. Kelly didn't even pause, and he watched her with that sinking feeling of dread permeating his very heart, aware that he was leaving the bedroom in cinematic slow motion. Leaving, leaving . . .

"Don't—"

The scream from beyond was right in his ears.

Scott opened his eyes and stared at the ceiling. The wind outside didn't moan or claw at the window, but the room felt a little colder than it had. A little more empty. He lay in bed and simply missed the feel of his long dead wife, missed the scent of her, cherishing those last few moments when the world was just fine and all he worried about was making enough to pay their rent. The dreams were so *real*, and while one could usually tell if a dream was going well or poorly, his always seemed to change from bliss to total terror in a capsizing wink.

He rolled his head to one side and met the gaze of the teddy bear. With the same hand he had touched his wife with—still feeling her skin on his fingertips—he reached out and, hesitantly, caressed the animal's soft head.

"This doesn't make me gay," he whispered, staring into the crystal brown eyes of the bear.

An hour later he was outside, decked out in full gear. He trudged forward through the snow, appreciating the snowshoes with each step and using another shovel he had found in a storage shed for balance. The sun hung low in the sky, brilliant and blinding, transforming the mounds of snow into fine, sparkling sculptures. Visor down, Scott travelled from backyard to backyard, stepping over fences the snow had blown up against. He broke into eight more sheds and garages without finding anything he needed.

He used snowdrifts as ramps over some of the fences, but that came to an abrupt end in one backyard, as the final, stained fence was much higher than the others, preventing him from seeing over it. That left the driveway, gorged with snow that resembled the long spine of some unknown frozen creature. He shuffled alongside the house in those long sweeping steps he'd learned to take while in snowshoes. Red siding covered the house, awash in a spray of frozen moisture that made him think of ships at sea. He walked into the road and saw, for the first time since taking refuge from the storm, that it was just off the main highway. Standing there, he turned in every direction searching for zombies, seeing none and hearing nothing. Shrugging, he made his way across the drifts in front of the next house, then made a beeline for the large shed out back.

Another padlock barred his way, and he snapped the silvery lock off with two cracks of the bat. The sound echoed eerily into nothing, and he waited for deadheads to appear.

None did.

Warily, he considered the structure before him. The windows appeared black, and he didn't bother lifting his visor to look inside.

He dug out the door enough to open it, a little awkward to do with the snowshoes on, and turned the lever after mentally preparing himself for the worst.

The door opened to reveal a dark interior full of band saws and worktables. Mallets and sanders hung off the walls, and a low row of fragrant birch wood was stacked next to a wood-burning stove. Scott stood on the threshold of the shed, obviously a craftsman's domain, and saw a worn-looking rocking chair perched high on one of the worktables, awaiting a final coat of paint or varnish that would never come.

Then he saw the rifle on the workbench, laid out underneath a window that allowed a slant of light into the room. He went to the bench and inspected the chestnut stock, not familiar with any weaponry other than his twelve gauge. The owner had mounted a large scope on the rifle, which reminded Scott of a telescope. A quick check of the nearby cabinets revealed three boxes of brass shells. He left it all, not wanting the extra weight and having more than enough shells for the shotgun.

He left the shed and closed the door. Once back on School Avenue, he started hiking, going past houses that didn't have any storage sheds or garages. Most had only driveways, glutted with snow. The tops of cars peeked out from under huge drifts, which would take a good two hours to uncover. Scott blinked. The blizzard had dumped a frozen sky upon the city.

But no undead.

That was heartening, but he knew they were nearby. Either underneath the snow he walked upon or inside the houses. It wasn't the first winter he'd lived through with corpses walking around, but there was every chance it could be his last.

The road's incline was perhaps a lazy ten degrees, and Scott walked until he spied another garage behind a house. He took in his surroundings, seeing tiny white wisps swirl off the street, marking a subtle increase in the wind.

Adjusting the straps on his backpack, he headed inside.

The garage was made of red brick with a black main door. He cleared away the snow at the base until he found the handle and hoisted up the door. Cranky wheels squealed.

Empty.

Not even a pot to piss in.

With a snarl, Scott shoved the door downward and looked at the sky. The sun just passed its zenith, and he figured he had two choices.

Continue on foot.

Or hole up in the house until the snow melted.

He didn't like either choice. In the end, he got walking. He'd packed enough food and water for a couple of days if he ate sparingly. Snowmelt would offset some intake of water. The thought of returning to Gus and Roxanne entered his mind, but he discarded it. That was a potential triangle he didn't want to get involved in.

With snow shovel in hand and gear slung across his back, he mushed.

The sky remained bright as he plodded deeper into the city, following what was the 102 until he reached an overpass. He lumbered over to the crossing's guardrail and gazed at the highway running underneath, north and south. Beyond, the land glistened under the midday sun. A forlorn breeze gave sound to the picture, and at that instant, a great feeling of loneliness swept through him. Even after two years, the desolation was still a chore to combat at times, even for a natural recluse like himself.

He continued on, making good time on the highway, until it split into two separate lanes marked by a white "No Engine Braking" sign. To his left lay a cluster of houses just past a metal tower holding up dead power cables. To his right and at the end of a curving road stood what appeared to be a hospital. The choice was easy. He stayed in the left lane and continued on, not wanting to venture anywhere near a hospital, apartment complex, or some other large building that could potentially be sheltering a large number of gimps.

Scott thought he was still on School Avenue. The land dipped and went by an open field on the left. No signs of life. More houses and power line towers on the left, a frozen collage of colours and cables. None of the houses appealed to him as a place to stop, and seeing as he still had an hour or two of daylight remaining, he decided to push on.

He stopped underneath a metalwork archway displaying the signs "WRONG WAY," "TRURO SOUTH SHORE ANNAPOLIS VALLEY," and "BAYER'S ROAD." There was little cover, so he selected one house painted sky blue and approached it. It only had the one level and snow surrounded the property, but Scott didn't care. He wanted to get out of the cold and eat something. The front door was easily accessible from the road, and he wasn't surprised to discover it locked. He went around back, walking by a set of bicycle handlebars that came up to his ankles. The back door was wooden, paint flaking, and also locked. Scowling, he had no choice but to enter through a side window. He punched out the glass with the shovel, cringing at the noise. He waited for anything to come to the window, and when nothing did, he unslung his pack and plopped it inside.

The search of the house went quickly and the place was unoccupied, much to his relief. There was a playroom for a young child, and he was thankful it was empty. He didn't want any part of putting down a kid deadhead. He closed the doors leading to the porch area he'd broken into and sat down at a kitchen table covered by a Christmas cloth. He removed his helmet and opened a can of ravioli from his backpack. He noticed a can of sweet corn in there as well, but he would save that for supper. Once again, the idea of turning around and heading back to the truck entered his mind, tempting him to leave his hopeless hunt and return to Gus's mountain.

Instead, he finished his meal and left the empty can in the sink.

7

The next morning, he trudged up the middle of a four lane road, toward the rise of a small hill. From the position of the sun, Scott estimated it was around ten in the morning. Massive snowdrifts ran northwest, reminding him of documentaries where divers mapped untouched ocean floors. He looked back every now and again, just to see how far he'd come and to see if anything was stalking him. His spoon-shaped tracks ran away from him until eventually fading from sight. Halifax was a sprawling city, but from what he saw of the numerous elm trees laid bare by winter, he imagined it was an incredibly green place in the spring and summer. He and Kelly had talked about visiting Halifax several times, but the opportunity never presented itself.

Kelly. Fragments of his latest dream sunk into his mind like wood splinters. He tried focusing on just the good parts and forgetting about the bad. He swore he could still feel her skin on his fingertips. That sensation lifted his spirits in ways a man could only appreciate in very dark times.

In fact, he became so focused on his inner memories he didn't realize the increasing lumps in his path. He stumbled on one, barely catching his balance and avoiding a fall by jabbing his shovel out in front of him. When he straightened up, he saw it and went cold inside.

An apartment building. Right next to the road. Four levels high, and God only knew how deep. Scott couldn't see around the structure, but he felt the need to distance himself from it.

Then he noticed what he'd tripped over.

It was a half-buried man, on a part of the street not entirely covered in snow. A road worker with the yellow reflective X crossing his chest. Ice glued his pasty flesh to the asphalt underneath, and Scott had managed to crack the body when he stumbled over it. A grimace of pain contorted the thing's features while snowflakes sprinkled its teeth and black gum lines. Numerous skin tags, as pointed as the tips of black pens, clustered about its mouth.

An eye cracked open in the gimp's head.

Worse, the barest of hisses issued from the creature's frozen jaw. Scott drew back.

The eye tracked him as far as it could. The head tried to move, but it was fixed to the pavement. An arm broke away from its body, waving stiffly in the air. The thing struggled to rise, groaning with the effort, but it stayed in place.

Scott realized he was standing in the middle of the road, countless other similar bumps dotting it.

An unnerving *crack* brought Scott's attention back to the gimp, which was lifting its head from its icy pillow. A long shred of skin stayed attached to the frozen ground like a piece of nailed-down black canvas. The monster's lips stretched before splitting, revealing a row of ebony teeth.

More moans cut the air around Scott as things awakened and crawled out from their white blankets. Arms slinked out of the snow. Fingers came forward slowly like the legs of spiders. Corpses pushed themselves upright, snow sloughing from their backs. One zombie sat up like a vampire rising from its coffin, its mouth clicking open in lockjaw fashion.

The zombie in front of Scott reached for him.

He whipped the shovel across the gimp's head, shattering the wide plastic blade. Scott took a step back and held up the handle in shock. He recovered quickly and plunged the tip of the wooden shaft into the dead thing's eye, feeling the ice hard resistance, but still spearing the zombie dead.

But others were near.

Scott reached back and gripped the shaft of the baseball bat. He scooted the weapon up and out of his backpack, immediately swinging at another gimp clambering toward him. He bashed the monster's skull, breaking it open in a single clattering note and driving it to the pavement. Brain matter spurted across the snow like a grisly bowl of overturned cornflakes. Wasting no time, Scott bolted past the unmoving body and through the awakening crowd. Zombies struggled to get to their feet behind and around him. He ran, taking great lopping strides so that he wouldn't trip in his snowshoes, holding the bat across his chest as he pumped up a small hill. The cries of the dead came from all sides, and from his peripheral vision, more dark shapes pulled themselves up through the snow, climbing to their feet. Zombies rose from the snow on the road ahead. Scott ran by them, not bothering to swing because they moved so very slow. The cold robbed them of their already limited mobility. He sprinted as fast as he was able until he reached the top of the hill.

And stopped to stare in disbelief at what lay beyond.

The very *land* was rising. Zombies as far as he could see oozed out from underneath the snow-covered streets, blotting out the white with black and grey. They stumbled stiff-legged into the sunlight from nearby houses. They pushed themselves free from tall drifts, getting up like long-lost mountaineers.

They all converged on him.

Scott's breath hitched in his throat. A small *army* was mobilizing around him. He sprinted ahead—too fast—and clacked his snow shoes together. He stumbled to the asphalt, the bat held before him. Shadows fell across him as he clawed at his snowshoes, struggling with the straps, but freeing himself in the end. He kicked them away. Something pulled on his backpack. He got up just as a zombie met him face to visor. Scott jabbed the bat's tip into the creature's chest, knocking it backward. He broke another zombie's knee in one swing, while another took the bat under the chin, straightening it out and knocking it off its bare feet.

Scott evaded three others seeking to entrap him, not wasting energy on dispatching them. He pushed through several more deadheads grasping at his limbs. Ahead on the right lay a wooden church with wide-arched windows. The thought of holing up in there didn't appeal to him. He continued running, the snow above his ankles in places, leeching away a little more strength with each step. He spotted a gas bar and convenience store ahead, its white and red protective canopy set high above six sets of fuel pumps. Something else grabbed his attention as well.

Just past the pumps and below a huge blue sign that read MILK lay a wire cage filled with propane tanks—the grey, ten kilogram variety. Newfound strength surging into his limbs, Scott quickly outpaced the zombies behind him and ran through the mass between him and the gas bar. He wouldn't have much time.

Reaching the propane tanks, a panting Scott saw the padlocks on the doors and groaned. Just inside stood a dozen of the barrel-shaped units, stacked on shelves in fours, all ready for a summer barbeque. Scowling, Scott lifted his bat and cracked it against the padlock, the ring echoing shrilly. The lock held, and he cursed at it.

The deadheads closed in. Scott didn't look at them. He didn't need the extra motivation.

With a frustrated grunt, he left the tanks and ran to the front door. It was unlocked, and he scrambled inside. He flipped the bolts on the door, locking himself in as shuffling zombies closed in on the shade of the canopy. Fear stabbed Scott through the heart. A veritable *concert* mass of cold stricken deadheads had gathered. Seeing the hunters thicken, he frantically glanced around.

Next to the door stood an open freezer, full of deflated and squished ice cream wrappers. The freezer had wheels, and Scott grimaced as he slid the long container over to reinforce the door. There wasn't anything else, and he wasn't certain if the glass would hold. Breathing hard, he searched up and down the shelving units. Most of the food and drinks were gone.

Zombies, made gloomier by the overhead canopy, crowded toward the window panes.

Inside, Scott located a long-neck barbeque lighter, still in its packaging. A clear vial was set into the grip, filled with jiggling butane. Snatching it up and ripping off the packaging, he looked for something to set alight and settled on a pack of men's socks. There were plenty of magazines littering the floor, but little of anything else. Frantically, he scoured the place.

The closest gimp smashed an arm into the glass panels, making Scott look up. Hissing and moans reached him. The thing smeared its face across the window with a squeal. More zombies thumped limbs against the clear surface. Even *more* undead arrived on the scene, pressing into their companions from behind and squishing them against the panels. The barrier shuddered. Milky eyes tracked Scott. Tongues lagged. Teeth gleamed.

Scott backed up toward the storage room entrance and stopped.

There, underneath a shelving unit, he could just see the corner of something black. He pounced on it and brought up a container of charcoal lighter fluid.

There had to be an exit in back, but Scott needed a distraction. He needed cover to escape the gathering army. He needed a *fire*.

He quickly made a nest of the discarded magazines, socks, and any other refuse littering the floor, then doused it all with the lighter fluid. He looked around for anything to add to the clump, found a garbage can with trash, and dumped that into the pile. Scott thought of the storeroom, and he slammed through the swinging door into the back.

The area was dark and virtually empty, filled with nothing but ravaged cardboard boxes and a wooden pallet. He grabbed it all and lugged it back to the front of the store, to the growing pile of combustibles.

Hands thumped the glass. Scott looked up and gasped. He could no longer see the pumps outside. The zombies blocked everything. The door trembled in its frame from the swelling weight against it.

Scott scurried back to the storeroom and searched the shadows. Whoever had been here before him had taken everything.

But then he found them, all standing to attention behind the washroom door.

Four egg-shaped, one pound cylinders, containing propane gas. Scott hissed when he saw them. Then he grabbed them and rushed them to the pallet, heart hammering in his chest. Moving the four cylinders to the pile in seconds, he positioned everything around them and held up the lighter.

On the other side of the glass, the chorus of voices sounded eerily like *"Nooooooo."*

Scott lit the pile. The fire danced through the cluttered material, merrily igniting the quickest to burn. He retreated from the small blaze, feeding it more trash, waiting for the wooden pallet to catch. Smoke filled the small interior of the convenience store, clouding the dark mass of bodies slammed tight against the window. The flames blazed when they touched the material doused in charcoal fluid, and bright ribbons licked the propane cylinders. More smoke billowed, and eventually the wooden pallet started glowing around the edges.

That was enough for Scott. Coughing, he turned and ran through the storage room.

The words *Escape route* flashed in his head. He slapped up his visor and stumbled through the aisles of empty shelving units until he found a heavy door leading outside, a push-down bar across its middle. He paused, catching his breath, not quite ready to venture back outside.

Limbs continued thumping against the glass at the front of the store, a perpetual pounding that tested the structure. The undead cried out, their voices chilling in the dark. Smoke oozed from underneath the door, eventually finding Scott and stinging his eyes. He wondered about staying inside for as long as it took to get the mob off his back. The fire was building inside, but for the moment he was safe.

An explosion rattled him and left him blinking at the door where orange light flickered around the edges. He knew that was the first of four propane bombs. Flames crackled, no longer the little thing he'd started minutes ago. It was all the encouragement he needed, and he turned and barged out the exit, slapping down his visor as he went.

The snow went up to his knees as he loped across an open lot. In the distance stood another church, but this one was made of brick and possessed much narrower windows than the wooden church, almost a throwback to medieval times. A low green mesh fence rose up before him and he vaulted over it, landing on his side. He climbed to his feet, picked up his bat, and looked back at the gas bar.

A wall of zombies slunk past the smoking conflagration the building was transforming into. Some of the dead spilling around the walls spotted him on the other side of the fence. They started pursuing in stiff-legged strides.

Scott turned and ran.

His chest was heaving when he reached the church. A pair of pointed, arched doors greeted him, and he threw one open. Ducking inside, he closed the door behind him. His visor made the interior gloomy, so he slapped it up and paused, trying to control his panting. The church was a wreck of shattered wood, hanging curtains, and black stains he was all too familiar with. He glanced at the main doors he came through and saw broken timbers on the floor, as if a great force from outside had smashed it in. Clumps of grey matter lay in between the debris, and he even spotted a single finger, wedding band still in place. A set of stairs were located at the far end, painted black. Scott walked quietly toward them, passing the archway that welcomed anyone into the main area for worship. He stopped and peered inside. A large ornate crucifix of Christ hung on the far wall, just past a pulpit, splayed against a backdrop of stained glass that was surprisingly intact. The figure presided over rows of pews. A low smell of rotting flesh, muted by the cold, accosted Scott, and he noted with dawning horror the aisle running up the middle of the church.

Bodies filled it.

One corpse in particular shocked him. A man lay on the carpeted wood, his thighs devoured right down to the bare, dull bone, while half of his upper torso appeared twisted around and gutted, as if the feeders had actually fought over him.

Scott held his bat at the ready, vacillating between drawing the Ruger or simply calling out, just to see if anything answered him. The rising fear in him made him quietly back away from the archway. Once out of sight, he went to the stairs and, treading lightly, started climbing.

When he reached the first landing, the stairway twisted around and up another flight. Black blood stained the wood, frozen like a gloomy berry glaze. Scott didn't like the unease forming in his guts. Blood covered everything, as if one of the defenders had dragged himself up and away to escape his pursuers.

Like a long evening shadow, Scott emerged from the stairwell into a darker upstairs loft, the stillness swelling, the shape of a body slowly coming into view with each step.

It was a woman, just beyond the last step, lying face down on the floor in a thick coating of black.

Scott exhaled heavily when he saw exposed ribs—broken and pried open, laid out like an open-air all-you-can-eat trough. Deadheads had opened her up from the back, chewing into the musculature of her body, from the back of her scalp all the way down to her ravaged feet. He leaned against a nearby wall, swallowing hard and trying not to look at the body. A set of open doors beckoned to him, and he moved around the remains, resisting the urge to gaze upon it. He moved into a balcony area. From there, he could see some of the foremost pews below, and the dead wedged in between them. The sight made his knees weak. *What the fuck am I doing here!* The scene elongated before his eyes as a feeling of light-headedness overcame him. *See! See!* his mind shrieked, as he realized how bad his situation had become, and then his knees *did* give out. He sat down heavily on a nearby pew, the backpack and shotgun preventing him from leaning back, brooding at the hanging body of Christ in the distance.

Unaware of the noise he'd made.

He leaned forward, bumping his helmet against the wood of the next pew, gripping his bat so he wouldn't lose it . . . and somehow he didn't.

He sucked in breaths and clenched his eyes shut, thankful for the chance to recover his wind.

He only rested for a minute before he heard the soft rustle of something moving behind him.

Well . . . shit.

A scratching came from the open doorway, followed by the sound of something heavy being dragged. He knew it was the woman, though he wished it wasn't. He should have risked the noise and bashed her head in when he first found her, just to be safe. Feeling spent from the adrenaline leaving his system, he quietly extracted the Ruger from his boot, before placing the bat across his lap. He racked the slide, wincing at the noise, and waited, listening to the shivering grind of fingernails digging into the wooden floor. The subtle popping of joints as the dark life force powering the wasted carcass hauled the creature toward him.

Scott looked down, waiting, hearing the soft slither of cloth and flesh draw closer.

A blue-grey hand slinked into sight. Broken nails hooked into a strip of wood and tensed as the corpse pulled itself closer. Scott wondered why he was waiting. The sight of the hand made him feel weak once more. It was soon quietly joined by a twin missing two fingers and a huge chunk of flesh from the edge of the palm. The top of its head seeped into view, its face twisting upward, the features hidden by its hair.

Dead flesh parted black strands of hair.

Lips split, and a ridge of teeth gleamed.

Scott didn't want to gaze upon any more features. He shot the dead thing in the side of its head, dropping it with the dull thud of a bowling ball. The sound of the suppressor lingered briefly in the church.

He discovered he had all but stopped breathing.

And for a moment, nothing happened.

Then, from below, the sounds of awakening zombies reached him. Low moans rose up like phantoms escaping a witch's cauldron. His spine went electric and he straightened up, peering over the edge of the last pew on the balcony level, into the pit below.

Scott winced.

Zombies, *many* zombies, rose up from between the pews, herky-jerky from the cold, but eager to locate the sound of whatever had disturbed them. A grisly collection of survivor types and Sunday-suited worshippers clawed their way to their swaying feet. Dead expressions and heads with broken necks gazed up and fastened onto Scott. Rising in the distant pulpit, a priest hauled himself into view, one arm lifting and praising the heavens for the living man in their midst. The father did not appear to have his other arm, but the one he did have stuck out like a tree limb and directed his congregation's attention. Their gravelly voices rose up in unholy celebration.

Scott turned around to leave and gasped at another zombie not two strides away from him and closing, its arms wide as if wanting a hug. The dead thing's face had been utterly chewed away, leaving only a partial skull blotted in dried blood and framed in shreds of skin. With a hiss, it launched itself at Scott, who threw up his arms and warded off the zombie. He twisted to one side and pushed the creature off balance. It fell between the pews across from him with a clatter, and Scott saw that the thing wore the uniform of a Halifax police officer.

He put a bullet into the deadhead's skull when it presented itself a second time. Scott wanted to run, but the notion of searching the officer for weapons came into his head, making him hesitate for a moment before waving off the idea. He could see the holster hanging off the officer's hip was empty. Gathering up his bat, Scott jammed the Ruger down his boot and retreated to the steps. He crashed down the two flights of stairs and hit the ground floor just as the congregation slunk into the main aisle, at least a hundred strong. As one, their faces turned to him.

Scott hesitated, unsure if he could get through them all. There were too many to shoot or take with the bat.

They drifted toward the stairs, pushed along by invisible currents.

With a gasp, Scott plunged into the zombies, charging through the entire mob. Hands grazed his face and arms, too frozen to close upon him. Horrid faces sped by, and he shoved them back until he burst through the doors into a sky mired by black clouds. Scott turned and saw thick, billowing clouds coiling and twisting upward from the direction of the gas bar, turning the sun into a stark, staring eye. Legions of undead walked the streets beneath the clouds, some visible, some obscured by the smoke.

They started for him.

The church zombies spilled outside, slipping on steps and landing in a tangle at the building's base. Scott crossed the road and chugged through a snow-covered driveway, fear pushing him onward. Breathing hard and feeling the weight of the backpack and shotgun for the first time, he slogged past a light-green house. A shirtless man lurched against the glass of a window, smashing through it in an attempt to grab him. Scott jerked away in fright, leaving the dead man hanging over the lip of the broken glass. It reached up and made a swipe for him, but Scott backed out of reach. Even so, the thing wriggled free of the window, the jagged ends of the glass sawing through the abdominal wall of the corpse and spilling thick coils of innards, which sparkled in the sunlight. Gasping in horror, Scott crushed its head like a bad piñata and left it hanging from the sill. He continued running, hoping he'd soon forget that scene, knowing there would be nightmares.

Onward he steamed, still hearing the concert of voices behind him, needing to get out of sight.

He passed through the backyards of several houses. In one place, the snow reached his waist almost immediately, grinding him to a halt and sucking the strength from his body. Out of the corner of his eye, dead people, still inside their houses, lurched toward the windows. Dark things he didn't need to see in greater detail. A moment later he heard them. Their pounding against wood and glass filled his ears. He pawed through the snow, using the bat as a third leg in places, until he reached the next street over. Stopping in the middle of the road to catch his wind, he saw that the lane ran to the left and ended in a T-intersection. He jogged up to it and peeked back the way he'd come.

Smoke far behind, dead things ambling through its veil.

Glass broke behind him. Across the street, a zombie rose up from a snowdrift, clumps falling from its shoulders. More shapes surged against the insides of houses. A corpse on the second story of a brown house punched its way through glass and half hung out the window, groaning in Scott's direction.

Scott didn't wait to see what would happen next. He plodded through another driveway and cut through yet another backyard. Cutting moans vibrated the very air and surrounded him. The sinking feeling of having made a very bad mistake entered him. Panic wasn't far behind. He should never have come to Halifax. A clothesline appeared out of nowhere and almost garrotted him off his feet. He ran over a small swimming pool coated in snow. A tall fence loomed in front of him and, putting his head down, he smashed through it with a horrendous sound of breaking wood. Splintered fragments raked the Nomex. Scott ran past more houses. The land sloped upward, sapping more energy from him.

He turned a corner and stopped.

Before him stood a wall of reanimated corpses.

His breath hitching in his chest, Scott staggered back as the dead turned on him. He dropped his bat and shrugged off his backpack. He unzipped it, groped for the extra magazines, and kept them near his leg. Grimacing, he drew the Ruger from his boot and clasped it in both hands. Deadheads walked toward him, slowed by the cold. He struggled with his breathing and took aim. They were coming in on two sides. The ones before him would expose him to the masses he left behind.

He was getting fucking tired of running.

Scott fired into the mob, taking his time and putting down a gimp with each shot as they closed the distance. They were no more than twenty feet away, and even with his heart hammering in his chest, they weren't hard to hit. The Ruger spat, the sound puncturing the frigid air, and something fell with each muted report. A teenage boy dressed in blue jeans. A bald man in a leather coat. A woman in a business suit. Skulls exploded. One shot missed and Scott adjusted, pulled the trigger, and the gun went dry. He ejected the magazine and slapped in a fresh one, racked it, and took aim at a zombie whose lower jaw dangled from its head like a swinging chin strap. Scott blew its brains out the back of its skull. He shot another through the eye. Three quick shots and three more corpses dropped to the ground. Two shots missed, causing him to bite his lower lip in frustration. Some zombies tripped over the fallen ones and crawled toward him. Scott looked to his left and found a creeper about to hook him by his hip. He twisted and fired point-blank into the creature's devastated face, exploding it and dropping the zombie to the snow.

A second magazine clicked dry.

Scott beat down a hoarse scream. Grimly, he snatched up a fresh magazine and slapped it home, then worked the slide.

A zombie stood right over him. He shot it under the chin, sprinkling the snow and other gimps with black matter. Another came too close and he fired a round into its belly, blowing the thing back on its frozen ass hard enough that its bare feet flipped up into the air. Scott rose to his feet and increased his tempo. He put down corpse after corpse until the third magazine emptied. Mounds of bodies littered the street, but a dozen more remained standing. He dropped down, pawing at the remaining mags. He fumbled one and it went flying out of reach. Whimpering, he let it go and drew the fourth magazine, concentrating on getting it in correctly. He inserted it and racked the slide.

Scott stood as a zombie placed a hand on his shoulder. He beat the arm aside and fired into the thing's face. It dropped to reveal another close behind. He killed that one as well, but the last few zombies were upon him. Hands pawed at him. Something gripped his helmet and grabbed his shoulders. The sounds of the hungry dead flooded his ears.

Scott freaked.

He fired the Ruger point-blank into faces and bodies, no longer caring about head shots. They crowded him, slamming into his body like a horrible wave of industrial sludge. They bit into his shoulders. They clawed into his midsection and chest. Scott lost the Ruger and grabbed the first head he saw. He violently twisted the skull. The crack splintered the harshness of the moans, but the zombie kept reaching for him—with open, hissing jaws and a broken neck. Scott jabbed and knocked it back, but it rebounded like a grinning punching bag. He kicked and twisted, wrenching free of frozen fingers attempting to keep a hold of him. He spotted the shaft of his bat and grabbed for it. Something hit his back with enough force to push him down, and he fell forward onto his hands and knees. Scott screamed and thrashed like an eel out of water, darting between legs. If he landed on the pavement and they flattened him out, he wouldn't be able to get back up—didn't have the strength to get back up—and they would heap on top of him like a ravenous defensive line.

Bent over, he scrambled through an opening in the forest of gimp limbs, feeling their hands slide off him. He stopped in a drift when he saw there weren't any zombies ahead. Whirling around, he straightened up and assumed a batting stance. There were perhaps ten or so deadheads focused on him, and they stumbled toward him, working frozen limbs as if attempting to keep their balance on rough seas.

Baseball wasn't his sport, but Scott would make an exception in this case.

He took the head clean off the first gimp within range, surprising even himself with the crack and snap of his victim's skull spinning off its shoulders, a fleeting ribbon of gore trailing the rotten bauble as it spun through the air. The bat smashed in the heads of the second and third zombies. Scott shifted in the snow when he had to, hoping to God he wouldn't hit a patch of ice. The fourth deadhead went down after two hard strikes to its forehead. Scott realized he was grunting with each swing and striking over the gimps' outstretched arms. They made no attempt to defend themselves. He bludgeoned their skulls from all angles, horrified to see it took more than one hit to kill them. Not only had their joints stiffened, but their heads as well, becoming a thick, icy ball of matter that took a lot more power to crack.

Sapping away what little strength he had left.

He crushed the skull of the last gimp attacking him, leaving a grotesque saddle-shape in the smashed bone. Other zombies approached in the closing distance, from the roads and between the houses. He'd only just put down the first wave. Then he gawked at the carnage he'd wrought. A *slew* of dead gimps lay in the road, face down, face up, or on their sides. Black soup seeped onto the white covering the ground.

But beyond them, and on an almost mechanical march, came more.

Hundreds more.

He had to get moving.

Gun, his mind cried out, and he realized with a drop in his stomach he'd lost the Ruger. He frantically moved to the area where he thought he'd dropped it, pawing at the fallen corpses and turning them over. The smell of the dead made him gag. He didn't have time for this. The snow was shin deep in places, more than enough to hide the weapon.

The dead stumbled toward him, uncaring of his plight, intent only on meat.

Scott picked up his backpack and struggled into the straps, eyeing the approaching mob while adjusting the shotgun until it hung off his back the way he wanted. Still no handgun, though.

The zombies were perhaps twenty meters away and closing, their numbers thickening, their icy features set on him. They wandered through driveways, around hedges, down the streets. Some tripped over the dead Scott had killed, but they slowly got to their feet. Others stepped around them, looking at the living man with their heads cocked curiously to one side.

Scott reached down and pulled on the shoulder of one dead gimp. He only had time for one more. Deadheads converged, moaning, while a few gnashed their jaws as if shivering in anticipation.

Scott rolled the corpse over and felt an explosion of relief.

There, grip facing up, was the Ruger.

He grabbed it and ran, gun in one hand and bat in the other. Only when he started moving did he feel the burning exhaustion in his limbs. He retreated back behind a row of houses, searching for a two-story with an attic. He needed to get out of their line of sight—and smell. He needed to get out of the open . . .

He needed to disappear.

Ducking under low-hanging clotheslines and avoiding lawn furniture, he sprinted past three houses before settling on a tall brown structure. He climbed the steps leading to a back porch and gasped.

There, shuffling toward the door, was the owner of the residence. Wearing only coveralls, and without eyes or lips, the elderly gentleman grinned hideously at his visitor as if he were welcoming a dear friend.

Scott fired two shots, puncturing the glass and killing the elderly gimp. He brought his elbow up, punched it through the damaged pane, and had the door open in seconds. Old linoleum coated the floor. Seeing the old codger crumpled just inside did nothing for him. It was only another dead thing.

Scott spun about and shut the door, then slid across two deadbolts. He withdrew from the porch area, seeing the festering tide of hundreds of zombies bleed into the backyard, making him wonder if it was possible for the things to actually track him in the snow. It wasn't something to dwell on. Holding the gun out before him like a crucifix, he backed into the shadows of an old kitchen. A green stove, scratched as if a cat had gone insane on its metal hide, squatted in one corner, while a worn hardwood table dominated the room. He checked under the table as he moved deeper into the house, into a living room with the remains of two ravaged victims on the floor—another man and woman, perhaps husband and wife. One body looked almost chopped in half, a grisly V separating its right shoulder from the rest of the torso. The axe that had undoubtedly done the job lay just beyond the victim, in front of a set of stairs and the door to the street.

Scott crushed the skulls of both with the bat. He left the axe and huffed his way to the second floor. A short hallway, painted white and spattered with black, with five open doorways lay before him. There was no trapdoor in the ceiling, and for a moment, Scott felt an almost overwhelming sense of terror strike him. He went from bedroom to bedroom until he located the entry to the attic—a wide hole covered by a piece of plywood.

Scott didn't have time to be picky.

He needed a chair to get up there.

Scurrying into one of the bedrooms, he grabbed an old-fashioned desk chair, the kind without any wheels, and returned to the main bedroom. He placed the chair directly under the attic hole and climbed. He pushed the cover to one side and peeked up into the gloom. Light from a vent dappled the place, but otherwise the space was dark and small, with bare timbers exposed. The shapes of boxes and suitcases were pressed into the dark recesses on either side, offering just a little space to hide.

Scott took it.

He shoved his backpack and weapons into the hole. A nearby closet held a few blankets, but Scott believed there were more somewhere in the house, and he heaved armfuls up into the dark attic.

A crash from below informed him he had no time to search.

Climbing onto the chair, he studied the room and saw that the bed was nowhere near the hole, but the chair would still remain once he was in the attic. He pulled himself up, burning through the last bits of energy he possessed, lay on his belly, and peered back into the room. The pounding far below became irregular, but insistent.

Scott took the bat and stretched his arm back down. He struck the back of the chair, bumping it along a little bit at a time as if it was a fine old day. Taking a breath, he swung the bat with one arm and knocked the chair over with a thump. The sound made him cringe, but he quickly retreated into the dark of the attic, replacing the cover and effectively sealing himself in.

Back in an attic. He swore to God if he lived long enough to find a place of his own, he'd make sure the top floor was prepped. As it was, boxes and suitcases choked this particular attic, and he took a few careful moments to arrange things. He located three sleeping bags and even two pillows, and one of those he placed flat in the middle of the floor, laying the other two on top. He heaped more blankets onto the pile. Scott placed his backpack nearby and got out the jug of water. He lay down his guns and the bat, pointing them at the hole, just in case he needed any of them. With a gasp, he pulled off his helmet and placed it to one side, feeling the sweat in his hair. He crawled into the nest of sleeping bags and blankets, still in his Nomex gear, and lay down with a deep sigh.

The sounds from below continued.

He waited, focusing on the covered hole to the attic. He snaked out a hand from under the blankets and rested it on the shotgun. His eyelids became heavy.

More thumping, far below.

Strangely enough, it didn't bother Scott much anymore.

8

He woke up to the sound of something shuffling along in the bedroom underneath, heard the chair being pushed around, and expected any moment for the attic cover to pop up and a gimp to lunge through. Loud bangs of wood against wood and other sounds of the searching dead seeped through the ceiling. Scott's hand, still on the shotgun, slunk away from the heavier weapon and stopped on the grip of the Ruger. He waited. More rumbling below. More moaning. Flesh thumped about as the dead navigated the entirety of the upstairs floor, searching for him. Perhaps they knew he was close by. He focused on the attic cover. The urge to creep forward and lift it— just a crack—so he could peek down on them became so strong that he began to think it was a good idea. What could it hurt? There was no way for them to reach him. He'd kicked the chair away from the hole, and no gimp had ever displayed any memory or knowledge of utilizing the comforts and tools of the old world. So where was the threat? The danger? He released the grip of the gun and bunched up his legs to shift himself forward. He could lift the cover with the tip of his Bowie and peek just for a *second*.

Then Gus's voice spoke in his head, warding off the notion and wondering—in typical Gus fashion—where the fuck were his brains? Scott blinked and had to wonder that himself. He stretched out underneath the mound and closed his eyes, opening them only when he heard noise directly beneath his hiding spot. With the racket the deadheads were making below, he swore they must have been a crew of furniture movers in their old lives.

The light in the attic receded, and Scott sensed the temperature dropping as well.

He closed his eyes again and somehow drifted off to sleep.

The next morning seemed a long time coming. He had woken several times during the night to sounds of something crashing or moaning below. Scott lay in his nest and stared at the wooden beams of the ceiling. After long minutes, he crawled out of his makeshift bed and relieved himself in a nearby suitcase. While he peed, a great crash came from the direction of the stairs, making him lose his concentration. A deadhead had fallen down the steps.

Stupid bastards.

Zombies still lumbered about below, but the noises they made were muted, like waves lapping against the hull of a ship. The realization that they were leaving the upstairs lifted his spirits and he relaxed a little more, burrowing back into the pile of blankets and sleeping bags.

Telling himself to be patient, Scott tried hard not to think of the old world. He stared at the bare ribs of the roof and waited for the undead to leave.

The day dragged on. Sometimes he was awake, and sometimes he slept. When he did sleep, he made certain his head was under the covers, just to muffle any potential snores. He didn't remember Kelly ever telling him he snored, or Gus that time they'd been trapped in an attic, but he saw no reason to risk it. He wormed out of his sleeping bag and blankets, opened up a can of spaghetti and meat balls, and feasted on them cold, eating a third in the morning, a third in the afternoon, and the rest just before the light left the attic. He drank his water in measured sips.

Waited.

Listened.

Thought.

He descended from the attic two days later, stiff, from lying on his back for so long, and thirsty, as his water ran out the previous night. The zombies had retreated from the house a day earlier, but he felt it wise to wait the extra day. The second floor was empty of zombies and he went to the bathroom, intent on sitting on the house throne. Filthy shreds of clothing and what appeared to be shrivelled strips of flesh covered the toilet, so he passed on sitting. There was no way Scott was plopping his ass down on that piece of porcelain, and he looked elsewhere to relieve himself.

The house was a shambles of broken furniture, walls smeared in grey-black grease, and that feeling of being soiled. The back and front doors hung open from where the deadheads had broken in, allowing light in. He kept to the shadows, peering at the zombies walking up and down the street in jerky motions. The slab of wood and broken glass that comprised the front porch door was crushed to one side, as if something huge had forced its way through. Some of the undead had even come through the picture window in the living room. The ones he'd put down appeared mangled and pulped, as if a herd of cattle had walked over them and did a little dance before moving on.

Warily, he retreated to the attic to retrieve his gear.

Descending once more to the first floor, he edged along the wall to the back porch. The backyard was empty, but the ground had been mashed with innumerable footprints. He had his water jug and wanted to fill it with snow before leaving. Snowmelt would have to do until he found something better. Across the yard, a white drift appeared untouched by the siege. It was only ten meters away, yet Scott felt as if he would be targeted the very instant he stepped outside. Laying his pack, bat, and shotgun in the porch area, he slapped his visor down and crept outside.

Sunlight glared down and he was thankful for the visor. He looked this way and that before trudging through a ridge of hard snow. Reaching the drift sculpted like the crest of a wave, he punched his hand through the outer ice. He started jamming fistfuls of snow into the jug, looking around the backyard every so often to ensure that the area was clear. Something compelled him to turn around toward the street. There, like slow-moving husks caught in a current, undead stopped in the road.

Scott froze. He fought down the urge to run back to the house and concentrated on filling the jug. None of the corpses looked in his direction. More snow crumbled and fell down the sides of the bottle, and he wormed his hand deeper inside the drift to get at the softer stuff.

In the street, the zombies started moving, drifting like sluggish black ice floes.

Scott had almost filled the bottle when he saw a gimp turning in his direction.

He dove to the right, cutting off the angle of sight with the corner of the house. Blood pumping in his ears, he kept low and treaded across the snow with crunching steps. Once he reached the back door, he edged along to the corner, crouched, and waited.

It didn't take long for a shadow to lengthen across the white ground. The moaning and shuffling grew louder.

Scott reached down to one boot and pulled out his Bowie knife. The foot-long blade gleamed dully in the daylight, and he positioned himself for a quick killing stroke.

The shadow swelled on the ground.

Scott tightened his grip on the Bowie, its tip in front of his visor.

The zombie shuffled forward with the creaking of frozen cloth, its arms hanging limp at its sides, and Scott surged upward and stabbed the corpse under the jaw. The tip of the knife punched through the undead's thin mat of hair. Scott twisted the blade, feeling the grainy resistance of frozen tissue and skull, and yanked the corpse around the corner. He lowered the body to the ground and placed a boot against the dead thing's head. The blade came out with a rasp of steel on bone.

One down. Scott leaned against the house and waited for more.

None came.

Breathing quickly, his heart hammering, Scott stepped away from the corner and peeked around the corner.

The dead roamed the street, but none came his way.

Thanking Christ above for that little bit of luck, he crept back toward his water bottle, mindful of the gimps popping in and out of view in the other backyards. Filling the jug wasn't pressing anymore, so he took it, stayed low, and returned to the house. Getting inside the open porch door was a huge relief. He found a blind spot and relaxed somewhat, out of sight of any deadheads unless they came through the doorway. The jug in his hand was practically full with snow, and Scott swore at himself—quietly—for taking the risk. He tightened the lid on the container and stuffed it into his backpack.

One thing done for the day. And one less zombie to deal with.

The dead roamed the streets. He flipped up his visor and pinched the bridge of his nose. With an army between him and the vehicle, getting back to the truck was a lost cause. The chances of him surviving Halifax were low, Scott had known that from the start, but now death seemed almost a certainty.

And he wasn't even sure Tenner had come to the city.

The more he thought about it, the greater the doubt clouding his mind.

Sniffing, he drew the Ruger and took inventory of his ammunition. Two magazines remained. One of those bullets would be for him if it came to that, as starving in an attic or being torn apart by a mob didn't appeal to him.

The lip of the broken window drew his attention, and he looked into the yard. Zombies groaned dismally outside and in the distance. Being a realist, which he believed was just a pleasant word pessimists called themselves, he started to think he had little chance of finding Tenner.

But he wasn't going to stop looking.

Not until he had to use that final bullet on himself.

He thought of the flattened snow outside and the dead populating the streets. So many. So goddamn many.

Give up and go back, his doubt whispered to him.

No, Scott *mentally replied.* This one's for Lea and Teddy . . . And anyone else left alive.

With that, he gathered up his gear, took a breath, and left the house.

Trying to look everywhere at once, he approached a neighbor's home, walking on a parallel course with the street out front. When he saw his chance, he darted across the driveway, keeping low and baring his teeth as he ran. His boots punched through the gathered snow with an audible crunch, making him wince. Reaching the corner, he crouched and slipped along the wall to the back door. Even when he placed a foot down as softly as possible, the snow would hold for only a second before breaking.

The back door had already been forced open. Scott cautiously entered a kitchen with a rotten apple skin of a linoleum floor. The pipes had broken at some point, flooding everything and eventually seeping through the wood. Frozen blooms of mould dotted the wooden windowsill facing the backyard, and the smell of something decayed wrinkled his nose. He wasn't going to stay long, and he didn't want to engage any zombies that might be inside. *Make like a ghost*, he thought.

After a few moments, he took a steadying breath and crept back outside. Zombies paced the street, mumbling as if asleep. He sprinted across the driveway toward the next house, with a deck and patio furniture blanketed in white. Diving in between wide railings, he scrambled to his knees and came to a sliding glass door with the drapes closed. Just beyond a work shed, figures walked aimlessly in the sun, forcing him to stay low. Scott slunk along the length of the sliding window until he reached the end, expecting another driveway—another fifteen feet of exposure to the main road.

What he found momentarily stunned him.

There *were* no houses.

Charred timbers, like frayed fence posts, stood on foundations smothered in twinkling snowdrifts. Scott leaned against the wall hiding him from the road and gaped at the open space. There was no chance of covering such a distance with the zombies around. They'd be on him right away if he tried to go that way. The gap of three or four house lengths was just as lethal as a bottomless pit.

Scott backed up to the sliding glass doors and tried them. Locked. Making a face, he took his bat and positioned it where he thought the lock would be. He didn't like doing this, but he didn't want to return to the previous house either, and each second spent debating endangered him all the more. The head of the bat crunched through the glass on the first punch, shattering it in long shards. Pieces tinkled to the floor. He reached inside and fumbled with the lock before opening it and sliding the door open. Slipping inside, he locked the slider, drew the curtains, and hoped that nothing would come to investigate.

Then he heard the hissing.

He'd stepped into an open area that was a combination of kitchen, living room, and dining room. From the kitchen, a decomposed dad dragged himself toward the intruder using the wall for support. The thing's right arm was missing. Rising up from behind a couch was the mother of the home, her blond hair a wild mop that did not cover her jawless mouth.

Then came the true horror show.

Pulling themselves along the floor like bloated snakes were two small boys, each perhaps ten years old. One of them had both legs gnawed off at the knees. Their mouths opened horribly in the dim light, like young birds waiting to feed.

The cold slowed the family, so Scott pulled the gun from his boot with time to spare. He shot the father through the forehead, dropping him before he even got around the black kitchen island. He put a bullet into the head of the mother next, flipping her over the back of the couch. The children were the worst. The children were *always* the worst.

But he shot them within seconds of each other.

Moments later, Scott discovered the front door wasn't locked. Crouched low, he secured it, keeping his head below the curtainless window. A stairway with rose-pink paint led to three bedrooms and a bathroom. An ensuite lay off the master bedroom, and it was there Scott stopped and dropped his drawers upon his bowels' insistence. Ordinarily he'd be somewhat constipated, but for some reason, things were flowing.

Once finished, he left the bathroom and set up in a boy's bedroom. Scott jerked the curtains across on a window facing the street below, shading the little room in summer blue, and peeked out from one corner.

Deadheads. A thick parade of them.

His heart sank. Realizing he wasn't going anywhere anytime soon, he decided to get comfortable. He plopped his gear down on a nearby desk and chair, and that alone made him feel tons lighter. The bed beckoned, but it was too early for that, and he didn't want to have to camp out here with the damaged sliding doors below. It didn't feel safe. So he stood at the window's edge, the wall at his back, and peered out at the world at a narrow angle. Something, he supposed, he'd done for most of his life.

He watched the zombies file by, risen from their icy graves by his hand. If he hadn't walked over the first few deadheads, perhaps they would have all stayed beneath that frozen carpet, swept by blustery gales that whistled at their strongest. The dead meandered through the street, staggering, searching, sometimes bumping into one another and falling on their asses. They would climb back to their feet with little gruesome grunts of protest, ignore each other, and stumble off in search of a bite. Opposing tides of zombies flowed in and out of sight, clotting at times, and Scott realized with dawning horror that there were more gimps out there than perhaps Annapolis and Saint John combined.

More than he had ammunition for.

Having nothing better to do, he continued watching the dead, wondering how he was going to continue on or even get out of Halifax alive. He remembered people-watching from when he was a baker, from behind the counter while on breaks, casually observing folks as they walked by the shop. All zombies now.

At some point Scott felt hungry, opened up a can of roast beef stew, and ate half. He left the rest on a nearby desk and covered it with a cloth. He pulled a chair away from the desk and placed it near the window so he could sit and look outside, studying the undead's movements. There would be another snowstorm soon, he was certain of that. Perhaps the temperature and snow would bury them again, enabling him to move on.

On the other hand, perhaps the currents of undead would maroon him in this upstairs bedroom for days, weeks even, turning the refuge into a cell.

Clouds drifted overhead, herded along by a heatless sun, and Scott watched the gimps slog away, flattening the drifts. He reflected on how the zombies sensed the living, which had been a popular topic of discussion with Teddy and Lea. None of them were certain if the creatures' eyes worked anymore. The gimps responded to movement, though, which suggested they used their eyes—at least the ones that still possessed them. The three of them had also established that the zombies got by on hearing or smell. The debate on whether or not the things were truly dead was never really settled. He remembered Lea had taken the position that in order to smell, they'd have to draw breath—voluntarily or involuntarily—which went against them being truly dead. The same went for the idea of seeing people move. Teddy had quietly countered that no one could live with the wounds some of the zombies sustained, running off a veritable horror list of undead creatures missing entire sections of their bodies. How could they be anything else than dead? They both agreed that perhaps the virus that transformed people into walking corpses might somehow commandeer the part of the brain controlling those senses and use them at will, much like a puppeteer, which had struck Scott as odd. He couldn't see how any virus could manage such a thing. And how could anything survive with the wounds some of the zombies walked around with?

They had decided that hearing seemed more plausible than smell or sight, but even sound had to be converted into signals for the brain and then interpreted somehow in order for the zombie to react.

He remembered throwing his two cents on the fire by simply saying, "They're undead," as if that explained everything. Arguing about what had reanimated them, the science behind it all, wasn't important. They were undead, and a blow to the brain killed them. Nothing else mattered.

Scott realized how short-sighted he had been. Fully understanding what attracted the zombies meant staying alive that much longer. Perhaps, depending on the corpse's wounds, they used whatever senses they had remaining to get by. He didn't know what a gimp did that had been robbed of its eyes, ears, and nose. Could he somehow fool the dead into thinking he was one of them? They did it on TV. Why not real life? Perhaps he could camouflage himself or imitate their movement, passing himself off as dead. The idea was worth exploring further, but how to do it?

Their clothes.

The notion made him straighten up and savour it. The clothes they wore stunk as much as their dead flesh. What would happen if he wore enough of it to mask his own scent? And if he did clothe himself in undead fashion, could he walk like them? To further strengthen the illusion?

With that simmering in his mind, Scott watched the zombies even more intently from behind the curtain. Some walked better than others, but even the best shambled as if they had downed a flask of booze. And they all made noise.

He rubbed his chin and growing beard and mulled over the problem. Hypothetically, it might work. If the zombies were getting by on the barest of brain impulses, emulating the smell, sound, and movement of one of their own just might save his ass. The only question was how to get what he needed.

Then he remembered the four dead people in the house.

The raw material was there and waiting.

NORSEMEN

9

Three cargo vans, black and bruised, cruised along Highway Two of the Trans-Canada Highway, slowing only when passing through the city of Edmundston. Long deserted cars, trucks, and transports littered the four lanes, and Pell navigated and led the others through the mire of leftover steel and rubber, at times leaving the asphalt entirely and driving on the shoulder to get around clumps of vehicles. The highway cleared once through the city, and it opened up into scenic views of hills and valleys dusted with light snow. The air was getting colder, and mornings gleamed with frosting as inviting as a cake.

To break the monotony, the drivers sometimes sped ahead to pass the leader, and even as Pell looked ahead at the countryside, one van overtook him and blasted away like a hot cannonball. Nightmarish men hung out the windows, screaming and shaking fists in excitement as they drove past. Pell looked at the boss man. An armored Fist sat and stared ahead, squinting at the daylight. He was like that most of the time while on the road. Sometimes silent, sometimes humming some indistinct tune to himself, barely heard above the engine. This was one of those times when the leader purred away. Pell thought it was a surprisingly melodious sound, broken only by Fist's deep breaths, which would fuel the next few bars. Given his leader's ferocious reputation, Pell was certain he was the only one who knew of this musical inclination. No one really knew much about Fist or what he had been before the Fall. Not that it mattered. One only needed to follow his commands.

In the back of the van dozed four killers, almost boneless in their seats, snoring and stinking up the interior with their rancid breath. Bare meat hooks hanging from overhead clicked off each other like gruesome chimes, adding to the rattling of the moving vehicle and Fist's oddly comforting humming.

Pell concentrated on the road, staring at the backside of the van ahead and waiting for word from the big man to stop. Scavenging had been fair in Quebec. They'd even left behind a garage full of excess gas they drained from vehicles, to be used for the trip back west. Meat was constantly an issue, and while they managed to take down two people and cook them, hopes were high the pickings would be better further east. They had stores of cured and smoked meat, but that would only last so long.

From the passenger seat, Fist took another breath before turning it into a slow song Pell knew he'd heard before, but couldn't place. That would bug the hell out of him for the rest of the day. The lines of the highway flashed by, ticks of distance and time, becoming brighter as the road pulsed into the graceful curve of an overpass, all channeled by guardrails.

Then their van hit ice.

The rig ahead of them suddenly swerved, crashed through a guardrail, and plunged into the valley between the opposing lanes. It flipped over, rolling onto its side, in a song of screaming engine revolutions and crumpling metal before disappearing below. Pell felt his own tires spin for a second, before momentum pushed his van past the crash site. The vehicle fishtailed and he turned into it, regaining control. His foot crushed the brake pedal as his heart gonged in his chest.

"Turn around!" Fist shouted, startling Pell more than the lead van doing a dog's trick.

They returned to the overpass and parked, blocking the road. The men from the third van got out, their boot heels clicking on asphalt, and stared down at the dead transport.

The crashed van had nosedived into the pavement below. It had smashed itself at an angle upon impact, crashing into the median. Steam rose from the crumpled engine block; a pair of legs stuck out from the shade of the concrete, as if someone was trying to hide under a bed.

For a while Fist said nothing, studying the scene with a grim patience and listening to the weak groan of wheels until they came to a stop.

"They're fucked," someone said into the rising wind.

Fist straightened and studied the countryside. Houses lined both sides of the road running underneath the highway. The road beneath led into a large town of sorts. Pell looked about and felt his anxiety rise just a bit. This wasn't the best of places to have an accident. But then, where was?

A hand slapped against the side window of the wrecked van. A face peered up at them, ghostly pale. Then another.

"Get down there and pull them out," Fist rumbled at the rig pigs standing around him. "Salvage what you can. Food and water. Gas."

Orders heard, the men jumped the guard rails and huffed down to the crash site. They swarmed the van and pried open the ruined rear doors with crowbars. Norsemen in tire armor and motorcycle helmets pulled their dazed companions out and heaped them on the ground. In a minute, five men were free. A sixth man, the driver, had been the guy trying to hide in the shade of the second overpass. He had flown through the windshield and skidded across two lanes and up a concrete incline. Most of his face had been cheese-grated away, but mercifully, a snapped neck had taken his life.

Pell was one of the men to flip the driver over.

"Dead," he yelled back to Fist, standing tall on the road above. Their leader brooded above them as grey clouds sped overheard. He stood with both hands on his hips, gunslinger style, with his elbows jutting out. The huge man drew a flat hand across his throat, then down his middle, and finished with the motion of tossing something away. *Waste not, want not*, Pell thought, knowing it was a saying of Fist's. He repeated the hand signs to three men nearby. The trio took out cleavers and knives and fell upon the dead man with gusto.

Meat was meat, regardless of where—or who—it came from.

Pell wandered to the front of the crashed van, studying the exposed underside of the vehicle as he went. Herman and a few others stood about the crumpled hood, which they had managed to pry back.

"Engine?" Pell asked in Norse speak.

"Dead," Herman said in English, shaking his head.

"Can't do anything?"

"To this?" Herman asked, sooty face incredulous. "It's dead."

Pell stepped away from the mechanic and looked up at the shadowy, cobra hood shape of their leader, who seemed to have taken a menacing interest in the conversation. He pointed at the van and drew a thumb across his throat.

Fist nodded once.

"Get the gas out of the tank, then," Pell said to Herman. Pell didn't mind being a mouthpiece, nor did he mind being something of a right hand to the boss, since he sat across from him when on the road. Such a privilege afforded him certain liberties, even when he stood low in the pecking order.

"Hey," grunted a man wearing Viking horns. He pointed beyond the shade of the concrete. Zombies, featureless in the distance, appeared in ones and twos on the road.

They staggered out from between houses. Some oozed from underneath cars like enormous worms. As the rising wind gave soundtrack to the scene, the dead mustered their forces and, with heavy steps, marched toward the wreck site.

Above, Fist turned and gazed on the small army.

Pell wasn't afraid of the dead. None of the Norsemen were. The dead weren't something to fear—in small bunches. Large numbers could be a problem.

"Get them into the vans," Murphy shouted, making Pell swivel around. Whether they needed to be told or not, the men bearing the weight of the dazed Norsemen complied, walking with their companions up over the slope to the vehicles.

"Get the food and water!" Murphy shouted. His emaciated face was covered by a visor spray-painted black. The man was a jackal amongst dogs and quick to bite.

"You're not in charge," Herman yelled back, gathering up plastic jugs of water. Pell looked at Fist, but the leader had disappeared to the other side of the highway.

Murphy stopped in his tracks long enough that Pell thought he was going to fight the mechanic, this time with a zombie mob bearing down on them all. If he did, Pell decided to shoot the man himself, and his hand strayed to the sawed-off shotgun hanging off his thigh. But Murphy reconsidered, spun away, and grabbed an armful of packaged food from the rear of the van before huffing back up the slope.

Pell stepped to the back of the wreck and was given a milk crate filled almost to the brim with loose shotgun shells. He scrambled up to the highway and his waiting van.

When he reached the top, Fist was gone.

Quickly depositing the shells into the back of the van, he went to the guardrail and stared at the zombies moving toward them. Several dozen of the creatures spread over the street like an infection of black pox.

Pell blinked. Casually walking toward the undead with two unsheathed Bowie knives was the grim and armored shape of Fist. He had donned his hockey helmet, and he strutted toward the dead without any backup. He took his time, looking this way and that, as if wondering which would be the first to perish.

The corpses drifted toward him, leering and challenging him with rotting voices.

In reply, the Norse leader stabbed the first creature through the face. He knifed two more, taking them through the sides of their skulls. A pair of zombies feebly reached for him, and he kicked both away with a boot and a grunt, clearing a killing zone. He decapitated one and crushed the head of another he'd thrown to the ground with a boot heel. More of the dead wobbled forth, focusing toward the man as if he were a gate, and Fist put down zombie after zombie, ending their moans with curt crunches of metal and bone, or the heavy, clay-like clatter of a shattering skull.

Pell watched, awestruck, as Fist decimated the approaching crowd in a slow cadence of violence, showing the dead what little concern he had for them. Though none of the Norsemen feared the dead, no one would wade into a crowd of them alone and start swinging. They had long since learned the best way to combat the decomposing legions was as a closed unit. Other warriors stopped at the guard rail and shouted, pumping fists, and for a moment, Pell imagined Fist not even hearing them, but simply humming to himself.

"Finish loading the vans!" Pell shouted.

"Done," someone called back.

Pell put his hands to his mouth and yelled, "We're clear!"

A moment later, Fist started backing up, disengaging from the reaching arms of the dead. The zombies pursued him, but like many times before, they did not heed what was underfoot and stumbled over the wrecks of their truly dead companions. One topless, grey-blue man dressed in sweatpants rushed Fist. The Norse leader's hands snapped out like thunderbolts, smashing into the dead thing's head and whisking it off its feet. The remaining zombies stumbled and flowed over the body, hiding it from sight.

Fist walked away from his pursuers and contemptuously showed them his back. He glanced back every ten steps or so, just in case another runner appeared.

The cheering died as Fist hiked up the incline to the waiting vans. No one had truly expected him to die.

"Saddle up," Fist bellowed as he reached the top, slapping a speechless Pell on the shoulder to get him moving. The driver didn't think his leader had been in danger either, but he hadn't seen anyone walk right into a crowd of the dead, alone, as Fist had just done.

Still moving, Fist walked up to Murphy, who stood his ground.

"Did I hear you giving orders, Murph?"

"You might have."

Fist's blackened face scowled behind his face cage. "Don't get used to it."

The other man blinked.

Warning delivered, Fist got aboard his van. Pell and several of the others had paused to watch the short exchange, and Pell thought for certain Murphy was about to be gutted. He'd seen Fist do it for less. Shaking his head, Pell and the others climbed into their rigs. Sitting in the passenger seat, the face-caged profile of Fist stared ahead at the open highway.

"Find an off ramp and take us down there," the leader rumbled. "Time for a show."

Pell settled in and pressed down on the gas pedal.

The vans rolled down an exit and went into an unnamed neighborhood, a collection of houses and small commercial buildings. Zombies tried to stop this invasion, blocking the road in small clumps, but the vans knocked them down and crept over their cold forms, their bones crackling underneath the tires. The rig pigs inside squealed in delight. Fist rolled down his window and repeatedly slapped the side of the door with a meaty hand. More walking corpses came into the street—attracted by the fleshy beat and the sound of engines—but not enough to stop the machines. They were crushed like the others, and once the convoy reached the end of the road, they turned about and drove back, flattening any remaining zombies. On the third pass, Fist released his Norsemen. Almost a dozen erupted from the side and rear doors, whooping and roaring and making quick work of anything moving. They decimated any zombies that came into view, striking them down with wild mirth. Heads were struck from bodies or cleaved in two. The men joked and became almost uncontrollable, but they ran to the vans when their rides started moving again, falling in and walking alongside the vehicles.

As the sun descended and the shadows lengthened upon a road littered with unmoving bodies, the Norsemen kicked in doors and smashed windows of businesses and houses. In twos and threes, they raided property after property. When they discovered something of use, they took it outside and dumped it on the curb. Once finished with their looting, they set fire to the houses. The homes of the day weren't the ones of yesteryear. While up to building code standards, open concept was the most popular floor plan, and coincidentally the best for allowing a fire to breathe. With no small rooms in a dwelling to contain a fire, cheap prefab building materials, and an overabundance of glue, open flames quickly grew into truly monstrous things and gutted houses from the inside out.

By nightfall, the Norsemen had ignited whole streets, still screaming, singing, and merrily basking in the heat and smoke from the impressive blazes.

In the morning, the fires still burned.

But the vans had moved on.

SCOTT

10

None of the corpses' clothes would fit Scott, not even if he took off his Nomex coat—which he had no intention of doing. It was hot and heavy, and running in it would probably give him a heart attack, but it was also the most protective gear he possessed.

Having crept downstairs to where he'd shot the family, Scott stood in their midst and quietly contemplated his next move, his thoughts broken by the cries of the undead outside, as dull and dreary as foghorns around a midnight bay. The father of the family had a smaller frame than Scott and he decided any clothing would have to be cut off. He pulled the Bowie knife out of his boot and held it up like a scalpel. He dropped to one knee and grimaced at the smell of dead flesh. Taking the clothes off the corpses was all well and good in theory, but the reality was going to be difficult to do without puking. Scott pulled the bottom edge of his firefighter's ninja mask up over his nose. He took a hold of one pant leg and inserted the knife. He sawed the length of the leg, straightening the dead limb out as needed, until he got to the upper thigh.

"Holy *shit*," Scott gasped and backed away, draping an arm across his face. The rancid cloth he peeled away from the dead man stunk to hell. The quivering of hairy fat rolls didn't help, either. He had played with the idea of gutting the father, or at least bleeding him a little, and wiping the blood on the cloth strips, but after smelling as well as tasting the foulness, he just couldn't bring himself to do it. The way the stench was making him nauseous, he wouldn't need to *act* like a deadhead. He resumed cutting around the dead dad, leaving him shirtless in a pair of cut-off Dockers. The mother received the same treatment, and she reeked just as badly. The danger of swooning made him stop once more, just to retreat to the living room to get some fresh air. Scott went back to her side and sliced away the arms of her dark, stained shirt and slacks. He stripped the T-shirts off the boys, but left the rest.

With the sour rags in his hands, Scott went into the kitchen and started cutting. He knotted strands together and tied the rotten material around his forearms, legs, and backpack. The father's shirt got turned into an uneven poncho. One boy's T-shirt became a hood to stretch over his helmet, something he wasn't looking forward to doing. If only he had some ointment to put under his nose, something to dilute the smell.

Inspecting himself when he was all done, Scott figured there was no better time than the present to go for a walk and test his theory. He gathered up his things, flipped down his visor, and pulled on the hood and poncho, praying to God above the fresh air outside would help him breathe.

Outside, the evening sky bled dusky red.

Scott opened the front door and eased himself outside, closing it behind him. He had his bat in one hand and the Ruger in the other, just in case. Standing on a set of short, worn steps, he hunched over and watched the zombies walk past, heedless of him. He hoped his nerves would hold out.

He shuffled down squealing steps, taking his time and making no rushed movements. *Act dead* flashed in his mind. A ragged crowd lay no more than fifteen feet ahead of him, and Scott scrunched a shoulder up to his ear and let loose with a moan of what he hoped was convincing zombie-talk. He dragged his feet as he moved toward the road. *Steady*, he told himself. *Don't rush anything.*

No sooner did he think it than his toes hooked into something under the snow and he stumbled, falling to his padded knees. His hands flashed out to stop his fall as his mind screamed *NO!*

The ground rushed up and slammed into him, bunching one arm uncomfortably against his chest. His bat rattled away, but he held on to the gun. Grinding his jaw, he reflexively drew his hands to his head and rolled over onto his back.

Too fast. A zombie detected the movement and slunk toward him, wheezing as if it possessed cancerous lungs. Scott watched the thing loom over him, its mouth hanging open in a frozen rictus. He forced himself to stay still while his heart screamed. The zombie came close enough for Scott to see its bare feet and the shredded flesh from soles that had once frozen to something. The urge to raise the Ruger, to blow the thing's head off, became unbearable, and Scott understood what it was like to play chicken for real, when the stakes were life or death.

The deadhead *stepped* on him, planting one of those tattered feet squarely on his stomach, squeezing the breath out of the man draped in corpses' clothing as it swung its weight across him, momentarily blotting out the sun.

Then the crushing pressure was gone, and the zombie moved away.

Scott lay on his back, composing himself before getting to his feet, acting as zombie-ish as his rattled mind could manage. He staggered a step and slowly picked up his bat from the ground. Something bumped into him and moved away, but he didn't react. Didn't move. Gimps staggered toward him, getting close enough for him to almost gag on their stench and weep at their horribly ravaged features. A woman walked toward him on a collision course, a nurse, with a huge chunk of meat missing from her bare left bicep, enough to see a generous amount of yellowed bone. Scott didn't even blink as the creature thudded into him. He let its momentum spin him in a lazy circle so that he faced the other way. The nurse sleepwalked by, and the sight of the mob choking the streets made him almost giddy in the knees. The feeling of a small dog being chummed and thrown into a tank with sharks came to mind, and Scott willed himself to stand and watch and act as if he was one of the dead instead of the living, even though his fear yammered at him to bolt for high hills.

Two more zombies shoulder-nudged him and pushed him aside like a block of ice bobbing in a river. Scott rolled with the hits, forcing himself to not react, keeping his shoulders slumped and his arms at his sides. The gimps left him alone.

It was working. The dark visor hid the near panicked smile he felt spread across his features.

It was working *better* than he had expected.

In a thunderclap moment of amazement, Scott saw that the zombies actually ignored him.

Turning around in the tide, he peered ahead at the masses made dark by his visor. *Act dead*, he told himself, and stepped forward carefully, picking a path through the walking slabs of cold, hungry meat. Some came at him headlong, bent on colliding with him, and when they hit, he spun like a ponderous top. Scott forced himself to remain a lump on two unsteady legs. The zombies milled about, but none raised a hand toward him. He paced himself, slackened his posture, and shuffled through the gimps and the deserted cars and walked.

He walked until the sun dropped out of sight and the sky purpled.

Brown paint covered the two-story house in flakes that fluttered in a breeze. There was no front lawn to speak of, just the bare concrete slab of a sidewalk glazed in dark ice. Three stone patio squares led to a front door of what appeared to be heavy oak— the kind of door a person would feel safe behind. Scott moved in the direction of the house, swaying as if he'd broken both hips and downed a pint of rye whiskey. He climbed the steps, feeling dead eyes on his back and ass, and latched onto the knob like it was life itself.

Taking a breath, he twisted it.

Lady Luck smiled on him once more. The door was unlocked.

He stood there for a moment, hunched over as if waiting for a bullet to the skull and ever so grateful to have made it this far. He pushed, and the door moved with slight, sticky resistance. It didn't open all the way, and he had to nudge it with his shoulder, making it squeal loud enough to make him cringe. He shambled inside, banging his shoulders off the frame as he went in and closing the door with a foot. The house was dark and he lingered in the entry, sizing up its dark hallway.

He waited, standing there in the dark, taking short, curt breaths and smelling the foul air.

"Anyone home?" he asked.

An answering hiss came from the kitchen, as startling as a snake's rattle. A sexless shadow, slouched and menacing, oozed into the dim doorway ahead with the grace of a slug.

Scott fired the Ruger twice before it collapsed with a fleshy clatter.

He waited, gazing both inside and out. A throaty rumble came from the end of the hallway, organic and decomposing. Then an unsteady clumping drew closer, as if the person wore heavy work boots and walked on bare floor. Adjusting his stance, Scott waited until a *huge* gimp came into view. The thing clacked its forehead against the top of the door frame, and Scott blinked. He couldn't remember ever seeing a taller specimen since the fall of civilization. The undead had to have been a basketball player in its life, but now it grunted and groaned as its skull prevented it from going any further.

Not wanting to wait, Scott walked up to it, taking zombie steps, and blasted its brain from underneath its chin. The gimp crashed to the ground in a heap. Scott listened for more zombies before finally figuring the place only had the pair of corpses. Relaxing, he returned to the door and locked it, then walked through an almost totally dark family room until he found the stairway to the upstairs.

He walked normally as he explored the rooms in the dark, fumbling as he went along. Locating the master bedroom and finding it empty, he took off his zombie clothes and placed them outside of the door, which he closed. A window overlooked a backyard almost swallowed up by the encroaching night.

Scott lay down on the bed without undressing, and while the smell of zombie flesh clung to him, it no longer bothered him as much.

He dreamt of Kelly and Suzy, the smell of rot surrounding them.

11

The next day, under an overcast sky, Scott once more walked with the dead.

Before he took to the road that morning, he had sliced up the clothes on the giant gimp and the smaller one, a pair of corpses that oddly complemented each other somehow, and used their 'fresh' clothing as additional camouflage.

He continued down Bayer's Road. The Ruger in his right hand, the bat in his left, he weaved in and out of derelict cars and trucks when he had to, body-checking deadheads when necessary. On multiple occasions he leaned into his shoulder a second before making contact with a gimp, usually hard enough to put them on their bony asses. The first check he delivered scared him quite badly, as he thought it would attract too much attention, but he soon realized the gimps weren't vindictive. None of them sought him out after he laid them out.

In fact, he had to pace his body checks, as it was far too much fun.

There was no wind, only the constant, freezing gnaw of winter and the eye-watering stench of his disguise, despite being outside in fresh air. Gimps walked, crawled, and slunk about the ground, complaining incessantly, and not taking notice of the hidden meal making a steady, but crooked line deeper into Halifax. Behind his visor, Scott's eyes darted this way and that, taking in each deadhead as it came close to him, deciding quickly on whether he should lay into a corpse or let it bounce off him. For an old hockey player, it wasn't a difficult rhythm to get into.

He paused at an intersection of Bayer's Road, Windsor, and Young Street and felt his stomach lurch. Empty lots the color of the purest cream waited for him, offering no shelter or refuge for several hundred meters. A huge apartment complex lay to his right, and gimps had spilled out onto the streets and populated the open expanse like drunken people enjoying a park.

Behind him, only the hordes he'd already passed through.

93

There was no retreat.

Steeling himself, Scott plunged forward.

One zombie slipped on ice and fell across his path. Scott resisted the impulse to walk around the body for fear of being detected, so he stepped over the dead thing without missing a beat. He kept on, focused on what lay ahead. More zombies congealed into a wall, blocking his way and forcing him to slow down. He hoped they would split apart. They didn't, however, and his course took him into two of them. He put his weight into his shoulder and broke through the pair, dropping one to the pavement. The flesh covering one bare knee broke open like a rotten potato, and blackness spurted out.

Scott stumbled along until the next scene stopped him dead in his tracks. His visor saved him, concealing his jaw just before it dropped in horror.

A van had crashed into a power pole, buckling the length of wood so that it leaned across its roof. A man hung from the T, crucified, his arms kept in place by what looked to be rope. His lower body, starting right at his waist, was gone. Devoured. Whoever had hung the man had done it so the zombies could feast on his legs and waist. Once it was gone, the undead had then reached up as far as they could into the rib cage, pulling down whatever had not simply dropped, perhaps even a rib or two, until the torso collapsed like a sloughed off snakeskin.

Scott tried very hard not to look at the reanimated upper half, moaning pitifully for release.

He lurched forward.

The intersection curved and Bayer's Road abruptly became Young Street. A red billboard blazed "Value and S," but the rest of the sign was covered with frost. Businesses drifted by his line of sight, some displaying signs announcing services and lunch specials, while underneath, zombies roamed aimlessly. A large Super Store rose above a parking lot teeming with the dead. An office building on his right had most of its windows smashed out. The dead cried out with decomposing vocal chords, making Scott wish they'd shut up for a moment. A transport trailer on the left had mowed down a tree before crashing into a power pole. A skeletal driver hung out of the cab, devoured from the waist down, a seat belt keeping the remains in place.

Scott passed it all, feeling the frayed seams of his sanity being tested from all angles.

He kept composed, stayed dead-looking, and avoided attention. At times he paused and slouched against a nearby car or truck and closed his eyes. In those moments, he concentrated on what the world had been like before the dead walked. In his mind's eye, it was a winter's day in the city; living people were all around him, carrying on with their business, heeding the slow pulse of traffic lights.

But as real as he managed to make these memories, they were only fleeting, like a painkiller that wore away far too soon. Then he was back in *this* world.

A feeling came over him as he walked down Young Street, passing once popular food chain restaurants and automotive service stations. The urge to stop and look around came upon him. Could he chance it? He decided he would and eased to a stop. A few seconds later, he turned around as if he possessed shattered hips.

Zombies passed in front of his vision—grisly, disfigured forms of rot, walking without direction.

Scott kept his posture slumped and studied the mob. Something would not allow him to tear his eyes away.

Then he saw it. A gimp walking with a pronounced sway to its shoulders as if it had trouble making its legs work. Covered in black gore, it strode straight ahead, pushing its way through.

Curiosity laced with growing dread hooked Scott's attention. The gimp was heading straight for him. He turned about and got walking, deviating slightly from his path and crossing the street at an angle. After lumbering ten meters or so, he slowed and glanced back as nonchalantly as any deadhead.

Fear gave his mind and heart a squeeze.

The same gimp continued to follow.

Fighting down his swelling panic, he turned and shambled off, slowly veering back on his original path. Gritting his teeth, he realized he was moving too fast and forced himself to slow down. After another fifteen meters, he looked over his shoulder once more. The zombie pursued him still. Worse, it mirrored his movements and cut the distance. Black gore covered the leathery face of the thing, frozen around empty eye sockets.

Well, shit! Doubt stabbed his mind. Had his disguise somehow failed him? Focusing on the road and the zombies ahead, Scott increased his speed just a little and hoped to God the next time he checked, his tail would be gone.

He limped over Robie Street by mid-morning, straining hard to remain in character, but a part of his mind, the evil part, excreted foul images of how things would go down. He saw the zombie behind him attracting the attention of other gimps, following him until he broke or they simply jumped him. Even now, he believed his follower was attracting the attention of others, and a long, strung-out herd was forming behind him.

A fallen sign welcoming people to the Lion's Head Tavern lay on his right, and Scott felt the overwhelming need to get off the road and out of sight. He stopped once again, half-turned in the street, and almost shit himself a second time in as many months when he saw that the zombie had not only *continued* stalking him, but had gained even more ground to come within a dozen strides of him. The empty caves of its eye sockets locked onto him.

What's going on? He couldn't shake the deadhead.

A white metro bus came into view, and he walked along its body until he got close to the driver's side mirror. Some other zombies slowed his pursuer, and it reached the rear of the bus as he moved past it. Scott kept his head fixed straight as he shifted his eyes and studied the sides of the street, wanting to find a place to lure his hunter. Somewhere secret so he could take care of business with one quick and quiet shot.

Skeletal hedges went by, and he spotted the huge sign of Oland Brewery on the side of one building up the street. The beer maker looked to have exploded from some massive unknown attack, leaving a devastated shell that spilled debris onto the street. To his right, another brown two-story house came into view, with limited windows and a front door that opened almost directly onto the sidewalk. The door was ajar, and Scott made a beeline for it. The zombies had ripped down the front fence, and Scott felt it rattle when he stepped on it. He nudged the door open with a shoulder and went inside.

The stairs to the second floor faced him, alongside a short hallway to a kitchen area. An open living room and dining area lay to the right. Even though the door was open, the smell of some unknown rotting material clung to the air. Once inside, Scott dispensed with his zombie gait and pulled himself halfway up the steps before turning around and waiting. He pointed the Ruger at the front door, wanting the zombie to be well inside so that once he shot it, the dead thing wouldn't block the entry and he could seal the house. Scott intended to go through the place afterward and do a cleaning, but first . . .

The form of his hunter bobbed into sight through the small circular window set in the door's surface. It drew closer, until a hand pushed it open. Scott straightened his arm and took aim where he expected the head to appear. The gimp shrugged past the door and its face came up in a snarl.

Scott started to squeeze.

"Oh, Jesus, *wait!*" a woman's voice squawked.

Scott gasped and jerked the gun toward the ceiling. The fright of those three words sent electric waves of what *almost* happened through his core. He collapsed on the stairs and stared at the thing in dumbfounded fascination.

"Oh, shit," the zombie said, before glancing behind her—at least, it sounded like a woman. She moved inside and closed the door. "I think they're coming."

The lips of the hideous face didn't move.

"Huh?" Scott blurted, utterly confused by what he was seeing.

"Listen, you idiot, we don't have the time. Just come on. We'll find the back door. There has to be one. Just pray to God it isn't blocked or anything is in our way."

With that, the gimp—who had followed him for almost half a kilometer—rushed to the kitchen in a totally lifelike manner.

"Holy shit." Scott got up and bounded over the steps, landing heavily in his excitement. He scrambled after the stranger. "Hey, wait!"

"Go fuck yourself!" she called back. "You were the one hauling ass up the goddamn street for the last fifteen minutes!"

"Huh?" Scott paused in the threshold to the kitchen. The zombie was pressed up against the back door, her hand on the knob.

"Listen." She raised a hand, her lips still paralyzed. "You follow me from now on, got it?"

Scott could only nod.

The zombie turned back to the door and opened it. She peered out and eased through. Scott followed. Outside, in cloud-muted daylight, the talking gimp, still looking as if it had the living shit kicked out of it, but in possession of a female voice, reverted back to a gunshot stagger. The sudden change left Scott standing and staring in amazement for all of three seconds. A crashing from the front of the house got him moving, and he left the door swinging as he followed the woman.

Back in the street, Scott didn't let her out of sight. He noticed two short handles sticking up from her back, which made her easy to distinguish from the surrounding gimps. She led him down the road toward Oland Brewery. Crashing wood echoed somewhere behind them. Zombies in the street paused and considered the direction of the sound, while Scott and his mysterious talking gimp slowly moved against the tide, forcing through it like wooden prows through Arctic ice. Two gimps jostled the woman, but she didn't cry out; she simply absorbed the hits, staggering for effect. She righted herself, staying in character, and pressed on. Deadheads wobbled by and Scott stayed three strides behind her, keeping in her wake. They came upon a row of independently owned shops. Across from them, bulldozers and cranes rested on an open construction site never to be finished.

She shuffled toward one of the shops, taking her time and moving through the walking corpses without drawing attention. She stopped at the glass door of a furniture shop and pushed it open, disappearing inside. Scott followed and, once he was inside, he saw her stop in an aisle surrounded by dusty-looking sofas. She looked to her left.

Scott saw the three deadheads a second later, lurking in parts of the shop, oblivious to them both.

She turned toward him and, with those mangled lips that didn't move, said, "Lock the door."

Scott complied, finding bolts at the top and bottom. The furniture shop contained beds of all sizes and colors, kitchen table sets, ovens, living room sets, and even washers and dryers. Funny, he hadn't really considered them as furniture in his previous life.

"Don't use the shotgun."

"How do you know about the shotgun?"

The dead face turned toward him. "You're kidding, right? How do you think I picked up on you? The thing's hanging off your back. The poncho doesn't hide it well, just makes you look like a walking pitched tent from behind. And I saw you come out of that place this morning. You closed the door behind yourself."

"Oh."

"Oh," the face mocked him in a husky voice. "Just don't use the shotgun."

As she said it, her hands went up behind her head. She extracted two nightsticks that were almost two feet long. Holding one in each hand, she moved down the aisle, approaching the zombies from their flank. Scott raised the Ruger. He followed her until he had a clear shot, then took aim.

She glanced back at him just as he pulled the trigger. A zombie's head snapped back before dropping to the floor in front of a beige sofa set with matching recliner. Gore speckled the upholstery.

"I think that was the shop manager," he reported.

"Don't waste your ammo, man."

The two remaining deadheads hissed, opening mouths ringed with black skin tags. They moved unsteadily through the gaps between furniture. The talking zombie with the nightsticks went to meet them. Scott shoved his Ruger into his right boot and lifted the bat. Lazy hisses came from the two zombies, but they did not move to attack.

Once she got close enough, the woman dropped the gimp façade. The nightsticks crashed over the first zombie's skull with enough power to make Scott cringe and glance fearfully to the store's front. She drove the gimp to its knees and laid the second nightstick upside its skull, breaking it open and staining another set of sofa chairs with brain matter. The second zombie turned at the noise, but had no time for anything else as she hit the thing, *one-two-three-four*, crumpling its brainpan. It collapsed in an aisle. She continued pummeling the dead thing, striking it long after it had stopped moving, increasing the power of her blows until Scott felt a chill slink up his back.

Eventually, with a mighty expulsion of breath, she straightened up and regarded him.

He stood with his bat in hand, feeling awkward and more than a little wary.

"There might be more. Let's search the place, okay? And meet over there in a minute." She pointed a nightstick toward an open window set into a wall, which was probably the administration office. She left him without waiting for an answer, stalking off in search of other undead prey. Scott watched her go in stunned amazement. With a jolt, he remembered his task, and he went about doing it.

The place was empty.

They met back at the office a few minutes later, entering from a side door that locked from the inside. The window gave a clear view of the storefront while shielding them from any zombies beyond. Light from the open window offered just enough to see. Two large chestnut desks filled the square room, facing each other, while a sizeable leather sofa with some duct tape bandaging an arm rest lined the north wall.

Scott plopped down on the sofa, pulling off his undead-scented poncho, hood, and removing his motorcycle helmet and ninja mask underneath. The air was cold against his sweating flesh, and he took a deep breath of stale air. The woman stood by one desk and placed her clubs on its surface.

Then her hands went to her scalp and she pulled off her face.

12

The mask came off with a *slurp*. She wore a hood underneath that covered her face, and that came off next. Eyeing him, she tousled her flattened hair as if trying to resuscitate it and took a deep breath. Blue eyes narrowed in his direction before she pulled off her own poncho and let it drop in a heap onto the floor. A black backpack came off next. She wore a dark snowmobile suit and plastic elbow and knee pads. She reached up to her neckline and unzipped her suit a startling four inches, revealing white skin underneath. Making a face, she kicked the pile of dead clothing out the door and motioned for him to do the same. When he had, she closed it and went back to the desk.

"Man," she said without looking at him. "I hate wearing that. Stinks. What were you doing out there?"

"Huh?" Scott asked as he sat back down.

She locked eyes with him, not bothering to repeat herself.

"Ah, well." Scott leaned back on the sofa. "I was looking for someone."

"Yeah? Who?"

Scott didn't want to tell her just yet. "A man. That's all I want to say right now."

She leaned against the desk and stared at him. Scott noted that the nightsticks were within easy grasp. She didn't trust him, and he didn't blame her.

"A man, eh? You're looking for a dude."

"Yeah."

"He's a friend of yours?"

Scott blinked. "You're asking a lot of questions."

"Guess I am," she said, breaking eye contact for a moment and squinting through the window, checking on the storefront. "What's your name?"

"Scott."

"I'm Amy."

He nodded. Neither offered to shake hands. She had a raspy voice, as if she had screamed herself hoarse at one time and never fully recovered.

"Spotted you first thing when you came out of the house this morning." Amy sized him up. "Not too many zombies take the time to close a door behind them."

Scott felt the color drain out of his face and Amy nodded, eyes widening again for emphasis. "Yeah, a little thing like that gave you away. Lucky for you, though, that Moe doesn't have the capacity to catch on to those little things."

"Moe?"

"Yeah, zombies."

Scott forced a little smile. "Nice."

"Nice?" The skin between Amy's eyes and forehead wrinkled. "Moe's nice, eh? I'll keep that in mind. What do you call them?"

"Gimps. Deadheads. Dees. Dead fuckers."

Amy snorted, momentarily cracking her otherwise fierce demeanor. "I like that one."

"It's popular."

"Yeah? With who?"

Scott realized it was just him and Gus.

Amy filled in the sudden quiet. "I'm sure whoever's still alive at this stage has a pet name for them. We call them Moes, on account they moan. And zombies, of course. Or just the dead. The boys might take to dead fuckers."

Scott didn't ask who "the boys" were. He felt it was best to just stay quiet.

"Where're you from?" Amy asked.

"Saint John. New Brunswick."

"Never been," Amy said curtly. She considered the desk behind her and hoisted herself up. "You're a long way from home."

"Came over here with some people I knew."

"Where are they?"

"Dead."

Amy didn't offer condolences, but rather kept on gauging him with her dusky blue eyes.

"You?" Scott asked.

"I'm from Halifax." She stopped from saying any more, and Scott realized she was a careful woman. "You're smarter than most."

"I am?" That was a surprise. "Why?"

"You figured out Moe can't tell us apart once we get all stinky."

"Oh, that. That only happened yesterday."

"Better late than never. Especially here."

"I guess."

"Well," Amy announced, as if deciding something. "You wanna come along with me, then? Meet the gang?"

Scott wasn't sure about that, and Amy picked up on it. "Don't worry. We're cool."

"Oh, uh, well . . ."

"Need time to think about it?"

"It'd be nice," Scott admitted.

"You have as long as it takes me to catch my breath and walk out of here."

Wow. He struggled to think of something to say. "That mask you have . . ."

"Something, ain't it? It's an old Brian Mulroney Halloween mask. Found it in a costume shop's bargain bin."

"Who?"

"Brian—never mind. Obviously before your time. Before my time, really. The benefits of a Poly-Sci education at Dal."

"Where you get the nightsticks?"

Amy's brow creased. "Nightsticks? Oh, these. They ain't nightsticks. They're tonfas."

"What?"

"Tonfas. Hardwood martial arts weapons. I don't have a gun. Wish I did, though. Something like that silencer you have there."

"Sound suppressor."

"Huh?"

"The proper term is—" Scott shook his head. "Where'd you get them?"

"From my teacher."

Scott truly didn't know what to make of Amy. Her brisk manner of conversation and her unwavering stare made him feel uncomfortable.

"We ran out of bullets long ago. One of the reasons we came to Halifax was to look for guns and ammo. There was an armory in town, you know."

"I didn't know that."

"Yeah, well, there was. One of our guys was there. Blown to hell, though. Too bad for us. You don't see it much around here, but downtown had the shit kicked out of it."

"What do you mean?"

"I *mean* it had the shit kicked out of it. Halifax explosion two point oh. The Army set up defenses around the place, blocking off whole streets with steel barricades, razor wire, and sandbags. Even buses in some cases. I wasn't around for it, but you'll see. Houses have been levelled, man. Some buildings look like blocks of cheese. The ones still there, I mean. We have theories on what might have happened, but before they died, the Forces kicked ass."

"They died?"

Amy nodded. "The ones that were lucky. A lot of them rose as the dead. Unfortunate for us. We ran into a few already."

"Why's it unfortunate for us?" Scott knew he wouldn't like the answer.

"The soldiers wore body armor, and it didn't come off if they were turned. It stayed on. Worse, their *helmets* stayed on. I doubt your little sidearm there could poke a hole in one of them. And a smack to the head with a tonfa does shit all."

"So how do you kill them?"

In answer, Amy reached down and pulled up a tonfa. The hilt of the weapon had been sharpened into a spike. Once Scott had an eyeful of that, Amy dropped it to the desk and pulled a survival knife out of her boot. She held it up, twisting it this way and that, showing off the serrated edge.

Scott was at a loss for words. The thought of facing zombies in full body armor made him uneasy.

"Through the eye or under the chin. The weather makes it harder than usual. You really have to punch the tip in hard, and it feels gross. Like you're plunging into a frozen watermelon or thick slush or something like that. All grainy."

"The cold freezes them," Scott added.

Amy nodded. "I guess you know all about it since you've lived for this long."

Scott supposed he did, but his mind still lingered on the zombie soldiers.

"So," Amy finally announced. "I'm ready. How about you?"

"You don't mind me coming along?"

"Nah. I think you're okay."

That surprised Scott. "Yeah, how so?"

"You have at least two guns on you, and you didn't try to use them on me."

Scott blinked. All this time, she'd been waiting for him to draw on her.

"And you didn't try to rape me," she said.

Stunned yet again, he couldn't look her in the eyes. "Oh . . . I guess that's a, uh, good indicator."

"Yep. Big man like you. Armed to the teeth. Little girl like me with a pair of sticks. I wouldn't have had much of a chance if you really wanted to bend me over the desk here."

"Uh," Scott said. He didn't feel comfortable with the sudden change in conversation. He scratched at his neck and remembered her destroying the gimp from earlier. "Well, I wasn't—"

"Thinking about it? I saw that. I have this thing about people. Hasn't failed me yet."

"Oh." Scott felt strangely, awkwardly, on the defensive. "Good . . . Glad we had this. This talk."

"Me too." She got up off the desk. "I'm getting ready to leave. You still have a choice, but once I walk out of here, I'm gone. Plain and simple."

"Where are you headed again?" Scott asked, standing.

"Downtown. It'll be a day-long trip, with all the snow and shit in the streets. And then there's Moe, of course. But you have the clothes, so that's fine. Gonna have to touch them up some time, though."

"What do you mean?"

"They're *clean*. You haven't saturated them in blood and guts. It's worked for you so far, but sooner or later, your own smell will come through. Once that happens, they'll be on you like a football in slow motion."

Scott wasn't sure he got the simile.

"We have a base downtown. Like I said, a bunch of streets were cut off and fortified. It didn't work for the soldiers, but it's all we got for now. And we all walk around in dead guts if we go beyond the fort."

Jesus Christ, Scott thought.

"Shall we, then?" Amy asked as she gestured to the door.

Feeling as if he could have worse options, Scott nodded.

13

"Wait a second," Amy said and went to one of the zombies she'd put down. Her knife appeared in her hand and she cut through the corpse's shirt, revealing the sallow belly. The knife flashed as she stabbed down, sinking it to the hilt. She sawed with some effort, making a slit in the fish-belly flesh, gasping at the end. The smell of rancid guts poisoned the air, and Scott held his breath, looking away for a moment.

"Here you go," Amy said and splashed a fistful of decomposing innards on Scott's poncho-covered chest.

"Oh Jesus," Scott gasped and bent over, suddenly sick. His hands went to his knees.

"You okay?"

Scott shook his head.

"You'll get used to it," she said.

He dry-heaved instead, suddenly thankful that he'd skipped breakfast. He spat and grunted, the powerful smell of intestinal juice making his eyes water.

Then he felt a splash against his back.

"All right," Amy declared. "You're done. Now do me."

"What?"

"Stand up, you big baby, and take this."

Scott glanced up and winced. Amy stood right before him holding a fistful of what appeared to be wet eels, grey-black, like something scooped out of a sewage line.

"Oh Jesus." Scott looked away and felt his stomach rumble in dangerous fashion.

"I was like that once," Amy said. "You get over it."

Scott wasn't sure he'd ever get over it, and rubbing the deadhead's intestinal tract over himself was something he had difficulty processing mentally and physically. Amy waited for him to compose himself, which he had trouble doing.

"Look, it's the best way."

"Guh . . ."

"You okay?"

Scott cracked an irritated eye at her, shook his head, and went back to fighting the upheaval in his stomach. After a few moments, he regained control and straightened up once more.

"You really are a wuss, aren'tcha?" Amy asked. Scott saw that she had smeared the innards over her front and lower back.

"Yeah," Scott muttered quietly. She had him there.

"Let's get going, then," she said and pulled on her hood and mask. Scott did the same, thanking God that he didn't have to smear any guts on his hood. As it was, he was still combatting some dizziness. He never thought smell could be so powerful, so debilitating.

"You ready?"

Scott nodded, not even wanting to open his mouth. He pulled on his own hood, making sure it covered his nose. Then his helmet went on, and finally the cloth hood.

"I need air," he informed her.

But she was already walking for the store's front door.

Scott lurched after her, feeling very *not* ready for what was coming, but not wanting to be left behind, either. He suspected Amy was quite capable of doing just that if she had to. She opened the door and left it swinging for him, and he followed her outside.

Into a river of zombies.

Scott watched Amy blend in almost seamlessly with the tide of undead thanks to the bulk of her disguise. Fighting down the impulse to catch up to her, he hunched over and waded in with slow, lengthy steps. The air cleared the stench clinging to his person and helped alleviate his queasiness, but the thought that he wore a gimp's insides on him was almost enough to make him barf. Once again, he thanked Christ above he hadn't eaten anything that morning. A deadhead hit his right shoulder, off-balance, and crumpled to the ground. Scott walked on, eyes fixed on Amy's back, doing as she did and hoping he was every bit as convincing.

They meandered along in undead fashion, passing a number of quaint houses submerged in finely sculpted drifts. Some houses were burnt out husks that gleamed with frost, while other lots were empty except for snow. Scott believed that if he dug, he'd find blasted foundations. Whatever the Army had in their armory, they hadn't hesitated to use it. Cars lay buried in driveways or parked on the sidewalks. Some dotted the road itself, no doubt once seeking to escape the city. The snow on the roads became more packed down as the dead trampled over it, pressing it until the main drags were relatively easy to walk.

They kept going until Scott noticed Amy deviating ever so subtly from her path. Then he saw why. Young Street narrowed to almost a single lane. Power poles criss-crossed the street, creating a logjam of wailing deadheads too brain dead to simply turn around and walk out of the trap.

Just over their heads, Scott thought he saw an ice bound harbour.

Amy turned to her left and walked up a long slope. More picturesque houses half destroyed. More Army destruction. Four houses in a row appeared to have been fire-bombed. Their blackened walls stood, but Scott didn't think they would stay that way for long. Deadheads fell into step alongside him, but he focused on Amy just ahead and slowly out-paced his unliving companions.

They passed a white dune where three torsos jutted from the snow bank, their horrid features staring into space, their mouths frozen open. Scott wasn't certain if they were deadheads or not, and they soon passed out of sight. He kicked at corpses at his feet, animated and groaning as they made do without legs and pulled them-selves forward. Two corpses didn't have limbs at all, and one tried to inchworm along the frozen asphalt with one arm that ended in a splintered wrist.

Amy marched on, ignoring the horrors and earning Scott's growing amazement. How did she *do* it? How did she simply walk by such gruesome displays and not lose it? It urged him to control his own frayed nerves.

The street ended in a wire fence and she eventually stopped against it, swaying as if a wind pushed her. Zombies stood on both sides of her, staring at the same thing, and she blended in. Scott stopped just behind her and forced himself to ignore the others, feeling that if one brushed up against him, he just might scream. A nearby sign read "Needham Memorial Park." Beyond the fence, *hundreds* of deadheads trudged aimlessly in a slow cadence through trampled down drifts. Some crested a hill, as if mulling their unlife, while others moped around its snow cap. Some bumped into a distant jungle gym. Scott spotted one that had somehow gotten tangled in the chains of a swing.

Well, shit, Scott thought, feeling a strong surge of unease bubble up, wanting to turn and run. His breathing picked up, and nervous energy was building up in his calves, causing them to ache. Some of the zombies on the other side of the fence were walking toward him, eyeing him evilly. Never had he seen so many undead. Not in Saint John, and not in Annapolis. He gaped at the horde enjoying the park, the words *"so many, so many"* pulsating in his skull. Control started slipping away. Zombies were closing in, sensing something off about him, something not quite dead. A hospital patient wearing light green pajamas dragged itself toward the fence, toward him. Sur-gical tubing and IV lines hung from its stomach and arms like horrible, bloodless veins. That one knew he was alive, Scott was suddenly sure of it. That one was coming right for him, and it would reach over the fence with a palsied hand and grip his poncho and rip it from his body. It would only take that one movement and one triumphant wail from the undead thing, and then *all* of them would pile on him like a sacked quarterback forced to the ground, where they would work their teeth into everything and *pull* until something gave in a burst of blood. All to his muffled shrieks.

Amy nudged him a little too hard, bumping him into the zombie next to him. She had turned around ever so casually, then began walking back the way they had come.

Struggling with the sense of imminent doom, Scott did the same, convinced that any second he would feel the groping hand of the hospital invalid on his shoulder. He couldn't move fast enough from the gate, and the urge to check on where the zombie was swelled up in his brain like a murderous tumor ready to pop. His legs went to rubber. His skin became clammy and his breath quickened. His *breathing!* They could hear his *breathing!* He sounded like a train! The dead things along the fence were watching him with graveyard amusement, daring him to give up the act. Who was he fooling? Any second he'd be halted and bitten.

But that didn't happen.

As he stumbled away from the fence and the vast mob in the park, nothing reached out to grab him. Nothing clamped rotting teeth onto his shoulder. Nothing tried to stop him.

Scott hoped that Amy would seek shelter in one of the houses soon. He'd had enough walking with the dead for one day. His mind redlined, and its needle quivered toward meltdown.

If they didn't get out of sight soon, he knew he would freak in epic proportions.

If that happens, *his mind stated clinically,* we'll both be well and truly fucked.

He opened his mouth and moaned, only half aware he was doing it. The zombie ahead of him stopped and turned around, and he saw it wasn't Amy; it was some hideous caricature of a face, and more zombies were gathering around its shoulders like a dark wall, damming him in. The lead gimp came for him, its lips smeared at the corners like a drowned clown's grin. Scott halted in his tracks and bent over for his gun, his fingers slipping on the textured metal grip. The zombie moved in a blur, startling him with its speed, and butted its chest against him. It raised its face and Scott saw the clearest blue eyes glaring at him, seemingly screaming at him to hold it together, to hold it in because if he *lost* it, they were both dead. They would be pulled apart in seconds. He tried to move away, but the thing grabbed him, and that almost made him shriek.

Then it was pulling away, taking him by the wrist and walking as if it had both knees blown out. Scott let himself be led, feeling an ocean of undead eyes watch with an unspoken query. They jostled him. Zombies crawled blindly at his feet and attempted to trip him. His vision became a wall of grey-blue faces, black skin tags, and parted, hungry mouths.

A house rose up before them. They inched their way toward the door, when Scott really wanted to sprint. Every muscle and fiber in his body wanted him to take off, but the zombie leading him dictated their pace. They crossed the magically elongating distance as if they were dragging granite blocks behind them, and *that* wait almost set him off.

Finally, after what felt like a year, they reached the front steps.

The zombie with the human eyes pulled him inside and nudged the door, allowing it to swing most of the way shut before finally pushing it closed with a click. Then the creature whirled on him and shoved him up against the wall. Scott grabbed the front of its clothing and snarled. The zombie clutched his wrist, twisted it somehow, and bent him over almost effortlessly. A surprised, breathless wheeze of pain broke from his lips. A foot crashed into the back of his knee, dropping him to the floor, and suddenly the deadhead before him was a head taller.

"Shut *up*, you bastard," a husky whisper urged. "Shut up or I swear to *God* I'll leave you here."

Scott's eyes clinched shut. Two years of holding it together and suddenly the wheels on his wagon didn't just drop off, they *flew*. His hearing went offline, leaving only a flat buzz that hummed shrilly deep inside his skull. He panted and moaned the weak wail of a kid left on a dock, watching the family boat pull away with everyone on it except *him*. He set his jaw, held on to the gimp with the woman's voice, and waited for the teeth. Images of his wife and child flashed through his mind to be replaced by this *thing* that smelled like rotting meat and shit. And Jesus! Oh, Jesus Christ! It finally had him! Finally had him at its mercy and any moment now . . .

Scott froze, paralyzed with fright, as if the mother of all black widows had just injected him with enough venom to blow off the top of his head.

He whimpered and waited for the teeth.

Instead, anaconda arms wrapped around his head in slow, murderous motions and drew him in and held on. Not crushing, but just . . . pressing against him, firmly. Warmly. The zombie held on to him like that until his breath subsided; until he realized that it wasn't biting him; until he relaxed in its arms; until he remembered that the thing had a name and it was Amy. He listened as the off-the-air whine in his ears resumed picking up real sound, and the moans were behind the closed door, in the street.

Far away.

And after a while, tears welled up in his eyes and he hugged her back.

14

They stayed upstairs in the empty house for the rest of the day. Amy had led him to the master bedroom after stripping off his clothes, then heaped him onto a queen-size bed with a red satin comforter. She rolled the blanket around him like a bloody California roll, said something comforting, and left the room. Scott heard her moving things around and he wanted to help, but his limbs had gone boneless, and his voice didn't seem to want to work. He closed his eyes instead and fell into an exhausted sleep where he dreamed fleetingly of the Mountain Man, on a sofa, nursing a bottle of Captain Morgan.

You fucked up, Gus informed him with a drunken smile. Booze didn't lie.

Shame flooded Scott. He'd jeopardized not only his life, but hers as well. So much for his mental toughness.

Fucked up big time, *Gus droned on.*

Scott had nothing to say to that.

But I think it'll be okay.

You think? Scott asked, suddenly hopeful.

Sure thing, Chico.

Scott sighed. *My fucking name* isn't *Chico.*

That set the Mountain Man laughing. Scott joined in, feeling better. He felt a hand across his mouth and opened his eyes to see an intense, round face peering at him.

"Hi," he said, but it came out as a mouse fart.

Amy frowned at the muffled squeal. "You back?" she asked.

Scott nodded.

"You aren't going to freak out again?"

That made him take a deep breath through his nose. Amy removed her hand, her blue eyes dark and hard like sharp rocks. She backed off and returned to the wooden chair she'd been sitting in beside the bed. Dull squeaks pierced the air as she sat down. Scott heard her sigh.

"I'm sorry," he whispered after a while.

Amy said nothing.

"I lost it out there. I . . . you didn't have to save my ass like that, but you did. I owe you one. Bigtime."

He heard a sigh from Amy's dark form near the bed. "Don't worry about it."

But Scott did. He felt the terrible, gnawing shame of letting her down, and he didn't even know her, but he knew he needed to redeem himself in her eyes.

"Hope you don't mind, I ate some of that beef stew in your backpack," Amy said.

Scott had to think about what exactly he had with him. Then he remembered. "What's mine is yours, now."

"Where'd you get that, anyway?"

"The stew?"

"Yeah."

"From a friend."

"He got any more?"

Scott smiled in the dark. "Yeah. Tons."

Amy grunted and folded her hands on her lap.

Scott cleared his throat. "I thought you were a deadhead out there. Thought you were going to bite me. I don't think I've ever seen so many gimps before, so close, clustered together like that. Crawling on the . . . on the ground. All around. I froze. Everything just got to me all at once. Something just snapped."

He stopped then and thought about what else to say. In the end, he softly said, "Thank you."

"You're welcome," she replied quietly. "Just don't let it happen again."

"I'll try."

Amy said nothing. Outside, the morbid chorus of the undying seemed distant and oh so cold. Scott listened to it for a while, feeling the contrast of the bed's warmth. No matter what it was like outside, there was perhaps nothing so grounding as the comfort of a warm bed.

"We stay here for the night?" Scott asked her.

"I don't think you're in any condition to go anywhere. Do you?"

"No . . . What about your friends?"

"They aren't going anywhere." She seemed pretty certain about that.

"Really?"

"Yeah. That stew was really good," she said.

"Did you eat it all?"

"No, only half. Hard to eat when Moe's around."

"I hear that."

"Never touched it when the world was still the world. Called it dog food." Amy sighed in the dark. "Never again."

"Funny, eh?" Scott agreed. "That, and the little things you miss. Go easy on it, 'cause once it's gone, you'll miss it."

"You know what I miss?"

"What?"

"Q-tips."

Scott felt his forehead crease. "Q-tips?"

"Yeah. I used to love cleaning my ears. Still do, I mean, but it's not like I can do it every day, anymore."

"Why not?"

"Well, I *can*." Amy backed up. "It's just that, sooner or later, they'll be all gone. And you know what?"

"Hm?"

"When the world was falling apart, I bet I went something like three months before I cleaned out my ears. Something, eh? And when I finally did, it was as gross as it sounds."

"Does sound gross."

"It was. Needed an ear pick."

"Ew."

The dead called out from outside, but Scott didn't care. They were outside, and he was fine. "What's the plan for tomorrow?"

Amy appeared to think. "First, we'll see how you're doing."

"I'll be fine."

Silence. "Then we'll see if we can make it down the street out there. Continue toward Barrington and make our way to the casino."

"Casino? There's a casino in Halifax?"

"There was. Once. Now it's next to home plate."

"Your boys are there?"

"Yep."

"How many?"

"You'll see."

"They anything like you?"

"No," Amy said quietly. "I'm special."

Scott almost said, *You certainly are,* but he didn't, realizing that it came close to actually flirting. Flirting with a stranger in a dark room while recovering from losing his mind, and with zombies outside in the cold, didn't appeal to him. So he stopped right there.

"Get some sleep," Amy said as if sensing his thoughts. "I'll keep watch. When you can't sleep anymore, it'll be your shift. Fair enough?"

"Yes."

"G'night, then."

"You'll be okay?" Scott asked and was immediately thankful for the dark. He felt his cheeks burn with embarrassment.

Amy didn't answer right away, but she turned ever so slightly in his direction. "Course I'll be okay," she said without any trace of annoyance. "Told you, I'm special."

Certainly are, Scott thought a second time. With that, he stopped talking.

And eventually tumbled into sleep.

In the morning, he woke up to find Amy already awake and moving. It didn't surprise him. In the short time he'd known her, he recognized that there was very little Amy couldn't do, and if there was something, she'd work around it somehow. A person had to respect that. Up until yesterday, Scott had thought he was the same way. The memory of losing his composure in front of her still burned in his craw and set him shaking.

"You okay?" she asked when she came in from the hallway.

"Yeah," he answered, tossing off the bedcovers. "Yeah. Breakfast?"

"Sure. Whad'ya got?"

From his pack, he pulled out a can of cold ravioli in meat sauce, opened it, and offered it to her while she pulled up a chair.

"Thanks," she said. She left the room and came back with a spoon from her pack. He sat at a nearby desk.

"Where'd you sleep last night?" he asked.

"Next room."

"Ah."

"They got nice beds in this place," she commented.

"You got any water?"

"Yeah, in the bag," she said, taking a bite and nodding. "Good. Actually had a case of this. The last can went about a week ago."

"We'll need to get more water soon," Scott stated, studying the bedroom.

"Not going to be easy," Amy said as she chewed. "But I know a place along the way. We actually have a bunch of bottled water at the base downtown. MREs as well."

"Those the ready-to-eat meals?"

Amy nodded. "After stuff like this, a chicken MRE is like Christmas dinner."

Scott bet it was. "You said you guys were looking for ammo here. One of the reasons you came to Halifax. What were the others?"

"Find other people. Strength in numbers and all that."

"City's a bad spot, though. I mean, by now most people are either out or long dead."

"Leaving all this wonderful stuff," Amy said. She pushed hair out of her eyes and studied the inside of the can, looking for the next chunk. "The city still offers a lot. It's just getting it is all. When we realized we could disguise ourselves to blend in, it seemed the way to go. Get searching, get what we were looking for, and then get out. One trip."

"People and ammo," Scott stated, looking at the bedroom's only window, hearing the dull, constant wail of the dead outside.

"And seeds."

"What?"

"Seeds. Fruit and vegetables. Most of the farmland still has stuff growing in it, but it's wild and weedy. And there's Moe. We were looking for a Home Hardware depot with a gardener's section, or anyplace else. I found one a few klicks away from where I spotted you and found a bunch of packets."

"You know anything about that?"

"Got a degree in agriculture."

"Thought you were a Poly-Sci grad."

"And agriculture," she stated, handing him the leftovers. "Thanks."

Scott took the can and dug into the remaining half. Freaking out left a person with an appetite. "You're welcome. Does it have to be a Home Hardware? I mean, I passed a Superstore on the way in."

"I think I know the one. I was in it the morning just before I spotted you. Actually camped out on a sofa up in the manager's office the night before. Nothing there, though."

"You got everything you were looking for in one stop?"

"Pretty much. Onions, carrots, some broccoli. A few others. I got a few packets of each. More than enough to get us started. But if I spot any other groceries or the like, I'll still check it out. Never know what you'll find."

"And the seeds are still good?"

"Oh, yeah. Most seeds are good for a few years, but the germination rates get lower as time goes on. I think we'll be fine. Some won't be any good at all, though. Like, say, parsnips."

Scott didn't really like parsnips anyway. "What happens when you're all finished with everything?"

"We move out. Been here almost two weeks as it is, looking for stuff. The Forces left a bunch of canned goods and MREs back at the base. Lots of supplies, but we can't stay here, obviously. Moe's too strong."

"Where are you headed after Halifax?"

"We have a safe place to start over." Amy glanced at him, her bangs falling over her face. "You interested?"

Start over. The words glowed in his mind's eye. Start over was oversimplified. "If it's okay with you, I'd like to think about it first."

Amy stood up. "When you're finished eating, let's get moving."

Scott nodded and dug into the cold leftovers.

"Who you looking for?"

He stopped eating. "A guy who . . ."

"Who what?"

"Killed some friends of mine."

Amy remained quiet for moment. "And you think he's in Halifax."

"Maybe. Decided this was as good a place to start, anyway."

"There are bad ones out there. Worse out west, I've heard. Road warrior shit happening out there."

"Yeah, well, I just want to take care of some business."

"You know this guy's name?"

"Tenner."

Amy grunted. "What's he look like?"

Scott swallowed some ravioli. "Don't really know. I never saw him. I heard his voice just before he shot me in the back and left me for dead. Then he went to work on my two friends. He got into a basement and cut them up."

"Jesus."

"Yeah," Scott said, finishing off his food, which had lost all taste. He left the empty can on the desk. "Well, I know his voice. If I hear it again, I'll know."

"Ready for the horror show?" Amy asked him after a moment.

"Yeah." But he didn't sound or know for certain. There was only one way to find out, and despite what had happened to him yesterday, Scott was always one for getting back into the saddle. Unless the saddle killed him first.

They finished up their morning routines in separate bathrooms, got dressed, and met in the living room. The bloody outerwear they gathered up and held at arms' length like old skin shavings. They put on the gear in silence, each thinking of what was to come, and Scott also wondering if he truly was up for walking with the dead. Amy was probably wondering the same, but she said nothing.

"All set?" she asked, her Brian Mulroney mask hiding her identity almost too well.

"Yeah."

"Don't shut the door this time," she warned as she gripped the knob.

Did she have to remind him of that? Scott felt like shit.

She opened the door to reveal a scene from a painting, white ruined with black. The cold air hit them in a gust and paralyzed them for a moment. The road teemed with undead, both walking and slinking along like worms coated in ice particles, moving in that half-frozen way that was so disturbing to watch.

Amy shuffled out the doorway and into the street. Scott followed, his anxiety rising, but not dangerously so. They headed down the slope and back the way they had come, then struck left, between two houses, bypassing the crunch of gimps at the nearing intersection. Scott was glad to see the backyards were small and the color of unspoiled porcelain. Amy moved through drifts, her feet punching through with little winded *pops*, and he did his best to keep up. He struggled through the snow, using the bat for balance and hoping the dead would not detect him. The thought embarrassed him. There weren't any in sight behind the houses, yet he was still worried.

Amy ambled by three houses painted light green, pink, and white, then she took a right and walked down a driveway, moving slowly around a German-made Jetta buried up to its windows. Scott followed, cheating by placing his feet in the holes she'd already made. Amy paused in the road beyond, and Scott didn't know if she was waiting for him or simply acting like a dead deer. He stopped beside her and looked ahead.

Halifax Harbour, plugged with ice floes that must have drifted in overnight. Nothing had ever looked colder. Amy started walking again, slower than before, and Scott realized why. They were headed down a hill glazed with snow. Ice slicked the pavement underneath the powder. There were grooves in the surface, and he realized they had been made by Moe trying to walk up over the hill, but slipping and sliding back down to the T-intersection at the base of the hill.

Scott's breath caught in his throat.

The road looked like a protest march of epic, undead proportions.

And they were walking right for it.

Underneath his hood and visor, Scott bared his teeth at the nearing mob, wondering if Amy truly meant to walk amongst the throngs on the lower road, dreading the notion. The woman had ice in her veins. Moe shambled along to a song of pity and horror, and Scott felt a sudden urge for rum, whiskey, *anything* to take the edge off, anything to armor his insides. Beyond the parade was a factory of some sort, but reaching it seemed impossible.

To his relief, Amy veered to the right, keeping close to a wire fence. A large billboard sign rose up after that, announcing a *SPRING SPECIAL* on carpet cleanings. The red building behind it was a ruined blossom of brick, steel girders, broken glass, and splintered wood. A bus shelter came into view, the glass walls intact, holding seven or eight deadheads in place like a tight fishbowl. One had its face pressed up hard against the glass, smearing the fleshy pulp of one cheek until it gave away like a piece of dry, crumbly cake, coating the glass in black and exposing a decayed rack of molars. The cheek stuck for a split second before dropping.

Scott didn't need to see any more of that.

Amy pushed past the things jammed into the bus shelter and zombie-walked up a furrow that might have had a sidewalk underneath. Scott walked in her slipstream, aware of the gimps milling about in the street to his left and feeling his armpits flood with sweat. He didn't falter, however, didn't break. That confidence galvanized him and made him feel back in control. He hoped his recent lapse was only a one-time thing.

Under an increasingly cloudy sky, they ambled past what Scott believed to be thousands of undead. Moe was everywhere on the street and sidewalk. It was the largest concentration of dead things he'd ever seen, bigger than what he had witnessed in Annapolis, and despair rose up into his gullet like an undigested lump. It had been a mistake to come into the city. Tenner had to have perished in such a hellish place. There was simply no place to run from them all.

The chalky glut of ice in the bay's throat appeared pristine, but then dark shapes, like tombstones, bobbed into sight. Deadheads moved on the ice, perhaps trapped, perhaps coming from the other side. A green sign marked the street Scott and Amy travelled as Barrington. Another sign designated the vast dock area on the bay as the Halifax Shipyard, but the buildings were wrecked, flattened into splintery lumps by some unknown force. Amy moved on, following Barrington Street to the south. An embankment of ice and snow rose up on their right, and in the distance, suspended almost magically over the bay, stood an enormous red bridge spanning the two sides.

The sense of going somewhere filled Scott as he lurched after his guide, fighting down the urge to stop and simply take in the majesty of the still-standing structure. Half-destroyed buildings of unknown purpose stood atop the embankment on his right, and at first Scott thought they were hotels. A knot of zombies gathered underneath a white sign stating that the maximum speed was fifty. Scott thought there were at least two hundred gimps around the pole, spilling out into the street. There was a morbid joke in there he couldn't pull the trigger on.

Amy sunk into them like a cell penetrating a permeable wall. The very sight of her going into the mass made his scrotum tighten. The woman was crazy. Either that, or she had the biggest pair of wrecking balls he'd ever seen. Even *worse* was that he was following her in. Taking a breath, Scott braced himself.

And then he was amongst them.

The smell of the things enveloped him, and he stretched out his neck so that he wouldn't lose sight of her. Walled in as they were, with the bay on the left and the tall embankment on the right, Moe seemed to have stopped and gathered in the road as if waiting for one to rise and begin belting out demands from a soap box. The gimps pushed and crowded Scott like a tightly-packed herd of cattle. They banged into his front, sides, and back, and he had to stop and slowly twirl to get around them. Several times he went sideways, and those were the worst. They pressed against his back with an almost maddening pressure, and had he suffered from agoraphobia, it would have been enough to drive him over the brink. He lost sight of Amy. If it weren't for the narrowness of the street, he might have gotten turned around and pushed away from her entirely. A railing kept him from falling over a ledge and into shipyard buildings just below the street. He pushed his way along the length of metal, ignoring the innumerable smiling faces confronting him.

Then the dead thinned out, and he broke through the crowd.

Relief surged through him when he saw Amy perhaps thirty meters up the street, stopped and waiting for him. A series of large, brown brick buildings stood behind her. Scott increased his speed ever so slightly and, minutes later, he drew up alongside her, even more relieved to see that it was indeed her and not some cruel trick.

Amy nodded approvingly—or at least he thought it was a nod, since she was still in zombie-mode—and started walking again.

They moved deeper into Halifax as the sun drifted past its apex. The landscape became even more of a warzone. Sections of the road actually had become glazed craters from massive explosions. Signs had been ripped from their posts. Cars and trucks were tipped onto their sides or crushed, as if by tanks. Some looked to have been blown apart in fiery glee. An Armed Forces G-Wagon, which Scott knew were militarized jeeps with machine gun mounts on the roof, lay buried in snow up to its grille. They moved past a green tank in the middle of the road, as dead as the patches of zombies crowding it, and Scott got his first look at the metal beast. Then he saw the soldier.

Amy walked by the thing as it stood at the heel of the armored vehicle, like a dog beside its master. It didn't wear a helmet, but a full flak vest covered its torso and green military-issued jacket. The soldier gimp's right arm had been chewed off just below the elbow, and the corpse used this to periodically beat upon the tank's bulk, like a lost child trying to get the attention of an elder. Amy continued on and Scott followed, fighting down the urge to stop and stare at the undead soldier.

Time dragged on, and the cold chewed on his extremities. A chill reached his core despite his Nomex protection and the clothing underneath. They didn't stop for lunch, and Scott began to admire the pace Amy set. The woman didn't slow down. She was military stock through and through.

They passed under the bridge's overpass and continued walking. Apartment buildings and houses came into view, blasted, burnt, and left for dead. A stone church rose up before them, just behind an apartment building in better shape than most. A garage door was opened three feet at the base of the building, and Amy veered toward it. Scott followed her in, bypassing the undead mobs.

She lowered herself to the snow and wormed her way underneath the door. Scott did the same and, once inside, she grabbed him by the wrist and led him along the door, the only light at their feet. The touch of her hand was far more comforting than he expected.

"There's a stairway over here and an apartment on the first floor," she whispered to him. "I cleared out the place a few days ago, but anything could be back in it. That's where we're going."

"Tired?" Scott asked good-naturedly, knowing they had to have walked a good twenty kilometers in the dead- and snow-filled street.

"A little, but I also left two jugs of water in the fridge here."

That information made Scott aware of his own parched throat. "Lead the way."

15

They blockaded the apartment's heavy door with a piece of two-by-four, then slid the pair of deadbolts on the upper and lower section of the frame. They took off their bloody clothes and tossed them into a bathtub, then closed the door to the washroom. They got out of their gear underneath and stretched. Scott figured it was nearing three in the afternoon, and Amy told him they wouldn't make the base until tomorrow. It was safer to camp out at the apartment.

It wasn't a bad place, in Scott's opinion. A little lower end than what he would have expected, but he imagined the harbor view had once demanded a hefty price. Feeling peckish, they returned to the kitchen table to eat something. She got the two jugs of water from the fridge and placed one down on the table in front of him. Scott opened a can of beans and wieners, much to the disdain of Amy.

"What?" he asked.

"Beans and wieners?"

"Yeah? What?"

"They give me gas."

"They give most people gas."

"No, you don't understand," Amy said in a serious tone. "They give me *gas*. I'm warning you now, okay?"

Scott shrugged. "Don't scare me. You act like women don't get gas or something. I was married, you know. And you don't have to eat it. Don't you have anything with you?"

"Ate it all before I met you. Last half of an MRE. I was on my way back to base. I don't eat much, actually." Amy sat down across from him as he scooped out half of the can onto a glass plate. "How long were you married?"

Scott smiled faintly. "Not long enough. This mine?" He pointed at the jug.
"Yeah."

"Thanks." He took the four liter jug and cracked it open. He drank almost a fourth of it before placing it back on the table. "Oh, that's good."

"Save it, because that's all there is."

"This is fine." Scott gasped. "Oh my."

They finished their meal. Afterward, they retired to the living room and pulled the sofa across the floor so it faced the bay. Sounds of the undead moving in the street some twenty feet below reached them. Scott feared that if he stepped up to the glass and peered over the balcony's edge, the deadheads would be there staring back up at him.

"Not a bad place," he commented quietly, not venturing any closer to the window.

"The view makes it. I call dibs on the bedroom."

"Okay."

"And I don't think there's a need for shifts. We're pretty safe in here. They can't open the door in the stairwell, and someone cleared out this whole floor ages ago."

"How many are you?"

Amy settled back into the couch. "Six total. There were seven, but one guy got himself killed. Man, I wish the water worked in this place."

"Sorry. Did you know him?"

"As well as I know you."

Scott hesitated and decided to change the subject. "I came from Annapolis before this. The guy I knew there had running water."

"No way!"

"Yeah. I even got to take a bath."

"Oh man, are you *serious?* I don't want to sound gross, especially after telling you about the ear thing, but I can't remember the last time I had a bath."

"Hot water, too."

"How?"

"The place he's got has solar panels, so when the power grid failed and the lights went off, his stayed on."

"Wow." Amy shook her head, impressed. "And you left all that?"

"I did."

"Hope you find your killer," Amy said, making herself comfortable. She stretched out her legs, covered in denim, and placed two sock-covered feet against the glass.

"We need that coffee table."

"I can get that." Scott stood and lifted the piece of furniture around the sofa so that she could set her feet on it. Once in place, he stepped over her legs and sat down on the opposite end, catching a lingering whiff of blood.

"You're useful," Amy said, eyeing him.

"Yeah, that's me," Scott replied, scratching at his growing beard. It was really starting to itch.

They sat and quietly gazed out over Halifax Harbour, the sun lashing the sky in swathes of red and gold. There were warships a little farther up in the harbor, shadowy, cold, and dead-looking. Amy got up and left and Scott followed her with his eyes, settling on the frumpy ass of her jeans for the briefest of moments, as if he were touching a reddening stove burner. She came back ten minutes later. She carried a stack of thick quilts, half of which she gave to Scott. They got underneath the blankets at opposite ends of the sofa. It felt good to relax, to get away from the dead.

"You know," Amy said softly, "if it weren't for the fact that Moe was right below outside, I'd say this was any other winter day."

"Well, let's just pretend it is."

"Good idea."

They became quite for a moment.

"Where's this place you guys are heading?" Scott finally asked. The warmth of the blankets and the softness of the sofa leeched the tension from him and made him weary.

"Big Tancook."

"What's that?"

"It's an island off of Blandford. Small population. Easy to get rid of Moe."

"An island," Scott whispered. "How far off?"

"A few kilometers off the mainland."

"That's a long boat ride."

"Longer when you're rowing, but we have that covered."

"How so?" Scott looked at her.

Amy met his inquiring gaze with a steady one of her own, her blue eyes locking with his, and Scott thought for a split second that she wasn't going to say anything. "We met up with a group from Antigonish who were on their way to Tancook. We got along and figured it was in both groups' best interests to join up. Repopulate the earth, y'know?"

Repopulate the earth for the Lord! a voice cried out in Scott's head, reminding him of the priest who had barricaded himself in an underground bunker with fifty women.

"There're about twenty-five of us. Seven of us decided to head into Halifax since it was on the way, while the others went to Blandford to try and secure a boat or something to carry us all across. We thought about going to PEI, but decided against it."

"Why?" Scott asked. "Better farming there."

"Bigger population as well. We'd exhaust ourselves trying to clear Moe outta the place. One of the smaller islands was decided upon, but not *too* small. Big Tancook was it. Only about a hundred people living on it. Or lived on it, I should say. We just wanted to see if we could find enough seeds to give us a chance. And if there were any more people around. We really . . . weren't expecting to find anyone."

"An island."

"Sounds good, eh?"

It did. "A few kilometers off the coast?"

"Yep. And Moe can't swim. And he sure as hell can't walk the bottom to the island. Currents will see to that. Fish'll probably eat 'em, too. At least we can hope. Once we're there and it's cleared, we should be safe."

"Should be? Do I detect a twinge of doubt?"

Amy scratched her brunette head with a pale hand, and her sleeve fell down a bit to reveal an even paler wrist. When she was done, she smoothed her hair into place. "Anything can happen. I've learned not to get my hopes up."

"Would be something," Scott finally said.

"What?"

"Seeing Moe swim."

"That would be. Would be," she said, pursing her lips. A strand of hair fell into her eyes, and she blew it away. Scott hesitated a second before looking back to the window and the darkening sky.

"Can you swim?" he asked.

"Yeah, a little freestyle. How about you?"

"Just doggie style."

Amy paused and regarded him with a question on her face.

Scott's eyes widened. "I mean dog style. Paddle. Dog paddle." He felt his face turn hot. Both hands fluttered before him to get his meaning across. "Dog paddle. I can . . . I can do that. Swim. I didn't mean anything else. Uh . . . sorry."

But Amy only looked at him, face unreadable. Scott cleared his throat in the suddenly uncomfortable silence.

"You okay?" she asked pointedly. "Look like you're about to choke."

Scott nodded, but didn't dare glance in her direction. He felt her shift on her end of the sofa.

Neither of them said another word until it was dark and time to sleep.

They rose the next morning from their separate sleeping quarters and met at the kitchen table. They ate the last of the food in Scott's pack: a can of ravioli.

"Don't worry, we're almost back," Amy told him when they finished the food. "We have plenty to eat in the box."

Scott didn't know what that was, but he trusted her. That thought stuck with him for a moment.

"You okay?" she asked him.

"Huh? Oh, yeah, I'm fine. Let's get moving."

Amy eyed him for a moment before moving to the tub where they had stored their outerwear, ponchos, and hoods. Scott followed. They got into their gear, then the bloody garments that kept them alive. Amy sniffed at her poncho and screwed up her face.

"What?" Scott asked.

"Not so pungent anymore."

"Is that bad?"

Amy's head see-sawed with uncertainty. "We should be okay for today, but we'll need to soak these things again first chance we get. Just to be on the safe side."

"Will they smell us?"

"I don't know. We never gave them the chance before. Just be careful out there. And stay close."

"Yeah," Scott said, intending to do just that.

"One more thing. When you see me lift my arms, you do the same, okay? Nice and slow."

"Why?"

"Because if you don't, someone might blow your head off. They didn't have any weapons when I left, but they might have found some since. Just put your arms up when I do."

Being so close to safety only to be gunned down was an image Scott didn't need.

Once fully ready, they slipped out the door and downstairs. Upon entering the garage, they heard the dismal cries cut the air outside, breaking the spell of all being well with the world. They went into zombie mode and exited the building the same way they had come in, crawling under the garage door. Getting to their feet, they started to walk along the street. Scott noted that it wasn't as full of gimps as it had been a day earlier, but there were still enough spotting the hard-packed snow to keep him nervous. He suddenly wished Amy hadn't told him of the potential lessening of their disguises. That didn't do anything for his confidence.

Nor did the image of her ass in frumpy jeans, and he stashed that thought away, feeling suddenly guilty. *Doggie style*, he scolded himself. Where the hell had *that* come from?

He glanced up and saw a tower of jade and broken glass in the distance, seemingly at the head of the harbor. They walked toward it, following the road and leaving the deadheads behind. More apartment buildings stood high on their right, their windows smashed and blackened by fire. The road rose up in a gentle slope, and prominent signs displaying *Scotiabank* and the *Delta* came into view. The signs were punctured and wrecked, with holes large enough to drive a truck through, and Scott wondered what the hell had been used on the structures to devastate them so.

The road split to the left and right. On the right, it rose and ran on, while to the left, it sunk to a pedestrian walkway that loomed over the road. The glass panes were smashed out, and sandbags were stacked up like battlements. Scott's jaw hung open. He saw machine guns up there, unmanned. Underneath, metal barriers with slots for weaponry crisscrossed the street; behind that, metro buses had been tipped over to further block the road, making one long, massive, and intimidating barrier. More sandbags were piled up to fill obvious gaps in the defensive wall. More G-Wagons with flat tires and half-open doors. Long spools of razor wire stuck up in places like the guts of a broken toy, mashed to the ground by unmoving bodies.

Scott's jaw dropped.

Hundreds of gimps coated in snow lay in the road some fifty meters before the defenses. Automatic gunfire had ripped their bodies into shreds and exploded their heads, leaving skulls resembling half-broken crockery pots. Several bodies didn't possess any heads at all, and Scott realized with dawning horror that the shards he began feeling underfoot weren't ice. They were jagged fragments of bone. The machine guns had ripped Moe several new assholes, and then some.

Amy walked toward the barricades, slowly raising her arms.

From the pedway above the street, a figure rose above one of the rows of sandbags and waved her through.

Following a path through the swaths of death and razor wire, Amy kept her hands up and walked toward the buses.

Taking a breath, Scott raised his arms above his head and followed.

16

sAn aluminum ladder dropped down from the belly of the pedway, right in front of the overturned bus. Scott kept his arms over his head, watching as Amy dropped the zombie walk once under the pedway and started climbing. He reached the base of the ladder just as she slipped between the gap separating the pedway and the bus, disappearing in a flutter of legs.

Scott looked back. There were deadheads far behind, but none moving in his direction. He took hold of the ladder and crawled up, one hand more than full because of his bat.

"Watch yerself now, watch it," a man's gravelly voice informed him. Scott spotted him through the gap. He was black, with grey in his short-cut hair and beard. The man stood back and allowed Scott to get above the street on his own power. This new individual was short, dressed in a dark snowmobile suit like Amy, with a body as thick as a wall. Once Scott was up and standing on iron sheets that covered the metro buses windows, the shorter man got about pulling up the ladder. Scott made to help, but was waved away.

With the ladder on top of the bus, the brick of a man straightened and sized up Scott.

"Jesus, yer a big one. Jesus, Jesus. Yer gonna haveta feed this one, Amy," he said, in a gruff voice that might have inhaled far too much cigarette smoke over the years. "Scott," Amy introduced him in her own scratchy voice, "Donny Buckle."

"Buckle," he corrected and nodded at Scott. "This one seems to insist on callin' me by me first name."

"What's wrong with that?" Amy asked him.

"Don't like it. Never did. Shitty."

Amy rolled her eyes. "Donny is not a shitty name. Is it a shitty name?" she asked Scott.

"Uh . . ."

"Not much of a talker," Buckle said. "Where'd ye find him?"

Newfoundland. Scott finally placed the accent. Buckle was from Newfoundland. Or Cape Breton.

"Out yonder," Amy said, taking the mask from her head and making a face of disgust. "He followed me home. Can we keep him?"

Buckle scowled at Scott. "He probably shits all over the place."

Scott blinked at the short stocky man and noted there was a weird gleam in his eye. Newfoundlanders were, on the whole, a hard bunch. Drinkers. Quick to befriend and quick to fight.

"Look, Donny, where's Vick?" Amy asked.

"Over yonder," Buckle growled, tipping his head in the direction of the building the pedway was connected to. "Taking inventory, no doubt."

"The others there?"

"I think," Buckle stated. "Joe's over on the other end, keepin' watch. I'll get him if it's important." Buckle pronounced the word im*part*ant.

"Yeah. Please. I think we'll need everyone about."

"Right-o. Hey," Buckle directed at Scott. "Don't shit the bed while you're here."

Scott looked questioningly at Amy. Buckle turned and picked up a nasty-looking length of steel bar, with a wedge resembling a hammer's claw on one end and another flat wedge and curved pick on the other. Scott had seen them before and knew it to be a firefighter's Halligan tool. With this fearsome weapon, the Newfoundlander walked off to the end of the pedway toward a set of stairs leading to street level.

"You come with me," Amy said, jumping up to the pedway. The glass that had once protected pedestrians from the elements had been mostly shattered. The sand-bags were piled high enough on the walkway to conceal Scott from his chest down. Amy probably couldn't be seen at all from street level. They walked past the machine gun emplacements, all of which were obviously ruined by the weather.

"Yeah, we already checked," Amy said, glancing back at him. "But this place is still a good base with all the walls. And Purdy's Wharf here still has a few offices intact. The Forces stockpiled supplies on the third floor and barricaded the base."

Scott realized they were walking toward the building seemingly built of jade and broken glass, which he'd seen when walking along Barrington. The building stood tall against a backdrop of sea and ice.

"What is this place?" he asked.

"Downtown area business section. The historical part is right over there. Not much left there, though. Army shot the hell out of it. But Purdy's managed to keep most of her windows. On this side, anyway."

They stopped at a closed black door, which Amy pulled open. Inside, they followed another walkway, this one's outer glass intact and with a metal railing leading up to a stairwell. Scott could look down to the first floor, and he saw ornate fountains that had run dry. The street-level windows were boarded up with heavy-looking sheets of iron. Amy held the door open as he walked through it.

"This place is big."

"There's another tower as well, but we found most of the stuff in this one, so we didn't bother moving it."

"How many floors?"

"Twenty or so, I think. But we don't go up there."

"Moe?"

"No Moe. We figured the Forces must have cleared them out. Just too damn far to go, anyway. You ever climb twenty flights of stairs in a cold building?"

"No."

"Well, there you go. Here." She reached the third floor landing and pulled the door open for him once again. "See how nice I am?"

Scott smiled faintly. Special *and* nice—a favorable combination.

Worn beige carpet and brown wood panelling covered the hallway. A current of fresh air flowed past Scott, and he wondered if perhaps a nearby window had been knocked out. Open doorways offered quick peeks to a number of reception areas, some of which had sofas draped in grey, military-issued blankets.

"Yeah, these are bedrooms," Amy said, gesturing with a hand. "This place was the cat's ass at one point in time. There's a gym here, too."

"A gym."

"You work out?"

Scott wanted to say life was a workout these days, but he decided that would sound snarky, so he shook his head.

Voices floated from a corner office up ahead that Scott guessed faced the pedway.

"In here first," Amy said and directed him into a room that had once been a cleaning station. Shelving units contained chemical cleaners as well as rolls of toilet paper. The toilet paper made Scott smile.

"What's so funny?" Amy asked, pausing in taking off her bloody poncho.

"Toilet paper."

He could see she didn't understand, and he didn't mention Gus. A minute later, they left their disguises behind and headed back down the corridor, toward the voices.

"Here we are," Amy announced and went in through an open doorway.

"There's my girl," a deep voice boomed with affection. Scott entered just in time to see another black man wrap his arms around the considerably smaller Amy and hold her close. He was bulkier and taller than Buckle. An even six foot by Scott's guess. He was perhaps the oldest as well, easily fifty. Maybe even fifty-five.

Amy broke away from the large man and indicated Scott. "Vick. Scott."

Vick came forward with a smile, holding out a hand. Scott took it and noted that the man's hands were as big as his own.

"Where did you find him?" Vick asked Amy, releasing his hand.

"Up on Bayer's Road."

"The hell you doing up there? That's supposed to be off limits."

Amy shrugged. "Found a bunch of seeds up there."

"You did?"

"Uh-huh."

"Well, that's wonderful news!" Vick declared. "And good to meet you," he directed at Scott. "Glad you made it. I'm Vick Tucker."

Other people stepped inside the office, introduced themselves, and either nodded or shook Scott's hand. Sam Koffer appeared like a wild child of sorts, with a mighty shock of dirty blond hair that Scott figured made Amy incredibly jealous. The man had a voice that suggested he could sing. Lance Shaffer was not quite as tall as Scott, and he appeared none too keen on the physical competition. He was another big man, with an athlete's build easily detected even underneath the thick winter coat he wore. When he took Scott's hand, he locked gazes and squeezed hard enough to deliver a message.

Don't fuck with me.

Shaffer even released his hand dismissively, leaving Scott momentarily stunned.

Vick smiled, seeing the exchange. "Don't worry about Lance. Everyone's on his shit list from the get-go. He gave Sammy there a hard time for the first three weeks."

"Still does," Sam protested.

"But then he warms up to you," Vick said.

"Don't fucking count on it," Shaffer warned and glared.

Vick frowned, but his hard features lit up again when he looked upon Amy. Scott knew right away that the man loved her. A pang of disappointment coursed through him then, as off-key as a guitar string snapping.

"Have a seat." Vick pointed at an office chair while he and Amy plopped down on a leather sofa, quite close together. "Any trouble out there?" he asked her as Scott sat down and gazed about the office area.

Amy shook her head.

"Well, the news on the seeds is great. Now then, where you'd find Scott again?"

"Bayer's Road. He was walking with the dead."

Vick looked approvingly at Scott. "You were? Not many know how to do that, my boy. Fewer still have the guts to even try it. I'm crazier than a shithouse rat, and I'm none too happy when I have to do it."

"Donny doesn't seem to mind," Amy pointed out.

"That's because Buckle's a different kind of crazy," Vick stated to Scott. "There's shithouse rat crazy . . . and then there's chemically unstable."

"He is special," Amy agreed.

"Not as special as you, though," Vick informed her with a wink. "Now then, Scott. You staying with us?"

Scott blinked and wasn't exactly sure what to say.

Amy dove in. "He might. He has to find a guy first. Someone who killed some of his friends."

Vick's happy face became drawn. "Sorry to hear that. There're savages out there these days. I'm ashamed to say some of the living have become worse than the dead."

"I hear that," Shaffer growled. "Fucking war zone to start, and crazies on top of that. Goddamn grim world."

Scott noted that Shaffer tended to stress the hard consonants in a word.

"Yes, well," Vick drew out, "we won't be here much longer. I don't see any need to hang on now that's Amy's back with the goods."

Amy's mouth arched into a smile.

"Get any broccoli?"

"I did."

"Well, that's just great," Shaffer said. "At least we don't haveta row to Norway and crack open the—whaddya call it? Doomsday Safe?"

"Doomsday Vault," Amy corrected him.

"Yeah, that thing."

"The what?" Scott asked.

"It's a storage facility on one of Norway's islands," Amy informed him. "Has all of the earth's 'spare' crop seeds packed away in it, in the event of a global disaster where most of the species is somehow wiped out. Or, in our case, where we want to borrow a few for our own survival."

130

"Never heard of it," Scott said.

"That's okay. Most people don't know about it. Or have forgotten."

"Amy knew," Vick added. "She's our resident farmer."

Scott noted Amy seemed uncomfortable with the title.

"So what do you bring to the group?" Shaffer asked him bluntly. "Any particular skillset, or are you just another mouth?"

The question left Scott blinking. "Huh?"

"What can you do?" Shaffer rephrased, none too pleased about it. "*Son*."

"Lance, it's a little—" Vick began.

But Shaffer dismissed him with a wave of his hand. "I'll ask what I want to ask. Problem is you guys aren't fucking asking enough. This guy could be a spy for all you know."

"He's not a spy," Amy stated in a tired voice.

"How do you know? He got a goddamn special badge or something? I sure as fuck don't see nothin'. No halo over his head. So how about it? Hm? What do you bring to the table?"

Scott shrugged. "Not much, really."

The scowl on Shaffer's face deepened.

"I was a baker."

"A baker," Shaffer purred, smirking at the others. "Well, fuck me gently. Nice to know we'll have cookies and muffins around the campfire at night. Can you fight?"

"A little."

"A little." Shaffer stood directly before Scott and tilted his head, gazing up at him. "What's that? Don't tell me you've only killed Moe, cuz that's easy. You got any training? Military? Self defense? Martial arts?"

Scott didn't like this guy. "Played hockey for a bit."

Shaffer visibly balked, not appreciating the joke in the least.

"Shaffer," Vick said, getting the man's attention. "Relax. You forget the other reason why we came here?"

"Your trouble is I remember all too goddamn well. You've heard the fuckin' stories about out west. This guy could be a plant."

Amy rubbed her face with a palm and looked out a window.

"He came in with Amy," Vick carried on. "That's good enough for me."

"Me too," Sam Koffer said.

"Nobody gives a good goddamn about what you think, meth head," Shaffer snarled. "What're you doing in the city?" he asked Scott pointedly.

"Looking for a guy. Killed some . . . some friends of mine."

"Got a name for this killer?"

"Tenner."

Shaffer blinked as if a hot blast of wind had smacked him between the eyes. Even Vick and Sam Koffer became silent for a moment. Amy regarded him with those blue eyes of hers and waited for what was coming.

"What?" Scott asked quietly, feeling the abrupt change in the air. He started twisting in the office chair, making the base squeak.

"Did you say Tenner?" Shaffer asked. Sam moved in on his flank, his own features screwed up, wanting things to be sorted out.

"Yeah."

"Joe Tenner?" Vick asked.

"Don't know his first name. Only Tenner."

"What's he look like?" Sam asked.

"How many fucking Tenners you think's around?" Shaffer snapped at the smaller man. "Christ almighty."

Sam recoiled as if slapped with an ice pick. "Just clarifying is all, man. Don't blow your asshole out."

Shaffer glowered as he reassessed Scott. "What's he look like?"

"I don't know," Scott answered after a moment. "All I know is his voice. He shot me in the back and left me for dead. Best thing that happened, I figured. I saw what he did to my friends."

"Yeah? What did he do?" Shaffer demanded, his glare intense and unwavering.

"Cut them up."

"Tenner," Shaffer hissed and looked at Sam, then Vick.

"Did you know about this?" Vick asked Amy.

"That he's looking for Tenner? Yeah, I knew. Didn't say anything, though. There's always a chance."

"Chance of what?" Scott asked.

But Shaffer overrode him. "Chance, my ass. There's only one Tenner in the phonebook at this point in the game."

"It might not be him," Vick said quietly.

"You *hope* it's not him," Sam added.

"So you believe what this guy says?" Shaffer pointed at Scott. "Just wanders on in here and says he's looking for a murderer?"

"I found Tickle," Amy said quietly.

That admission silenced the men.

"What?" Vick asked.

"I found him. Up on Bayer's Road."

If the first bit of information had quieted the men, this new piece stunned them. Even the angry Shaffer straightened up and blinked in confusion, as dazed as if a horse had kicked him in the face.

"Tenner said not to go up there," Sam said, piquing Scott's interest even more. "Said Moe got Dan."

"Moe didn't get Dan." Amy frowned and met Scott's eyes. "Well, not in the way we thought. Scott saw him, too. I saw him see him. You remember the one I'm talking about?"

Scott's innards chilled as if thrown and stuck to a block of ice. "The guy . . . the guy who was crucified?"

Amy nodded.

"The fuck you mean, crucified?" Shaffer wanted to know.

Amy didn't flinch. "Tenner said he saw Dan get pulled down and killed by Moe. I'm telling you . . . we both saw Tickle tied to a power pole like a hunk of meat left to be cured. Moe didn't take the time to hang him from the pole . . . someone living did that. Hung him just high enough so that Moe could reach his legs and lower abs."

"Oh, Jesus Christ," Vick whispered, pulling back from her.

"The rest of him turned," Scott said quietly.

"This fucker could've done that," Shaffer spat, jabbing a thumb at Scott.

"Think about it," Amy countered. "Think about that day. The more I do, the more I think Tenner *wanted* Tickle to go with him. Dan called the shots then. He was the one giving out orders, and Tenner got Dan to go along with him into an area we already knew was infested with Moe. And this is Dan Tickle we're talking about. He was a careful man. It's . . . difficult to see him taking any unnecessary risks. And we only just met Tenner. Been with him a week. He said a lot of things that seemed right at the time, and really played upon Dan's sense of not placing the rest of us in unnecessary risk, but now I'm thinking . . ."

Amy stopped for a moment, considering her words carefully. "I'm thinking he manipulated us in that short time. Saw right away that Dan was the leader. Played the rest of us off against each other. Tried to get us alone. Like he did with Dan."

"You really think he killed Dan?" Shaffer asked.

"Course he did," Amy stated. "After what Scott's told us? No doubt."

Sam cleared his throat. "Y'know, I thought—"

"Fuck what you thought," Shaffer snipped, silencing the shorter man before staring at Vick. "You hearing this?"

"I'm hearing."

"And?"

Vick inhaled sharply, as if the rush of air cleared his brain. "I think we wait. Buckle will be bringing him up here soon. Then we'll do introductions again, I guess. Find out what's what."

Vick made this last statement while eyeing Scott.

"Wait," Scott said softly. "Tenner's here?"

They ignored him. "Buckle might be in danger," Sam stated.

Shaffer turned on him. "Buckle? You fucking serious?"

Vick agreed with Shaffer. "Buckle can smell shit before it happens."

"I think Sam might have a point," Amy said. "Dan was good, too."

"Fucker wants me to go off with him and look for another armory tomorrow." Shaffer scoffed and shook his head.

"Might not be him," Sam offered.

"Shut the fuck up, Sam," Shaffer fired off quietly. "Just shut the fuck up."

"But why would he do it?" Sam insisted. No one had an answer. Scott had an idea, but he didn't want to say it just yet. Not with these people who thought they knew Tenner, who might have been in his company for a while, heedless of who the man was or what he was capable of. The excitement of the hunt drawing to a close rushed through him, and he fought to control it. Scott's idea was simple. Tenner was insane. Worse, Tenner had a taste for killing. In a new world where the law was decided by the strongest, what was there to stop the man? Scott realized Tenner might have been killing people for a very long time. Working his way east.

Vick's eyes were on Amy. "So, what do you think we should do?"

At that precise moment, men could be heard approaching the room.

"Depends on him," Amy said simply, focusing on Scott sitting in his office chair. No sooner did the words rasp from her mouth when Buckle entered the room.

Behind him stood a tall man wearing a thick black winter coat with a hood fringed with fur.

A man with his hair tied off in a fox's tail, which draped over one shoulder.

17

"What's going on?" Buckle asked gruffly, taking in the sour faces in the room. He finally nodded at Scott. "Someone shit in an MRE?"

"Just talking to the new guy," Vick said.

"New guy, huh?" the tall man said. He stepped around Buckle and held out his hand. The corners of his eyes crinkled up, and he bared his teeth in what he no doubt thought passed for a smile, making Scott freeze. "How you doing? Name's Tenner."

Name's Tenner.

My name's Tenner.

Don't shoot me, okay? I have a gun, see? My name's Tenner.

He heard the screams of Lea and Teddy in his head as Tenner took their lives, as if he were back in that terrible house of death and undead, floating in the black of unconsciousness.

Tenner remained beaming at him with that toothy expression meant to convey friendship, extending a hand. The silver in his bound hair gleamed like exposed wires. The smile dissipated from Tenner's eyes and he frowned a little, noticing Scott wasn't going for his hand like he should have, perhaps even sensing the swelling silence in the room. He offered his hand again as if completing a magic trick.

Scott stared into his black eyes. The eyes of a predator. "What was your name again?"

The corners of his grin wilted altogether. "Tenner. You gonna shake my hand or what?"

Scott got to his feet, eye-to-eye with Tenner, the killer of Lea and Teddy and God above only knew how many more. He had never really wondered what he would do once he caught up with the murderer. Perhaps he'd secretly known that the odds against actually finding Tenner were so incredibly high that he would just search and search until Moe finally caught him, or he ran out of supplies, or any other unforeseen thing caught and killed him. But he would never *really* catch him.

But here he was. Standing right in front of him. Smiling as if he shat gold and pissed silver.

Scott pursed his lips, anger welling inside him.

Life had a funny way of working things out.

He grabbed for his Ruger and caught his hand on the lip of his boot. His fingers scrabbled over the butt of the weapon. Tenner's eyes went wide. A heavy boot came up, snapped out, and kicked Scott square in the chest, sending him flying over the office chair. As Scott tumbled over, Tenner lifted up the back of his coat and yanked free something tucked in the waistband of his jeans.

"Gun!" Buckle roared, knocking the weapon toward the ceiling and breaking the paralysis of the onlookers. Tenner snarled and belted a plastic padded elbow into Buckle's nose, breaking it instantly. Blood spurted out of both nostrils as the Newfoundlander crashed against a nearby wall.

"Holy shit!" Sam yelled out, incredulous.

Vick jumped off the couch. "Tenner, wai—"

But Tenner didn't wait. He opened fire instead, spraying the room. A loud burp of shells from the Glock 18 drove most of them to the floor. The blaze ripped into and exploded Sam Koffer's head, blasting brain matter out the back of his skull and dousing the window behind him with pulp as dark and viscous as spilled pudding. Sam's body crunched up against the window, abruptly faceless, and slid down, revealing the gruesome, spidery punches the bullets left in the pane.

Tenner paused to aim at Scott.

A chair flew at the gunman. It struck him across the body, spurting a killing chatter from the Glock that violently stitched a line across another pane of glass. Tenner fell back toward the open doorway. Vick rose up from the ground, and Amy darted to one side.

"Ease up goddammit, Joe!" Vick shouted, bringing up a length of pipe. Scott got himself free of the chair, lifting the Ruger.

Another gush of Glock fire tore into the room, driving everyone to the floor. Scott fired back. The Ruger coughed and at least six rounds sizzled through the doorway, two ripping out puffs of dusty debris from the frame after Tenner disappeared outside.

Scott lay still for a moment, keeping his gun trained on the doorway.

"Fucker jacked up me nose," Buckle raged.

"Stay down!" Vick ordered, crouching near the door and holding a length of steel pipe like a katana.

"Like fuck!" Shaffer said, slamming into the other side of the doorframe. "The bastard killed Sammy!"

He brought up a bat and held it to his chest.

"He still out there?" Vick asked Shaffer.

"Can't see him from this angle."

Tentatively, Shaffer peeked around the corner. Next to Scott, Sammy's right leg did a little reflexive jerk at the knee. Blood pooled around the body, as bright as paint.

"Bastard's gone," Shaffer announced.

That wasn't good enough for Scott. He sprinted out the door, gun at the ready, and headed down the corridor. Cries of *"Wait!"* followed him, but he wasn't listening. They were only just discovering what Tenner could do. Scott, however, fully understood what the killer was capable of.

He bolted to the opposite wall and hurried along it, his shoulder rasping against the drywall. Some of the doors he passed were open and Scott gave each a quick peek, but he thought Tenner was trying to escape. He'd exposed the murderer for what he was, and the man was trying to get away, like an uncovered spider.

Up ahead, the dead exit sign above the stairwell came into view. Scott ran for it and didn't realize that the door was still open until it slammed into his helmet. He bounced off the frame. A hand came down over his wrist, sending his gun flying.

"The fuck are you, huh?" a savage voice hissed at him. Hands gripped Scott and pulled him into the stairwell before tossing him down a flight of steps. Scott landed hard on his back, sliding down the metal edges of the stairs and rattling toward the next landing.

His hand snapped out and held onto the railing a second before he stopped. He spun on his back, got to his knees, and looked—

Tenner's foot landed squarely on his chest, knocking Scott against the wall and robbing him of his wind. Tenner closed in, snarling and punching, slamming fist after fist into Scott's midsection. He cracked elbows across the motorcycle helmet, going for Scott's eyes. Scott was jolted left and right with each connection, his head flopping. Then hands gripped the sides of his helmet.

"How'd you know?" Tenner seethed. "Tell me that before I—"

Scott punched him in the gut, buckling the man. That crazy fox tail came into view and Scott grabbed it, yanking it and the owner to one side and sending him crashing into the concrete wall. Scott threw his own mass into Tenner's and squashed him into a corner. He punched the man's back, his kidneys, and the back of his head, causing Tenner to bunch up. He kneed him with a furious energy. The killer shuddered in the trap before unexpectedly standing up, trying to shove Scott back. Scott wouldn't allow it. He heaved him back once more. Both men tried to knee the other at the same time, knocking their padded joints off each other.

Tenner dropped down, threw his arms around Scott's waist, and lifted him off his feet, propelling him forward to crash into the far wall. The air in Scott's lungs left him in a rush. He gasped, throwing up his arms to defend himself, only half-aware of just how vulnerable he'd become.

Instead of taking advantage of the situation, Tenner snarled in frustration, turned, and bolted down the steps.

Then Scott heard the voices.

Faces crowded around him.

"Where'd he go?" someone asked.

Then Amy was there, pulling him to his feet. "Get him back to the office. Help me, Donny."

"My gun," Scott gasped and felt it pushed into his hand a moment later.

They brought him halfway up the steps before Scott's senses returned. Amy and Buckle let him walk on his own power, and soon he was rushing back to the office with the others behind him.

"Tenner's outside by now," Scott said as he went through the door.

"And probably away," Vick muttered behind him.

Cold air came into the office from the bullet holes in the windows. Sam Koffer's corpse littered the floor, all bled out. Scott went by the body to an untouched window. He looked down into the street, just before the pedway and the wall of overturned buses. Nothing. He looked toward the historical section. The Ruger might make the shot if—

Tenner came into view, running away from the building and heading toward downtown. A rush of adrenaline took Scott, and he aimed with both hands. Tenner whirled about uncannily and sprayed the windows to Scott's left with bullets, puncturing the glass in a connect-the-dots line and driving him to the floor.

"Fucking hand cannon he's got there!" Shaffer said, staying low.

"Jesus, Jesus, *Jesus*," Buckle growled from nearby, holding tissues bright with blood to his nose.

"Thought you were a cop once upon a time?" Shaffer threw at Buckle.

"Was—got the gun up and away, didn't I?" Buckle replied testily. "Never really liked that one."

"Me neither," Shaffer said. "He still out there?"

Vick and Scott raised their heads above the windowsill and peeked outside. The street was empty.

"Gone," Vick informed them. "Like a baby's fart in a thunderstorm."

"You should've grabbed him instead," Shaffer hissed at Buckle.

"Fuck off." Amy crouched over Sam's corpse, a sad expression on her features. The leg slowed its jerky twitching. She stepped back from the growing pool of blood.

"Might be time to go," Shaffer said to the rest. "I don't know about you guys, but I sure as hell don't want to be around when he decides to come back."

"Seconded, Jesus, seconded," Buckle said, a nasal tone to his words. One hand kept the bloody tissue pressed to his face, while his other hand hefted the Halligan tool.

"Third," Shaffer said.

"Amy?" Vick asked her.

"Yeah. Let's boot."

"Scott?"

"Huh?"

"You coming with us?"

Scott stepped away from the window, mindful of where Sam lay, and regarded them all. Tenner was out there. He should be going after him. He studied the now-still body of Sam Koffer and wondered if he was responsible for his death. He probably was. In his rush to punish the murderer, he'd gotten Sam killed.

"For a bit. Just in case," he muttered.

"Just in case of what?" Shaffer demanded, gripping his bat with both hands.

"He comes after you."

That made them stop and stare.

"You think he will?" Amy asked.

"I don't know. But I do know he's crazy. You really think he killed off one of your guys?"

"After this?" Amy asked in shock.

"Yeah, me too," Scott agreed. "And he was going to go somewhere with you tomorrow?"

Shaffer nodded, a distasteful expression on his rough features.

"Yeah," Scott said, reading his thoughts. "I think you were next on the menu."

"While you were looking for an armory. Or anything," Amy added.

"Fucking pig-sucking bastard," Shaffer seethed.

"Afterward, he'd probably make up another story," Scott continued on. "Waited a few more days and who knows. Maybe one more. Or maybe something else."

"You make it sound like he's drawing out the fun," Vick said, rubbing his chin.

"Yeah. Sounds like that, doesn't it?"

"Let's get to the van and boot," Shaffer said. "Hell with him."

"One thing," Buckle said, gesturing in the direction Tenner had gone. "He was *goin'* in the direction of the van."

"Well, shit," Shaffer said. "And hey, wait, where are you going like that?"

Over the heap of scarlet tissue held to his face, Buckle's eyes widened in genuine surprise. "Wha?" he asked innocently enough.

"You're fucking *bleeding* all over the place!" Shaffer roared.

"I'm all right."

Shaffer looked to Vick for support, but before the older man could say anything, Shaffer went off again. "You're not fucking all right, you moron! You're gushing like a tied-off foreskin, for Christ's sake. Why don't you just go out there and ring a fucking dinner bell while you're at it? It'll take Moe off our backs, anyway."

Buckle took the wad of sopping tissue from his face and inspected it thoughtfully. Bloody strands clung to his silver-streaked beard.

"I'll slice up a blanket," he finally said.

"A goddamn piece of blanket ain't going to make it better. Vick, come *on*."

"Buckle'll be okay with the blanket," Vick said, throwing his support into his friend's corner. "Not like Moe's right outside anyway."

"Should've known better saying anything to you," Shaffer fumed. Even as the words came out, Buckle went over to a grey blanket on the desk and drew a survival knife. In seconds, he'd cut out lengthy wads. He fitted a black hood over his face, growling when he pulled the mask down over his nose, and stuffed the wads of blanket underneath and around his nostrils. The mask bulged from the blanket, but seemed to do the trick.

"That doesn't look good," Vick said.

"Who gives a shit if it looks good or not?" Shaffer said, and pointed a finger at Buckle. "You just make sure that you keep it there."

"Go fuck yourself."

"*What* did you say to me?" Shaffer stepped toward Buckle, and for a moment Scott thought the two men would actually go at each other, as incredible as it seemed.

"Ease off," Vick said, halting Shaffer in his tracks. "We got other things to do. You okay with the blanket, Buckle?"

"I'm okay."

"Then, that's it," Vick concluded. "Let's get a move on."

They left the room, not bothering to cover themselves in any camouflage gear. Down through the stairwell they pounded, carrying their weapons and sprinting across the lower floor to the open door. Outside, the sky was the color of concrete. Their exertions armored them against the cold, and they rushed through a narrow street between two historic stone buildings.

And in doing so, they lost Tenner.

18

As Tenner took the steps three at a time down to the first floor, one glaring thought went off in his head like a klaxon. How?

Another thought shoved aside the first. Who was the stranger?

He didn't recognize the man, and he'd certainly taken measures to ensure no one knew his true intentions or who he was. He ran through the historic section for a short distance, came to an intersection, and veered toward the water.

Who was he?

A friend of one of his victims? Possible, but he doubted it. Tenner made certain that he was well alone with all of his potential prey. Someone he'd left for dead, but had been mistaken? Another possibility, but unlikely. He checked all of his kills to ensure they were truly dead and, realistically, no one was in any shape to come searching for him once he'd finished playing with his toys.

So, who was he?

He didn't have any idea. All he knew was his plan to leisurely kill the survivors—one at a time and in secret, savoring each death like a fine and incredibly rare bottle of wine—was finished. He turned another corner and made his way toward the main entrance of a hotel near Purdy's Wharf. Like the office building, the hotel was surprisingly free of the destruction that had gutted the other buildings. Tenner suspected the place, whose name was ripped off the front, had been used as a barracks and command post due to the number of MRE caches and discarded packaging tossed into the numerous garbage receptacles outside the building. He quickly strode by a check-in counter dulled by dust and grime. Tenner stooped and felt underneath the counter for the self-generating flashlight he'd found and left there days earlier. He grabbed it and took a carpeted stairway down to the basement.

Before he'd met up with the six wanderers, he'd taken the time to search the surrounding premises for anything of interest besides the ruined automatic weapons. He had found several things that made him cock an eyebrow, but the one that had surprised him the most lay in the guts of this particular hotel.

He descended into the black soup at the bottom of the stairs. He held up his flashlight and thumbed the switch. Light blazed ahead of him. Wasting no time, he went past a laundry area stuffed with partially-filled bins of soiled bedding that would never be washed. Just beyond that was another room filled with metal piping, ventilation ductwork, boilers, and huge air-conditioning units. He ignored smaller storage areas along the dark corridor, half-expecting an undead fright at any moment. The light illuminated a heavy, grey-painted door at the end of the corridor, with "No Admittance" stamped across its surface in block letters. Any locked door begged Tenner to open it, no matter the cost. This one in particular had proven to be a stubborn son of a bitch, but in the end, he'd pried it open with a crowbar. The locks had been ruined in the process, but he didn't give a damn about that.

Tenner pulled the door open with a squeal and left it that way. He was certain the others hadn't discovered this place, nor had he revealed the location of the passageway to them. If they did catch his scent and followed, he'd be somewhat disappointed, but for reasons his pursuers wouldn't understand. The light revealed another stone stairway, surrounded by carefully cut rock leading down into the depths of the earth.

Tenner knew Halifax had been a prized harbor for Allied shipping during the Second World War and had been heavily defended against the threat of Nazi incursions. What he hadn't known until he'd started exploring the area was the addition of a tunnel system that ran from the downtown waterfront, now labeled the historic section of the city, to Citadel Hill, once known as Fort George.

He descended three flights of steps. The fitted stone wall ended before a wide entryway and a concrete corridor with exposed lengths of iron braces. The passage stretched off into darkness, toward Citadel Hill. The way was musty, the air stale, and as cold as a freezer. It had been good fortune to discover the secret tunnel, and he'd been even more fortunate when he found what waited at the end. The national armories of the city had all been ravaged and destroyed in a battle that had to have been truly epic, leaving Tenner at his journey's end and feeling despondent.

But he discovered not all of the munitions had been used or rendered useless.

They had only been moved.

Tenner plunged through the underground depths, threading a tunnel wide enough to drive a jeep through if one could be found. Pipes ran along the otherwise bare walls of the tunnel, plunging into the concrete at points and re-emerging further down the line. Iron railway tracks, stamped into the concrete, slunk off into the dark void ahead, and he knew that three old rail carts lay draped in cobwebs perhaps a kilometer away, positioned at the bottom of the stairwell underneath the Citadel. Munitions had no doubt been transported back and forth along the passage at one point in time, and Tenner suspected that there were other underground tunnel systems and chambers besides this one. He couldn't imagine what other secrets lay underneath Halifax, but he envisioned the complex to be huge. Once he took care of the people above, he planned to do some more exploring.

If there was anything else down here, he'd find it. But that was for another day.

The light zigzagged on the walls as he ran. He controlled his breathing so he wouldn't exhaust himself. Tenner eventually slowed to a walk, placing one hand on a hip as he caught his breath. He tipped the flashlight up at the ceiling, not six inches above his head, seeing hairline cracks in the surface.

It was while he studied the cracks he heard it.

A subtle whisper of movement, coming from the darkness ahead, soft enough that if he were truly deep in thought, he would have missed it entirely. As it was, his senses snapped into alertness, and he used his free hand to pull out the Glock. Tenner crossed his wrists like he'd seen done in the movies, penetrating the dark with the flashlight while pointing the gun in the same direction. He held his breath.

And heard it again.

The sound made a crease appear in Tenner's forehead. There weren't any zombies down here—Moe as the rest of the survivors had referred to the dead. He'd made certain of that when he came through the first time. He supposed there was a possibility that a zombie had entered the main tunnel from a side passage he'd missed.

"I hear you," Tenner said slyly, waiting for the answering moan. One advantage of Moe being mindless was that they became predictable. There was nothing devious about the undead. If they heard you, they would moan. It was simply an undefined motor reflex, not a warning or a call to others of similar decomposing ilk. Moe didn't utilize any cunning hunting tactics, nor did they sit and wait for their prey. As feeders, they were as mindless as any single-celled organism. The only thing one had to be careful about with Moe was numbers, and when and where they appeared.

He hadn't checked the load, but Tenner knew he had a few rounds remaining in the Glock, and he had two extra magazines in his coat. And of course there were all manner of goodies waiting for him back at the truck. He only had to get there.

But something was approaching from up ahead.

The sound increased. It grew from a whisper to an unending scratching that sounded as if it were close to the floor.

A crawler, no doubt. Many a zombie had had its legs chewed away or its feet worn down to raw ivory knobs by walking barefoot. The horror of walking the earth fascinated Tenner. The dead would walk until their shoes gave way, until the asphalt rubbed the padding off the soles of their feet, wearing them down to the bone, then shaving the bone away and causing Moe to walk on stubs of flesh, until even that wore away and they toppled over. Tenner had never seen the entire process. The virus that turned people into reanimated corpses also had the surprising side effect of toughening human flesh—which made him think they weren't entirely dead—but he could envision the timeline sped up, seeing a turned person wearing away their shoes, then their feet, then even their shins. They'd fall over at some point and start crawling, then the ground would wear away the front of their clothes, their skin, the tissue underneath, until finally getting to the bone. At some point, the musculature would no longer be able to pull its mass along, so Moe would eventually be rendered immobile. Until . . .

The murmuring of movement drew closer, still hidden by darkness. Tenner did not proceed any farther. It was always best to let the creature come to you. The sound seemed to spread out along the width of the floor, like the satiny touch of a blanket being dragged along the ground.

Or branches.

Lots of branches.

Tenner tensed up, no longer certain what was coming toward him in the dark was Moe. He flexed his fingers on the grip of the gun. Something was getting closer, and it wasn't a corpse. Nor was it a group of corpses, which held no fear for him.

This was something else.

The sound became louder, until it filled his ears and caused him to cringe in puzzlement. Tenner held his breath and let the sound slowly bloat in the tunnel, loud enough that he felt his scrotum go tight with unease. He took a step backward involuntarily, then stopped himself. There was nothing in the new world that he feared. Nothing.

The hissing of branches grew louder, and he could almost detect grainy crashes within the noise itself, like a radio channel spewing static. A smell hit him then, as putrid as any clustering of Moe.

The stench of dead flesh.

But what *was* it? He pointed the beam of light at the farthest possible point, thrusting back the black and illuminating only bare concrete, pipes, and iron railroad tracks. He swept the light from one side of the wall to the other, thinking he detected movement in the vault-like dark.

Seconds passed, and Tenner took a breath.

The sound grew, swelling in the blackness, until . . .

Rats entered the field of light in an ebony front that caused him to back up two steps in shock. He panned the wide beam back and forth to uncover a veritable *flood* of rodents moving along the concrete floor, no more than twenty feet from him, their claws causing the raspy cacophony that had so puzzled him. The tunnel channeled the tide of rats directly at him. They filled the width of the tunnel and beyond the reach of the flashlight. Tenner stopped for a moment and stared in stunned disbelief.

Rats! A wall of rats!

The creatures moved strangely, however. They didn't move in that cautious, scampering flurry of legs normal rats used to find cover from predators.

Then it became obvious to him, as obvious as seeing the vermin—some with bodies longer than his hand. Exposed ribs and backbones gleamed in the flashlight's glare. The foremost ranks of this new foe were a decaying mash of flesh and hair and bone on a scale Tenner had never contemplated. Like their human cousins, the virus powered their undead flesh along in a nasty, mouldy carpet of unending hunger, the ground wearing down their claws and no doubt fraying their underbellies—but Tenner couldn't see that just yet. All he could see were these wretched creatures, no longer fearful, dragging themselves toward him en masse, on whatever limbs still worked, seeking only to fasten their rodent maws upon his flesh and chew.

Tenner backed up another step while panning the light right to left, surveying the sheer scope of the army seeping toward him with all the intensity of a burst vat of tar. He pointed his gun at the front ranks, knowing that a mere bullet would have little effect on the swarm.

Then something latched onto his boots from behind.

He shined the flashlight at his own feet and stared at the layer of rats teeming about his ankles, attacking him from behind. Rats gnawed on his boots, stretched themselves up past his ankles, whiskers oddly unmoving. Tenner did an awkward jig on the spot, dancing on the heads of several horrid attackers and crushing them underfoot. Some he only partially flattened, and he saw the creatures haul their squished flanks or shoulders off the concrete to pursue him, until a second and third layer of rats crawled over their injured brothers, seeming to swallow them. The sight of these half-crumpled creatures still moving unnerved him in a way he never thought possible. People didn't bother him in the least, but rats and spiders had always had a creepy hold of his psyche.

Jerking his feet high above the swarm, he energetically tip-toed to one side. The options open to him were few. He could proceed ahead, or he could retreat.

Tenner plunged forward into the dark. He slipped in places as he stepped on several rats at once, but he didn't fall. He drifted closer to the wall and took a second to stuff his Glock into a side pocket while switching his flashlight to his right hand. With his left hand placed against the wall for extra support, he forged ahead. The rank smell coming off the creatures filled his lungs with each breath and threatened to do more than just screw up his face. *Everywhere.* The rats covered the floor, and he pulled several along with him with every second step as they tried gnawing through his motorcycle boots. Their claws scrabbling on the concrete sounded like muted fingernails across a chalkboard, and Tenner knew anyone of lesser mental fortitude would have been driven to the brink of losing control from both the sight and sound of the dead things in the tunnel. Some scurried along the pipes he clung to, and he had to swat them from the metal. The light beam bobbed and weaved over the creatures' backs, and Tenner believed for a moment that the furry tide was actually becoming thicker. He couldn't see where the rats had gotten into the tunnel; he slogged through their depths, halfway up to his shins. Their voices hummed in his ears. A stumble almost brought him to his knees, forcing him to keep both feet on the floor, and he started sliding his feet forward as if cross-country skiing, bulldozing through the swarm sloshing heavily around his lower legs. He could feel the little jaws attempting to latch onto his boots, actually pinching the leather against his flesh. For a moment, the morbid thought of actually *lying* down in them, like a seething meadow, occurred to him.

The swarm would undoubtedly devour him right to the bone in less than a minute.

Pushing the image away, he pressed on, shoving aside rats. They ranged in size, some as big as his hand, others half the length of his forearm, but they all moved sluggishly. Glimpses of teeth and bone flashed in the light. Tenner tramped through it all, mindful that they were almost to his knees. The rats foamed about him. He swatted more rodents from the pipes. One leaped and landed on his shoulder, biting into his fox tail almost immediately. He crushed it against the wall. Twice he slowed and whipped the flashlight back the way he'd come, illuminating the knobby mass he'd only just waded through. It was as if the heavens had opened up and vermin had poured down. He didn't intend to stop, for fear of giving the rats time to climb up his legs. Already the lower parts of his winter coat had had its foamy stuffing ripped away. Worse, the constant pushing against their bodies began to leech away his energy.

No sooner had he realized he was tiring when he misstepped, falling to his knees.

The rats flowed over his lower legs and nipped at the ends of his coat, his jeans, and the backs of his legs, no longer slow-moving. Tenner sprung to his feet, gripping a length of pipe to stabilize himself and keeping his unprotected hands above the mass of undead animals. Rats clung to the edges of his coat and dug into the black denim covering his thighs. He started moving, knocking the dead things away with his fists in a flurry of frantic energy. The flashlight beam weaved and bobbled like a warped lightshow, showing the swarm at his feet one moment and the arch of the ceiling overhead the next. He crushed several rats, knocking them from his person, their grotesque forms swallowed up by the rising, furry surge. Tenner cleaned himself off in a frenzy and ran, no longer content to wade patiently through the deluge of bodies. Twice more he stumbled against the current, and once almost fell, but he caught himself on a nearby pipe.

Seconds later the rats thinned out and fell behind. He ran a few more meters before stopping and examining himself for bites. He wore two pairs of jeans, and the furry little bastards had shredded the first layer of denim. Some tears went deep, exposing hairy white flesh, even though he'd only been exposed for a few seconds. The vermin's destructive energy fascinated Tenner.

The scrabbling of claws made him look up and shine the light on the tunnel floor.

The volume grew. They had turned about and were coming after him.

This realization might have frozen anyone of a lesser mind, but not Tenner. He lingered, until the rats charged into the light's beam, before turning and jogging deeper into the tunnel, leaving the bulk of the rats behind. They could not keep pace with their longer-legged prey, and eventually they became nothing more than a presence in the dark somewhere behind him.

Sometime later, a ragged-looking Tenner reached the set of circular steps leading to Citadel Hill, some ten-plus stories of secret brickwork that bore straight upward. He shone the light up, briefly illuminating the stairs and tall shaft overhead, and paused to listen.

Nothing.

A low rustling made him jerk the flashlight in the direction he'd come. The sound could have easily been mistaken for the shifting of pebbles or twigs over a hard surface, and he would have missed it if he hadn't been listening. They were still coming after him. He craned his neck and regarded the flights of stairs that would take him up. He'd lose them above. There was a steel door at the very top, and not even undead rats could gnaw through stone and concrete. How long had this new threat been festering underneath the city? And how had the virus managed to jump from people to rats? Rats would feed on carrion if available, and just sniffing around an infected corpse was probably all it took. From there, one rat could infect whatever else was around and simply continue spreading the virus.

Tenner envisioned entire litters being infected, and those rats infecting whole populations in short time, only to infect rats outside of the city . . .

The thought was more than a little disconcerting.

He started climbing the stairs to the surface.

19

They moved down one of the waterfront historical streets, alternating between a jog and a brisk walk. Hard-packed snow covered the grey pavement; large icy lumps dotted the road like white cairns. Figures with their faces covered lay against building foundations like bleached, featureless mannequins. Cars were also present, but they were pushed to the side to allow a clear pathway through the street. The men didn't seem too concerned about deadheads, yet Scott attempted to see everything at once. Buckle and Shaffer were the farthest ahead; Vick walked just ahead of him and Amy, who stayed close by his side. All of them had their weapons at the ready. He spotted a sign for a ferry crossing just as Amy spoke up.

"You looking for Moe?"

"Yeah."

"Just keep an eye out for Tenner. Don't worry about Moe. Well . . . worry a little, but Moe was mostly all cleaned out from this section."

"Those guys?" Scott pointed at the fallen snowmen.

"Only part of it, but yeah."

"They're either soldiers or Moe. Dead, of course," Vick said in his deep voice. Scott thought the man could have easily had a career in narrating books if the world still functioned. "This whole area was sealed off. Buses and anything they could make into a barricade and fortify."

"So what happened?" Scott asked, frowning.

"Moe happened, o' course," Vick explained. "You'll see soon enough."

Through open spaces between buildings, Scott could see the water.

"We think they boxed themselves in down here with their back against the harbor." Amy kept close to Scott, and every now and again her shoulder brushed against his arm. "And duked it out. That crowd we walked through to the tower?"

"Yeah?"

"Nothing compared to what's up ahead."

"What?"

"It was the city's population against entrenched soldiers," Vick picked up from ahead. "And at some point in time, our boys started using the heavy stuff."

That explained the devastation in the area. To Scott's right, buildings had been blasted and their guts had spilled into side streets, covering them with piles of snow-covered rubble and making their passage a chore. They passed a parking lot on the left that had taken a direct hit from an artillery shell. The pavement and shredded vehicles lay spread out like the ragged design of an immense winter blossom surrounding a deep crater. Statues ended at blasted knees. Bullet holes stitched lines in the nearby storefronts, and huge bites of destruction had been taken from building corners and walls.

The heavy stuff, Scott's mind repeated. Yet they had all perished anyway.

"Where are we now?" he asked after practically speed-walking for a few more minutes.

"Water Street," Amy informed him, and pointed to the far right, to another bus barricade lodged in between wrecked buildings. Beyond that and back a ways was what appeared to be a distant ski slope. "That's Citadel Hill up there. Tenner said that was the worst of it."

"The worst?"

"All open ground up there, if you can believe Tenner. He said when he was up there, the hillside was nothing but torn up bodies of Moe. That might've been the head of whatever fortifications they had here, as it's the highest ground around. Army boys dug in, laid charges around the base of the hill, and when Moe came for them, they blew it all."

"Jesus," Scott said. The sliver of slope winked from sight as they marched past the corner of a building. They moved on, through more parking lots and defensive positions filled with corpses that lay stretched out like overgrown creepers. The open space appeared as a vanilla killing ground of monstrous proportions. If he had to make a guess, the Army had fired into an advancing crowd of Moe until they ran simply out of bullets and were overrun.

Jeeeesus, Scott mouthed in mute awe.

"Here's where it got gruesome." Vick looked back at him with a sly smile. "You can be thankful we've had snow to cover things up. But you can still see the shapes. And the size of it all."

He was right.

Up ahead, Scott saw a wall of buses parked at the head of an intersection of three-, four-, and five-story apartment buildings. A wide slope ran up to the top of the buses, where sandbagged machine-gun nests were placed, and bodies hung over them like emptied sacks. Arms and legs stuck up through the layer of snow at irregular crooks and angles, leaving no doubt in Scott's mind what comprised the ramp. Several white scaffolding planks went up the middle of it all, saving anyone from having to actually walk on the dead.

"Where'd you park?" Scott gasped.

"Over the wall there," Amy told him. "We couldn't get over the buses, so we found a place."

"Awfully far to get back," he observed.

"We're okay," Amy told him. Scott disagreed on that point, but he kept his mouth shut.

Buckle and Shaffer were already on top of the buses and disappearing on the other side. Shaffer glanced back at them with a face full of impatience. He motioned for them to hurry, and Vick increased his pace. Amy and Scott followed.

"Shaffer was our unelected leader before Tenner arrived," Amy told him under her breath. "Nothing like having two alpha males jostling for position."

That was something Scott didn't miss, and he got the feeling that Amy didn't care for it either. Underfoot, the scaffolding rattled as they stepped onto it and walked to the top of the buses.

Scott's mouth hung open at what he saw on the other side.

If the open parking lots behind him were secondary defensive lines with wide killing fields, then the street ahead, now a choked chute of bodies, was a firing range from hell. The apartment buildings and shops that stretched out for perhaps fifty meters had their fronts ripped down by whatever explosive devices the Army had once commanded. Bodies, chunks of bodies, and lost limbs appeared imbedded into raw wood and concrete, which stretched down one side of the street and up the other. It struck Scott as a half-pipe of shredded frozen meat that started out beyond the buildings, but slowly built itself up like frosty coffee grounds, until it begin to rise in a second slope that breached the first wall of buses. Blasted corpses even decorated rooftops for as far as he could see. Huge menacing machine guns of unknown caliber, ruined by the weather, lined both levels of barricades. He stopped and gawked at the spectacle of carnage on either side of the bus, measuring which side was worse, and easily deciding on the front. Dead soldiers filled metal dumpsters. They had taken up positions inside the metal boxes, perhaps fifteen feet out from the buses to create the first battle line, with the machine gun fire overlapping and joining theirs from over the buses. With these two lines of fire, it seemed probable that the Army had lured or waited for the gimps to walk toward them en masse before they unleashed hell. The firing attracted more deadheads, and Moe kept on coming while the soldiers behind the line, eager at the prospect of using their weapons to their full destructive potential, ripped their targets new assholes. Scott wondered how many deadheads had been mowed down before magazines went dry, or how long the Army had waited until they started using the heavy guns, or if they broke and ran when Moe kept marching down this ungodly throat of death, taking losses that had no doubt eroded the soldiers' resolve, until the first corpses scratched at the outer trash dumpsters, crawled over them, and feasted on what was inside.

And how long might it have lasted? A day? Two? Three, perhaps?

Doesn't matter, Scott supposed. In the end, Moe had eaten them all.

The stench of frozen corpses and the magnitude of the fight threatened to make him gag.

"C'mon," Amy said, saving Scott from the bottomless well of hopelessness he suddenly dangled over. He looked into her round, pale face and couldn't bring himself to say a word. These were once people who walked, worked, and breathed, and now . . . Amy took him gently by the arm and guided him down the ramp on the other side. Scott gazed ahead, past the raw ruin that stretched out for a whole block and then some, and silently noted that if she wasn't there, he might have lost it a second time.

Up ahead, Buckle, wearing a black mask and hood that transformed him into a short, stout ninja, had stopped and turned around. "You all right, b'y?" he asked pensively, saying the word as *bye*, the Newfoundland equivalent of boy or buddy. The sound of his voice was uncomfortably loud in the street, which was lined with icy chunks of unmoving meat.

"Just a little shaken up," Amy answered for him, still holding onto his arm.

"S'aright," Buckle said in a new, nasal whine. "Vick's like that all the time. Ain'tcha, Vicky, me ol' trout."

Vick rolled his dark eyes. "Told you to stop calling me that."

Buckle shrugged and looked away.

Vick took to inspecting the rooftops for reasons unknown to Scott. "Been looking at this mess for the last few days, and I'm still not used to it. All them people. What was once people."

"You okay?" Amy asked Scott.

"Course he's not okay," Buckle observed. "He looks like he shat himself."

"Hey, shut up," Shaffer ordered, stressing the words as if he was all out of patience. "Before you burst something and starting bleeding all over the place."

"I'll make sure it's you, then."

"I *said* shut up, goddammit. I'll put my boot up your ass if you don't quiet down." This time, Buckle let it go.

Scott was grateful for the silence. He regained control of his emotions, but the scale of the shooting fest still left him awestruck. The ruined buildings scrolled as he followed Amy, past an apartment building on the left and a ravaged parking lot on the right. The lay of the land tilted, becoming a slope that faced the water. Scott thought that back in the day, this particular patch of real estate must have commanded top dollar. Some very wealthy people had been infected here.

Another parking lot came into view. Waiting amongst a scattering of vehicles topped off with white cones was a beige passenger van, its ass pointed toward them.

"You came here in that?" Scott asked Amy.

"Yeah. It's Vick's baby. We're loading stuff onboard. There's a lot of room in the back."

"Y'know something?" Buckle turned and asked Vick.

"What's that?"

"I don't think Tenner came this way."

"What?"

"I don't see any new tracks."

"Too hard to tell. Snow's packed down," Shaffer exclaimed. "We've been back and forth today and yesterday. He's probably around here somewhere. Be on guard."

Buckle rolled his eyes at Vick.

They stopped before the van without incident, and Scott and Amy studied the streets for deadheads. The coast seemed clear.

"Baby looks good," Vick exclaimed as he opened the door and did a quick take of the inventory. "Everything's still in the back. Looks fine."

Buckle and Shaffer stood in front of the van as Vick climbed aboard, tossing his pipe onto the passenger seat. Behind the wheel, Vick frowned. The engine refused to start.

"Nothing."

Buckle stepped forward and motioned for Vick to pop the hood.

"What are you waiting for, shithead?" Shaffer asked as Buckle struggled with the hood's latch.

"Suck me."

"Can't open a *hood?* Jesus Christ, *move.*" Shaffer pushed Buckle away and reached underneath the hood. "Leave it to you to . . . ah, there it is. See what a real man can—"

Shaffer lifted the hood and the engine cavity exploded, enveloping him in a sheet of flame and tossing Buckle into the snow. Shaffer did not scream. The front of the van jumped. The hood ripped free of its hinges and smashed into the windshield, crumpling it inward. Shrapnel sliced and sizzled through the air. Vick tumbled out of the driver's seat as smoke billowed from the vehicle. Amy pulled Scott back and into a crouch beside her. Buckle stood up and inspected the fallen Shaffer.

"How is he?" Vick called out.

Buckle straightened, partially obscured by the smoke billowing from the engine. "Dead," he muttered.

"What was that?" Amy asked, still partially in shock.

"Booby-trapped," Vick declared in his deep voice. They gathered around the smoldering wreck of the van. Buckle kicked snow on top of Shaffer's blackened body. The skin crackled and popped when the ice particles struck it.

"Rigged," Buckle said in his nasal twang. "Our mister Tenner. He had no intention of coming here. Had this rigged to blow. Smart prick. Knew eventually y'get around to poppin' the hood."

"An explosion like that?"

"Seen something like this when I was on the force. Old codger had barricaded himself in his house with a load of shotguns. Had grenades hooked up to his doors so that if you jerked them open, out came the pins."

"Grenades, huh?" Vick asked, his gaze alternating between Shaffer's cooked body and the still-smoking engine block.

"Grenades," Buckle confirmed. "Don't ask me how the old bastard got them. He put a round into his brain before we got to him."

"Where the hell did Tenner find grenades?" Vick pondered.

"Tenner could've found anything and put it in there," Amy said. "Remember, we found him here first."

"Maybe he found some other toys, too," Buckle added. "Maybe he's been holding back."

"And he knew we'd be driving out of here at some point in time," Vick said. "Course by then, the game would be afoot, I suppose. With or without your appearance," he directed at Scott.

"What now?" Buckle asked.

"We should get back to the tower," Amy said. "Gear up right this time. Tenner's out here somewhere, but we should be able to lose him."

"The fucker might've heard this." Buckle nodded at the van.

"I have an SUV," Scott said.

They all turned to him.

"It runs," Scott explained. "Drove it up here and left it in a garage on School Street. Got gas and food there. We could hike back there if we can't find anything else."

For a moment none of them said anything, and all they heard was the occasional snapping of fire.

"Up on School Street," Amy said. "That's a long hike. There's a lot of Moe if we go back the same way you and I came."

"We could go around," Scott suggested.

"Take longer. No guarantee it'd be safer, either. Moe's everywhere."

"Tenner's out there, too," Vick said.

"Well, he might be."

"What do you think?" Vick asked Amy and Buckle.

"Sure, why not?" Buckle immediately smirked. "Beats the hell outta this."

"Amy?"

Amy stood there, a little bit shorter than Buckle beside her. She reached up and hooked a strand of hair that had fallen over her face and tucked it behind a very white ear. In that pose, that moment, Scott felt something switch on inside.

"Can't leave a good vehicle behind. Not in wintertime. We could probably find something somewhere, but there's always the chance it'd be an older make, or the battery would be dead. Might not start. Or it's trapped in between a bunch of wrecks. Not to mention the risk if the thing is out in the open. The cars here on the lot, well, we already took the gas from them and put it in the van."

"Can't put it back?" Scott asked.

"We punched holes in the tanks." Amy smiled weakly.

Buckle nodded. "Right. Let's go with the sure thing."

"Yeah," Amy said. "Let's go back to the tower, though, and suit up right. Get some of the MREs."

Vick started throwing snow and ice onto the engine block, dousing the fire.

"What about him?" Scott asked, indicating the dead man.

Buckle answered that. He stooped and hooked Shaffer underneath the arms and lifted the corpse. Vick grabbed the legs. They carried him to a nearby car and, after a moment, got him inside and left him bunched up on the back seat. Buckle closed the door and, once done, he and Vick faced the others.

"An above-ground coffin for him," Buckle said. "Didn't care for the man, but can't leave him for Moe. Now what?"

"We head back," Amy told him.

"He didn't touch the MREs in the van." Vick pointed at the marked boxes in the back seat.

"Leave them there. He might have tampered with them."

That thought quieted them.

"We pick up what we have at the tower and move out. I don't want to stay there tonight," Amy said in her raspy tone. "We can always come back later and get the rest. Like, *much* later. He could be hanging around, too. Awright? Then let's go."

Without waiting for them, she about-faced and started marching. Buckle rubbed at his beard and shrugged. "She's your daughter," he said.

Vick looked at Scott, his craggy face pouting. "She's not my daughter."

They started moving.

After a few seconds, Vick added quietly, "Not by blood, anyway."

NORSEMEN

20

The land became whiter as snow flurries struck with greater frequency, and the air grew colder still. Winter was upon them, and Fist wanted to be in Halifax before the storms started kicking in. They made good time along Highway 2 until it became Highway 104. Towns appeared on the edges of the Trans-Canada Highway, and Fist allowed the Norsemen a few days hunting and scavenging in each. They bypassed Moncton entirely, not wanting to get tangled up in the city. Fist's orders were to strike east to Halifax, scout the surrounding areas, and return to the west with his report. Fist thought it prudent to stay with the smaller towns because the dead weren't as populous as they were in urban areas. They would not avoid Halifax, however. The nuclear plant there had been mothballed years ago, and the city was regarded as a gem of possibilities.

The sky stayed a morgue grey, and light snow fell. Being on the road for so long was beginning to grate on Fist's nerves—and his ass. A sign materialized in the distance, drawing his weary attention.

"Sackville." Fist tasted the word and liked it. *"Litterae, Religio, Scientia,"* he muttered, making Pell glance at him.

"Drive into town," Fist commanded. "Let's see what . . . Sackville has to offer."

Nodding, Pell did as told, as he'd better. Fist believed the man to be loyal, at least as loyal as any of the dogs at his beck and call, but he kept watch and had no reservations at all about killing him if needed. Behind him, the other warriors rustled and chortled at the thought of getting out of the van. Fresh meat was getting scarce, and they would soon start cutting into their dwindling stores of smoked flesh. They all hoped the hunting would be better in Sackville.

As the snow continued to fall, Pell drove through the inner roads of Sackville, going deeper, passing large red brick buildings that appeared to be dormitories.

"What is this?" the driver hissed, staring out his window.

"University of Mount A," Fist rumbled. "A for . . . Allison."

"A university?"

"Yes."

Once carefully sculpted grounds were now littered with abandoned cars, fallen trees, and power lines, as well as scattered debris, all coated with a thin sheet of snow. Victorian-styled houses lined the road on the opposite side of the residences, their windows smashed out. Grey figures, almost incorporeal, paused on crests of low hills and watched the vans go by. Fist stared back at them. Zombies. They were truly everywhere.

The road became increasingly rough.

"Stop here," Fist ordered and opened his door. "Everyone out 'cept Pell. Get hunting."

Pell braked in the middle of an intersection of what appeared to be a small downtown area. Signs for banks, ATMs, coffee places, and once-quaint shopping stores hung off of storefronts. The van's side door slid open with a rattle and a half-dozen Norsemen eagerly got out, readying clubs, axes, and bats. Fist went to the back of the van and grabbed his maul. His hockey helmet went on last.

The second van pulled up behind them.

"What's up?" Murphy asked, leaning back in the passenger seat. He seemed quite relaxed.

"Gonna do some hunting," Fist answered him.

"Here?"

Fist slowly turned toward Murphy and glared. Murphy did not flinch.

"Only asking," the man finally grumbled.

"Get your ass out of the fucking van," Fist growled. "Before I stab it."

Murphy slowly did as he was told, his expression saying he didn't like the threat. Fist didn't give a shit what he liked or didn't. When one followed, one didn't ask questions. Not in *his* pack of dogs.

Men leaped from the other transport and geared up for a hunt. Fist walked to the front of the two vans and waved an arm. The two vehicles, encircled by walking Norsemen, crept down the street.

"Anyone here?" Fist called. "Anyone? Hey?"

When he paused, another man called out. Snow continued to fall in lethargic bits of fluff, and the town took on a ghostly hue.

The shouting attracted the dead.

They crept toward the living, dragging their feet, and the living put them down with smiles. A string of dead bodies marked their passage into town, and the snow did its best to cover up the husks.

"We're looking for gas," Fist yelled, which was true, although they could have gotten it from any of the derelict vehicles lining the road. "And a place to stay. If anyone can help."

"We're hungry, too," a man with Viking horns shouted, making those around him smile.

The Norsemen came to another intersection, and Fist directed them to veer to the right. A ravaged grocery store appeared out of the curtain of light snow, but they didn't stop. More dead tried to eat them, but had their existence ended instead.

Two hours into the hunt, they looped back to their starting point and continued doing a slow circuit, until past two in the afternoon.

"This place is dead," Fist heard Murphy declare behind him, impatience in his voice. The man was beginning to irritate him.

"Hey!" a woman's voice shouted.

The vans stopped in a squeal of brakes.

Fist watched as four people emerged from the grocery store they had passed and dismissed as being empty. Silhouetted by the snow, she was perhaps in her thirties, plain-looking and hopeful. She carried a scoped rifle, aimed at the ground. Three men followed her, all dressed in heavy winter clothing. Fist noted the hunting shotguns and forced himself to smile.

"We were about to give up," Fist burst out.

"So we heard," the woman said, studying the others. A dash of uncertainly marred her features for all of a second, then she pushed on. "You're a fierce looking bunch."

"This?" Fist exclaimed good naturedly, looking over his armor. "Keeps us alive. Zombies can't bite through it. And we try to save our ammo, so . . ." He hefted the maul.

"So I see," the woman went on. "I'm Claire."

"Fist," Fist introduced himself.

"No first name?"

Another smile. Fist felt his cheek starting to ache. "That is my first name."

"Strange. Where you guys from?"

"Out west."

"We heard it was hell out there," one of the men said, cradling a shotgun in his arms, not as welcoming as Claire.

Fist dropped the smile. "It is. Damn scary. Alberta's the worst of it. Nuclear plants melted down when the power grid went. It's a mess. We lost people trying to get out here. The dead aren't the only worry, I can tell you."

"How you get here?"

Always with the same questions, Fist thought in annoyance. "Sackville? Just saw the sign and decided to drive through. Looking for supplies, things to eat. This place looked promising, but we went by the shop. Didn't look the greatest."

"Nah, the store's been picked clean almost five months now," Claire said. "But we're doing fine. It's a day to day thing."

"Tell me about it," Fist said. The snow wasn't letting up, but he thought he detected movement on the roof of the store. These were cautious people. "Pays off to be careful," he said without thinking.

Claire didn't say anything to that, and for a moment, an awkward silence stretched between them.

"Well," she said, making the effort. "We don't really know you, but wanted to take the chance, you know. See if you were all right."

Fist nodded amicably. "Understandable. Understandable. So what do you want to do?"

"Well, you're going to want to stay somewhere. There's plenty of empty houses if you drive straight on and take a left at the intersection. There's also a Rosie's Hotel just outside of town, but that one is filled with stinks."

"Stinks?"

"Stinks or stinkers. What we call the dead."

"I see." Fist smiled again, even though it was the stupidest thing he'd ever heard. Impatience swelled in him. He didn't like conversing or smiling in large quantities. "And then what?"

"Well, let's just play it by ear, if that's okay with you?" Claire said, hope once again back in her voice.

"Sure, where are you staying?" *Too fast.* Fist chastised himself.

"We'll be around," Claire replied. "See ya."

"Later," Fist said and watched them back into the shop. He took a breath. There were six, possibly seven of them. Some very good eating—and at least one woman. Fist gnawed on his lip as they disappeared into the shop. Women were . . . prizes.

Snow continued to fall. It would be an easy thing to allow them a head start and track them down. They had done it many times before.

At least six, with the chance of more. Fist felt the stares of his dogs behind him. They waited for the word, but he slapped the passenger side of the van and started walking down the street. The houses they had mentioned sounded good to him, and if Claire were truly cautious, he suspected they would be watched. That was fine, too. The game was afoot.

Fist *so* enjoyed a good hunt.

*

Hunt they did.

Within a day, the Norsemen tracked down the house of Claire and her people. They had taken up refuge in a large house that had a ten-foot-high stone wall around the entire property. Fist and his boys attacked at night, quietly killing the men on watch and scaling the walls. Moments later, they were in the house.

After that, chaos.

There had been ten of them, including a boy and a young girl, which Fist executed outright. In the gunfight that ensued, Claire was gut shot and died slowly, quite the opposite of what Fist had planned. There were two other women, and he let his boys have them. By morning, all of them had been killed, gutted, and quartered, and the kitchen had been turned into a smoke house with chunks of fresh meat hanging from hooks.

They stayed at the house two more days, just in case they had missed anyone.

They hadn't.

On the third day, the two vans did one final exploration of Sackville, searching for crumbs. They left in midafternoon, driving through town and onto the highway, only to pull off after travelling a short distance. The days were getting shorter, and Fist spied a roadside service station and truck stop, with the small Rosie's Hotel nearby, just as Claire had said. Fist remembered her screams, her white skin dappled with dark blood, then tuned it all out.

Stopping in front of the main door of the hotel, he organized a party of seven, including Murphy. They tooled up and entered the hotel, Fist in the lead. As expected, the dead haunted the halls of the establishment, and the Norsemen cleared the first floor within minutes. The second was cleared in equally short order. Fist allowed a short, but terse smoke break in one of the rooms of the third floor, eyeing Murphy, before finally clearing the rest.

Once the bloody evictions were completed, Fist had the vans back up to the main doors of the hotel, noses out in case they needed to leave quickly. As the cold winter dark deepened, the Norsemen conducted searches of the hotel's kitchen and storerooms. The propane lines for a set of stainless steel burners were still functional, and three men were charged with heating supper while the rest roamed the lower floors.

Later that evening, they all gathered and ate in the large and relatively untouched dining area. Bottles of gin, vodka, whiskey, and other spirits were liberated from the hotel's untouched bar. Shadowy from flashlights and lamps, red carpet covered the entire floor and made Pell think of haunted places. As expected, the men sat and ate mostly with those they usually shared a van with. There was some movement between tables, but one group seemed to stay put. Pell looked at Fist and saw him take in the gathering of four in a corner. A castle of bottles was being assembled before the men.

Murphy sat and drank there.

Mealtimes were loud affairs, but the discovery of the booze made this one exceptionally loud as they ate and spoke with the enthusiasm and revelry of a true Viking hall. Murphy's table seemed to laugh the longest and the hardest. Fist, nursing a bottle of port wine, found his attention coming back to them time and time again. They would hunker down and whisper before bursting into laughter, as if sharing in a conspiracy. Sitting at his leader's table, Pell could smell trouble, despite being half cut on rye whiskey.

Nearby, Fist took a long gulp of wine. He'd gotten quieter, more attentive to what was happening across the room.

Murphy felt eyes on him and glanced over, meeting his leader's gaze. He didn't linger, but went right back to whispering to the men gathered about him.

Another eruption of scalding laughter.

Pell took a shot of rye and barely felt the burn. He watched Fist. The man had tensed up in his chair, and the two other men sitting nearby felt the heat coming from him. Fist was a pressure cooker warming up.

Then Murphy made his mistake. The jackal looked across the way and nodded at Fist, even hefted a bottle in his direction, before whispering once again to his boys. There was another short conference and a snickering from all three. Murphy leaned back in his chair, grinning as if exhausted from the last joke, and took a long pull from his drink.

Pell was only a little surprised when Fist got slowly to his feet and placed the bottle of port down carefully.

The nearby Norsemen quieted one by one as Fist removed his tire tread cuirass, fashioned from the image of a Roman legionnaire. Then he stripped off the leather jacket underneath and tossed it on an empty table nearby.

That got the attention of Murphy and his companions.

Working at something lodged in his teeth, Fist pulled off his tight T-shirt, revealing the progression of evil tattoos up the length of both arms, his neck, and the snarling green dragons on each pectoral muscle. Fist had been a large man before the Fall. Powerfully built, but with a sheen of fat. His current diet had allowed him to slim down to a chiseled form, and his midsection appeared as rows of corrugated iron.

Murphy leaned back in his chair. If he was worried, he didn't show it.

With exaggerated nonchalance, Fist reached into his left boot and extracted a Bowie knife, a huge blade that could've been mistaken for a machete. Holding the weapon in his fist, blade pointed at the floor, the leader of the eastern foray stepped away from his table, moved to the middle of the room, and started overturning anything within reach. Three Norsemen sat at a table in the middle of the room, but deserted it seconds before Fist lifted it from the ground and threw it against a wall.

He cleared a ragged space in the middle of the floor.

"Murph," Fist growled in his subterranean bass voice. "Get up."

Instead of obeying, Murphy smiled at his companions, appearing at ease. He was the only one at his table who appeared relaxed. The others had tensed up.

"Why?" Murphy asked insolently.

Pell considered himself to be a brute, but he was fighting not to shit himself, and it wasn't even him being called out.

"Stand the fuck up," Fist exhaled mightily, his voice like released steam.

"Looks like you got something on your mind." Murphy leered. "Imagine that."

"I have."

"Yeah?" Murphy countered as he got to his feet. The men at his table scrambled away before he flipped it and rolled it away, white dishes, bottles, and gnawed bones scattering across the carpeted floor.

"Well, I've been thinking, too. Been thinking you ain't been doing your job good enough. Might be time for a change," Murphy seethed, his face darkening in the shadows of the room. He didn't remove his riot gear, but he did produce a long serrated blade, every bit as evil-looking as the eager gleam in his eyes.

Fist said nothing.

"Fuckin' aye," Murphy said, gathering up wind before switching to the harsh Norse speak. "Maybe I kill you now. Take lead of pack."

He flipped his blade and caught it by the handle.

Fist glowered.

"Huh?" Murphy's eyes widened with indignation. "You think you can take me?"

"Son," Fist finally said in his deep, deep voice. "I'm gonna cut your balls off."

The silence that fell over the room after that line gave Pell shivers. A man could've heard a corpse squeak-fart six feet under, it had gotten so quiet.

Murphy didn't appreciate the threat or the stillness in the least. He roared and lunged forward.

Fist slapped Murphy's rushed stab aside, leaving his attacker wide open. He grabbed his would-be usurper's weapon arm and doubled it over, dropping and splitting the elbow joint over his knee. Murphy shrieked and dropped his weapon. He clawed at Fist's face, but the Norse leader slapped the pommel of the Bowie square into his nose, stunning him.

Then Fist stabbed him, pulled the knife out, and bent the challenger over. A second man lunged at the leader then, swinging a bat.

Fist caught the weapon, the brazen slap of flesh on wood echoing in the room. Then he knifed his attacker through the eye, burying the steel in his head. The body dropped, and Fist had to stoop to rip his knife free.

The third man held up his hands and backed against a wall, his frame trembling. Fist spared him, but pounced on Murphy, who lay on the floor holding in his guts. Fist held him by the throat as he punched the Bowie through his flesh. The thrust came fast and hard enough to pierce the carpet and the wood beyond. There was a soft *yurk* from the impaled man, then Fist's heavily muscled torso rippled as he swirled the blade in a sawing fashion. Murphy trembled briefly, all fight gone.

Fist kept on cutting.

He stood up a few moments later, Murphy's bloody heart squishing in his hand, and glared at the men around him. No one dared move for fear of being next.

Fist walked up to the last one of Murphy's group. "Open your hand," he said.

Not knowing what to expect, the man did as he was told.

Fist slapped the raw heart into it. "Fry that up," the leader hissed. "I'm not finished eating."

The Norseman hesitated for only a moment, then fled the room with the organ. Fist remained and sized up the remaining pair of dogs.

"Anyone else think I'm not doing my job?"

Heads shook no.

Not satisfied with their answers, Fist gazed about the room, meeting even Pell's eyes for a moment and unnerving him in an instant. His point made, the leader returned to the two men before him.

"Cut that up," he ordered, indicating Murphy's body.

They jumped to the task.

"Tomorrow," Fist informed them all, "we hit Nova Scotia. By the end of the week . . . Halifax."

SCOTT

21

They reached Purdy's Wharf without incident and quickly ascended to the floor designated as base camp. The afternoon sun had gone behind some clouds, and the air inside the building seemed just as chilling as outside, perhaps even more so with Sam's corpse decorating the meeting room. They gathered around the body, and Buckle took the initiative and covered him with the dead man's coat.

Amy took charge over the men. "Gather up everything you got now. And grab everything you can carry in your packs."

"We can't take it all now, Amy," Buckle protested.

"No, but maybe we can bring Scott's rig back here and transfer it all into the back?" She glanced at them for approval, then at Scott. "Where did you say you parked?"

"School Street."

"School Street? I don't know that one."

Scott thought about it. "Maybe I'm wrong, then."

Vick and Buckle exchanged pensive looks.

"School Avenue?" Amy asked.

"Yeah, that's the one."

"You're sure?"

"Yeah, pretty sure."

"Our Amy knows the city like the back of your hand," Vick joked. "I'll be in my powder room. What's the plan, by the way?"

Amy scratched her head. "We take the long way around. Might take a few days, but we'll have food and water with us, so that's okay. School Avenue is right on the 102."

She paused for a moment, collecting her thoughts. "We came through a lot of Moe to get here. I say we go around them. We can trek up South Street to Oxford, then jump over to Connaught, and eventually get onto Bayer's Road. If we meet Moe, we'll sidestep him if we can."

"And Tenner?" Vick asked.

"I'll do him," Buckle growled, then considered Scott. "That is, if you don't mind."

Scott didn't reply right away. There wasn't any other punishment to fit the crimes Tenner had done, other than feeding him to the gimps. He had thought about it earlier, but was he ready to kill another living person? He sighed. It was the wrong time to start questioning his resolve.

"Yeah," he replied.

Buckle's forehead mashed up. "A noncommittal answer if I ever heard one. Tell you what. If we meet up with the bastard, I'll give you first dibs."

"Feeling bloodthirsty?" Vick asked.

"You're not?" Buckle retorted.

"No, I am," Vick stated. "I liked Sammy and Tickle tons better than Shaffer, but . . . can't believe they're gone. That Tenner killed them. Still expect Shaffer to start screaming any time."

"Get ready," Amy ordered them all, "and we'll meet back here."

Buckle followed Vick out the door. Scott was about to fall into step behind them when Amy stopped him with a shake of her head.

"You stay with me," she said.

"Why?"

"Those guys have their armor in the same room. I don't think any of us should be separated right now."

Made sense.

"You get to watch me dress," Amy stated with a wry little smile, which both startled him . . . and made him smile back.

"Um . . . body armor?" Scott asked as Amy moved past him and into the corridor.

"Yeah. Some they pulled off dead soldiers in the streets. Took a little while to find something to fit over their winter gear, but they got some."

"You too?"

"Yeah, well, I have some. Mostly joint protection. I'm too small for the other stuff."

They went into her room—another office waiting area with a leather sofa draped in grey blankets, which resembled more of a neat nest than a reception area. She walked to the desk, slapping her elbow and knee pads as she went, ensuring they were in place. From a corner she picked up a small protective vest, white and heavily padded.

"Don't like putting this thing on," she said as she pulled it on. "Squishes my boobs."

Scott didn't comment and looked out the only window in the place. A view of Halifax Harbour lay beyond, shaded by the clouds.

"You knew about Tenner," he finally said.

"Yeah. Well, I suspected."

"You didn't say anything earlier, when we first met." Scott turned to face her.

Amy didn't back down. "Didn't know for certain, is all. Didn't want to get your hopes up. Sorry if I did anything wrong."

Scott reflected on it. Had she done anything wrong? No, he supposed. She really hadn't. She was only making sure that *he* was sure.

"I thought there was something weird about him," Amy stated. "Pretty much from the first day we met. I'm good at getting vibes from people, and he had a bad one. Not like you."

"I have a good vibe?"

"Something like that. You never . . . well . . . you look me in the eyes when you talk. He wouldn't. He'd . . . look at other things."

"Like what?"

"My girly parts."

"Oh."

"Yeah. Oh. And he'd do it in a slimy way, too. I made it a point not to be alone with him. Even talked about it with Vick. He knew. But, well, that was all. I meant to confront him if he really got weird about it."

"Why didn't you?"

"We started scouting for things, and he was either gone when I was back or vice versa."

Scott nodded and looked back to the harbor. If she noticed his sudden uncomfortable silence, she didn't show it. Amy resumed fitting the vest over her snowsuit and, once secured, produced what looked to be a riot helmet with a clear visor.

"You won't be able to wear your mask over that," Scott observed.

"Tired of the mask anyway," she said and pulled the dark hood over her head. The helmet went on next.

"Heavy padding," Scott said, indicating the vest. "Where you get that?"

"Tae Kwon Do gear. Vick used to run a school."

Scott felt his face go slack in surprise, and Amy saw it.

"Who do you think has made it this far? If people don't have any special training or skills, they're pretty lucky. That's the way we see it, anyway."

"I don't have any special training."

"Except hockey."

Scott smiled sheepishly, remembering. "Minor hockey."

"Oh." Amy kept a straight face. "Even better. Well, you're one of the lucky ones." She grabbed her tonfas. "Which is to say, very lucky. We had a conversation on that very subject one night. We figure anyone who's left alive and survived up to this point isn't your average person. Some might be survivalists, some might have some training, or even ex-military."

"Buckle that?"

Amy didn't answer right away. "No, he's a cop."

"A cop?"

"Yeah, ex-RCMP."

"Shit."

"He was based in Newfoundland, but got transferred to Nova Scotia. Attended university down in the Valley, I think he said. Anyway, let's get going."

Scott followed her to another room where cardboard boxes were stacked almost chest high. MEAL, READY-TO-EAT were stamped on the sides, as well as the different kinds inside. Roast chicken, beef, spaghetti and meat balls, even meat loaf, and those were just the ones he spotted in a glance. Plastic four liter jugs of water were stored on shelving units nearby.

"Wow," he said.

"Something, eh?" Amy said, opening her backpack and placing a jug of water inside. "We found about two months' worth of food here. And water. Moving it all was the biggest obstacle. MREs last for years."

Scott opened a box of roast beef and eyed several metallic, re-sealable baggy units.

"Get some water, too," Amy told him as he started transferring the bags to his backpack.

The sound of boots made Scott turn around. Vick and Buckle stood just outside the doorway, waiting their turn at the food and water stores. Both wore black body armor over their snow suits, with high sturdy collars to protect their necks. Padding was strapped to their elbows and knees, and both wore the same type of battle helmet Amy wore, complete with matching black masks. Scott figured the armor to be Kevlar or whatever material soldiers wore in the field. The armor protected their limbs to a degree, Scott saw, but the thick snow suits would probably also save them from a bite long enough to put down the attacker.

"You guys all shop at the same place?" Scott asked.

"Looks that way, doesn't it?" Vick answered. "Plenty to go around if you want an extra suit. Formally make you part of the group."

Scott inspected their protection, then looked at his own Nomex coat and pants. "No, thanks. This is fine."

"Good idea," Buckle said with a deep nasal sound to his voice. "Your gear's got overall better protection, I think. And it's fireproof, if you feel the need to light yourself up anytime."

"Why didn't we check out the fire stations?" Vick asked Buckle.

"*You* wanted to play soldier," Buckle reminded him.

"Finished," Amy announced and made her way to them, getting her backpack on in place. "You're sounding worse."

"Me?" Buckle asked.

"Yeah, you."

"Tenner broke me nose, 'member?" Buckle replied. "Got more blanket in there. The last one got saturated. Got it in both nostrils now."

"Ew," Amy stated.

"Yeah, fuckin' ew." Buckle scoffed in agreement.

"We'll have to come back here," Vick said, changing the subject.

"Yeah," Amy agreed, her expression hidden behind the black mask. "Sometime."

Buckle and Scott exchanged places. "Better not've hogged all the meat loaf," the Newfoundlander warned him as he went past.

They finished loading what they could comfortably carry in food and water and left the room. Next they picked up their camouflage, Moe-stained ponchos that reeked, stinking up the room.

"Gonna have to reapply these," Vick said as he threw his poncho over his head. A ripped T-shirt went on next, covering almost all of his face plate. Amy and Buckle did the same. A moment later, Amy motioned Scott to bend over while she placed a similar shirt over his motorcycle helmet.

"This was Sam's. Yours now."

Scott nodded.

"You got ammo for that shotgun of yours?" Vick asked him.

"Yeah, in my pockets."

"That's fine, just don't use it unless you have to. That Glock is better if you have to."

"Ruger," Scott corrected him.

"Whatever. We don't kill Moe unless we have to. Got it?"

"Got it."

Vick seemed satisfied with that and turned to the others. "I'm ready. You guys?"

"Ready, me son," Buckle said in his gruff-turned-nasal voice.

"Ready," Amy echoed.

"Me, too," Scott threw in.

Vick appraised them all for a moment, his dark eyes the only part visible through the masks he wore, and brought his length of steel pipe to his shoulder. Seconds passed and he still made no move to leave.

"You okay?" Amy asked him.

The man with the steel pipe hesitated. "Just figured . . . there would be more of us leaving this place, is all," he finished with a half-shrug.

The silence that came after his words was almost solemn.

"All right, then," Vick finally said, as if convincing himself that all would be well. "Let's get it on."

22

Having finally reached the top of the stairs, Tenner felt like shit. He was in good shape, but running that last distance, the adrenaline dump, and climbing a mountain of stairs had taken a lot out of him. Pausing at the closed metal door only long enough to ensure that nothing was coming after him, he turned and strode through a short stone passageway, toward an archway of brick, snow, and light. He emerged from the tunnel into a wide, wintry courtyard as large as a football field. Thick brick walls rose up to ramparts and slick-looking concrete platforms. Artillery emplacements ringed the heights, and Tenner had gone up there to see where Purdy's Wharf was situated and to look out over Halifax Harbour, as well as the city behind the old fortress. Several buildings in the Citadel possessed shaggy white plumes of withered grass, bent over from the weight of snow and ice. Trucks, jeeps, and even four frosty-looking green tanks filled the open space before him, creating a ragged maze of metallic lumps. Bodies lay scattered throughout, some fresher than others—all soldiers and all dead. When Tenner came upon the fort, there were perhaps three dozen turned soldiers that sought to devour him. No Philistines these, as they wore full battle suits and proved to be a challenge even for Tenner. Most of the soldiers wore helmets that were resistant to his Glocks, so he killed them with his ceremonial knives—sinking the blades into brains by way of stabbing up under chins. The flesh was frozen, and gouging it with a length of steel felt strange to Tenner, as if he were stabbing stout slush, but they died all the same. It merely took a little more effort on his part.

Then he got to searching.

The Army had chosen well in positioning a sizeable force on Citadel Hill. The grounds around the fort were cleared and grassy, giving the defenders the best shot at any dead thing attempting to walk up the slopes. Though the grounds where draped in deep snow, crooked arms and torsos were still visible from the rampart heights, where snipers and machine guns had wreaked second-death upon the advancing legions of zombies on a mesmerizing scale. Whatever battles fought were all for naught, unfortunately, for the virus had finally penetrated the fort and wrecked deadly havoc from within. Tenner had no idea what the timeline might have been, from the time the Army barricaded itself in the fort to the time it finally fell, but he suspected it had been at least a year.

He didn't really care.

All he cared about . . . were the toys.

He moved through the clutter of tanks and other military vehicles. The tanks he'd inspected first, but for reasons unknown, they would not start for him. The jeeps also would not start, and the mechanical riddles of their engines only made him scratch his head. The weapon systems were likewise a puzzle and, exposed to the elements for as long as they were, he left them alone. Sidearms and all manner of assault rifles lay on the frozen dirt, half-buried in white drifts; some even had detached hands, forearm bones gnawed clean, clutching grips. He left those. Empty casings filled with and partially obscured by snow were sprinkled just about everywhere underfoot—shiny leftovers from a final firefight. Some were his, but most were not. There were even some untouched box magazines left in the open, which Tenner left behind. Whatever was in the courtyard would stay in the courtyard.

Tenner arrived at an archway set into a stone building, where a smaller door was inset into a larger garage frame. He grasped the old-fashioned latch on the wooden door and opened it. He stepped just inside the threshold and smiled.

The room was a storage chamber of sorts. Three crates of carefully sealed and packaged AR-20s, the Canadian Forces assault rifle of choice, lay atop one another. He knew they were the upgraded version of the AR-15 tactical carbine. One crate's weapons came with attached laser designator sighting systems, as well as fitted grenade launchers. Another crate contained rifles with scopes, without any further bells and whistles. For some reason, Tenner preferred the simpler designs. There were side arms and futuristic submachine guns of a manner beyond his understanding. One crate contained what he believed to be light machine guns from the folded-up bipods underneath their fluted barrels, ugly-looking snakes that could no doubt rip out whole chunks of flesh. Another crate held several small wooden boxes filled with black egg-sized grenades, dimpled for improved grip. Even better, there were crates filled with intact magazines—several thousand rounds if Tenner wasn't mistaken.

The harbor-front armory had been wrecked. He hadn't been lying about that to the others.

But it didn't matter.

He'd found everything he'd wanted in the fort.

Just in time, too. The week he spent below the hill had almost depleted his stores of ammunition. Forays to the national armory, street searches, and fighting dead things had placed a strain on the supplies he'd brought with him in the SUV. That had been an adventure in itself. But he'd done it.

Even better, he'd done it only days before meeting up with his living, breathing toys, grown from the finest stock. He had intended to lead them on for as long as he could without raising suspicions. Take them out, one by one if possible, on patrols or searches for other survivors in the city. The very thought of looking for survivors had made him scoff secretly when they had suggested it. The city was a scorched battleground populated only by the reanimated dead, but whatever kept up their hopes. Even watching them eat the food untouched by the Army, supplies he considered rightfully *his*, had been quite difficult to do. There were enough MREs about to feed a single person for a year, perhaps even two if he was extremely conservative. Tenner had helped transfer boxes of supplies from Purdy's Wharf to their van, but he'd mentally vowed none of it would leave the area. Though he was no mechanic, it didn't take any skill to disconnect a few wires and hoses in the engine, then rig a grenade to the inside of the hood. He had even listened to Amy talk about going back to basics and the need to grow their own food, but the thought of working a farm had made him sick. However, Tenner believed keeping up morale was a good thing and a useful carrot to lead the mule with. So he continued listening to them, inwardly marvelling at his ability to act like a normal person, to actually *blend in* with them. Over time, he'd gotten to know them. Vick was the fatherly type and obviously thought the world of Amy. Buckle was the enforcer and, with his police training, was potentially a bigger threat than Vick, whom Tenner understood had taught martial arts for a living before the demise of civilization. Shaffer was the loudmouth cynic, probably a bully back in the day, the kind of asshole a person would despise having to work with day in and out. Sam and Tickle were merely dogs following their leaders. Tenner had, in fact, considered Sam to be his next plaything, before changing his mind and deciding on Shaffer. He'd thought of lashing the loudmouth to a telephone pole and allowing the dead to feed upon his lower extremities, the same as he'd done to Tickle. He'd also come up with another idea. There were craters out there. Perhaps binding Shaffer with duct tape and burying him in snow up to his neck would be fun. Of course he'd notify *Moe* that dinner was in the fridge and waiting.

Amy, on the other hand.

Amy was special. Even better, the female was still alive.

There weren't many women left in the world, and certainly none as physically and intellectually appealing as Amy. He'd watched her at times, quietly sizing her up, measuring her strengths; he had to admit, he'd been impressed. He'd be even more impressed when he was strapping her arms and legs with duct tape, rendering her helpless, while he worked his magic with his knives. The possibility of impregnating her, creating a brood, had entered his mind. A *superior* species of man. A mutant, even. Tenner believed he was superior in every way to those around him. An alpha male's alpha male. He eventually discarded the notion of creating more in his mould, however. Keeping a female alive and docile until she came to term would be a hassle he didn't really have time for. There was also the risk of siring a daughter. Having a female would only force him to reset Amy in another attempt at a male offshoot. Even then the odds of success were only slim as, by that time, Amy would no doubt be in rougher condition than when he first impregnated her.

Still, he had to admit, having her around for even a short while would entertain him in ways the sport would not.

The sport—his *game*—had gone on quite well and would have no doubt continued going on well until the appearance of the mystery man. *And who the fuck was he, anyway?* Nothing came to him. The face drew a blank. But the new meat knew *him*. Knew *of* him.

Didn't matter.

Whoever he was, he was only an extra piece of meat to slaughter.

Tenner pulled up the body armor he'd found in another part of the fort from yet another storage container with several suits of different sizes. He selected the biggest one that would fit over his winter coat and brought it back to the room with the weapons and ammunition. The black plates went on with an ease that suggested Tenner was *born* to wear such gear, shackling them around his thighs, lower legs, chest, and arms. Wearing his coat underneath was tight, but he didn't mind. He strapped on twin thigh holsters for Glock 18s, then filled a backpack with extra magazines for the guns and the AR-20 he'd chosen. He was lucky to have found ample ammunition for the Glocks, as he had nearly run out. The assault rifle had a cache of extended magazines. The rounds were of a size unknown to him, but they looked incredibly large and lethal. He lashed a death vest to his chest: eight egg-sized grenades attached to the front of a vest of synthetic material, semi-protected by pouches of Velcro, that allowed him to use the explosives one at a time, or he could undo a wire cord and, with one yank, detonate them all at once. The vest also had several loops and pockets for extra magazines. A dark hood covered his mouth and nose. A combat helmet with tight-fitting goggles went over his head, giving him the appearance of a secretive Special Forces soldier. His bush of hair made the fit a little awkward, but it was his pride and joy, and so he put up with it.

Finally, his precious knives went into sheaths that hung off his belt at the base of his back, overlapping each over with hilts outward so that if he had to reach behind and grab them, they'd be in his hands in a flash.

There was a box of MREs nearby, and Tenner took four as well as a jug of water and made room for it all in his backpack. Once that was done, he stopped and looked around the room. He'd thought about taking two assault rifles, one as a backup, but carrying the pair would be too cumbersome. If he somehow lost one, he'd assess the situation and consider coming back for another. The light machine gun was also an option and he had to admit it was tempting, but there was no sport in that. He would've taken his hunting rifle, the Bushmaster, but he'd nearly depleted the ammunition. His AR-20 possessed a scope as well as three modes of fire—single shot, semi-automatic, and full electric *rock n' rolla.*

The best his prey had were handguns. However, he did seem to remember a gun barrel slung over the shoulder of the mystery man—a shotgun probably, or a hunting rifle, and no doubt limited ammunition. There was also the mystery man's handgun, but that didn't bother Tenner. He thought about sniping the bastard from a distance, just blowing his head off in the middle of a street somewhere, which would lay to rest the man's puzzling existence, as well as scare the living shit out of the remaining targets.

Then something occurred to him, an image that brought him up cold and abruptly speechless.

The rats.

What about them?

Replaying the chase in the tunnel left a disquieting image in his head. Was the appearance of the rats some sort of tragic foreshadowing for him? Or were they merely another lowly physical manifestation of the virus to be dealt with while he went about his true purpose? Where would they play out in the cosmic scheme of events? Was it safe to assume they couldn't breach the fort? He didn't have an answer to any of those questions.

Zombie rodents. *He sighed mentally.* What would be next? *As Buckle so often said,* Jesus, Jesus, Jesus.

Tenner hefted the backpack and strapped it on. He looped his assault rifle over a shoulder by its strap. He took one last look around the chamber and believed he had everything he needed for the hunt. After it was over—he figured a day at the earliest, four at the most—he'd come back and plan his next move. Perhaps he could actually convert the fort into something liveable. Or maybe he'd move back to one of the higher floors of Purdy's Wharf and enjoy the view. Mexico could wait a few months. *Hellifax* had so much to offer, and with the newfound stores of supplies, it would be stupid of him to leave so soon—even with the knowledge of zombie rats in the city's metal guts.

Hefting the AR-20 and placing the skeletal butt stock firmly against his shoulder, he turned and started walking toward the door, wondering where he should start hunting.

The words *at the beginning* popped into his head.

It was as good a place as any.

23

The four of them left Purdy's Wharf and quickly made their way back toward the main wall. The snow squeaked underneath their boots, and the cold wormed itself into their limbs. Scott thought of how he'd wished he had been able to see Halifax under different conditions. Buckle was about a dozen steps ahead of him, seemingly staring straight ahead. Vick walked across from him on the right. The older man looked around, studying the stone corners and listening to the sound of their march, the only noise to be heard. Scott glanced at Amy to his right, who finished the wide box the four of them made.

They moved along without speaking, approaching the killing fields as Scott thought of them—that second line of machine gun nests spread out in front of the parking lots. Vick produced a pair of spiked knuckles that almost made Scott balk. The spikes looked to be at least a fearsome three inches long. Vick quietly fitted them on one hand and then the other, trapping his steel bar underneath an armpit as he did so.

"Scary, aren't they?" Amy asked. She had noticed him gawking and stepped in close. "Most of the items from his shop weren't the best thing for putting down Moe. But he took a liking to those."

Hearing her, Vick turned and raised his fist in a grim salute. A tattered hood made from a T-shirt covered his battle helmet, but Scott guessed there was a ready smile hidden underneath it all.

"That where you got your sticks?" Scott asked her.

"They're tonfas," Amy corrected him. "And yes, that's where I got them. And the chest protector. All sparring gear."

"Havin' a nice chat back there?" Buckle asked over his shoulder. "Why not a little louder, eh?"

"Sorry," Amy said and lowered her voice. "He can be cranky sometimes."

Vick looked over at Buckle and said, "You *can* be cranky at times."

The Newfoundlander didn't comment.

"Any more of that around?" Scott asked her in a much quieter tone.

"Tonfas?"

"And spiked knuckles."

"You know how to punch?"

"Huh?"

"Throw a punch. You know how to throw one properly?"

Scott had never thought of it before. "No."

"Then it'd be kind of a waste."

"Thought they were for people who couldn't throw a punch."

"Oh, they are," Amy said, stepping in closer until she was only an arm's length away. "But on someone like Vick, they're lethal."

With spikes like that, anyone's lethal, *Scott thought darkly.*

The bus and the ramp of corpses came into view. As they drew closer, Buckle slowed to a stop and surveyed something that caught his attention.

"What's up?" Vick asked.

Buckle shook his head. "That one corpse there . . . I remember it 'cause it's a soldier."

"Yeah? So?"

"I was sure it had legs before."

Vick and the others stopped and studied the dead body for a moment, perched on top of the rest and partially covered by a thin dusting of frost. The legs were gone at mid-thigh, leaving only ragged chunks of frozen meat.

"Looks . . . gnawed on," Amy observed. "Not like the others."

"Dogs, maybe?" Vick suggested.

"Haven't seen a dog in a year. Sure as hell haven't seen one around here," Buckle said.

"What else could it be, then?" Amy asked.

"We got other things to worry about right now. Let's keep on," Vick said. "Get moving. Don't like just standing here wasting daylight."

They left the corpse, but Scott lingered. Something about the missing legs disturbed him. Eventually, he turned and saw Amy waiting for him. They walked through the half-pipe of wrecked and gun-blasted flesh, and Scott was once again amazed at how much damage the zombies had absorbed, yet they had still been able to advance to the inner defenses.

But the body with the chewed off legs continued to bother him.

It brought up another mystery, one unsolved, back in the valley. In Annapolis.

He stepped in close to Amy as they passed through the mess of frozen dead. "I need to talk to you about something."

She half-turned. "Can it wait?"

He supposed it could. "Yeah."

Then they were through it all. They didn't stop at their demolished van, nor did they turn up what a sign declared as Morris Street. Scott kept quiet as they marched toward a T-intersection and what looked to be a huge building that had taken an explosive round right through the front. The rooftop was charred and blackened. Not a window in the place was intact.

A choice loomed up as the road came to an end—left or right. Another sign read TERMINAL ROAD.

Underneath his motorcycle helmet, half of Scott's face hitched up in a sorry smile.

To his surprise, Vick and Buckle turned right and headed up Terminal Road. Scott and Amy followed at a comfortable distance.

Then he saw the dead, about forty or so. Stragglers compared to what he had seen before, but more than enough to be a problem.

The men stalked them as if they were a couple of gunslingers instead of virus survivors, not disguising their movements in the least. Their heads flicked right and left, studying the perpendicular street. Amy's right hand fluttered in a *come on* gesture, and he followed. Together, they closed the gap between the pair of men.

"What are they doing?" Scott whispered.

"Picking a fight," she murmured.

On cue, Buckle's Halligan bar came up while Vick raised his length of steel pipe. There was a gap between the walking corpses, delivery men and hotel staff still in their decomposing uniforms. Some of the white clothing had turned black from wounds that no mortal could have survived. Huge chunks of flesh were torn of out some of the zombies, while others had been disemboweled and feasted upon until only a black cavity remained. Scott glimpsed backbones, shifting as the dead shambled about without direction.

Buckle and Vick went into dead mode, adopting limps and shuffling through the forty or so gimps filling the street. They waded into them as if crossing a deep river, heading toward an open parking lot across the road surrounded by three buildings. Scott and Amy entered the small mob just as the men reached the lot. Why were they heading into what looked to be a dead end?

Something bumped into him, and Scott rolled with the solid connection as if drunk. Another hard hit and he pulled away from it, alarm creeping in. A zombie had paused and seemed to be considering Amy's form just ahead.

A hand came down on Scott's arm.

The deadhead reached out with all the gentleness of a grandmother's touch, and Scott had enough of an angle to see a woman, stick thin and wearing the remains of an exercise suit. Two huge, seemingly cracked cue balls filled her orbital cavities, and Scott saw she had no eyelids. Or cheek flesh, for that matter. Black skin tags festered around a mouth that badly needed to be wiped.

He brushed her aside, but a moan chased him. Other gimps turned. Something was wrong, he realized with surging fright. They weren't buying the act. Moe *knew* there was something about him, and some primitive intelligence urged them to bump him, to touch him, to see if there was a reaction.

Ahead and well inside the parking lot, Vick and Buckle turned around and stood like a two-man wall. Amy pushed ahead, still walking like a corpse and trailing three curious souls. Something tugged on Scott's poncho, and any moment he feared he'd hear the jogger behind him shriek *"Meat!"* and that would be that.

Vick dragged the tip of his steel pipe across a strip of bare asphalt, making a death rattle that startled Scott.

Suddenly, the hand on Scott's poncho was gone. Moans and hisses cut the air from the zombies around him, alerting the rest of the pack. Zombies lurched toward the two men, who were no longer imitating the dead. Amy slowly held out an arm until her hand touched Scott's padded midsection, making him slow all the more and keeping him out of the parking lot. His fingers clenched his bat. Scott wanted to ask what was happening when Vick's steel pipe crashed down on a gimp's skull, a second before Buckle whipped his Halligan bar across the face of another. The deadheads clattered to the ground, and the two men swung again. Buckle thrust with the claw of the firefighter's tool, taking the tops off decomposed skulls like they were old aluminum cans.

But the one who truly made Scott stand and gawk in utter zombie fashion, the one who ripped a swath of destruction through the moldering ranks of Moe, was Vick.

Wielding the pipe as if it were a sword, Vick ducked and weaved, cranking his weapon and smashing faces, the sides of skulls, even taking a head completely off at the shoulders. Steel and armored arms batted aside limbs that reached for him. One Moe had its arm twisted up and torn from its socket a second before a spiked fist knocked it off its feet. Vick jabbed his pipe between legs, upending corpses and building a barrier between himself and the deadheads. He crunched three heads in the span of two or three seconds with all of the grace of a samurai, then he was killing *more*.

But Moe didn't falter.

Moe advanced.

Vick suddenly went down, and a wide group of undead collapsed a second later as if the entire front ranks had tripped. Then the man's armored form loomed up from the ground, somehow trapping limbs with his own and snapping them like kindling. The pipe started humming in the air loud enough that Scott heard it through his helmet. He understood then why Amy had kept him back.

It wasn't for safety.

It was to *watch*.

The length of steel split air and decaying flesh. Zombies attempting to get over their brothers on the ground had their heads bashed in. Vick stomped on the skulls of anything moving at his feet and speared the cut end of the pipe through brainpans in startling crunches of bone that reminded Scott of cracking eggshells. The last corpse reaching for the martial artist had its arms pushed aside before being tripped. It fell to the ground, and Vick drove his boot through its face.

"Jesus," Scott whispered in awe. "The man's Bruce Lee."

Amy tugged on his wrist, leading him out of the street and into a parking lot that had once been empty, but was now full of bodies—all gone in no more than a minute. Buckle crouched over one and scooped out black innards. Scott only gave him a second's attention before switching back to Vick.

"What the hell was *that?*" he asked, remembering at the last moment to keep his voice low.

"That was Vick keeping the peace," Amy informed him.

"Time to get covered up now," Vick huffed in a strained voice. He gestured to where Buckle stood, his hands full of dark viscera.

"Come and get it 'fore I throw it out," Buckle said. Amy stepped up, and Buckle wasted no time splashing her front and back.

"Go on," Vick told Scott. "Get some on you. Moe won't be picking up on you with a fresh coat."

Scott did as he was told, catching an unholy whiff of raw guts and marvelling over how smell could stop a person in their tracks. Buckle retrieved more guts from another unmoving deadhead and, with one last flourish, slapped an oily gob on the side of Scott's head. He felt the impact through his helmet. He hadn't known the man for long, but he thought Buckle was taking his work a little too eagerly.

"You wanted the guts?" he asked.

"Uh-huh," Buckle said. "Needed the fresh stuff. Although it's really kinda chunky with the cold and all."

Scott saw the plan. "You guys lured them back here, off the main road. Got them out of sight to butcher them."

"That's right," Buckle said, motioning him to step aside so he could touch up Vick's protective coating.

"Vick's been teaching and doing martial arts for thirty years," Amy informed him. "Third degree black belt Tae Kwon Do, Second Degree Kempo, a little Black Dragon Kung Fu, a touch of Brazilian Jiu Jitsu, and exotic weapons training."

"How do you know all this?" Scott asked.

"He's my teacher," she said simply. "I got all the goods on him. I'll tell you about him sometime. It's interesting stuff. If you like MMA, that is. You should see him when he has a pair of Sai in his hands."

"Your teacher?" Scott blurted, computing the rest.

"For twenty years."

His voice didn't work anymore. "How old are you, again?"

"Not supposed to ask a girl her age, nerd."

Scott balked at that, but before he could say anything, he noted that Vick was ensuring that Buckle got zombie guts on his back.

"Stunnin', eh?" Buckle asked Scott.

"Not the words I'd use. I didn't even see you after . . . that."

"Just as well. I'm not near as graceful as the man here. Deadly Vicky."

Vick stopped for a moment, regarded the Newfoundlander, and shook his head before continuing to paint him, a little more aggressively this time.

"What was it you do again?" Scott asked Buckle.

"Shoot shit."

"Oh."

"When I have the equipment, that is."

Vick slapped Buckle's shoulder, letting him know all was done. They gathered up their weapons and stood in a loose square for a moment, very much aware of the stillness.

"Buckle comes from a long line of professional snipers. Ain't that right?" Vick asked.

"Yeah," Buckle said, indifferent. "How you feelin'?"

Vick shrugged. "Not bad. Still getting my wind back. Getting old's shitty."

"Vick's not as young as he used to be," Amy stated.

"Don't have to be young to kick the shit out of Moe. Just got to be careful, is all." Vick looked at Scott. "You hear me?"

"I do," he answered. He remembered Amy's words from not so long ago. *Well, you're one of the lucky ones. Which is to say, very lucky.*

He didn't realize just *how* lucky he'd been up to this point, especially to find these people, until now.

"All right, listen now," Vick directed at him. "You've done this before with Amy. Ain't no different today. Got that?"

"Got it," Scott answered, suddenly bursting with respect for the older man.

"You stay in a box formation. Buckle and I will be in the front. We'll head straight through the city, back to where you parked, and not one of those fuckers will know the difference. Just act dead. Or like you've just downed a case of Moosehead."

Beer. Scott suddenly wished he had a bottle.

"You ready, smartass?" Vick asked Buckle.

"Born ready, me son."

"How about you, hell-child?"

"Ready," Amy said.

"All right, then," Vick said with satisfaction. "The walk in the park is over. We've done this before, and we're doing it today. Got a ride to catch, a city to leave behind, and an island resort waiting for us. And if I have my way, I intend on getting shit-faced on cocktails with little umbrellas in 'em. Let's *do* this."

With that, Vick marched back out into the street, and the rest of them followed.

24

Freshly coated with Moe's slushy innards, the four of them reached a *South Street* sign. Old fashioned brick and mortar buildings stood on the right, somehow eluding the fire show the Army had laid down in an effort to subdue Moe. A white unblemished field of snow with a few lonely swings and slides lay across the way from the houses, the centerpiece an artsy aqua-green statue. Scott was taken by how the city might have once looked in the summer. If only.

Ice glazed the slope they marched up, slippery in places, causing them to stumble. Drifts had been visibly beaten down by gimps no longer in sight. A yellow Victorian-style three-story building came into view on the right, perhaps a hotel. A short stairway led to a wide porch, complete with green lawn chairs. The soft squeals of metal and wood joints gave them pause.

Scott blinked in surprise.

A gimp, dressed in a formal grey suit and sporting a resplendent red tie, sat on the porch in a lover's swing. The thing rocked itself gently, facing the street, baring the leering, lipless smile of a ghoul that might have just fed. Black eyes, which Scott wasn't entirely sure were there, stared off into space, ignoring them as they shuffled past. The creature remained rooted to the chair. Scott believed the dead man would soon stop rocking, get to its feet with all the elegance of someone clawing their way out of a grave, and bellow at them. Except it wouldn't come out as words, it would only come out in that frightening hiss of frayed vocal chords.

But it didn't.

The well-dressed zombie stayed in its summer swing, rocking itself while staring over their heads. The creaking of the rusty joints stayed with them as they passed in front of the porch, then gradually died away.

They continued walking, leaving the watcher in the swing and passing through an intersection. The grade of the road increased, and Scott thought for a moment of the hills back in New Brunswick and the thrill of sliding over them in the wintertime. The memory faded as quickly as it had popped into his mind. In ones and twos, deadheads wandered around discarded cars parked on sidewalks, heedless of the disguised living passing by. Keeping in formation, they crossed over Barrington Street and continued to plod up the incline. Scott felt a light trickle of sweat down his back and armpits, not entirely the result of walking. Gruesome displays of reanimated flesh caught his attention, and he struggled for a moment to keep his head pointed straight ahead. The dead came in all shapes and sizes, and he didn't think he'd ever get used to them. Scott was ever so thankful for the visor and ragged T-shirt concealing his face.

He focused on the hill.

The burn seeped into his calves like hot poison trying to slow him down. The others marched on without any visible effort, and he strove to keep pace. Coming into Halifax had been easy, he realized. It was all practically flat or downhill, with only a few exceptions. Escaping the waterfront was something different. They passed houses, some still in livable condition, others suffering. Three houses in a row had gone up in a fire and lay covered in snow, the remains of structural beams sticking out of the main floor like charred spears.

Ahead, Buckle bumped into a zombie and knocked it to the ground. The thing fell flat on its back and, when Scott reached it, it flailed its withered arms and legs about as if puzzling over the best way to stand. More zombies filled the street, drifting into sight from driveways like sea mines pulled free of their rusty moorings. One gimp, a business man, walked toward Vick, its dead hips swaying as if it were working the hell out of an invisible hula hoop. It missed Vick by inches, and Scott noted Amy slowed her pace just enough to allow the zombie to walk in front of her. More zombies appeared on the crest of the hill, their vague, grey shapes slowly coalescing as they drew closer. Another gimp had half of his neck chewed into, right down to the segmented bone. Two grandmothers pulled themselves along the ground with feeble tugs, and one was near enough to Scott to graze his ankle with a spider's touch. More horrors came into view, some hanging around the doorways of the houses lining both sides of the street, while others simply walked past.

They plodded to the top of the hill and continued walking. Amy slid toward him, closing the distance between them just as he saw the graveyard on the right through a fence of iron bars. The dead shuffled amongst snowcapped headstones and elaborate marble crosses. Hundreds of the things took halting steps, seemingly headed in no real direction. A barrier of cars and trucks lined the streets, cocooned by snow drifts not yet beaten down by the meandering dead. A row of brown brick apartment buildings stood on the opposite side of the street. Scott's breath caught in his throat when a figure fell ten stories, rags fluttering savagely in the descent, to burst upon white concrete with the sound of a dried-up watermelon.

They walked by the gimp and saw it was a boy. It whimpered once like a lonely dog.

Scott felt his breathing increase. His anxiety swelled. Halifax started to close in about him. The gimps knew who he was. They *knew*. And they were making a bee-line for him. He slowed in his tracks and grimaced against the rising panic in his lower legs and chest. *Not again . . .*

Something bumped him on his right.

Amy's hand closed about his and squeezed. Her shoulder felt firm against him. Like a soothing rock, the contact brought him back. He closed his eyes a few times, only opening them to ensure Vick and Buckle were still ahead. Forcing slow breaths into lungs that wanted much, much more, he squeezed her hand back. A silent *I'm okay.*

Neither of them released the other.

Bonded, they crept along the street, walking as stiffly as anything just risen from the grave. Scott took a few moments to compose himself, closing his eyes and allowing Amy to guide him. A weight brushed against his side, but he ignored it. The smell of the dead seemed to penetrate his every pore until each breath was an invasion. But he kept walking and did not let go of Amy's hand.

After a few moments he opened his eyes, defeating the panic attack for a second time and wondering why the hell they were happening to him *now*. After so long living with the dead, the day-to-day survival and risking his own life, why *now*? Then it hit him. It was as obvious as the bodies moving about him.

He was *amongst* them, trying to keep his life a secret from an army of predators—a goldfish swimming in a river full of piranha. He watched Vick and Buckle as they eased through the zombies. Some bumped into the two men, but they absorbed the impact or rolled with it. Neither stopped.

The memory of Amy's voice came back to him. *You're one of the lucky ones.*

Two years of being on the run from these things. Two years. Scott felt a touch of chagrin then, which burned away any lingering anxiety. He had stayed *alive* for *two fucking years*. That wasn't luck.

That was skill.

With that realization, he mentally armored himself against any further panic attacks and let go of Amy's hand.

To his surprise, she didn't let go of his.

He didn't dwell on it and closed his fingers upon hers. Around them, the zombies moved in the same direction.

That last thought stayed with him and sunk into his brain. *The zombies were heading in the* same *direction.* Scott slowed and eventually stopped, pulling Amy to a questioning halt. He turned into her, bumping her with his chest, and looked back the way they had come.

He felt his skin crawl when he saw the flow of gimps moving up the street, *away* from the waterfront. Even the zombies that were bleeding out into the main drag from side avenues weren't heading toward the waterfront. They shambled in the same direction as the rest, almost as if some unseen barrier prevented them from turning toward the harbor.

They're tidal, he'd heard Gus say, but this struck Scott as something else. This *had* to be something else. The street resembled a mass of bomb-blasted refugees fleeing their homes before the next wave of shells hit.

Amy tugged on his hand and this time he relented. They turned back into the stream and moved with it. Vick and Buckle were far ahead, but Scott stood tall and spotted the two men doing their best to blend in. He watched Moe from the corners of his eyes, wondering what was going on in those black brains. What was spurring them on to apparently mass evacuate an area? Did they possess a sense to detect impending disaster, like dogs seconds before earthquakes? Did that mean that, on some microscopic level, the creatures were still alive?

Scott prepared himself for the worst. One thing was certain—he dared not do anything to appear remotely *alive* amongst the horde.

To do so would get him and Amy ripped to pieces.

25

While four of the living retreated from the Halifax waterfront, Tenner marched down the white slope of Citadel Hill, making no bones about the fact that he was alive. Arrogant? Perhaps. Stupid? Hardly. *Defiant* was more like it. This was his world. Here, he was God. The corpses were beneath him, little more than dogs gone wild. He feared the undead no more than houseflies.

He trudged over the hill, seeing corpses lurking around car wrecks and abandoned vehicles. Upon reaching a low metal fence, he lifted one leg and then the other and dropped six feet to the snow-covered sidewalk. His head held high, Tenner reached Duke Street. The roof of the Halifax Metro Center had been devastated by artillery fire. Around him, the wearisome, all too familiar moans sounded in his wake.

If they truly wanted a taste of him, they'd have a fight on their hands.

He drew his Glocks, having already racked their slides. On his right, a woman staggered into daylight from an open door of the Metro Center's parking lots. Beyond her, more shadows followed. The woman opened a mouth that looked stretched. She fixed onto him with eyes that had been gouged from her face and left crushed on her cheeks.

Tenner casually took aim and put a round into her forehead, snapping her head back and jerking her off her feet as if abruptly clotheslined. She landed with a clatter as he walked on, mindful of the side streets and any potential threats lurking there. He marched past the Scotia Square Mall, not bothering to go inside. Such places were ripe with Moe. Perhaps even more than that, he thought, remembering a tunnel swarming with ragged rats.

A zombie rose up from behind an SUV parked under a dead streetlight. Tenner blew its black brains out, splashing a wall as white as porcelain. Corpses slapped their limbs against the glass doors leading into the mall, trying to attract his attention for just a few more seconds. The crosswalk ahead of him was empty one moment, then a handful of zombies skittered into view, slipping on ice slicked pavement. A boy of perhaps fifteen got within an arm's length of Tenner when the Glock cracked and sheared away a chunk of skull and scalp. He shot another gimp at close range, the front and back of its head exploding instantly.

The others he allowed to follow him—if they dared.

Above him loomed a pedway connecting two business buildings, their signs blasted away by gunfire. Two empty machine gun emplacements were up there, pointed at the sky. Tenner proceeded under the concrete connector. Something crashed into the streets behind him and he turned to see a soldier, encased in full combat gear, pushing itself up from the pavement. The dozen or so zombies following were almost upon the soldier. The armored corpse got to its knees, black viscera hanging from a hole that was once a mouth. Individual teeth gleamed like oily pearls.

As long as they were behind him, all was fine. If they got in his way, he'd ruin them with extreme prejudice.

He turned right at Hollis Street and aimed himself at Purdy's Wharf like a laser. No zombies sought to stop him. He halted and glanced around. He remembered putting down a few Philistines on this street, but their unmoving husks were nowhere to be seen.

The soldier zombie dragged itself in pursuit, rattling something off the street. Tenner turned around and switched his firing modes on both guns. The sound would no doubt alert anyone around, but he didn't care. He'd kill them as well.

He opened fire with the Glocks, and brains pollinated the air in violent puffs of inky white. He brought the twin hand cannons side by side, exploding heads like lines of cheap light bulbs overloaded with electricity, then spread them apart once more.

The soldier staggered back until it fell, and Tenner saw that the helmet protected its head. He stepped forward and jammed one barrel underneath the destroyed chin of the infantryman. When he pulled the trigger, the sound of the shell ricocheting off the inside of the helmet reminded him of the muffled clanging of pots and pans. The soldier dropped dead in the street, and Tenner waited for anything else to come at him.

Nothing did.

He listened and heard only the diminishing buzz of the Glocks. Once again dead bodies lay splayed out in the street, and something odd occurred to Tenner. Certainly there were a few zombies lingering in the zone the Army had established, but there were large bodies of roaming corpses just beyond Citadel Hill. Amy had even reported that sections of Barrington had been swamped with the reanimated dead. How many soldiers had been in the area? The numbers made him question the true population of Halifax at the time the virus broke out.

However many there had been, they had *not* returned to this area. They kept clear of the waterfront almost entirely. Was the reason for this aversion the devastation wrought by the Army fortified here? Possible, but that would mean the things were capable of thinking—not that that meant anything to him either way.

Then he considered the rats.

Could they have anything to do with the undead avoiding the area?

Or be responsible for the disappearing corpses?

The memory of stumbling in the tunnel and feeling their claws upon him made him contemplate the rats once more. Did they pose a bigger threat than what he was allowing for? He placed his back against the stone wall of a historical building and peered across the street at Purdy's Wharf. Time was a-wasting.

The floor and room designated as the meeting area could be seen from the street, and Tenner had no trouble seeing the bullet holes he'd made earlier. He intended to do a lot worse. Checking the area once more, he holstered his side arms and got out the AR-20. He trained it on the window. He took a breath and bolted out from his position, racing across the open space while keeping an eye on the building's face.

The front entryway to Purdy's Wharf came into view and he went through, ran to the stairway, and chugged upward in relative darkness, keeping one shoulder against the wall for both guidance and support. The heavy armor slowed him noticeably.

Moments later, he entered the floor where the others had set up their base camp, half-expecting to meet Bowman once again. He dropped to a knee and pointed his rifle down the dark corridor, the gloom pierced by light from the windows inside the rooms. He couldn't hear anyone, but his helmet and hood restricted his hearing somewhat. A draft made a notice on the wall flutter ever so slightly. Tenner watched the paper for a while before getting to his feet, proceeding with extreme caution.

He paused for a second at each open doorway before swinging inward barrel-first, ready to fire or grant mercy—for a little while, anyway. Tenner noticed he was sweating. Excitement coursed through his person, and he struggled to control his breathing. He remembered a time back in Windsor, Ontario, in an old house he had converted into a private little abattoir, where he'd deposit unconscious prostitutes after hiring them and finally chloroforming them. He wasn't sure how the police found the house, or who had tipped them off, but the OPP were there in force on a Friday, busting both doors and charging in like human trains armed with submachine guns. Tenner had arrived perhaps twenty minutes later, on his mountain bike of all things, opting that day to leave behind the car he usually used. He watched the home invasion from behind the police lines. There hadn't been any guests in the house at the time of the forceful entry, but Tenner knew there was probably plenty of evidence.

But what he'd wondered about, from an officer's point of view, was the *rush* of invading a house, the adrenaline high from not knowing what might be lurking inside. He suspected it was probably almost as good as the release he got from tenderizing his victims with a sledgehammer.

Now he knew. Potential danger lurked behind every corner. He checked each room before proceeding to the next. A couple of times he thought he heard something and pulled back to the corridor to wait, only long enough to calm his warning tingles. He reached the main office where the others had slung their gore-soaked outerwear, then the rooms of each individual. Equipment was missing. Food was missing from the MRE storage area. By the time he got to the office where they'd held meetings, he knew his prey had vanished. Poor old Sam lay stiff and cooling on the floor, covered with his own coat.

Tenner crouched near the dead man's head and pulled back the death shroud. He inspected his handiwork and smiled slowly. Ol' Sam had got off easy. If he'd had the chance to do what he'd *wanted* to do to him . . .

"You hear me?" Tenner whispered, peering into the destroyed face. "You got off lucky. Damn lucky, Sam my son. You'll see. When I send the others over. You'll understand."

"They're wise to you, Joe," Sam whispered, causing Tenner's forehead to knot. It wasn't often his victims spoke back to him, but it happened sometimes. Sam wasn't a zombie, just a lingering shade drawn to the power of the Almighty, hoping to get a few last words in before traveling on to oblivion. Or so Tenner suspected.

"I know that." Tenner *pshawed*. "Tell me something I don't know."

"They're getting out of Halifax, Joe. They're leaving the city to you. Want no part of it."

"Really?"

"Figure you'll die here. Chewed up like a dog's toy."

Tenner smirked. These dead fuckers got mouthy in the afterlife.

"You hear me, Joe? You might've got me, got me good, but you won't do them. They're too smart for you. Too quick. Too dangerous, now. You really think you could take on Vick bare knuckle? *Amy*, even?"

That wiped the smile off Tenner's face. Without a word, he placed the mouth of the assault rifle to Sam's face.

"Killing me a second time won't—"

He squeezed the trigger and disintegrated Sam's head. Sam didn't speak after that, which suited Tenner just fine. He lingered a few seconds more, idly studying the mess on the floor. He got to his feet and looked at the window, examining the spidery dots ventilating the room. He remembered that shot. Took it on the run and still got it right. Didn't get anyone else apparently, but that was fine by him. Tenner didn't want to shoot them all.

Not if he could get his knives on them.

They're getting out of Halifax, Sam had said. That meant by van. Tenner smiled. The van was beyond the wall. It felt right. They'd gone there first thing, no doubt.

"Take it easy, Sammy," Tenner said and left the room. Minutes later he was walking briskly down Water Street. He kept the AR-20's stock braced against his shoulder, ready to pull up and blast something if needed. When he reached the bus barricade and the ramp, he noticed the body with the missing legs. Could the rats have been responsible for that?

His boots clattered on the top of the bus and, for a moment, he considered the street of corpses ahead. There was an awful lot of meat in this area, an awful lot of meat that had been around for a while. Aboveground no less, which meant the rats were no doubt crawling to the surface to feed. Holding onto his rifle, Tenner suddenly had a very bad feeling about the place. Underground, left unchecked, with a readily accessible food supply, how could the virus *not* have jumped from the corpses to the rats?

"Well, well," Tenner breathed as he completed a full three-sixty. "Might just be something worse than Philistines in town."

With that, he chugged down the other side of the barricade and along the street, no longer wanting to be anywhere near such a large stockpile of frozen dinners.

Minutes later he arrived at the wreck of the van. The booby-trapped hood had gone off just the way he'd hoped. Brown boxes of clearly-marked MREs lay in the back, untouched, and that was fine by him. He'd get them later. Looking around, he spotted tracks leading to a car. There he found a charred Shaffer.

"Hello, Mr. Shaffer," Tenner purred, gazing down at the burnt body scrunched up on the back seat. "Best not to lay around this neighborhood. Think we got a rat problem. No . . . I mean a *rat problem*. Hm? What's that? Sure, stay here if you like. Not me, though. I got some business with your buddies."

He paused for a moment, allowing Shaffer to speak. Unlike Sammy, Shaffer was exceptionally quiet. Perhaps he somehow knew about Sammy? The dead liked to blab.

"No friends of yours, eh?" That made Tenner smile. "I knew there was some friction between you and Buckle there, but I kinda got the impression you liked Amy, in your own way. And that ass? Oh *my*. Well! You're dead now, so . . ." he shrugged dramatically, "what the hell, right? What's that? Get them? Wow."

Tenner chuckled. The dead were also out to fuck up the living.

"Spiteful bastard, ain't ya? Just so you know, I do intend to get them. And I fully plan to send them your way, piece by piece. So you just relax. Stay comfortable. Tell you what—you watch my back and, when I get back this way, I'll make it so the rats don't get you."

Shaffer started speaking again, but Tenner left him. Truth be known, he couldn't stand the man's guts, either.

Tenner took a few steps into the street and studied the ground. He chuckled. The jig would soon be up, he supposed, knowing what the remaining foursome might find if they stuck to the roads. He'd told them not to venture into *that* part of the city. It was for their own good—or so he'd said. It was all for him. They'd soon discover Bowman. Tenner wished he could see their faces when they did. No doubt they were making good time with those shit-rags they'd peeled off the dead and wore like suits. The very thought made him curl his lips in distaste. No one would catch him wearing such filth.

Tenner started walking and glanced at the skies. It would be dark soon.

And oh how he wanted to get his hands on the living.

26

Walking like he was death cooked over by an industrial-grade torch, Buckle didn't feel so good. In fact, he felt like shit. His nose was broken, and what was worse, the gobs of blanket that he had stuffed into his nostrils had become saturated with blood again. He'd changed the wad when they'd returned for their gear at Purdy's Wharf, but he feared the replacement had long since reached its capacity. Thinking on it further as he walked down a street filled with dead things out for a late after-noon stroll, he decided that his nose *had* to have stopped bleeding. Except he was *tasting* it when he breathed through his mouth. Moe smelled like cold shit, even with the mask on, but this mix of his own blood and decaying flesh was getting to him. He figured it must've started bleeding during the last fight, remembering some-thing popping in his nose when he swung his pipe. He wanted to swap the wad of blanket around his nostrils for another strip he had in his pocket, but he certainly couldn't do it here. The thought of even attempting something so stupid almost made him chuckle.

Then he saw the body in the street.

Well, shit. No doubt the others had seen the corpse. There wasn't any way to miss it; it was right there. Tenner had been busy. The interesting thing was, they had come to Halifax to see if they could find a number of things in the city. Vick and Amy had thought it a good idea to risk it, and he liked listening to them far more than that shithead Shaffer. Buckle didn't mind taking orders. He'd made a career of taking orders while he was with the RCMP in Clarenville, and he'd carried on with it willingly enough when he transferred over to Halifax. Besides, after living in Halifax for almost twenty years, Vick had become his oldest and best friend. What made things even easier was that Vick knew what was what.

But he had to admit, both Vick and Amy had messed up when they'd allowed Tenner to join the group. Twenty-five years on the force counted for something, and his age had only sharpened his bullshit detector. That was one thing that had stayed intact when the dead started pulling themselves up from the grave. *Oh, yuh.* That piece of equipment worked just fine, just like the twelve gauge dangling between his legs. When Tenner had heard he was a cop, Buckle had caught the sudden tensing around the man's mouth, the subtle narrowing of his eyes, and the smallest of pauses followed by long-winded bullshit answers to the most innocuous questions. Buckle wondered if the others had noticed how Tenner would leave the room after just a few inquiries. Even when he'd gone to bring Tenner back to the main office there, just before Scott pulled the Ruger—he'd recognized the make right away, but had no idea where he'd gotten the silencer, unless it was a custom job—he had tried too hard to be cool.

No, sir. It had once been Buckle's job to sniff out bullshit, and Tenner was a walking pile of it.

Trouble was, Buckle had made the mistake of underestimating the scope of Tenner's crimes. He'd thought the man was a criminal in the old world, maybe with gangland connections or a jacker of sorts, even. He couldn't have proved anything, but he'd decided he could keep an eye on the man.

But a goddamn *killer*?

Moe walking about wasn't the only way the world was still fucked up.

And now this.

There was a dead man in the middle of the street. He wasn't one of their group. In fact, if Buckle had to guess, he'd hazard Tenner'd been lying out of his ass when he'd spoken of not finding any other survivors in the city. There was at least one person left, and woe to him that the likes of Tenner had found him.

Vick didn't slow down, and that was all right with Buckle. He'd seen worse. Once, as a first responder back on the island, he'd come across a poor bastard who had run into a moose on the highway in the dead of night. Moose crossings on the highways were always a danger, and the driver—a young guy in his twenties out of Gander—had driven his sedan right under the tall spindly legs of the animal, taking two of them clean off and plowing into its seven hundred kilogram wreaking ball of a body. The moose had crashed through the driver's windshield and mashed the youngster's face and head into a bloody pulp. The worst part was that the man's face, flattened and blackened as it had been, could still be identified.

That had been the worst incident in Buckle's twenty-five year career. Not even the people he'd *shot* had looked as bad as that dead man whose head had been squished by sixteen hundred pounds of freefalling meat.

But this one was bad.

A transport truck had rammed into the base of a power pole, bending the whole thing over another car. A corpse hung from the pole at an awkward angle, which was painful to look upon. Extension cords and duct tape kept the body in place. Moe had ravaged the poor bastard's lower extremities, eating him right down to the grisly bones. There wasn't even any flesh on his face. The footprints on the car hood suggested Moe had got up there to finish chowing down. The frost and snow on the remains informed Buckle the man had died a while ago. Tenner had done whatever to his victim, probably gagging him—or worse—then left him in the street. He and his fellow officers had learned never to ask for details. No good ever came of it. Right, ready, and served up for Moe. And Moe had partaken. Buckle had to consciously refrain from opening his mouth and cutting loose with what all cops eventually acquired—very morbid humor.

Buckle eyed the remains as they slipped into his peripheral vision, then finally slipped away behind him. He restrained himself from stopping in the street, amongst innumerable undead, and investigating the body just a smidgen longer. Even the thought brought a mental rebuke that he deserved. He hadn't even been an investigator at the end of the world.

Just ahead, not ten feet away and closing, Moe was studying him.

In fact, Moe—a dude decked out in what looked to be a power linesman's neon yellow work suit—was standing right in front of Buckle. Worse—never ask how worse—the thing regarded him as if it was out for a just *loverly* stroll along the graveyard and suddenly remembered something. Only it hadn't just remembered something, it seemed to have recognized Buckle for what he was. This particular Moe had its scalp removed right down to its Cro-Magnon brow. One ear hung off the side of its head like a fleshy, albeit shrivelled, decoration. And its eyes, grey and blazing with bright recognition, were locked onto Buckle.

It knows! his mind shrieked, despite the T-shirt hanging over his riot visor. *The blood. It smells the blood!*

When the creature was five strides away, Buckle angled the Halligan bar, held in both hands, so he could spear the thing through the skull.

One of Moe's hands came up, only it wasn't a hand; it was a creamy knob of bone where a hand should have been attached to the wrist.

Buckle pulled back his Halligan. Perhaps if he stabbed the zombie under the chin and left it there, he might still be able to—

Phewp.

The Moe's head exploded, and Buckle knew it had just caught a bullet. The zombie crumpled to the ground, and the march went on without him. Buckle resisted the urge to look behind him because, if he did, there was no doubt he'd see an arm still stretched out, holding onto a silenced Ruger.

Donny Buckle reminded himself to thank Scott the first chance he got.

The current of undead carried the four survivors past the graveyard, a parking lot full of snow-covered cars, the Canadian Cancer Society building, the IWK Health Centre, and several apartment buildings. As daylight diminished, they shuffled past Robie Street, and Scott thanked God when Vick began to alter his course, turning toward Buckle on his left. The Newfoundlander caught the movement and stopped in his tracks. Deadheads moved by in an ever present stream, but the four of them made their way to a two-story house on the left, situated not seven feet off the main drag. It was white with a short railed fence surrounding a deck right on the doorstep. Vick stepped to the front door and, very carefully, tried the knob. It opened with a click.

Vick stepped inside. Buckle placed his back against the frame, standing guard until Scott and Amy entered. Then he backed inside and closed the door, shutting out the trailing voices.

Once inside, they did not immediately relax. They crammed inside a short entryway filled with shoes and sneakers. Vick went further into the house, disappearing from sight. Amy pointed to a set of stairs, and Scott nodded. Bringing up the Ruger, he took the stairs two at a time as quietly as possible, pausing once when he heard the clatter of metal on bone coming from the kitchen. Scott reached the landing and rapped his fingers on the wall, then waited. Nothing. He quickly searched through an upstairs bathroom and three empty bedrooms. He came out of the master bedroom and saw Amy standing guard on the landing.

"Clear."

Scott joined her and saw Buckle pulling the curtain across the window by the front door. Once that was done, he did the same to the living room curtains, covering up a picture window facing the street.

"All clear," Vick stated below. Amy slouched and descended the stairs. Scott followed her. They both dropped onto a huge sofa, which squeaked under their weight.

Buckle sat down in a nearby matching chair, while Vick simply collapsed and stretched out on the floor.

"Hey," Buckle said, his mask turning in Scott's direction. "Thank you for out there."

"You're welcome. What happened, anyway?"

"Figured it smelled the blood from my nose. Just zeroed in on me."

"Saw that, too," Amy added. "It was scary how it did that. Lucky there weren't more. You better get that taken care of before we go back out there tomorrow."

"I'll do it right now," Buckle said and got to it.

"Tomorrow?" Scott asked, looking at Amy.

"Tomorrow," Vick said. "We're not going anywhere at night. Here's where we board up, rest up, and in the morning, ship out."

"Did you see what was happening out there?" Scott asked, feeling his tension slip away. It felt good to be able to let his guard down, even if it was just for a little while.

"You mean Moe? Walking the other way?" Amy asked.

"Yeah."

"Yeah," Vick stressed. "What's up with that? That was freaky. And I'd thought I'd gotten used to freaky—after seeing dead people eat people and all."

"They were walking away from the waterfront," Scott said. "Just walking."

"Still are," Buckle reported. He had hooked the curtain back a little and peeked out at the road. "Like there's a town meeting somewhere."

"Where're they going?" Vick asked.

"I think the more important question is why?" Amy stated. "They've never done anything on a scale like this before, and I agree with Vick. It's creepy. I mean, they're usually drawn by noise and smell, but I didn't hear anything."

"Then there was that poor bastard in the street," Vick said and looked at Buckle. "And that flesh-eating banana that almost took a run at you."

Buckle grimaced and dabbed a fresh cloth about his nose.

The sofa was seductive and, with one weary effort, Scott pulled off his poncho and headgear and plopped it on the floor, wrinkling his face. *Nasty business*, he thought, and got even more comfortable.

"We'll have to keep an eye on it," Amy said. Her voice sounded distant to him. "Because I don't like it in the least. If they're moving away from the waterfront, there has to be a reason. That's *a lot* of Moe out there. Lots of shit can happen in a crowd that size. If we're unlucky, if something happens and we get separated, we need some-place to link up. I say we meet up at Scott's house on School Avenue."

"Agreed," Vick said.

"Right on," Buckle added.

"Scott?"

But Scott was asleep.

Amy studied the blond giant for a while before settling back into the sofa, the faintest of smiles on her round face, her blue eyes reflective. Vick smiled inwardly. He'd known that girl since her father had first brought her into his Tae Kwon Do academy when she was ten, and though he would never say it, he thought of her not only as his finest student, but the daughter he'd never had. He figured he knew her just as well as she knew herself, and certainly as well as her parents had, if not better. He knew the side of Amy that her mom and dad didn't get to see—the competitive side. The work ethic. The intellect she'd certainly displayed with her university schooling. Vick knew first-hand how quick she was to pick up on things, how voracious her appetite to learn. She had learned her first forms in a week and earned her yellow belt in two months. Orange in another two, all culminating in a black belt at age twelve, and that was only because he'd intentionally slowed her progress. She'd come into a young man's school that was barely making ends meet and stayed with him for years to learn all that an aging Vick Tucker had to teach. He knew that Amy didn't get frustrated easily; she flowed with events as supple as water.

He also knew when Amy liked something.

And he could see, just by the barest of pauses that so many people would misinterpret as nothing at all, that Amy Jenner, Little Amy as he privately thought of her as, was starting to take a shine to the new guy, Scott. He wasn't sure what he thought about that or how he felt. Scott hadn't been around long enough for Vick to get a solid read on him, but he believed he was a good man. He'd taught enough students, kids and adults alike, to see the ugly side of human nature. He could tell the ones who learned martial arts for exercise, for relaxation, for self-defense, and to be able to kick the living shit out of their fellow citizens. Vick didn't like those, and over his years of instruction in the various arts, he'd given walking papers to nine people—men and women who'd used too much power during practices and sparring sessions, who treated their classmates like dirt. They were the ones who would sometimes look to Vick to see if he'd caught an over vigorous body flip or repeated strikes that were much too hard. They knew Vick knew. He saw most of the garbage that went on in his school, and three strikes were enough to jettison the ones he didn't like or who wouldn't conform to his rules. Violators were warned twice, then told to leave on the third, always behind closed doors.

Vick had almost always detected the bad ones.

But he hadn't gotten anything off Tenner. That one had fooled him completely.

For now, Vick eyed Amy from where he lay on the floor, a rug underneath him. He didn't say anything to draw attention to her, because he knew while she didn't get flustered, she could be easy to embarrass. Vick wasn't one of those people who enjoyed embarrassing other folks, and he didn't like people who did.

"Well, someone just nodded off," Amy said.

"Mmmhm," Vick said and propped himself up with a groan. "Looks like a good idea. Let him have the couch. There're beds upstairs?"

Amy nodded.

"Unoccupied?" Many a suicide victim seemed to prefer taking the final plunge in their own beds. It was a disturbing trend that Vick had noticed in the last couple of years of scavenging houses for supplies. He pulled off his own innards-soaked camouflage and plopped them on the floor.

"Shit's gonna stink up the place," Buckle observed.

"The little old lady in the kitchen is gonna stink up the place," Vick deadpanned.

Buckle grunted. "I'll take care of it. I think I can put her outside. Believe it or not, the street's clearing up."

"What?" Vick asked, and both he and Amy went to opposite ends of the curtains and peeked outside.

Buckle spoke truth. Where once there had been a black rush of corpses, only a trickle seemed to be stumbling by, heading away from the downtown area.

"Gotta be a reason for it," Amy said, letting the curtain fall back into place. She went to Scott and shook him lightly, urging him to straighten out on the couch. "Your neck will thank me for it later."

Vick glanced back at her, then looked at the scene outside. As he did, Buckle caught his attention with a knowing look and a sly smile. Buckle saw Amy's interest in Scott, too, and he'd only known her half as long. Vick went right back to looking outside and hoped Buckle would follow his lead. Unlike him, Buckle didn't mind teasing people, Amy in particular.

"Y'gonna tuck us all in, darlin'?" Buckle inquired innocently.

"You can tuck yourself in," Amy informed him and went upstairs. Buckle grinned and winked at Vick. Vick shook his head in silent warning.

"G'wan and turn in, me son," Buckle told him. "I'll take first watch."

"Thanks, man."

"No sweat. I'll lug out the old lady corpse as well," he said, pronouncing the word as *carpse*. "Put her on the front porch. No need to stink up the place."

"Wake me up in a few hours."

"Fair enough."

Vick stretched and regarded the sleeping man on the couch. Was he fooling them as Tenner had done? He didn't think so. God above, he hoped not.

Climbing the stairs was a chore for Vick, and his fifty-six years seemed to be getting heavier with each passing day. He was grateful for the mask he wore. The last fight in the parking lot had taken more out of him than he wanted to share with the others, and the thought of a prolonged confrontation with the dead didn't make him happy.

That thought made him smile. The last two years had been one prolonged confrontation.

He met Amy at the top of the stairs. She carried a thick blanket in her arms.

"Nice of you," Vick said, keeping his voice as neutral as possible.

"Plenty more where that came from. There's a linen closet back there."

"I'll make do with the beds."

"G'night then," Amy said, moving around him, and descended the stairs.

Vick had the idea of lingering just long enough to see her cover Scott on the couch, but decided against it in the end. He saw no point in potentially ruining the path nature was taking.

He'd keep an eye on Scott all the same.

Amy was, after all, like a daughter to him.

27

The water ended in a line that was almost impossible to distinguish from the sky. The sun warmed the sand, which was surprisingly soft and bespoke the heat of the day. The smell of surf as it rolled in was pure and clean and heady.

Suzy was out in the water with her flutter wings on, standing up, splashing, grimacing, and laughing her butt off. Her long dark hair splayed out wetly on her back. Scott and Kelly watched from the beach, laid out on a blue towel sporting tropical fish.

"Look, Mommy!" Suzy cried, and tried to swim again.

"You watching her?" Scott asked.

"I'm watching her," Kelly said and flashed him a smile. Sunglasses that were too big for her face and yet fit her perfectly hid her eyes. "She swims like you."

"She does not."

Kelly made little puppy paws in front of her chest, fluttering them energetically.

"She does *not*." Scott laughed, feeling good. "Leave me alone or you'll be paying for dinner."

Kelly snorted and looked at their daughter swimming in the surf. The sun, huge and high overhead, had browned her back to an almost well-done tone. "You're paying for dinner, buster. I didn't bring my purse."

"You don't have any money?"

Kelly regarded him with a look of mock disdain. "I came out here to swim."

"Can't believe a woman goes anywhere without her purse. You don't have any money on you? At all?"

"Look at me." She grabbed her breasts, covered by one part of a modest two-piece bikini that she'd earlier claimed showed off too much. He'd disagreed. "Where am I going hide it? Here? Down here?"

"Strippers do it."

"You better not be comparing me to strippers, mister. I'll *so* pummel you, right here."

"*Some* women would be flattered to be compared to strippers. You got the chops for it."

"I got the chops for it?" Kelly looked back at Suzy, still kicking away in the water and crying out *look at me, look at me!* "Man, you are just digging that hole deeper."

"What I meant is I'd never guess you were in your thirties."

Kelly simmered. "Keep it up." She rolled toward him on the beach towel, the curve of her breasts shifting, kept in check by some thin material. Scott could just make out her nipples. A tan line, only a millimeter thick, marked how much skin the sun had gotten.

Scott felt another smile building.

"Hey, I'm up here."

Scott met her eyes. Over her shoulder, Suzy's silhouette ran out of the water and down the beach. Water glistened in his daughter's wake.

"Yes, ma'am?"

"Do I have to bring you back to the room and beat you?"

Scott's expression shifted into something sardonic, and he made a show of thinking deeply on the offer. "You just said 'beat' . . . right?"

Mommy, look at me! Look at me!

"Sicko. Get your mind out of the gutter."

"Only if I can drop it into the cleavage."

Squeals of delight rose over Kelly's sun-browned shoulder, but Scott could only pay attention to his wife's eyes, peeking softly at him over her large sunglasses.

"What am I going to do with you?" she asked.

"Don't know. But if you keep giving me those kinds of lead-in lines . . ."

"You've got a dirty mouth," Kelly informed him.

Scott clamped down hard on what he wanted to say, but his grin said it all.

"That's it," Kelly warned him. "You keep that in check. Now, about dinner . . ."

Suzy leaned over Kelly's bare shoulder and bit savagely into her mother's unprotected skin, ripping the flesh to white bone in a flash. Kelly shrieked. Scott shrieked. Blood spouted from her. Suzy grabbed her mother's hair in a fist and, when she opened her mouth for another bite, the meat fell out. It wasn't their Suzy anymore. It was a slimy thing with pasty white flesh, wrinkled from being in the water for too long. Skin tags as long as barnacles decorated the thing's bloody maw. The flutter wings she still wore squeaked. Suzy didn't even make a sound as she chomped into Kelly's cheek and ripped . . .

He woke with a jolt, both legs kicking as if someone had staked him through the heart. The house was dark, but from the window where the sofa chair was stationed, a voice asked him, "You okay?"

"Yeah," Scott lied and hoped Buckle wouldn't ask any questions.

Instead the Newfoundlander went back to peeking out through the window.

"What time is it?" Scott asked.

"Dunno. Nighttime."

Smartass. "I'll take over for you," Scott offered.

"That's my shift your taking," Vick said from the steps. In the house, he appeared as a shadow against shadows. Buckle stood up from the sofa chair and cracked his back.

"Y'can duke it out, now," Buckle said. The ex-cop and Vick tapped fists as they passed on the stairs. Seconds later, Vick was at the window looking outside. Satisfied with what he saw, he placed his steel pipe against the wall and sat down heavily in the chair.

"Go on back to sleep," Vick said.

"Can't now," Scott replied. "But that might change in a few minutes."

"Not the company, I hope."

"No, no, not at all. Once I get over waking up, I can usually fall back. Might be an hour, but I'll get there."

"Bad dream was it?" Vick said in the dark, his silhouette leaning toward the window.

Scott didn't see any reason to lie. "Yeah."

"Hm. You still get them?"

"Every now and again."

"Of who?"

He sighed. "Wife and daughter."

Vick didn't ask where they were or anything else, and for that Scott was grateful.

"Had my share of bad dreams," Vick said. "We all have. Hope you sleep easy soon."

"Me too. Hey . . . you were something else in that parking lot today."

"You liked that?"

"Sure did. Hell, could you teach me that stuff?"

Vick chuckled. "Sure. Free of charge, too."

"Thanks. I mean it. Once we get out of here."

"Deal."

"Take you long to learn?"

"The arts?"

"Yeah. Them. Take long?"

Vick leaned toward the window and glanced out. Moonlight silvered a sliver of his features and sparkled off one eye. Seeing nothing of interest, he dropped the curtain.

"Quiet out there. Streets are empty. What was your question?"

"How long did it take you to learn?"

"I'm still learning," Vick answered him. "That's the . . . the spiritual answer, I guess. The answer you want is all my life. From when I was ten. Learned right here in the city, too."

"Wow."

"Yeah, wow," Vick said, sounding pleased. "Course Halifax was changing back then. Still a beautiful city to live in. Safe, too, as long as you minded where you went. Like all places, there were some areas a person just didn't go alone."

"You made a career of it?"

"A career," Vick purred, tasting the word. "Yeah, I guess I did. Had my own little hagwon down on Quinpool. That's Korean for private school. Had a little side business selling exotic weapons. Did some of that online as well. I've done okay by it, I suppose."

"What I saw in the lot there, man, you did just fine."

Vick smiled. "What you didn't see was how I was out of breath almost right away. My conditioning ain't what it used to be. I like to think it's the same, but it ain't. A career. Hm. You know something? People around me accepted me for what I did, for what I taught them. But I dare say you're the first to call it a career. I don't have a teaching degree, yet I taught people—a lot of people now know how to defend themselves because of me."

"Pretty noble."

"Noble, eh?" Vick chuckled softly. "Some didn't think so. Had one guy once tell me to my face that I was preaching violence to our city's youth. That I was a violent person. I remember him plain as day. Old fella, in his early sixties. Big set of dentures on him that were much too white, y'know? Like they were over-bleached or something. Anyway, yeah, he stood right in front of me, my height he was, and waved his finger in my nose telling me how I was a bad person for teaching what I was teaching. Selling weapons and such. All legal, I says. Not in the eyes of decent folks, he says, wagging his fingers at me, as wild-eyed and aggressive as anyone I've ever met in a street fight. Those big teeth flashing, too. Told me I should be ashamed of myself and that I should close everything down. Ask God for forgiveness. Hm."

Scott waited. "And?"

"Oh, well, that was that. He left me then. I think he even confronted my students and their parents once outside my hagwon and ranted at them for a while. That was a bad scene. Some of those moms and dads weren't as understanding as I was. Anyway, I remember one day the same guy, white dentures and all, was being mugged in an alleyway near the school. I went down there and no sooner did the punk grab his watch—he'd already gotten the wallet—I was on him. Kicked him in the guts and laid him out cold. Knocked the wind out of him. I thought he was going to die, but he didn't. I got the watch and the wallet from him and handed it back to . . . Rumstead, that was his name. Handed it back to him. You know what he said?"

Scott shook his head.

"He looked at me, then the kid on the street, and back to me again and goes 'Did you have to kick him *so hard?* Why the hell you have to kick him so hard?' And then went on about charges, about how the kid would be within his rights to sue me. Man, oh man."

"Whoa. That's one real asshole."

"Yeah, well, I admired him in a way," Vick confessed. "He stood up for what he believed in. Didn't like the way he did it—loud as he was—but he had the balls to do it anyway. Especially to my face. I mean, for all he'd have known, I could've hurt him. Course I wouldn't, you understand, but he didn't know that. All he knew was that I taught kids and adults how to kick the shit out of others."

"Why the pipe?"

"The pipe?"

Scott pointed at the weapon leaning against the wall.

"Oh, that. I had katanas and an assortment of weapons at the shop when Moe started walking around. First used a sword on them, too, but a sword's not much good against an enemy that has no regard for its own safety. Also, if you chop deep enough into a head, there's the risk that you'd get it stuck in there. Takes too much time to pry it loose. Axe is the same way. All the blades I had didn't really do the job. I had one set of tonfas, but Amy took those. Better off. She's faster than I ever was."

Scott nodded, remembering the display.

"Simple bat like you have there isn't bad, but it isn't balanced properly. This," Vick gestured to the pipe with a dark hand, "was in my basement. I added the leather for extra grip and, yeah. Works fine. Well balanced. If it were a foot or so longer, I could use it as a quarterstaff."

"Works good," Scott agreed. Then something came to him. "What did you think of those gimps out there today?"

Vick yawned. "Just Moe. Except they were headed in the same direction we were. I think it's a bad omen, to tell the truth."

"I agree. Never seen a group of them do something like that before. Before I came to Halifax, I lived with a man for a few months. A friend. We had something of a mystery going on down in the Valley."

"Yeah? What?"

"The bodies were disappearing. I mean the bodies of Moe. We'd put a deadhead down, and the next time we came across that place, the body would be gone."

"Strange. Dogs, maybe?"

"We thought about that, but we never heard anything. Never did find out what it was. I left to come up here."

"Ah. Well, I figure . . . it's something they don't like. Really, we don't know anything about them. Don't have the means to study them. And the way I figure it, even something as brainless as a slug has the instinct to sense and avoid danger."

Scott mulled that over for a moment. He wondered if Vick had just realized what he'd said. "You think something dangerous is coming?"

"Possible. Something elemental, maybe. Fire, perhaps. Bad storm."

"Don't think it's a storm. When I drove up here, it was pretty bad. Moe was standing out in it, just freezing in place."

"Hm. That's right. Not a blizzard, then. But . . . something," Vick said softly.

"Something," Scott agreed.

"Hey, thanks, by the way."

"Huh? What for?"

"Exposing Tenner for what he was." Vick took a breath. "That prick would've gone right on murdering us if you weren't around."

"Oh, well, don't mention it. Sorry for pulling the gun when I saw him. When I heard his voice, I knew it was him. The gun thing wasn't cool."

"You were going to kill him, eh?"

Scott looked at his hands in the dark. "Yeah. I think so."

"You think so?"

"Pretty certain. I mean, yeah. He killed my friends. Who knows how many others he's done?"

"Hm," Vick said, and neither man said anything for a while. "Y'know, I've taught students techniques that will put an attacker down for the count: joint locks, choke-holds, ball shots. Done it for years. Never had to use it, really."

"Think you could?"

"Never been pushed far enough. Depends on the person, too, I guess. In times like these, it might be pretty easy to kill someone. There're no consequences, as far as I can see. Except maybe spiritually."

"Killing the dead is easy," Scott said.

"It is that. But another living person?" Vick drew in a breath through clenched teeth. "I wish you well on that one."

"You gonna tell me I gotta live with it or something? That it won't bring back the dead?"

"Oh, fuck no. Not at all. Call Tenner crazy or whatever you want. I'm just a firm believer that evil is out there, and it ain't just gonna go away. There's no talking to it. Ain't in its nature. And in this world? Where's there's no police, no laws, no rules, no clinics . . ."

"He's gotta be stopped."

"Yeah, he does. I understand that. And I hope that . . . when the time comes, you can pull the trigger."

There was a moment of silence then, so deep that the silence itself could be heard, and Vick sat up slowly, looking to the window. "You hear that?"

"No. What?"

Vick's face was half-covered by shadows when he turned to him. "Don't know, but be on guard."

He got up and grabbed his pipe. Scott stood with him. He'd never stopped to take off his Nomex coat or pants, and Vick, if he had taken the armor off upstairs, had on everything except his helmet and spiked knuckles.

Vick bent over slightly. "You sure you don't hear that?"

Scott shook his head.

Without another word, Vick went to the door and drew back the curtain covering the large window. He looked left and right. A moment later, he unlocked the door and stepped outside. Scott followed.

Cold air cupped his face like a hand. Scott tiptoed onto the front porch, stepping over the legs of the granny zombie that Buckle had deposited just outside the front door. Vick wandered onto the front step and held onto the railing, still listening. Scott strained to hear, but as soon as he seemed to be about to detect something, it faded away, teasing him.

Vick walked into the icy street made blue-black by the moon. The sky overhead had cleared and a full moon blazed, a halo of such intensity that Scott momentarily forgot about everything else and stared up at it. Moons like these made him feel all was right with the world. Vick wandered cautiously into the middle of the street, alert and straining, staring off in the direction of the waterfront. No moans scratched the night. The deadheads had all moved on. Haltingly, Scott stepped off the front porch, onto the sidewalk, and took two testing steps before Vick glanced back at him and lifted a hand for silence.

Then Scott heard it.

The barest murmuring of movement, like the softest surf, glided toward them. Vick pointed down the street and Scott strained to see, hoping his night vision was good enough. The way they had come was a mess of dead traffic covered in snow, but through the main drag, straight down the middle of the road, a dark lip of viscous oil bubbled toward them, almost soundless. It covered the white road in a slow, but steady flood.

"What is . . . *that?*" Scott whispered, barely aware he'd spoken.

"No idea," Vick responded, answering as if in a trance and gripping his pipe as if drawing comfort from it. "Never heard the like before. Listen."

The darkness crept over the snowy roads like a vat of watery coffee grounds that had burst and spilled forth. It enveloped cars. It went around unmoving lumps and swallowed them whole. Bases of trees were swamped. The sound became louder, a low guttural rustling of some unknown material, like walking on a forest floor at midnight, when a person's senses are almost achingly aware of everything.

It rooted Scott to the ground.

"Oh, my God," Vick whispered, and Scott could almost hear the man's jaw drop.

Then he, too, saw what was approaching.

Awash in moonlight and under a sky dimpled with stars, the blackness moving over the ground gradually took on shape, as if it were a foggy nightmare solidifying. They moved in little jerks, strangely different from what he might have expected, and he realized the subterranean humming was the sound of hair and the press of bodies rubbing against one another. A new sound perked his ears, just underneath that dreadful drone, which could only be claws clicking on patches of black ice.

There were millions of them, channeled by the street that Scott, Vick, and the others had slunk along while pretending to be dead.

Rats.

The street was alive with rats.

28

Scott couldn't tear his eyes away from the horrific tsunami rushing toward him. The rats' terrible hushed cacophony grew in his ears, freezing him with fear, willing him to just stay right there, just *wait*, and all would be settled in a few seconds.

Vick clamped a hand onto Scott's shoulder. "Come on," he whispered urgently.

"Those are *rats!*" Scott burst out, following the man back into the house. Vick slammed the door and locked it as Scott slipped by him. They entered the living room and went to opposite ends of the curtains, immediately peeking outside. Vick had the greater range of vision, being able to see farther down the street, while Scott had to make do with much less.

"How the hell could there be so many of the things?" Scott asked.

"I don't know, man," Vick muttered. "But I think it's a good idea to just stay inside on this one. What do you say?"

"Yeah."

"Oh, shit."

"What?" Scott could see Vick's dismayed face lit by a beam of moonlight.

A moment later, it didn't matter.

Rats surged in front of the house. They covered the width of the pavement, the cars across the street, and the land beyond. Across the way stood another house, painted white, with a black foundation. Rats bobbed and rose against the foundation, their wet ragged backs arched as they undulated along the concrete. As the two men watched, the vermin rose up and over the front porch's steps in a violent deluge. They continued on past the street, but a wave of them clawed their way onto the porch and quickly located the dead granny gimp in front of the door. Rats located the unmoving heap of flesh in ones and twos, biting into toes and thighs, before a swarm swamped the area and covered the body in a frightening blink. The unmoving gimp jerked from hundreds of little bites, as if being jolted with live wires, before being pulled under the rising torrent of black backs and pale tails. The humming increased, a white noise punctuated by little cracks and pops. An arm was ripped from the body and dragged away in jerks before disappearing below the furry tide. Scott felt his guts freeze. Some of the rats were huge, the size of ferrets, with hairless tails as long as a man's forearm. He glimpsed some with terrible wounds, deep enough to expose bone. The creatures moved with spastic twitches that spoke of something not entirely natural.

The things swarming the porch area were undead.

"See that?" Scott whispered.

"I do," Vick replied pensively.

The gimp's arm popped back into view, bare of flesh and gnawed to the gleaming bone. A human skull bobbed above the mass of flesh, teeth smirking, before disappearing underneath the rats once more. The creatures scurried over each other, layer upon twisting, teeming layer. Hairless tails, white and ghoulish, dragged over the frenzy.

In the road, the rats had risen to shin level—if one were brave enough to walk amongst them.

"Jesus Christ," Scott breathed, snarling in both fright and loathing.

Then the front door shivered.

The two men scrambled to the entryway and saw the wood tremble. It only rattled softly at first, but then it thrummed as if suffering a violent seizure. Claws raked the outer wood, deep and penetrating. The scratching intensified.

"What's up with that?" Vick said, aghast.

"They know we're in here."

"How do they know *that?*"

"They can smell."

"Smell?"

"Rats have a great sense of smell. If they got the virus, God knows what it did to them," Scott said.

"Shit, the virus sure as fuck's in them. You saw the street."

"Hey," Amy called out from the top of the stairs, making both men jump. "What's going on?" Her shadow bent over to see.

"We have a problem," Scott informed her, stepping out of the way to give her a view.

Her outline froze against the dark of the house. "What the fuck is *that?*"

"Rats," Vick reported.

A second shadow joined Amy at the top of the stairs. "D'fuck is that?"

The door bucked as if convulsing. Scott edged around Vick and peeked outside, pulling back the curtain.

Rats were scrambling at the sill. Little white claws lashed the wood, seeking purchase. Some even rapped their snouts against the glass.

Scott let the curtain fall back. "They're crawling on the backs of each other. Is that normal?"

A horrified Vick shrugged.

"I don't know anything about rats," Amy said from the stairs.

"You studied every other fucking thing in university!" Scott protested.

The scratching intensified at the door, rattling the wood in the frame and capturing the attention of the people inside.

Buckle bounded down the steps. "I'll look for something to brace the door."

Brace the door? Scott thought, looking back at the shuddering slab of wood and glass as the rats tried to work their way through. From the kitchen, Buckle manhandled a large table cloaked in darkness. Vick pulled Scott out of the entryway to allow Buckle to dump the heavy table and press it firmly against the door.

"Some furniture," Vick said, grabbing a sofa chair and shoving it against the table, adding its weight to the barricade. Buckle and Scott wrestled the sofa over so one end pressed up against the chair.

"Where did they come from?" Amy asked from the stairs.

"Looked like from the waterfront," Vick answered her. "That's why Moe was marching away from the area. They knew what was up."

"They knew?"

"Sensed it somehow," Scott added. "Not so dead after all."

"Get your gear on, Amy!" Vick yelled, turning at the creaks coming from the front of the house.

Buckle took two steps at a time to the second floor, following Amy's dark outline into the gloom.

Scott and Vick stood in the center of the almost empty living room. Scott passed Vick his hood and helmet and quickly donned his own. The sides of the house groaned like a ship's timbers at sea. On impulse, Scott headed to the kitchen.

"Where you goin'?" Vick shouted.

"Checking out the back yard!" Scott yelled. He hurried into the kitchen and saw a door with white curtains covering the window. He hauled back the material and peered outside.

The land dipped somewhat in the backyard, but rats teemed over everything. Scott saw the outside top step to the back door disappear under the rising tide of undead vermin. Claws worked furiously at the base of the door.

"Jesus," Scott muttered, and stepped back. The kitchen had nothing to brace the door with. There were two bolt locks and he secured them both, but he knew that it wouldn't last long before . . .

Before what?

He remembered his time in Saint John, when the doughnut shop had a problem with rats. The night's garbage bags were stowed in a wooden shed, secured by padlocks, where they would sit until pick-up. The shed was there to deter people from looking for the stale leftovers and, as such, made only out of sheets of cheap wood. It was enough to keep the homeless out, but not the rats. In fact, the rats had slowly worked their way into the shed, ravaging a garbage bag before their hole by the back corner was discovered.

They had chewed their way through.

A sudden quivering of the back door brought him back to the present, and Scott watched for a few seconds before Vick shouted from the living room.

"What's it look like back there?" he asked.

"Bad. We're surrounded."

Scott returned to see Buckle and Amy on the main floor in full gear, lifting their outerwear over their heads. The walls of the house groaned and softly crackled under the pressure of the undead siege. Scott glanced at Amy tossing the poncho over herself. He stooped and threw on his own. In seconds, all four of them were dressed and ready to move.

"Now what?" Buckle wanted to know.

As if in answer, the distinct sound of something puncturing through wood made them turn toward the front door. Claws clicked off glass.

"That was the door," Scott said.

"The table's next," Amy stated.

"Options?" Vick asked.

"We can stay and fight," Amy said, "or we can bust out of here and run for it."

"Bust out," Buckle voted.

"They're ankle deep out there," Scott informed them. "Maybe more."

"Well, then, what?"

Scott looked to the upstairs. "Come on."

They raced up the steps, following Scott as he went from one room to another. After inspecting them all, he stopped and shook his head in disbelief.

"What?" Amy asked him.

"No attic," Scott burst out. "Who doesn't have a fucking attic in their house?"

Buckle went into one room and ripped the curtains from a window. Perhaps twelve feet across the way and below them was another window. "What about this?"

"What about that?" Vick asked him.

"Oh, sweet Mary and Joseph," Buckle said, peering below. Scott crowded inside, mouth hanging open. It was a driveway with a car parked just underneath, its white roof luminous. Surging around it was a black river of rats, stretching from the street and into the backyard, flooding everything.

"Can't jump twelve feet, you idiot," Vick snapped.

"Didn't say jump across, Vicky," Buckle said. "But I'm looking at that."

The car between the two houses was well above the rising moat of flesh-seeking vermin. Just above that, and much closer, was a wide, old-fashioned window.

Vick pulled back and smiled at his friend.

From the first floor, a crackling of wood and glass reached their ears, startling them all.

"Who goes first?"

"Your idea, Buckle," Amy said.

"Right on." With that, the Newfoundlander smashed out the window with his Halligan. He lifted one leg outside and then the other, sitting briefly on the sill.

"Shit," he muttered.

Then he pushed off.

With a roar, Buckle landed hard on the roof of the car, squashing it inward and cartwheeling his arms for a brief second before getting his balance. He righted himself, arms outstretched, while rats gushed around his island.

"Holy fuck! They stink as bad as Moe!"

"Watch yourself!" Vick yelled back.

Buckle waved and leaned toward the other house. He smashed out the window with the Halligan bar, swiping it around the frame to clear away any remaining shards of glass. Once done, he tossed the tool through the window, made two test swings with his arms, and leaped.

He hit the window too hard.

Buckle slipped, latched onto the windowsill, and managed to hook it underneath his armpit. He hung there for a moment, feet scrabbling against the side of the house as rats nipped at his boots. Slowly, he pulled himself up and through the window, snagging his body armor before yanking it free. In seconds, he popped back out the window and waved the others down.

"Amy," Vick directed, getting out of the woman's way. Amy got her legs over the sill, dropped out of the window, and onto the roof of the car without any trouble. She jumped for the window and landed against the lower sill with a solid clap. Buckle grabbed her torso and hauled her inside.

"You go on," Vick said to Scott. "Watch your feet."

"Watch your ass," Scott answered, hearing more wood splinter from the first floor. He wasted no further time and jumped out the window, crashing down on a roof that was looking more like a crater. He landed hard, clanging his bat off the edge of the car's roof and grabbing for the shotgun slung over his shoulder. Buckle took the shotgun and bat from him and gestured for him to jump. The rats swamped the lower part of the car, as if sensing the meat just above them. Scott focused on the window and sprang toward it, crashing into the sill and holding on for dear life. Buckle and Amy pulled him in and dumped him on an open living room floor.

"Move your fat ass, Vicky!" Buckle bellowed.

There was a crash as Vick landed on the car. He teetered on the roof and fell forward with a grunt. Holding onto his steel pipe, his arms shot up and slammed awkwardly against the house.

"Take the pipe," Vick gasped.

Buckle reached out and pulled the weapon free of his friend's hands.

With a groan, Vick shuffled along the wall until he reached the window. Seconds later, they hauled him through and deposited him in the living room.

"Well, this place looks nice," Scott said, picking up his bat.

"Smarten up," Amy said, slapping his helmet as she moved past him, toward the windows.

"I'll check out back," Buckle said and got moving. Scott got to his feet and righted his helmet.

Amy pulled back a set of white drapes and looked out the windows. "They're out there, but maybe not as thick. Clustered around the other house."

"Not for long, then," Vick said.

Scott agreed.

Buckle came back into the living room. "They're out back. Ankle deep."

"Out the back, then."

They piled into the kitchen, banging against a round table and chairs, and gathered at the back door. Scott glanced out the window there and saw the rats were indeed thick on the ground, but they were still clustered about the previous house in greater numbers. Vick slid the bolts across on the door, unlocking it.

"All right, we get out of here and run to the right. When I get some space, I'm going to cut out to the road again."

"Why?" Scott asked.

"'Cause I don't want to be jumping fences and ducking through swing sets out there. They might be infected rats, but we have the longer legs. You all ready?"

They were.

"Let's do this," Vick said and threw open the door.

They spilled out into the backyard, and Scott was momentarily stunned by the assault upon the house they'd only just occupied. The baseboards were gnawed down to fibrous white, while a black river continued to pour around the foundation.

So many, Scott thought in awe.

"Come on!" Buckle roared at him. Scott felt rats scrabbling over his boots and Nomex pants. He pawed them off in disgusted reflex, turned, and bolted after his three companions. They crushed several rats underfoot as they ran, but the backyards of the houses were choked with searching rodents.

After running through the backyards of three more houses, Vick led them toward the street. They passed through another narrow driveway between the houses, stomping through streamers of rats. They pressed through dead things and emerged at the side of the street.

The moon was high in the night sky, and its light illuminated a tenebrous layer of pulsating vermin, surrounding the nearest houses and the road. The creatures filled the street, a seemingly unending carpet in the stark moonlight. They swamped Scott and the others' ankles, clawing and biting at the protective material. Scott danced on the spot, crushing several underfoot before Vick started jogging away from the creatures. He stopped killing and followed.

"Where are the damn things coming from?" Buckle huffed as he caught up to Vick.

"Waterfront."

"We were on the waterfront for almost two weeks! Never saw anything like this before."

"Something brought them up," Amy panted nearby. "Maybe it was a lack of food?"

"Or they wanted something fresh," Vick said, as they tromped through the thinner outer rim of the swarm.

"Maybe they just got braver," Scott threw out, feeling a chill as he said the words. The thought of the virus making rats hunger for human meat and driving them above the surface to hunt wasn't something he wanted to consider.

He glanced over his shoulder.

"Well, shit."

The rats pursued them. The outer edges of the mass scuttled up the street while far behind, drifts of blackness crawled through the houses where they'd sheltered. Scott thought the rats were massed knee-high at points. What would they do to a person if they caught one? The image of the disappearing granny zombie on the front porch appeared in his mind. Another image followed, the detached arm turning in the tide of ragged hair before slipping under, as if swept away by a savage undercurrent.

He felt his balls draw up in fright.

The mystery of the disappearing dead down in Annapolis.

Well, shit!

He turned back to face the street, seeing tendrils of rats scurrying across the surface.

And ran.

29

The sound of boots on ice and snow-covered asphalt split the night's silence as they quickly outpaced the swarm. Vick kept them on South Street, periodically coughing and wheezing as he chugged along the road made eerily luminous by the moon. The cold air had gotten into Scott's lungs as well, and he knew from experience he would be hacking later on. It had been ages since he'd had to do any lengthy running, but since coming to Halifax, it seemed it was all he did. He was quickly running out of gas.

"Wait," Scott gasped and halted. He bent over and held his knees, hissing in air through his nose and letting it out through his mouth. "I need a break."

The other three stopped in the street and regarded Scott in silence, breathing hard, but not out of breath. Vick lifted the visor of his helmet and spat.

"We should get off this street," he said.

"We can do that," Amy nodded. "We can cut in right here if you want."

"Wait," Buckle said, holding out his hand. "Listen."

It didn't take long to hear it. The low rustling noise crept along the curbs and crawled into their ears. It wouldn't be long before the rats caught up to them.

Up ahead lay a T-intersection, cutting across South Street. It was too dark to see the sign, but Buckle gestured for them to stay where they were while he investigated. He walked a dozen steps, cutting to his right and placing his back against a stone wall. Scott watched the man peer around the corner.

He straightened.

And ran back.

"Run!" he whispered in a harsh voice and raced across the street and behind a house.

The others followed, but were slow to pick up speed, not understanding what had driven Buckle back. Then the foremost rank of rats poured around the corner in a wide sweep that forever cut them off from South Street. They tumbled across the road like a rush of spilled apples, sensing fresh flesh and turning in their direction.

The living bolted after Buckle and caught up to him at a high wire fence in a backyard gleaming in moonlight. Buckle kicked the mesh twice, trying to bring it down; when he couldn't, he decided to climb it. He flipped himself up and over at the same time that Scott reached the fence and practically dived over it.

Scott landed hard and struggled through a deep drift of white. The shotgun slid off his shoulder, and he snatched it and his bat. He drove the bat into the snow and readied the shotgun.

"I'm getting tired of running, man," Buckle said as he straightened up alongside Scott. Amy and Vick cleared the fence, and they all looked back the way they had come.

The rats flooded the driveway.

"What the hell?" Buckle burst out in exasperation.

"Come on," Vick roared and started racing through backyards. Scott snatched up his bat and ran after him. They followed in a close line, looking over their shoulders every few seconds. They crossed one backyard and came out into another driveway and onto a smaller deserted side street. Vick led them up the road before cutting into another driveway. He repeated this twice, attempting to get the rats off their trail.

At the corner of one house, they stopped to compose themselves, placing their backs to the wall and staying in the shadows.

"What do you think?" Buckle asked, breathing hard. "We lose them?"

"We zigzagged a couple of times there," Vick answered, gasping.

But they could hear the hum in the distance.

"Lord Jesus," Buckle whispered.

"Man up." Vick punched his shoulder. "Amy's handling these things better than you."

"Actually, I'm about to defecate myself," Amy deadpanned. "Sorry if that's too much information."

"I see them," Scott whispered, pressing himself harder against the side of the house and willing its shadow to hide him. The others did the same and waited, hoping the rats would go around them. The white noise of the rats' approach grew. The crackling of wire fences reached their ears.

"We were going in and around houses, trying to be cute," Buckle whispered. "And they're just *coming on*."

Scott stuck out his head and blinked. At the edge of his vision, rats flooded the entire street and homed in on their position.

"We gotta go," Scott said.

"This way." Amy took the lead. The others followed her silhouette, a black wisp against snow banks of ghostly white. They passed behind several houses before she slowed and started testing doors, plunging inside the first one that opened. Scott went straight to the kitchen. He unslung his twelve gauge and placed it on a dark table while the others spread out, searching for deadheads. Buckle found a set of stairs, and he and Vick headed up to the second floor. Moments later, they reconvened in the kitchen.

"Empty," Vick reported.

"Let's lay up here for a bit," Scott said. "I need to catch my breath."

"We put some distance between us and those little fuckers anyway," Buckle said. Still, he went to the back door and locked it.

"What the hell?" Vick said in disbelief. "Never seen anything like that before."

"We're going to have to get back on South Street further down the line," Amy said. "Once we catch our breaths here, we can stay ahead of them. Get around them."

"They're like a fucking wave," Vick muttered. "Like that helicopter shot, the one covering the tsunami that hit Japan, where the water was rushing across the flatlands. Just like that."

"We can wait here for a bit, see if they give up the chase," Scott offered.

"They *can't* find us now," Vick said. "We're in a house again. The last house I can see how they found us—the body that was out on the front step."

"Sorry, man," Buckle said.

"Hey, I was only stating a fact, not pointing fingers. How would you know there was a swarm of rats heading up the street? You couldn't. There was no way. They came up the street and found the body. From there, they must've smelled us inside."

Amy inspected herself. "The ponchos. They could smell the ponchos. And the hoods. Anything coated in blood and guts."

There was a moment of silence as those words sunk into their heads.

"Christ, you're right," Scott said. "Gimps can smell. Rats can, too. And if they're feeding on the dead, this probably isn't helping us too much at the moment."

"What do we do, then?" Vick asked. "We drop them? What if we come up against a pack of Moe? We got nothing. Sure as hell can't walk through them like before."

"Rather square off against Moe than rats," Buckle stated. "But I see your point. We're fucked either way."

"Fucked more with the rats. Those things were chewing their way through the wood. Moe doesn't do that," Vick said.

Scott shifted from one foot to another. "We can test to see if their sense of smell is better than Moe's."

"How?" Amy asked.

"Look. We're ahead of them. I say we stay ahead of them. Let's drop the clothes here and bug out. Get back on track."

"And if we run into Moe?" Vick asked.

"We try and avoid them. If not, we go through them."

"Anything we kill might attract the rats. It'll be a massive connect the dots," Amy pointed out.

"And if we wear the shit, the rats might find us anyway," Scott countered. "You got any better ideas?"

Amy shook her head.

"You guys?"

Neither Vick nor Buckle opened their mouths.

"Okay, then. Another minute tops and we go. All right?"

They agreed.

"Fucking rats, man," Buckle muttered. "And I thought *zombies* creeped me out."

Scott mentally ticked off the seconds, feeling his wind return. Once it was up, he stripped off the blood-soaked garments camouflaging him from the gimps and threw it onto the floor. The others did the same.

"We just leave it there?" Buckle asked.

"Yeah. Maybe it'll throw them off, give us chance to get away. Everyone ready?" Scott looked at each of their faces, dark, but visible through the clear visors attached to their helmets.

"Let's go."

Opening the back door, they once again stepped out into the night, listening to the rats in the distance. They darted across two backyards, then walked down another driveway and into a road glutted with low drifts and half-buried cars. Their boots crunched through the frozen snow, making them cringe. They proceeded in a zig-zagging line, jogging past swing sets, marble fountains, work sheds, and benches hidden amongst tall, skeletal clumps of trees.

Amy went through another driveway and stopped, the menfolk behind her. A truck parked between two houses was almost covered in snow, but the first thing Scott noticed was the lack of noise—other than their own heavy breathing.

"Can't hear a thing," he panted.

"Lost them?" Vick wanted to know.

"I think."

"Let's go, man," Buckle urged.

Amy went ahead with her tonfas in her hands and checked out the street ahead. Against the backdrop of the moon, she seemed almost ninja-like. She returned to the shadows of the houses a few seconds later.

"We've got to head down to the end of the street here so I can see where we are, okay? Once that's done, we can get a better bearing on where to go. That sound good to you guys?"

"All in," Buckle said.

"Lead on," Vick added. Scott didn't say anything.

"You with me?" she asked him.

"Oh, yeah," he said suddenly. "Just thinking, is all."

"Anything we should know about?"

Where's Tenner now? *"No. Nothing."*

Amy's gaze lingered on him for a few seconds, as if wondering if she should press him further. But she didn't.

She led them out of the shadows.

30

Tenner heard the rats minutes before he saw them.

He had moved down South Street, following the tracks that made him think a parade had gone through town—a notion that was further supported by spying the rear of a huge zombie migration away from the downtown section. He had crept along, not wanting to attract the dead's attention, drifting toward Spring Garden Road. When he'd realized he had strayed so far off his intended path, he started retracing his steps back to South Street, which he believed his quarry was following. The undead were on the march, and he'd figured they were in pursuit of the living, so he would stay a hundred meters behind the lot of them, moving stealthily from cover to cover and staying out of sight.

When the sun dropped behind a concrete-and-steel horizon, he'd kept on, moving on a slant that would bring him back on the trail of the four last surviving people in Hellifax. He'd turned a corner, and a massive graveyard spread out before him. Seeing the coast was clear, he'd turned to his right and moved parallel with the graveyard, thinking he would reconnect with South Street on the other side.

That was, until he'd heard the noise.

Something told him that getting his ass to higher ground was probably a good thing.

Slinging his rifle over a shoulder, he spotted a fire escape ladder on a nearby brick building and jumped for the lowest rung. He caught it and hoisted himself up until he got his feet underneath him, breathing hard from the exertion. Up he climbed, panting, and pulled himself onto a metal landing three levels aboveground. He elbowed the glass, smashing it, and climbed through the window, noticing right away the stench coming from within the dark room.

Two lanky corpses sat at a narrow kitchen table and turned in a half-frozen way, baring teeth in lipless mouths. They were dressed in summer clothes, and Tenner got to his feet as they tipped over chairs to get to their own. They didn't hiss or moan, and the only thing brighter than the moonlight shining in through the shattered window were the zombie's teeth, which appeared in remarkably good shape.

Philistines.

His rifle slid off his shoulder, hindering his right arm, but his left was free. Tenner knocked away a hand and reached behind his back, gripping one of his two ceremonial knives. He unsheathed the blade and stabbed the head of the female zombie coming for him, who was dressed in cut-off shorts that hung from bony hips. The woman dropped in front of him and, for a moment, the blade hooked into her jawbone and he struggled to free it. The male loomed over him, his fingers caressing Tenner's back like fat worms. Tenner straightened up and shook his arm free of the rifle, which clattered to the floor. He took a hold of the zombie's head and drove a boot into the side of its knee. The joint snapped like an icicle and the zombie fell, still attempting to hold on to Tenner. The killer gripped the zombie's head and twisted it around as if trying to pull up a deeply-rooted weed. The pop and crinkle of vertebrae actually made Tenner cringe, although he wasn't sure why—he'd done much worse to his victims.

The dead thing still moved and pawed at his body armor.

Tenner saw a chair leg sticking out a few feet away. He bent the zombie over, taking his time, and impaled the creature's eye and skull with the piece of wood. There was resistance, like plunging a finger into sugar, but the zombie stopped moving. Only then did Tenner release it and examine his surroundings.

At the end of the room and next to a gleaming marble countertop was an open doorway.

Then he heard the shuffling.

Tenner went to the doorway and blinked at a corridor filled with carnivorous shadows. The closest one hissed at him, revealing a mouth full of broken teeth.

Tenner slammed the door and pressed his weight against it. A second later a heavy thumping moved him just a bit, but he set his legs and pushed back. The weight from the other side increased, and he knew he would not be able to hold the deadheads back for long. The rifle lay on the floor, but to get to it would mean allowing them to rush in. Tenner snarled and placed his back against the door's surface. He pulled out his Glocks.

Then he opened the door.

The first dozen or so heads packed into the hall exploded in chunks and startled jumps, as if he were spraying bullets into a mosh pit. He emptied one gun, then brought up the second. The Glock's lengthy burp devastated another dozen corpses, silencing their wailing.

But more were coming around the corner.

Apartment building, Tenner's mind giggled in scathing dismay. In getting to high ground, he'd inadvertently climbed into a goddamn nest.

Tenner emptied the mag and *tried* slamming the door, but legs from the fallen corpse stopped him. Growling, he stomped on the limbs and kicked the zombies savagely. In the corridor, zombies, like unrelenting ghouls on the hunt, crept over the piles of wasted flesh, stumbling against the walls, but advancing on his position.

Tenner got the door closed and reloaded both guns.

When he opened the door again, *more* zombies entered the fray. Setting his jaw, he poured a full magazine into the mass, making them dance. Faces burst. Skull fragments bounced off the walls. Dark streaks lashed the corridor's length. The gun went dry and he unloaded with the other, hosing the corpses that remained and mowing them down in a chatter of bullets.

The gun emptied.

But the zombies continued to enter the corridor, drawn to the fight.

Could be at this all night, Tenner thought in exasperation. He didn't feel like playing anymore. Holstering his side arms, he grabbed a grenade from his vest, pulled the pin, and baseball pitched it over the heads of the reforming Philistines looking for a fight. It bounced off a far wall, and Tenner slammed the door once again.

This time he placed his back against a wall.

The explosion shook the floor, and a mass of flesh blew open the door. Tenner grimaced and peered outside. The blast took out the wall thirty feet away, and surprising moonlight revealed what looked to be a chunk of missing floor as well, making a ragged pit that nothing was about to breach.

Tenner kicked the limbs clear, torsos and blast-severed heads, into the hall, and shut the door for the last time, marveling at what it was like to call down holy fire to smite one's foes. He turned his attention back to the kitchen. Darkness shrouded most of the room, but he could make out the refrigerator and countertops. The putrid smell of the place made his eyes water, and he was glad for the smashed window. He turned around and went to the woman he'd put down only a minute earlier—Philistine filth. There was no excitement in killing the undead. It was just a chore that had to be done, not at all as interesting as executing the living. Grabbing her arms, he hoisted her up—not surprised at how light the once reanimated cadaver was—and threw her onto the metal landing. Once she was out of the place, he turned his attention to the second zombie and went about pulling the chair leg from the zombie's eye cavity.

The willowy figure was also shoved out the window. Tenner stepped onto the metal platform and grabbed one leg of the woman, upsetting her and sending her falling to the road with a fleshy splat. He did the same for the other before crawling back through the apartment window. Once inside, he righted one of the fallen chairs and sat down.

Then he heard the noise again, forgotten in the brief battle.

He stuck his head back out the window and peered back the way he'd come, but he couldn't see anything. The road appeared black and wet under the clear night sky, but something struck him as strange.

A feeling he couldn't identify—fear?—lanced through his consciousness. He realized what the blackness truly was when it advanced. It oozed steadily over the snowy pavement below, and Tenner could only stare. The rats slowly came into view, some of the faster ones scrambling ahead and outpacing the mass. The vermin located the two fallen zombies at the base of the building and pitched into the corpses. More rats joined in twos and threes, until the creatures covered the carcasses like a shifting jigsaw puzzle. The unmoving zombies disappeared quickly in a writhing, twisting carpet. Tenner stayed where he was, watching them consume the carcasses and witnessing the darkness flow down the street. Thousands of rats, perhaps *hundreds* of thousands, passed the building. He was suddenly grateful that the fire escape's ladder was well out of their reach. He wouldn't put it past the little furry bastards to be able to climb.

Tenner flipped up his goggles, lifted his mask, and wiped his face with his palm.

Then he saw the graveyard in the distance.

The rats flooded the area as far as his eyes could see. An undulating *sea* of undead turned the pale glow of white into sewage black. The bases of tombstones stood against the rush, and the rats flowed around them. Tenner realized then that what he'd encountered in the tunnel was *nothing* compared to what was crawling over the earth. He looked down to where the two zombies once lay. Dull bones bobbed as every last morsel was gnawed clean.

He could've been *them*.

This wasn't just a horde anymore.

This was something . . . *biblical*.

Tenner picked up his rifle and placed it against one wall. With one hand on his chin, he watched the undead churn. They crawled over each other like black maggots, and he believed he saw faces in their patterns, crying out in terrible pain just before splitting apart. Time and time again faces formed and dissolved. After a while, the rats began to thin out.

Framed in wood and shadow, he pushed himself back from the window and stared out at the graveyard, pondering the existence of the rats as the swarm rippled away. The Philistines were only the beginning. If the vermin were rising in Halifax, they would be in every city. He'd planned to journey to Mexico. If the cities were infested, what would be left for him? Who would have thought it? Perhaps he wasn't the one to scour the last few souls from the earth. Maybe the rats were more efficient. They were certainly awesome to behold.

The rifle lay propped up against the wall, and his eyes flicked to it.

Perhaps he shouldn't be here at all, anymore.

He took the weapon and eyed the fluted barrel.

Perhaps he should just be on his way . . .

He tipped the weapon until the muzzle's black eye stared straight back at him and waited. His thumb found the trigger, and he squeezed just a fraction. Just a little more pressure and he would travel. The mouth of the weapon touched the top of his nose, right between his eyes, the metal cold to the touch. He waited for something to entice him to go that little bit further.

Nothing.

He eased off on the trigger. "Suicides," he scoffed. "Not so easy to do."

Or I'm just not motivated, *he thought.*

"No." He grabbed the rifle and examined its length. "Not yet, anyway."

He sprang up from the chair, knocking it over with a clatter. "Not yet."

Besides, if he killed himself, the whole world would wink out of existence with him.

The street below was empty, and the drone of the rats had diminished. He slunk back out the window and quietly made his way down the ladder, dropping the last meter. A skull lay at his feet, which he tapped with his toe. Tenner slunk along the wall, searching for rats ahead and eyeing the graveyard to his left. After the way the rats had devoured the two Philistines, he suspected the others had fled. The zombies knew about the rats, knew what they were capable of.

A part of him wanted to educate the dead that he should be *equally* feared.

He continued walking, keeping to the shadows and moving as stealthily as possible across intersections. Trash bins lay half-buried in snow and a low distant murmuring came from ahead, but otherwise Halifax was dead. He took no chances and stopped twice, listening to the city and hoping for some clue as to which way to proceed.

He hoped Vick, Amy, Buckle, and the mystery man had encountered the rats and had taken some form of refuge. In the dark, the chance of walking past clues as to their whereabouts would be quite high. Tracks could no longer be trusted either, as all the roads had tracks on them. He would need a thunderbolt of luck to find them, and even then—

A shotgun blast rang out over the city, haunting it, and Tenner froze in his tracks. More shots made him turn in the direction of the noise.

Then nothing.

Tenner smiled, felt a burst of hope, and started to jog.

31

If Scott was right about the time, it was somewhere close to midnight. The moon remained almost impossibly bright, transforming the city into a solemn dreamscape. They kept under the shadowy archway of the bare trees whose limbs reached overhead. Darkness draped across driveways and reminded Scott of open graves or entrances to family tombs, and he couldn't quite shake the feeling something was watching him.

Amy was just ahead, stooped over slightly and hustling with barely a sound. The others trailed behind her in a straight line. She paused once at an intersection, checking a dark sign that informed them they walked along Oakland Road. Amy shook her head. In losing the rats, Scott thought they must have gone really far out of their way. He trusted Amy's guidance to get them back on track.

She looked back and was about to say something when she stopped, staring past Scott. He turned, as did Vick and Buckle.

Emerging out of the midnight gloom was a mob of deadheads.

A *lot* of deadheads.

"Well, shit," Buckle hissed.

The foremost rancid zombie raised an arm and cried out. Other gimps zeroed in on the living, and soon the street was a slow stampede of shadows, made extra creepy by the shadowy lashings of branches.

"Hurry!" Amy whispered and started jogging. They ran around snow-trapped vehicles and linked up with a larger road, where the drifts had been trampled. Amy slowed down. Twenty meters away stood another crowd of deadheads, barring the way. She looked back quickly, and Scott suddenly felt the space between the two bodies of undead close in on them. The houses in the area were generously spaced, considering how tightly packed they'd been on previous streets, and drifts rose up like serpentine spines, covering lawns.

Amy broke into a run.

Toward the zombies now fifteen meters ahead of her.

Holy shit! Scott thought as he increased his own speed. What the hell was she doing?

He glimpsed one of the corpses before them, wearing the body armor and battle helmet of a soldier. A black visor hid its upper face, while its lower jaws remained visible.

Amy altered her path and stomped across a lawn, her feet driving deep into the snow. The men struggled to keep up, and Scott's legs sunk to his knees—deep enough to suck the energy from him. The two separate groups of zombies joined forces behind them and pursued. Voices of the dead sang out, making Scott run faster.

They slogged around a two-story house and through a backyard filled with deep snow. Amy got halfway up the drift and looked over a fence. She turned around and waved off the men.

"Too deep," she huffed. "Get to the house."

Scott turned around and saw Buckle and Vick sunk to their knees. Behind them was a condensed featureless knot of heads, torsos, and arms, all blackened by the shadow of the nearby houses, blocking any retreat.

"Can't go back!" Vick waved. "They'll have more trouble than us."

Amy didn't argue. She struggled up the drift and crawled over the fence. Scott went after her, feeling the round tops of the fence pickets through his Nomex coat. Vick and Buckle struggled through the snow, their energy being sapped away. The zombies came under the full glare of the moon. The soldier marched forward, outpacing the others, its mouth hanging open almost sadly.

Closing in on Buckle.

"Donny!" Amy cried.

Buckle glanced over his shoulder and spotted the dead thing. He flipped himself over the fence, right behind Vick, flicking up snow as he went. The soldier staggered and bogged down in the drift's depths.

"This way," Amy yelled and waded onward, arms flailing, toward a copse of bare trees.

Scott and the other men pulled away from their pursuers, but he glanced back to see the undead crawling over each other to clear the fence.

"We could've made a stand there," Scott blurted.

"Plenty of time to make a stand," Amy answered, pointing. To their right, more dark figures plodded through someone's garden.

"The hell they come from?" Scott asked.

"Don't worry about them—just move!" Vick urged.

Through the frozen brush they went, each step leeching away a little more energy. They outpaced the zombies on the right, but the night was no longer quiet. All around them, Moe wailed in hunger. A wall of glowing snow rose up before them. The trees ended and they stumbled onto a walkway, closer to the towering wall in front of them. Scott realized it wasn't a snow bank, but the side of a very large concrete structure.

"Dalplex," Amy said and went to the right.

"Dalplex?" Scott echoed.

"Sports arena," Vick informed him.

Amy came back and Scott saw why: huge chunks of debris had fallen from the building to the tree line, effectively blocking any further progress.

"Back the other way," Amy told them. "The Army or Navy must've hit the place with something. The place's shot to shit."

They turned around and stopped in their tracks.

A crowd of undead came around the corner of the building, slinking and smiling as if they had just heard a truly amusing joke. They swayed on their feet, gesturing with limbs that, in some cases, were not whole. The humans moved forward as a dark wave of Moe—the ones chasing them for the last few minutes—struggled through the nearby trees.

"Lord Jesus," Buckle said softly, seeing they were penned in.

"We have to go through them. It's the fastest way," Amy said, flicking out her tonfas.

"Then, we go through," Vick said, stepping up to stand at her side. He slipped on his spiked knuckles, weapons Scott knew would have scared the shit out of the living.

"What do we do?" Scott asked.

"Watch their backs," Buckle answered. "And keep an eye on the bunch behind us."

There was a pause as teacher and student prepared themselves for the coming battle, then they were swinging. Amy and Vick attacked the dead with an energy that took Scott's breath away. Back in the parking lot it had been Buckle and Vick facing Moe, but now Scott saw teacher and student united against a morbid enemy. Giving each other room, Vick and Amy greeted the dead with steel and hard wood.

The display was nothing short of stunning.

Scott stood dumbfounded, watching both martial artists as they created a close combat spectacle unimpeded by the inhibitions that would have been present if their attackers were alive. Whatever combat skills they had acquired over the years and finely tuned, they unleashed. The whirling tonfas and flashing steel pipe inflicted devastating blows to the advancing deadheads. Vick and Amy pounded in skulls, broke knees, and snapped arms, ripping out zombies like unpleasant weeds. Vick pumped his spikes into faces and temples while Amy attacked legs, upending corpses before bashing or spiking heads. She flipped one zombie over her back, and Buckle darted forward and brained it with his Halligan. He worked the weapon free with a crunch and pulled back to Scott.

Who just continued to watch.

It wasn't because he was awestruck anymore or even scared.

He simply realized he would be in the way.

Vick made magic with his pipe and spiked knuckles, thrashing and destroying gimps before they could lay their frozen hands on him. He seemed to be laboring as the fight went on, and the whirling, destructive energy of the steel pipe slowed.

Amy, on the other hand, appeared to just be warming up.

And kicking ass.

She spun the tonfas in her hands so fast that they resembled propellers. Her speed and fury made Scott think of Bruce Lee. She blocked hands with the weapons, spread the arms of her attackers wide, and spiked faces with the pointed ends. The resounding clatter of skulls being smashed became a gruesome rhythm. A soldier got his face bashed to one side before being spiked under the chin. An obese office worker with a rug of a beard had his knee broken and his temple crumpled. She cracked the skulls of three boys so fast Scott wasn't sure what had happened, hearing only the angry clack of a dancer's castanets. A female zombie reached for Amy with a skeletal arm and had it snapped into rubber before being swatted to the ground. One bash to another's jaw sent a hail of broken teeth bouncing off the concrete wall.

Amy darted left and right against the decomposing tide, not standing in any one place, but somehow aware of Vick and his steel pipe. Her movements blurred against the backdrop of slow-moving zombies. A low wall of unmoving Moe lay at her feet, and the zombies struggled to cross it, stumbling frequently. Several times Scott thought to rush to her side to stop a gimp reaching for her leg, only to see her kill it with frightening force.

Then Vick dropped back, chest heaving and arms drooping.

Buckle moved forward, kicking zombies and lashing out with the Halligan tool. Vick had been a symphony of destruction, a smooth-moving flow of practiced strikes; Buckle was brutal force. The Halligan broke bones with each heavy swing. With surprising speed, three zombies appeared out of the shadows and fell upon the former cop. Then Amy was there, hooking two zombies off their feet with her tonfas. Buckle crushed the skull of the last, but more crowded in.

Scott dropped his bat and drew the Ruger. He fired with both hands and emptied the magazine into the heads of three zombies, the exit holes bursting loudly. The weapon clicked dry and he didn't have time to reload, so he shoved the gun into his boot and shouldered the shotgun.

Boom. A face exploded. Both Amy and Buckle ducked out of the way, giving Scott all the room he needed.

Boom. A huge chunk flew from a stomach. *Boom.* The head followed, flying from its shoulders.

Boom. Boom. Two more gimps fell, their skulls shredded.

Buckle crushed the last deadhead's skull, embedding the Halligan into the zombie's temple with a harsh crunch.

"Five shots in that thing?" Buckle turned and asked with a wry smile. "That's a firearm violation, me son."

"Sorry, Officer," Scott said.

"I'm not fucking sorry," Vick muttered, steaming past them. "Get moving!"

The zombies still pursuing them were through the trees, getting closer.

Scott grabbed his bat and ran after the others. Following the wall, they raced around the building and arrived at the main entrance. The clear glass doors were unlocked, but the interior appeared as a starless void. The doors were the automatic kind, and the dead sensors would not allow them entry. With a grunt, Vick shoved one spiked fist into a crease and pried the door back enough so he could get his fingers in. Buckle jammed his Halligan into the widening slot and pulled, his back bending with the strain. The doors finally opened, and Vick waved them inside. Once in, they pushed the doors shut.

"The glass should hold for a while," he said, eyeing countless dark figures making their way across a snow-filled parking lot. "I think we're hitting the ones that went by the house."

"And any others in the area," Buckle added. Amy looked inside to a second set of doors. She pushed one open and went into the building, seeing soft light deeper inside, at the end of a corridor of blackness.

"Where you heading?" Vick asked.

"Can't go that way. Gotta find another exit."

"There's light ahead," Scott said.

"Probably a hole made by the same thing that blew that wall to hell," Amy figured. "Just don't make any noise. We don't want to have to go back the way we came."

"Suppose not," Scott said. He ejected the empty magazine from his Ruger and slapped in a fresh one.

"How many of those you got?" Buckle asked.

"Last one."

"Too bad."

"You said you shoot shit?"

"When I have a gun, yeah."

"Here, then." Scott handed him the shotgun. He dug out the remaining two dozen or so shells he had in his pockets and backpack. Buckle took the shells and the weapon, but regarded the shotgun in one hand and the Halligan in the other.

"Kinda awkward," he said, but slung the shotgun over his shoulders.

"They're getting close," Vick whispered, watching the zombies in the parking lot. A gimp abruptly stepped into view at the edge of the glass doors, rapping its face against the clear surface and bouncing back two steps. It moaned and smeared its features across the glass, making it squeal, while others drifted in from the sides. The soldier was amongst them.

"They can't see us," Amy said. "We're too far back from the doors and in the dark. They'll give up after a while, I bet."

"Lose the scent?" Scott asked.

"Exactly."

"Hold on for a bit, then. Let me catch my breath," Vick whispered.

"Seconded," Buckle said.

"If you oldtimers can't keep up, we might have to leave you behind."

"Jesus, Vick," Buckle's voice issued from the dark. "Where's the respect for seniors?"

"Couldn't take the strap to Amy," Vick explained. "Too damn fast. And you know how social services are, man. One phone call and you'd be arresting me."

"True," Buckle agreed. "World went to hell long before Moe."

Amy and Scott eyed the outer doors. The zombies thumped against the glass panes, but they didn't break. The dead groaned, the sound muted by glass. More came up from the rear, attracted by the others. Seconds became minutes, and a sizeable crowd gathered outside, thumping against the glass. Scott's unease grew. He didn't want to stay here much longer, even though he was sure Moe couldn't see them.

"Time to go," Amy said after a few moments, perhaps feeling the same way. She held her tonfas in one hand and grabbed Scott's right arm. "Link up."

"Ready, then," Buckle said, latching onto Vick.

"Those are my balls, man," Vick said, his tone as serious as only a man could be when his boys were being violated. "Just kidding. He really only grabbed my ass."

Amy groaned and turned toward the men. "Fifties, my ass. You guys are like twelve-year-olds."

"Just some levity," Vick went on. "Lord knows *he's* probably laughing up there."

"Yeah, well, he's up there and your ass is down here," Amy said, pulling Scott after her. "So just remember that next time you make a funny, 'cause I'll kick the shit out of it."

Vick had his free hand on Scott's shoulder. "How you doing?"

Scott wasn't quite sure how to answer.

As a train, they slunk toward the shards of light further inside the building.

"Wish to Christ we had a flashlight," Buckle muttered.

Scott did, too.

32

After killing Murphy, Fist felt one problem had been resolved, but he was more than eager to address any others, should they arise. Interestingly enough, none did, and their foraging went relatively smoothly over the next few days. They eventually rolled over the Nova Scotian provincial border, with a stop in the town of Truro. From there, Fist decided to drive for the heart of the province. Winter storms had made driving terrible. Hunting had been non-existent, forcing them to subsist on their Sackville kills, which they consumed quickly. They had cans of food, but no one was ready to eat only vegetables. It was the one thing they agreed upon with the reanimated corpses.

Fresh meat was best.

They drove down the 102 and slipped unnoticed into Halifax, arriving by early afternoon after a major storm that had clogged the roads with snow. They wrapped the tires in chains, which gave the vans better traction as they pressed deeper into the city. Zombies attempted to welcome them, and the vans pushed through several, their ravaged limbs slapping against the vehicles' sides with fleshy thuds. The Norsemen eventually lost these greeters and made their way downtown, wary of roads rendered impassable by snow or abandoned vehicles, until they came out on the other side of an enormous office building with a gaping mouth at its base.

An underground parking lot.

It had been an easy thing to drive both vans into the darkness and use them to block the entrance with the vehicles. They cleaned out the two dozen or so zombies that inhabited the underground darkness, killing them with savage efficiency.

And they camped there for two days.

A campfire blazed a few feet away from the vans, fueled by old garbage taken from a nearby bin. Seven of the remaining eleven Norsemen gathered around the flames while the others stood guard at the entrance. They cooked up the last victim of Sackville and supplemented their meal with tins of watery carrots and peas.

It was about then, just after Fist had returned from the dark after urinating against a wall, when they heard the distant gunshots.

Around the fire, the others stopped talking and listened and, for a moment, the crackling of the flames was the only sound. Fist's soot-blackened eyes narrowed, and he looked in the direction the shots had come from. Farther into the city, but not so far away from where they were camped.

The others didn't move, waiting expectantly for more gunfire. When it didn't come, they looked to their leader expectantly, like dogs waiting to be fed. No one would dare move before he gave the word, not after the example made of Murphy, and Fist liked that just fine.

He waited few more seconds before grunting as if he'd heard an amusing remark. The open fire pit burned, casting an evil hue over his men and the nearby area.

Fist got moving toward the van, waving a hand as he went.

Behind him, the others jumped to their feet in savage glee.

The darkness enveloped them and made their passage difficult. Several times, Amy bumped up against something, stopped for a moment as if in pain, and continued walking. They went through a gate and another doorway, and light from the moon suddenly gave the dark some semblance of shape.

"Where we heading?" Scott leaned forward and whispered.

"The pool. I've been here before, after the renovations," Amy whispered back. "We'll cut through the pool area and make our way to the exit on the other side. Get back onto South Street."

Even though they both wore gloves, he liked being led along in the dark by Amy.

"Do we have to keep holding on?" Buckle whispered.

"Unless you want to fumble around in the dark, yes," Amy told him. "All right, the pool's this way."

They entered a room where chunks of the roof had been destroyed, large enough for snow to blow into the area and coat everything in sparkling, ceramic white. Night sky, lighter than the building's interior, shone through, and Scott saw stars twinkling between hanging banners. A pile of rubble lay in a heap underneath the rippling cloth. It was as if someone had blown away one section of the roof and left the rest. Snow coated the floor tiles, and even the pool glowed with eerie wonder.

"Holy shit," Amy said. "Well, this will go faster."

"What?"

"The water's frozen."

"Oh?"

"Hold on," Amy said and broke away. She stepped to the edge of the pool and stabbed a tonfa through the layer of snow. "Feels solid."

She tapped again, harder.

Two arms rose from under the snow and grabbed Amy's wrists, pulling her forward. She shrieked and landed on the powdery surface, where more zombies straightened up, clumps of snow slipping from their frames. Vick yelled and jumped after her, swinging his steel pipe. Buckle went to the pool's edge and brained a rising zombie with one strike of the Halligan.

Scott kicked one zombie that came up to his knees and bent him backward, only to have the thing come lurching back at him. He realized the dead thing was frozen in the water, from the waist down. Dead fingers grazed the lower parts of Scott's legs, seeking purchase, before he squashed its head with two blows from his bat. The emerging zombies stayed in place, grasping for the living, but unable to close hands around them. Vick dispatched three deadheads and stood guard while Amy killed her attacker and struggled to her feet. The dead cried out, their voices echoing in the devastated pool area. The creatures reached and clawed for the living, but made no attempt to move forward.

"Well, Christ," Scott said. All the deadheads had become trapped in the pool. At some point, they had stumbled into the shallow end and stayed there until the water eventually froze them in place.

Amy pulled Scott back by the shoulder, breaking the spell of fascination.

"Fuckers are frozen in there," Buckle declared, and the four of them simply stood and stared at the writhing figures trapped in the water.

"They probably wandered in here, dropped in, and couldn't get out. Then it got cold." Amy shrugged, giving her arms a quick rub. "My tapping woke them up."

"Just like a dinner bell," Buckle said.

"We don't have to go through, right? Just hang to the walls?" Scott asked.

"Yeah, sure," Amy said, over her fright. There was plenty of room to avoid crossing the pool. The zombies continued wailing as the four of them threaded their way around the tiled edge of the pool. More gimps straightened up in the area where the living had first entered, while corpses in the deeper sections became shorter and didn't move at all. The water trapped zombies up to their midsections, their lower chests, their shoulders, until . . .

Scott stopped and stared.

Heads like ruined bowling balls groaned feebly at them, as if the living were the reason for their situation. Other heads appeared as white lumps whose surfaces split apart when their mouths opened. Still *more* heads, deeper in the pool, didn't move at all. They were just there, like snowballs waiting to be pushed under the surface. If he cleared away the snow covering the deep end, he was certain he'd find the tops of submerged heads. Perhaps even upturned faces, unmoving and staring up at the water's surface.

"Move on," Vick ordered him. Scott suddenly felt as if his own limbs had become blocks of ice.

"Un-fucking believable," he said in wonder.

"Ain't it," Buckle agreed. "The places they get themselves into and still make a grab for you? Kills me, I swear to Jesus."

"This way," Amy called to them, standing to the right of a dark doorway.

They pressed on, moving farther into darkness. Amy groped for Scott's arm again and led him along a concrete wall.

"Here we go," she finally said.

"You okay?" Scott asked.

"Yeah." She sniffed and adjusted her helmet. "Just got the jump on me, is all. Poppa Vick had me covered."

Scott felt a pang of guilt. She was right. He'd stood by as if glued in place while Vick dove in and started swinging.

"I'll cover it next time," he vowed in a quiet voice.

Amy looked back at him. "Didn't mean that as a cheap dig. Just that he and Buckle and I have been around awhile. Understand?"

Scott nodded. He still meant what he'd said, but he kept quiet.

"Did you just nod?" Amy asked.

"Huh? Oh, uh, yeah."

"Barely saw that, mister. You watch yourself." He could tell she was smiling. Scott found himself starting to like this woman. She was no-nonsense, tough, and possessed a sense of humor that he was only now starting to understand. Kelly had been like that—without the tonfas.

"Hold on a few minutes," Vick said in the dark. "We're safe here, I think."

"Another breather?"

Silence. "Yeah. Sorry."

"Me, too," Buckle added.

"Don't worry about it," Amy quietly assured them in the dark. "Ain't leaving you behind. Even though you're hard to clean up after."

The group waited and collected themselves for a few minutes.

"All ready?" Amy finally asked.

They were.

"Let's go, then."

They heard the metallic clink of an emergency exit bar being pushed down, and the door swung open. They emerged from the Dalplex and looked around cautiously, checking the corners and trees ahead of them. Scott wondered what other horrors Halifax had in store for them. He suspected that if his hair hadn't already turned grey from the constant frights, it would simply fall out.

No Moe could be seen.

Amy walked a few paces, the snow rising up to her shins, and peered into the darkness ahead. After confirming the coast was clear, she turned around and abruptly held up a hand.

"You hear that?" she whispered.

Scott listened, hearing that familiar low, rustling hum coming from their left, polluting the clean silence of the night. It was coming from the not-so-distant parking lot where the zombies had once pursued them. Moans rose above the humming, which struck Scott as odd.

"You want to check it out?" Amy asked.

"No," Vick said.

"Fuck no," Buckle added.

But Amy moved to a fire ladder nailed into the wall, just ten feet to the right of the exit. She unslung her pack and dropped it in a drift with a soft thud. "You guys hold on here, then."

"Don't do it, Amy," Buckle said.

"I want to see," Amy replied. "Besides, I'm on the roof."

"We don't have time for this."

Vick didn't protest, nor did he tell her to be careful, and Buckle shut up as well.

"I'll come along," Scott said, not really wanting to. He suspected he was going to see something he didn't like, but he didn't want her to go alone. Amy jumped to the lower rung and pulled herself up with surprising speed considering the weight of the padding and gear she wore. Once she got her boots onto the lower rungs, Scott followed.

They climbed fifteen feet to the top. Snow piled on the roof, almost knee-high in places, rising like pale dunes. Once Scott got to his feet, Amy pointed at the dark holes nearby that dotted the roof of the Dalplex.

"Army?" Scott asked.

"Army. This way."

They made their way toward the parking lot area, avoiding any holes in the roof where the structure might have been weakened by the shelling. The cars farthest away came slowly into view.

Scott faltered to a stop when he saw the scope of what was swarming amongst the deserted vehicles.

"You okay?" Amy turned and asked.

"We have to go back."

"Just a moment."

"Amy," Scott grated. "If this was a movie, this would be the part where the audience would be slapping their foreheads and screaming at us to head back."

"Listen, we're above them. Okay? And last time I checked, they can't climb."

"*Amy* . . . Goddamn it."

"You coming, then?" Without waiting for an answer, she left him, obviously not bothered if he accompanied her further or not. Scott hesitated, threw his head back in exasperation, and followed. They hunkered down as they got closer to the edge, not wanting to be seen.

Then they saw it.

The zombies on the lot, perhaps a hundred or more, writhed and wailed as rats devoured them from the ground up. Figures staggered from car to car, some falling on hoods as the vermin coated them from head to foot in a wriggling mass. Some gimps reached out to the moon, holding up arms covered in swinging rodents. Other did nothing, muddling along the cars as the teeming tide chewed away at their feet and ankles until they collapsed. When the corpses fell, they disappeared from sight in seconds, covered in hairy crawlers. Scott saw the soldier gimp marching away from the doors, as if trying to escape. Rats piled onto the figure, clinging by jaws and claws, and the deadhead did nothing to stop them. They ripped the unprotected parts of its person, bypassing the body armor. The soldier cried out, some inarticulate whale song that Scott thought haunting, as the rats burrowed inside its still upright carcass. Within seconds, the figure toppled to its hands and knees, and rats swarmed it in a gush. A moment later, its torso sunk to the ground, as if its hands had been gnawed away from underneath it. The soldier rolled to a sitting position, like a chunk of ice righting itself in water. An arm gave way and it toppled over onto its back, then disappeared under the diseased deluge.

"I've seen enough," Amy whispered.

"Huh?" Scott blurted, freaked out by the feeding frenzy.

"Let's go," she said and started backing away from the edge of the roof. Scott followed, perhaps never so grateful to run from something in all of his life. He watched where they both walked, not wanting to plunge through an unseen skylight or have some other freak accident and alert the veritable blob just behind them.

"They're something, eh?" Amy asked, dropping back to his side.

"I can't believe the things exist."

"Funny, too. Viruses don't usually jump from one organism to another. Unless it's mutated. But this one did. I wonder if it's gotten to any other animal?"

"Christ, I hope not."

They retraced their footsteps in the snow.

"See anything interesting?" Buckle asked as they climbed down on the ladder.

Scott shook his head, visions of rats devouring deadheads still in his mind. He knew he'd have nightmares sooner or later.

"We have to get away from here. Not much time."

"What's over there?" Vick asked. "We could hear Moe."

"Moe was being eaten alive," Amy replied.

"Rats?" Vick asked.

Amy started walking. "Yeah."

They labored through the snow, away from the parking lot area, and eventually disappeared into the trees. They left the Dalplex center and made their way through high, unblemished drifts, heading for the road.

Fortunately, the rats did not follow them.

Not right away.

33

After several minutes, Tenner crossed onto South Street and jogged for two blocks, over cluttered avenues where the snow had been trampled by countless feet, creating an icy mat that threatened to upend him if he moved much faster. There were no Philistines about and, more importantly, no rats. The vermin seemed to be swinging far to the left, drawn to dead meat. He felt like a gunslinger, swaggering down a deserted street and waiting for anyone to step into view to challenge him. He knew he was on the right path for some reason, and he had learned long ago to trust his instincts. The armor he wore slowed him, its weight considerable, but he wasn't about to relinquish it. Not after what he'd seen.

Far ahead in a street that glowed in the moonlight, stepping out from between trapped vehicles like shooting targets popping into existence, he saw two shadows. Tenner scurried behind a car, flattening his upper body over the trunk. With the moon still full in the sky and a backdrop of white snow, it was easy to make out the shadows crossing the road, four in total.

Holy shit. He'd found them.

Well, he'd found *someone.* The city attracted the odd survivor into its web, for whatever reasons. With such a high number of undead running around, not to mention the new and oddly fascinating presence of the rats, Tenner had made the decision to get the hell out of Dodge once he finished his hunt. He fully intended to load up whatever curry and supplies he could aboard his SUV and move out.

But first . . . First he'd finish what he'd set out to do.

When the dark figures slipped out of view, he crept from his hiding place and double-timed it up the street, his AR-20 shouldered and pointed at the ground. He jogged only as fast as necessary, to keep things from rattling. He looked around at times, scouring the shadows and ensuring there were no zombies or rats nearby.

Mustn't spook them. Mustn't, mustn't. He repeated the words in his mind. The shadows were out of sight, one with the dark, and he hoped he wouldn't lose the trail. A waist-high stone wall lay on his right, and behind that a great empty space opened up behind a high, wire mesh fence. An athletic field, perhaps. Across the street, a series of townhouses or low apartment buildings blocked any further view. He hoped the buildings were empty. He didn't need to run into another nest. As he got closer to where he'd last spied the four figures, he slowed down and studied the snow. There were plenty of tracks, but he wasn't certain if they belonged to his prey or to Philistines.

Once Tenner reached the area where he believed the others had crossed, he stooped over, keeping a row of cars on his right, and peeked in between the derelict wrecks, looking for signs of passage. There were several, but he still wasn't sure if they belonged to the living. Checking his rear flanks and seeing the coast was clear, he continued his hunt. Ahead, towering trees spread their bare limbs across the night sky, fracturing the moonlight. Behind them, low buildings birthed a courtyard of darkness and made it difficult to see.

Tenner crouched and trotted toward the rows of dark buildings, raising his weapon and hoping he was heading in the right direction. He kept checking the snow for tracks, hoping his quarry would not be caught by the rats or Philistines.

That would piss him off to no end.

Led by Amy, they left the road and skirted further inward, aiming to cut though a cluster of buildings when that plan became suddenly impossible. Underneath the dark shape of a pedway, walking as if asleep, was another crowd of zombies, lingering in the space between the buildings as if trapped. They swayed and cried out softly, oblivious to the approaching living. Under Amy's direction, they dropped to their bellies and lay flat in the snow.

"We're heading over there," Amy whispered. "Just follow me. I think I saw an open door at the bottom of that one place. A dormitory's fire exit, maybe."

"A residence?" Scott almost stopped in his tracks. "That could be a nest."

"That's a nest out there," Amy said. "But I think I can get us around them."

"How do you know this place?"

"My husband stayed here for a year. He went to Dalhousie."

Oh. His stomach suddenly fell away. *She's married?* For the first time that night, he was grateful for the dark.

"Lead on, Amy," Vick huffed. "Get us out of this shit."

Hugging trees and ducking behind cars, the four kept out of sight and crept toward the open portal. Reaching it, they quickly disappeared inside. Buckle quietly closed the door, and they found themselves in a stairwell. Amy went down a level and disappeared into darkness. The men followed reluctantly, finding her at another closed door at the bottom level.

"Through here and out another door and we're into a parking area," Amy said. "Okay?"

The men grunted; they were fine with the idea.

Amy pulled the door open and went inside. Scott breathed in air that felt more like a meat freezer than a student residence. Darkness swallowed them, sending waves of unease through Scott. He couldn't see Amy.

"Can't see shit," Buckle whispered.

"Keep a hand on the right wall," Amy said from ahead. "Just stay out of the rooms."

Thankful that there weren't too many turns, they reached out and used the wall to guide themselves down the hall. Some of the surfaces were grainy, but some were knobby and sticky with an unknown substance. The dark became a rhythm of wall and door. Amy tripped on something—twice—and warned Scott and the others of whatever was on the floor. He nudged the floor with his toes, feeling his way down the hall. A faint smell of decomposed flesh or something similar caught his attention. The wall they followed disappeared twice, indicating open doors or hallways, but there were no lights. None of them stopped or fell, despite whatever littered the tiles underfoot. Scott was thankful he couldn't see what filled the corridor, as he suspected it wasn't pretty.

"Turn on the right coming up and one flight of steps down," Amy whispered, the words floating back to him. He felt along the wall until it fell away. He made the turn, descending carefully until his foot touched a step.

There was something stretched out on it.

"What the hell," Scott muttered.

"Something's on the steps," Amy said before he could say any more. "So be careful."

"That's a man," Vick said.

"A dead man," Buckle said, his voice hanging in place as if he'd stopped to inspect the shape. The notion didn't set well with Scott. It was a fucking *void* in here, and any moment he fully expected something to clamp around his wrist or ankle and pull him down into oblivion.

"Leave it, Buckle," Vick insisted.

"Just making sure," Buckle said, his voice a whisper in the dark, heightening Scott's growing stress.

"Shit."

That was something Scott didn't need to hear. "What?"

"I must've missed a turn or something," Amy stated.

"Huh?"

"There was supposed to be a door down here. The dark is messing me up. And it's been years since I've been here. Hold on."

Hands groped Scott's chest, and Amy passed him in the dark. The others shuffled in the featureless soup until she walked past.

"All right, keep up."

They retraced their steps, the wall on the left now, moving through pitch blackness as cold and deep as some undiscovered arctic cave. Scott brought up the rear, pausing for a moment.

He'd heard something behind him.

"You guys hear that?"

He peered back the way he'd come, but he could see nothing. The dark was so utterly devoid of shape it was as if someone had gouged out his eyes.

Except sound.

It was back there, somewhere, in the dark. It seemed to stop when Scott did, advancing only when he did. But that couldn't be right. Gimps made noise.

He heard it again. Scott's senses became completely aware, everything coming online, trying to detect the exact location of the noise.

Ssssshumt.

The soft, definitely *organic* sound was somewhere behind them and slinking forward.

"You guys hear that?" he repeated, wondering why the hell they hadn't answered him.

But the others had marched ahead.

Jesus, Scott thought, keeping his hand on the wall and shuffling forward. He stumbled up the steps, feeling the weight of whatever it was on the steps.

"Scott?" someone called out ahead. Amy's voice.

Ssssshumt . . . Ssssshumt.

Panic rose up in Scott's chest and, for a moment, he was certain whatever was following in his wake was going to grab him—grab him and haul him back *there*, where it would nail him to the ground and gut him with hooks or claws or something even worse. He plodded forward, sightless, keeping one hand against the wall and leaning against it for support. The noise seemed to be only ten paces away and getting closer. That same soft squishing sound, like something wet and dangling being dragged along the tiles, just tickling it, before a heavy weight came down upon it and another ponderous step was taken.

"Scott?" Amy called again, and he could hear Vick's and Buckle's grumblings in the void.

"Here! I'm here!" Scott called, not loudly, but certainly no longer whispering.

"Hurry," Amy called. Why did she sound so far away?

Then he was falling.

In his haste to get back to the main floor, he'd forgotten about the open doors and had fallen right through one, landing on his side in a huff and expulsion of air.

"Scott!" Buckle cried.

Sssshumt. Sssshumt. The sound was much closer than Buckle.

Scott scrambled to his feet and tightened his grip on his bat. If there was something out there, he'd crack open its skull before it got him. All at once, visions of terrible things—giant eyeballs with fanged mouths or worms the size of trains—flashed before his mind's eye. He pushed them away and reached out in the total dark, wondering—hoping—he'd touch something familiar.

"Scott," Buckle whispered nearby. "Where y'be, me son?"

"Here." Scott stepped forward and bumped into something. He tried to grab it, but it landed with a crash on the floor, shattered pieces suddenly playing piano. He didn't think a nuke could've made more noise.

Then a hand grabbed him.

"Gotcha," Buckle said, his hand gripping Scott's shoulder. "You okay? Breathing awfully hard."

"Something was following me," Scott managed to say.

"What?" Buckle pulled him back to the doorway, where he finally regained his bearings.

"Listen, and get ready just in case," Scott warned.

But after ten seconds, it was Amy's voice that broke the tomb-like silence. "Hurry, you guys."

"Don't hear anything," Buckle said to Scott.

"It was catching up to me," Scott said, fear in his voice. "Then I forgot about the open door and fell through."

Silence. "Nothing out there now. Would've come for us after you broke the lamp or vase or whatever that was, I think."

There was no mistaking that. So what had he heard?

"C'mon," Buckle said, reaching out and guiding him back by the shoulder. Scott puzzled over the noise he'd heard all the way back to Amy and Vick.

"What happened to you?" Amy asked.

He shook his head and then realized no one could see it. "I don't know. Heard something back there."

"What?"

"Don't know. It slacked off when Buckle reached me."

For a moment they listened, not hearing a thing.

"Don't want to scare you guys, but . . ." Amy began.

"But what?" Vick's voice.

"This place had a reputation at one time. Back in the day. I never believed it, but . . ."

"But what?" Scott wanted to know.

"Well . . . just that there were a couple of suicides in the place. Some kids hanged themselves. Around exam time, I think. I remember Jordy—my husband—talking about it. Guys would hear things at night. Only hear things, never see. Sounds outside their doors or late at night in the laundry room. Whenever someone investigated, nothing was found."

"Amy?" Vick asked.

"Yeah?"

"Can we get the fuck out of here?"

Amy hesitated before answering. "This way."

"Thank you," Vick said, annoyance in the martial artist's voice—but Scott also thought that, in a world where corpses walked, it was very possible that Vick *believed* in such stories. There was a hint that perhaps the older man's nerves were also starting to fray in the constant blackness.

Giving directions when needed, Amy led them once more through the dark, taking longer this time, until they turned another corner and a distant window oozed moonlight. Scott exhaled in relief.

"Almost there," Amy whispered, her coarse voice sounding impish. Seconds later, they gathered before a door to the outside. The window offered a view of an empty parking space underneath the residence, and an opening that led out into a lane and, beyond that, a road.

"Well, shit. Almost home," Amy said, looking out the window.

Scott took a peek and shrugged. "Nothing. I was expecting deadheads. Where are they, do you think?"

"You want to see Moe?" Amy asked.

"Hell no, I'm happy." Scott smiled, relieved to be out of the dark.

"Ready, oldtimers?" Amy directed at Vick and Buckle.

"Gonna slap your ass you ever call me that again," Buckle warned her softly.

"I like 'oldtimer,' myself," Vick said. His steel pipe rasped against floor tiling.

"Anything's an improvement over pussy, eh?" Buckle said.

Scott made a face and shook his head.

The Newfoundlander caught the movement. "Don't worry about us, me son. Them's only terms of endearment. Besides, old Vick won't remember any of it two minutes from now."

"I'll remember kicking your ass just fine," Vick deadpanned. "Just keep it up."

The abrupt opening of the door quieted them all, and Scott suspected that was Amy's intent. She entered the parking area and the rest of the men filed out after her. Beyond the parking area, an empty lane and parallel road beckoned. Amy stopped and peered around the corner, ensuring everything was clear. They took in the gleaming road frosted in white. Across the way, a large gathering of empty-looking condos loomed in the sky.

"All right, the way looks clear," Amy said. "We're on Oxford. We keep going straight, or at least parallel with it, until we reach Connaught."

"Not a lot of places for cover out there, Amy," Buckle said, frowning. "Except for the cars."

"We'll make do with that, then. Unless you have a better idea?"

Scott didn't. Neither did Vick or Buckle.

"All right, then," Amy stated. "We go."

34

Tenner moved stealthily through the snow, hearing the moans from the dead up ahead and concealing himself when necessary. He didn't want to stir them up, not when he felt he was close to his quarry. He ducked behind a car and studied his surroundings. A mob of zombies stood within the confines of what appeared to be a courtyard up ahead, and he didn't think Vick or the others had gone that way. They'd be avoiding the Philistines.

So . . . where?

The tracks around him were of no help; there were simply too many. He looked at the closest building, a stone structure with every window dark and forbidding. His attention drifted to its base. The dark rectangular shape of a closed door captured his attention.

He checked on the zombies, making sure they hadn't seen him, and kept low to the ground as he moved toward the closed door. When he reached it, he dropped into a crouch and extended his fingers, feeling the snow and appreciating that a section of it had been swept over in a fan shape, as a door might do if it had been opened and then closed. The marks were recent. It wasn't a certainty, but he liked the odds that his old gang might have ducked inside the building to avoid the zombies lurking in the courtyard.

The moon hung fat in the sky, but it was dropping. He found the door handle and opened it; he could barely see the stairwell inside it was so dark. He paused and listened, not hearing anything. Staying bent over, he left the door open and crept around the corner of the building, taking the long way around. Ahead lay the white strip of the street. His boots sunk into deep drifts, slowing him, but he eventually reached the far corner and edged around it.

Holy shit.

Just topping what might have been a rise in the land, he spied shadows on the pavement, moving away from him.

They might have been zombies.

But Tenner didn't think they were.

He treaded softly ahead in pursuit, passing a parking area on his right, empty and uninteresting. Fresh tracks of a small number of people lay in the snow. They were grouped together and seemingly in a line, not at all like a crowd of undead. They went to the edge of the parking lane and dropped five feet, over a stony embankment and to the main street's sidewalk. Tenner reached the corner of the building and placed his back to it. Off in the distance, he heard the restless dead.

The little devils, he thought. They had come this way and stayed out of sight of the zombies by crouching below the embankment, which appeared to run beyond the length of the street. The building he had his back against was built on a low mound, as were the others surrounding it.

He retreated to a snow-covered car and placed his AR-20 on the roof, the butt of the weapon firm against his shoulder. He lifted the goggles to his forehead and squinted through the scope, moving the weapon until he spotted the retreating shadows sinking behind a rise in the street. They were spread out and, for a moment, Tenner wasn't sure who he'd be firing at. He selected one shadow, targeted its head, and flipped the selector switch to single-shot mode.

Then he took aim once more, baring teeth.

Which one are you? Vick? The mystery man? *He focused on his target.* What might this bullet bring?

They were almost over the crest and out of sight, the asphalt gobbling them down to their waists, then their torsos. One winked out of sight—probably Amy. She was the shortest. Tenner centered the lines of the scope on the head of his target and held the weapon steady. He had no idea who he held in his sights. A ripple of excitement coursed through him, and he welcomed it with a shiver. *Someone* was about to die. Thoughts of what they might be talking about went through Tenner's head, and he smiled. Whatever the conversation, it was about to be disrupted.

That familiar rush burned through his frame and nerve endings, the same chill that came before any killing. Then he reconsidered, frowning just a little.

He shifted his aim.

And squeezed the trigger.

35

Placing some distance between the gimps behind them, they straightened up and drifted toward the middle of the road. The street ahead was thankfully empty of both rat and Moe, and cars on either side provided enough cover so that the need to crouch wasn't so great. Scott glanced up at the moon. He figured it was perhaps one in the morning of a very long day. Stars winked back at him, clear and sparkling bright enough for him to almost wish he could just lie down on the icy pavement and simply watch them all. Ahead, the road stretched out and narrowed to some dark, unseen point.

He stepped closer to Amy. "How much further?"

"Depends. If it was a straight walk, maybe six or seven hours." She turned to look at him, her face and eyes dark under her visor. "But it isn't a straight walk."

"Okay."

"Shhh," Buckle hissed from the rear.

Scott winced at Amy, who gave him a little smile. For a long second, Scott saw just how attractive she was.

A gunshot punched the stillness and knocked Vick off his feet, belting him over as if a heavy plank had hit him upside the head and knocking him flat on his back. Scott and Amy froze in their tracks, processing what had just happened.

"*Get down!*" Buckle cried, all attempts at silence forgotten.

They flattened, scrambling toward Vick and seeing the puddle of blackness spreading around his head.

Amy let out a barely suppressed shriek, which came out like a muffled five o' clock whistle.

"Shhh," Buckle said, grabbing Vick's armor and flipping him over. "Shhh, I got you. I got you. Shhh."

He pushed Vick's visor up over his face and peered into his open eyes. Vick groaned. His arm hung from his shoulder at an awkward angle, and blood spurted rhythmically from under the Kevlar plates, which made Amy moan as loud as any Moe.

"Shush, Amy. *Shhh!*" Buckle hissed. He quickly ripped open the padding of the man's snowsuit with a wet sound.

"Is he okay?" Amy asked, leaning in and placing a hand against Vick's rough cheek.

"No," Buckle said. The Newfoundlander tried to turn his friend onto his side, but he gave up. He widened the tear in the snowsuit material and grimaced at the sight of raw meat. The round had bitten a chunk out of flesh and bone, and only a thread of sinewy tissue kept Vick's lower arm attached. "Jesus, Jesus, Jesus," Buckle whispered.

"What?" Amy asked frantically.

Buckle gripped Vick's sizeable bicep and probed the flesh with his fingers. "See how the blood's squirting out here? In bursts? That's not a vein opened up. That's an artery. Listen now, I'm going to keep pressure on this for as long as I have to. Head over to those apartments back there and find me something to tourniquet his upper arm, okay? And a lighter and something to burn—paper or cloth or anything. Okay? *Go!*"

Amy stood and bolted for the row of apartments. Scott watched her run off before looking back at Buckle, who did a double take.

"The fuck you waiting for?" Buckle snarled. *"Get after her!"*

Scott did just that, leaving the former cop to tend to his friend.

Watching them go, Buckle turned his attention back to Vick. He pulled the man's hood down with bloody fingers and placed a cheek over Vick's face. The old bastard was breathing, but Buckle knew how bad gunshot wounds could be. Worse, it was clear to him that this particular shot had pretty much destroyed the bone in the upper arm and shredded the artery there, resulting in the *spurt—spurt—spurt* of blood. No vein did that. A vein would only ooze blood.

"I gotcha, buddy," Buckle breathed, staying in control and releasing a hand so that he could unsling the shotgun and place it on the icy road. He saw the strap then, and scoffed at himself. With his free hand, he reached down and grabbed his knife. It was going to be tight. Buckle took a breath and quickly cut the hemp strap off the shotgun. Baring his teeth, he looped it around Vick's arm and pulled tight, cutting off the flow. He looked up and couldn't see if anything was approaching over the crest of the street, but it didn't really matter.

"Don't you worry one bit now, me son," Buckle whispered to his old friend. He looked at the blood on the road. There would be company soon, and he expected he'd hear their wailing long before he could see them.

"I gotcha," Buckle said, and adjusted the strap on Vick's arm, trying hard to focus, to maintain tension, and hoping that Amy and Scott would return soon.

36

When the shadows crumpled together and disappeared, Tenner knew he'd hit the mark right where he wanted. Who'd he hit? Tenner stood up and listened, the AR-20 pressed firmly against his shoulder. Two shadows fluttered away from where the wounded man lay, disappearing in the gloom of an apartment complex near a stone church. That was interesting. Tenner didn't think they were simply abandoning one of their own, which got him wondering if he'd killed his target. He wasn't completely familiar with the rifle, and he wondered if it fired something more powerful than a standard 5.56 mm round. Memories came back to him, reports suggesting the Army had developed an explosive-tipped shell. That brought a wry smile to his face. He really wanted to use his knives on his quarry, but the idea of accidently killing someone with a bullet amused him.

That still left three to hunt down and cut up.

He figured it was time to get over there and check things out.

Tenner straightened up and moved around the car he'd set his rifle on, then stopped in his tracks. The undead were wailing, alerted by the shot and drawn to the commotion. He went to the building on his right and peeked around the corner.

Undead. A hundred of them at least. Probably more. Attracted to the blood.

In his haste to slow his old companions, he'd made the mistake of not considering what the Philistines would do. It was a stupid mistake, one born from uncharacteristic impatience. If nothing else, the dead were predictable. Once attracted to something, they would investigate, alone or en masse.

It was just his luck that *this* time, they were investigating en masse.

Placing his back against the stone wall of the building, he thought about his next move. High ground came to mind, and he looked at a nearby window just to his left.

He wheeled toward it and kicked, putting a boot through the glass. A moment later, he'd cleared away the shards and squirmed into a student's dorm room, with a mussed up bed and desk. Tenner went to the door, opened it, and entered a corridor where windows allowed moonlight to transform the opposite wall into a length of wide piano keys.

He located a stairwell and huffed up three floors, emerging into a similar corridor and entering an identical room. He took up position at the window, facing the street below from a higher vantage point. Tenner smashed out the glass with his elbow. Dropping to his knees, he pointed the barrel of the assault rifle out the window, resting its length on the sill, and panned from side to side. He immediately spotted two figures, their faces swathed in shadow. One was bent over the other, who appeared quite dead.

Tenner took his eye away from the scope. Zombies were approaching their position, walking through a smattering of trees and heading for the street. Though the cold had slowed them, it wouldn't take them long at all to reach their stricken prey. Tenner felt a bit of disappointment. He'd already played a game of "Dead Invaders" with the old mechanic—he couldn't remember the guy's name. It had been weary work shooting all those zombies bearing down on the man, and he really didn't want to do the same again.

He settled in to watch. If anything, it would be interesting to see just what kind of person the attending shadow would turn out to be. Would he or she stay with their fallen comrade to the last? Or perhaps try to move the wounded, which Tenner dismissed. *Better than reality television*, he thought, smiling faintly with his cheek against the scope.

Right at that moment, two sets of headlight beams lit up the street.

Tenner's brow crumpled up in puzzlement a second before he saw what was coming and heard the growl of engines.

Buckle's heart leapt in his chest when he saw the headlights. Two sets of great, harsh eyes bore down on him and Vick. The engines got louder, and he hoped beyond hope that whoever they were, they were friendly. He heard Moe coming, but he wasn't about to leave his *compadre* to bleed out on the pavement. If things looked bleak . . . He had the shotgun and would do them both. Not that he wanted to die—he might actually enjoy living in a world where survival was day to day.

If it weren't for all of the fucking zombies.

So, with Moe heading their way, he hoped for a miracle.

The machines steamed toward them, slowed, and stopped not ten feet away from where he and Vick lay in the road. The brakes squealed, and the angry glare of the headlights made Buckle squint and raise a hand to shield his eyes. It seemed like a long time since he'd last seen a moving vehicle, and the headlights on this one made him feel exposed. The grisly extent of the blood pooling around Vick heightened his worry.

Doors opened and boots hit the pavement. Shadows formed. Big men, covered in slabs of something that Buckle couldn't quite distinguish in the harsh light. They spread out without identifying themselves. The engines idled, creating a grim chugging that did nothing to allay Buckle's growing trepidation.

Three figures sauntered over to where he still clenched Vick's arm, their boots scuffing up snow. The slabs covering their bodies were a collection of sports gear or body armor, seemingly nailed to their persons or lashed on with strips of leather twine. One wore a hockey face cage, but he couldn't see the man's face. It took him a second to realize that the newcomer had blackened his face with paint or some other substance.

The one with the face cage spoke. It came out in a guttural bark that sounded exhausting to produce. Buckle was no linguist, but it sounded like a hodgepodge of Slavic languages.

Others came into view on the Face Cage's flanks. Buckle saw their spiked clubs and shotguns, all short-barreled and swinging from hip holsters.

For a few seconds, they stood in the wash of the headlights and stared down at the pair of men.

"Who the fuck—" Buckle started.

Face Cage stepped forward and kicked Buckle in the face, crumpling him. He turned his head at the last possible moment, so the steel-toed boot connected with the edge of his helmet. The force was still enough to knock him away from Vick. He felt something grab him and drag him by his arms, away from Vick.

"Hey," Buckle tried to say, in a loopy daze. Someone hauled him to his feet and slammed him against the van. A massive paw clamped about his throat. The pressure increased, choking off any more words.

The others stood around Vick. They talked, but Buckle couldn't understand a word. Five of the warriors made a skirmish line facing the zombies shambling toward the street.

Buckle grimaced. Only five?

Behind the line, Face Cage beckoned to another man, who looked as if he wore chopped-up tire treads. The warrior brought forth a heavy-looking cleaver and bent down over Vick.

Buckle struggled, and the man holding him punched him twice, and then a third time—quick, powerful blows to his stomach and liver. His body armor absorbed most of the force, but then an elbow slammed into his jaw, snapping his head to the right and bringing sparkling motes to his vision.

"Relax," a floating head said. The face had a huge grinning mouth filled with white fangs. "We're going to operate on your friend."

Buckle saw figures kneeling beside Vick. He saw the cleaver rise up and strike down, then heard the muted chink of steel on asphalt and ice, echoing in his daze. Laughter rose up then, deep and cruel-sounding, and he saw one of the brutes lift Vick's arm into the air, pumping it in mocking victory.

Then Buckle smelled the tang of gas.

The men around Vick set fire to the stump of his arm. It ignited with a *whoosh*, and they let it burn until they decided to stomp out the flame. In nightmare fashion, the man with Vick's arm jokingly reached out with it to paw at his companion. A hand swatted the limb away with a curse.

Another elbow slammed across Buckle's face, clipping his already broken nose and refocusing his attention. The impact made his eyes water and his vision go hazy. He struggled to see, and gradually a black line of warriors standing before a crowd of Moe came into view. The zombies approached the end of the slope and, heedless of the five-foot embankment, fell and landed flat on their faces. The line of men moved forward, and the reaving began. Axes and mauls rose and fell in time with war cries and the wail of the dead. A few shotgun blasts punctuated the air. The warriors allowed the zombies to come forward, fall, then dispatch them as they tried to stand. The brute holding Buckle up by the throat laughed and cried out in a foreign tongue and, when the Newfoundlander looked down, he saw his captor's forearms were covered in writhing black and green eels.

Face Cage appeared at the edge of Buckle's vision and barked something at the man holding him. He didn't sound overly impressed. Face Cage loomed in front of him, and the warrior held up a scarred fist that looked to be the size of a bony melon.

Just before it crashed into Buckle's face.

37

The door to the apartment Scott and Amy chose wasn't locked. They went in and began frantically searching for something that would serve as a tourniquet for Vick's arm. The apartment was a small two-bedroom that smelled of stale animal hair, suggesting the owners had owned a dog or cat. The darkness hid no gimps, and for that they were thankful.

Scott fumbled his way through kitchen drawers and cupboards and located an extension cord, a tablecloth, dish towels, and a box of matches, all the while listening to Amy tear through a room behind the kitchen.

"You got anything?" he called, dumping his goods into the table cloth and bundling it into a makeshift sack. The matches went into his pocket.

"Yeah," Amy said as her shadow emerged from the bedroom. "I got a belt."

Amy's voice became distracted. "Who are those guys?"

"Huh?" Scott turned. She pointed to the still open door and the light in the street. Outside, a good fifty meters away, stood two large vans. Men got out of the vehicles and surrounded Vick and Buckle.

Then one almost kicked Buckle's head off.

Scott made for the door, but Amy grabbed him by the arm. "Wait," she hissed.

"They're kicking them!"

"I can see that," Amy said, visibly straining to keep her control. "But there's more of them than us. Just *wait*."

"But Vick—"

"Vick would do the same."

Scott blinked at her before turning back to the scene on the street. Buckle was being dragged to a van, while several men had made a line facing a crowd of dark deadheads moving in from the slope. In the glare of headlights, a figure crouched over Vick's body, lifted what looked to be a cleaver, and chopped down.

Amy gasped and clamped a hand over her mouth. Scott said nothing, not even when the chopper stood with Vick's severed limb and made jokes with it.

Scott pulled out the Ruger. Amy caught the movement and didn't say anything to stop him this time.

Gunshots made them both crouch and hang back from the door, hiding in the apartment's darkness. Zombies on the slope fell, partially illuminated by headlights. Men stepped toward the front ranks of the mob and started swinging axes and clubs. More gunshots cut the air. Howls and cries rose up from the newcomers. One of them hacked off a gimp's head and held it up to the night, screaming as he shook it fiercely, before slinging it into the snow. The gimps continued to attack, but the men that fought them didn't back down. They kept on dispatching the dead with enthusiastic efficiency. More zombies shambled in front of the headlights—white, half-naked forms that clutched and clawed at the front of a van. One van lurched forward with a drag-on's growl, pushing some zombies back and running over others. Rib cages crinkled before being crushed. Skulls popped like knots in burning wood. Human voices cried out in an unrecognizable language.

"You hear that?" Scott asked.

"Yeah," Amy said. "What language is that?"

Scott listened and brought the Ruger up to his waist. "Don't know. Hey, I've still got this."

"There's about eight of them out there," Amy said. "And they've got guns, too. We can't do anything right now."

"Thought they were your friends?"

That got a reaction from her. She turned to face him, displaying what Scott recognized as barely suppressed fury.

"They are," she said at last. "So . . . *wait.*"

Suddenly feeling like shit for saying such a thing, Scott took a deep breath. "Sorry," he got out. "That was dickish of me."

Amy looked back to the road. "It's okay," she muttered.

He wasn't sure if it was or not, but he still stung a little from the exchange. He stepped back, dealing with the maddening urge to rush out there and start shooting. There were now seven men that he could see, with drivers still in the van. It finally occurred to him to ask *who* had shot Vick. He believed it was Tenner. Somehow, the sick bastard had gotten his hands on a rifle. But who were these *other* guys?

"I think Tenner shot Vick," Scott said.

"I agree," Amy said, not taking her eyes off what was happening outside. "So who are these guys?"

"Just thinking the exact same thing."

"And?"

A second shot split the night air, and one of the newcomers fighting the zombies fell.

Tenner didn't know who the hell these new guys were, but he knew they were taking away two people he wanted to finish off himself. Through the scope, he watched the newly arrived road warriors spread out, subdue Buckle, and drag him away—easy to distinguish with the headlights lighting up the entire scene. And he saw the field surgery performed on the man he'd gunned down while others put down zombie after zombie, holding a line and systematically killing the dead. They looked like a line of assembly workers the way they were stretched out, taking apart any corpse that got close.

Two of the men picked up the carcass of the man Tenner had shot and carried it back behind one of the vans, where Buckle had gone. He realized these warriors weren't hanging around for long, and that bothered him. Two of his former companions were still out there, perhaps watching as he was. Waiting. And why exactly was he waiting? These guys could obviously take care of themselves, yet they were nothing compared to Tenner. He was the *man*. Even better, he was the man with the gun. He watched them through the scope, merrily killing zombies. They were having far too much fun, it seemed. They had no fear, and Tenner believed that was just unhealthy. Fear was a defense mechanism. *He* didn't need it, but others did. He'd give them something to be scared of. It was his world, after all, and anyone existing in it had to realize that glaring fact.

Tenner adjusted the rifle's butt against his shoulder. He caressed the trigger of the AR-20 as if it were spider's silk, and he drew a bead on one unfortunate brute hacking away at Philistines with a fire axe. He drifted from the man with the axe to the windshield of one of the vans. He couldn't see the driver, but he imagined he'd be there, right behind the wheel.

None of them were going to leave the area.

Fist walked up and down the battle line, swearing at his killers as they hacked the dead to pieces. Some of the dead tried to flank them, and Fist stepped in to stop them.

Pell joined him, and both of the Norsemen took to bashing in the skulls of the slow-moving corpses or shooting them outright. Fist had to admit, he never tired of killing the dead.

But then he heard two shots—shots that weren't from his lads.

He turned around in puzzlement and saw two bullet holes in the windshield of the nearest van.

"The fuck . . . ?" Fist exhaled in shock. Pell looked to him in wide-eyed confusion.

Then the other windshield crinkled as two rounds went through it, puncturing the glass in lacy white blooms. Fist looked beyond the range of the headlights to the dark buildings farther down the street.

A fifth shot made him duck. The other men dropped into crouches, trying to bunch themselves up into as small a target as possible. Zombies still advanced on the line, and some of the men swung their weapons at the dead things' legs, chopping them down to the ground.

Someone's trying to get their buddies back, Fist realized. He stormed to the nearest van and slapped the door, making it shudder.

"Get out of here!" he roared.

One of his men, a large grunt actually wearing Viking horns, emerged from the back and jumped into the driver's seat. He started the engine and stomped on the gas. The van's wheels spun on the icy roads for a few seconds, and the engine bloomed before the tires finally caught traction. The vehicle blasted away, speeding from the gunfire. Fist marched toward the second van and yanked open the door. The driver was there, staring at the ceiling with a spurting hole in his hockey vest. A second shredded wound in his neck dribbled blood over his clothes and seat.

Fist ducked and turned, just in time to hear the shot and see another of his men go down, his head sheared from his shoulders. The body landed at an angle from the head, the limbs shivering as if electrified.

A zombie loomed over the crouching Pell, but the big Albertan gripped the thing's knees and manhandled it into the street. Two brutal elbow strikes broke open its skull, spilling a rotten cauliflower pulp. There were no more zombies seeking to make meals of the Norsemen.

There was only the shooter.

"Sniper!" Fist roared, scanning the nearby buildings. "Pell!"

A head jerked up.

"Stay with the van, Herman!"

A riot helmet came into sight.

"With him! Everyone else, with me. Zigzag!"

Fist sprang forward, carrying a heavy maul and making himself as difficult a target as possible. Three other men got to their feet and followed. Their howls were low at first, gradually becoming undulating shrieks of glee.

A zombie wearing the body armor of a soldier appeared out of the gloom and confronted Fist. He swung his maul and half-tore off the head, killing it with one blow. Fist barrelled over it, whooping war cries meant to petrify the shooter, cause him to make mistakes—or make him run.

Either way, Fist and his boys would catch up with the one who had fired upon them. They'd hunt the shooter down until they caught him. Fist knew from past victims how long they could keep a person alive, and they'd gotten exceptionally well-versed in making those final moments as mind-blowingly torturous as possible.

When the four shadows charged down the street, punctuating their displeasure with a graphic beheading of one of the Philistines, Tenner drew back from the scope and chewed thoughtfully on his inner cheek. He watched the four men race down the icy roadway, pounding their way toward the building he was in, screaming as if their asses were on fire. That was a good guess on their part. Perhaps it was the angle of the shot that gave his position away? In any case, they were coming, and they sounded pissed, if not a little ridiculous.

The shouting was intended to frighten him, to get him off his game. It reminded him of a playground story he'd once heard, of a spider who had spun a web large enough to catch a cow. When the animal stepped into the sticky strands, the spider stuck its head out of its hiding hole, blinked, and instead of staying away from the larger animal, exclaimed "Fuck *yeah!*"

Tenner leisurely withdrew the rifle from the window. He reached to his death vest and ripped open one of the Velcro strips holding a grenade in place. With a spider's grace, his fingers wrapped around the egg-shaped explosive. There were only four men charging. He watched as, halfway to the building, their screams died away to loud huffing.

Just like dogs.

Dogs, Tenner thought, tugging on the grenade. It came free and left its pin and ring rattling against his vest.

Fuck yeah, he thought and tossed the live grenade out the window.

Two seconds later, the resulting explosion lit up the night and rocked the building's foundation.

The blast screwed up Scott's vision and prompted both him and Amy to drop to the floor. He took great gulping breaths, trying to calm his shaken nerves. Only seconds before, four howlers had been storming down the street, their vicious wailing petering out into the occasional grunt, becoming quiet and serious as they reached the parking lot of the dormitory.

Then . . . *boom*.

Scott thought he saw a fragment of something being flung backward into the night, lit up against something as fiery as the sun. A split second later, Amy was pulling him down.

"What the fuck was that?" she hissed in his ear.

"I think . . ." Scott shook his head to clear it. "I think it was a mine or some shit."

"Couldn't have been a mine," Amy retorted, getting to her hands and knees and pushing her back against a wall. "More like a rocket or something."

"A rocket? Where the hell he get something like that?"

"Same place he got the gun to snipe those guys out there." Amy made a distasteful face. "Bastard must've found some weapons somewhere."

"I think so," Scott agreed. He crawled toward the open door and looked out as Amy peered out a window. Smoke wafted from the direction of the building, but all else was quiet.

"Can't see shit," Amy said. "But the residence is still standing."

Screams split the night, causing Scott to tense up. Tenner hadn't gotten all of his attackers. The smoke began clearing, and the base of the building materialized out of the gloom. Scott couldn't see anyone over there.

"Van's still there," Amy informed him.

She was right. One of the vehicles was right in the middle of the street, its headlights still blazing. That didn't seem particularly smart to Scott. Running into a bomb wasn't especially bright either, but who could've known that Tenner had gotten his hands on explosives?

"We should take the van," Amy said, meeting his eyes.

"And leave?"

"Yeah."

"I can't leave, Amy. Not with him still out there."

"Vick and Buckle are in trouble."

"Do you know where they've gone with them?"

"No, but I saw two of those bastards out there getting into the van. You've got the gun. We can make them talk."

"And then?"

"We go," Amy said simply.

Scott exhaled. "I'm right with you until that last part. We can meet up at the house, if anything."

Amy hesitated for a moment, thinking things over, her face dark. "All right. We go now."

She got to her feet and readied her tonfas. Scott climbed to his and readied his gun.

"You ready?" she asked.

"Yeah."

Amy went to the door, stayed low, and slipped outside. Scott followed her, crouching and staying in the shadows of the apartments as they crept toward the van.

38

The sensation of swaying coaxed Buckle back to consciousness. He'd been in a few good fistfights in his career as a cop, but never had he been sucker punched. There was always the courtship, when the guys who wanted to fight would wave their fists in his face seconds before actually committing to a swing—a swing with a lot of pent-up, nervous energy behind it. That first punch was usually a dandy. There had been no pent-up nervousness with the guy that had bopped him, however. No, sir. There was only long experience there. Buckle wanted another shot at the fucker.

But first . . .

His shoulders and wrists ached. They had stripped him of his helmet, mask, and cloth bandage. He cracked open an eye and slowly gazed upward. His hands were handcuffed, and he appeared to be hanging from a meat hook fastened to a thick metal strut. His legs dragged below and bent behind him, grazing the wall, as if he were in a painful prayer. Darkness bathed the interior of the van. There were two men up front, both concentrating on driving. One of them wore a helmet with thick horns; the other had removed his, revealing a dark bulb of semi-spiked hair. A third man sat on a sofa seat parked against the opposite wall, his helmet turned, peering at the drivers. Things shook and jangled, chains and meat hooks. The smell of rancid blood and burnt flesh forced Buckle to wrinkle his face, and his broken nose reminded him *not* to do that again.

He moaned before he could stop himself, wincing immediately after.

"He's awake," the guy sitting on the sofa declared. One of the drivers said something in a language that reminded Buckle of Klingons, but that couldn't be right—it wasn't even a real language, for Christ's sake.

Laughter from the front. Buckle couldn't see anything beyond the drivers, but he could see Vick's dark form sprawled out near the back door.

The guy on the sofa stood, placed a hand on pipes that ran the length of the van's ceiling, and peered into Buckle's battered face. He wore a face mask, the visor blackened with paint; he had etched a smile with serrated teeth on the surface. The man's eyes were visible, although Buckle wished he couldn't see them. They scrunched up at the corners in evil mirth, as if the brute was grinning behind the visor. Buckle didn't like that idea. He and other cops would talk about human nature at down times, and they agreed that if there were no laws, no consequences, and no peace officers, some individuals would run rampant through the streets and do things purely on whim— until someone with balls stopped them. The *thing* before him appeared tickled to have a live subject, and it didn't seem inhibited by morals. Dread coursed through Buckle. This brute was exactly what he and his cop buddies had imagined so very long ago. A prime specimen of chaos, to be avoided and feared, and here he was, standing right in front of Buckle, who was in no condition to do anything about it.

Things, the Newfoundlander suspected, were about to get very bad.

"Gonna tenderize ya," a voice hissed eagerly from the grinning maw. Much to Buckle's dismay, the grinner held up a fist wearing metal knuckles. They weren't spiked, which made him thankful for all of a second. Almost carefully, the man undid the clasps fastening Buckle's body armor to his body. Grinner couldn't remove it entirely, as that would require unhooking him, but he loosened the armor enough so he could peel the plates back to expose his stomach and ribs.

"This," the happy face declared, "is gonna hurt. Might even kill you. Not that I give a shit."

The first punch crushed a rib and robbed Buckle of breath. Pain made him squeeze his eyes shut and he gasped, each expansion of his ribs lighting up his nerve endings as if they were being held to a flame. He swung from the hook and got his feet underneath him.

Grinner saw the attempt to stand and didn't like it.

He held on to the pipes overhead and stomped on Buckle's left ankle, shattering the joint. Buckle shrieked, swayed from the hooks, and blacked out.

The punches brought him back.

The punisher took his time while the van moved, regaining his balance just before unleashing blows that snapped out from the shoulder and pistoned into Buckle's body, the pain increased tenfold by the metal knuckles. One punch to the face and Buckle forgot about the screaming sirens in his mashed ankle. A flurry of strikes, some catching on Kevlar, ripped into his hanging mass and rocked him like a slab of beef, bouncing him off the wall and placing even more tension on his wrists. A hand gripped the Newfoundlander's chin, squeezed, and crunched an elbow into it. Teeth flew.

Another elbow, and Buckle's jaw snapped with a crack. Grinner studied him for a moment, eyes narrowed above the cannibalistic smile. He rammed an open palm into Buckle's nose. Not happy with the lack of sound, Grinner squished Buckle's nose to the left and right, as if working a knob on an old radio, before pushing his head back until he was looking at the ceiling.

Buckle swooned on the edge of consciousness when a hard hand gripped his chin. The contact made him burp out a little cry of agony.

"Don't you pass out on me, you little shit," Grinner warned. "You pass out on me and I'll hurt you *bad*. You *understand?* I'll fuck you up so bad not even God above will want to lay on hands. And the Devil himself will send you back here. So don't pass out, hear me?"

Buckle felt the fat pad of a finger on his right eye.

"You ever have a thumb in your eye?" Grinner asked softly. "Ever have one just go right on in there? Huh? Oh, you can scrunch up your face and all, but if . . ."

Oh, Jesus. Buckle could feel the thumb start to press.

"If I push hard enough," Grinner went on, "it's . . . going . . . *in.*"

The pressure increased. Motes of light penetrated his personal darkness, and Buckle squealed. The van bumped over something, jostling Grinner for a moment and causing him to remove his thumb, come back, and adjust his grip.

"I had this one guy," Grinner continued on conversationally, "hanging from a post. Got mouthy with me. After I stuck one thumb in his head, well, that *really* got him going. Wouldn't shut up. Not even after I shook his head around like a bowling ball. That was something to see. I'm not good at much . . ."

That statement was emphasized by more pressure on Buckle's eye. He tried to twist away, but another hand clamped on his face, holding him in a vise, and a second thumb wormed its way around his other eye, probing.

"Not good at much at all, really," the voice went on.

Buckle tried to turn his head, to hide it in his arms overhead, but the hands held him fast.

"But if there's *one* thing I'm getting a reputation for, it's putting a hurt on people. Just . . . fucking them up. Y'know what I mean? Don't care what it is, really. Blinding them, cutting them, mashing their balls. S'all fun."

Grinner's breath expelled as if a real smile matched the mirth projected on his visor.

Then the thumbs dug in.

"You feel that?" the voice asked. Buckle did. His torturer was in position and had a good grip. Playtime was coming to an end. He felt the jagged ends of chewed nails grind into his scrunched up eyes, causing him to mew involuntarily, a sound he'd never made in his life.

"Well, goddamn." Grinner chuckled darkly as his thumbs pressed further inward. "This fucker's about to shit himself."

Feeling something about to give horribly, Buckle's mouth dropped open to scream. "Hey."

Vick drove his spiked knuckles under the chin of the torturer. The impact bounced Grinner's head off the ceiling of the van. He released Buckle, who opened his eyes as if he'd been underground for years. Vick stepped forward, cocking his one arm and driving it into the man's throat. Grinner went down with a bloody-sounding gurgle, and the driver with the horns whipped around. The one with the short, spiked hair lunged out of the passenger seat, his face a horrible snarl of rage.

Buckle grappled with his shattered ankle and battered body, but still managed to get one leg under himself and stand. Pain exploded in his skull like a halogen light on full power. Buckle tried to get his hands unhooked from overhead and fell back, out of strength and out of breath. The new attacker reached out and grabbed the front of Vick's body armor. Vick twisted, wrapping his remaining arm around the man's elbow joint, and heaved up against it. The man with the spiked hair screamed. Vick kicked out a knee and Spike went down. Vick went to punch him and blinked in confusion. He realized he *couldn't* finish off his foe.

He was one arm short.

Growling, Spike surged forward, lifting Vick off his feet, and even with his arm still locked up, heaved him into the ceiling. The impact rattled the van's still-moving frame. The driver shrieked gibberish. Vick grimaced and released Spike. They toppled to the sofa, Vick landing underneath the other man. His boot heel flashed up and cracked Spike's chin. Blood burst from the man's face. Spike shouted something in that Klingon-sounding language. He swarmed the one-armed sensei and rained punches down into Vick's midsection, huge haymakers that dropped like fifty-ton bombs falling from heaven. Even from where he hung, Buckle heard the furious rhythm of meat on metal plates.

Filling his lungs with air, Buckle got his one good leg under him. He straightened, unhooked himself from above, and suddenly dropped to the floor. He rolled over the still-gurgling Grinner lying on the bare metal, the sounds of punching just next to him crashing into his ears like fleshy cymbals. He felt the butt of something on Grinner's waist. Buckle grabbed it, lifting it free with a rasp of leather on metal.

He brought up a sawed-off pump shotgun.

"Hey, buddy!"

Spike looked up and, for the briefest of moments, looked utterly gobsmacked, a split second before Buckle blew the man's head apart like an overripe melon.

The ex-cop roared, jacked the weapon, and sent a spent cartridge flying into the dark. He placed his back against the wall of the vehicle. Amazingly, Grinner pushed himself up on his elbows, a dark froth spilling from the ruined meat of his throat.

Buckle shot him through the base of his skull, dropping the man like a reanimated Moe.

The van veered wildly, eliciting cries of pain from both Buckle and Vick. Buckle pumped the shotgun a second time and slapped an arm against the wall for support. He steadied his gun arm, *willed* it to be still. The Viking at the wheel looked back, saw the barrel pointed at him, and fumbled at the door. Buckle fired just as the horns clattered off the man's head in his haste to fling himself out of the moving van.

Vick groaned as he pushed the corpse away. "Is that all of—"

The van crashed, slamming into something that refused to move. The impact turned Vick's words into a startled grunt, jolting both men and flinging them into darkness where everything stopped at once.

39

With a brute of a henchman behind him, Fist entered the parking area of the dormitory and took a moment to compose himself. He adjusted the hockey helmet covering his head, sticking his fingers into the cage that protected his face and rubbing an itch around his nose. Then he snarled.

"That was a grenade," he hissed to Shipp.

"Grenade?" Shipp asked, his eyes almost bulging behind his black painted visor. "Where the fuck did he get that?"

"Don't know," Fist said. "Leftovers from a soldier, maybe? But that's valuable property, in any case. Where the others?"

"Gone around. Looking for another way in from the sides."

Fist grunted. He spotted a door facing the parking area, leading up into the guts of the building. Hefting his maul with one muscled arm, he briskly walked toward it with Shipp at his heels. They stopped at the door and studied the dark interior.

"All sorts of nasty shit could be in there," Shipp said warily, holding a spiked club.

Fist's eyes, blackened with soot, fixed on the other man and narrowed evilly. "*We're* nasty shit."

Shipp quickly nodded his agreement. That was good. Fist knew he had to get his boys in the right frame of mind before an ass stomping, and this was a *fight*—not the slaughter they'd grown accustomed to.

Not bothering to ask if Shipp was ready, Fist opened the door and entered the building.

In the crinkling of brick and the weedy sound of dust and debris settling, Tenner sat and waited. He carefully stuck his head out over the windowsill and scanned the ground. Brick, concrete, and shards of wooden beams sprinkled the snow, as if the foundation had taken a direct artillery shell. The amount of destruction made him touch the six remaining grenades at his chest and give them an affectionate rub through the Velcro. He couldn't see any of the remaining screamers down there, but he believed he'd gotten at least one. The safest thing was to assume the remainder were in the building, looking for him. Naturally, they would be coming upstairs—the highest point in the building, where a sniper could inflict the most damage. He wasn't at the highest point. There was at least one more level above him, but they would probably search the entire place, just to be certain—unless they were idiots.

Evil. Delicious and pungent. He sensed their raw presence closing in. Packs like this might have a purpose in the new world, but Tenner didn't want them around. Their methods were raw and unrefined compared to Tenner's silky approach. He was well aware that, unlike good, evil fed upon evil. Even if he could've somehow rolled back time, perhaps even been able to converse with them and establish an alliance of sorts, he knew eventually he'd kill them or they'd kill him.

No, it was best to execute the whole fucking lot.

The remaining van was still in the street. Tenner knew he'd sniped the driver, and chances were good he would be able to drive away in the vehicle. But first he had to kill some people. He slunk to the door and dropped to his chest, feeling the weight of his body armor. Just outside and to his right was the stairwell he'd used earlier. Ahead was an indistinct corridor, its length slashed in two places by moonlight coming from open doors. The spectral light cut up an otherwise haunting darkness. He had a choice: go hunting or stay here and wait for them to find him. Exhaling, he climbed to his feet and went to the stairwell door. It opened with a whine, making him cringe. He listened. Nothing. Tenner returned to the room and rummaged around until he found some paper, which he immediately folded. He took the wedge and jammed it between the door and the floor, keeping it open and in place. He would hear anything coming up that stairwell, and one grenade would mangle the lot of them.

Tenner hefted the AR-20 and flicked the rate of fire switch. He couldn't see exactly what he'd selected, but he'd find out eventually. Hopes of getting the full electric *rock and rolla* show filled him. Dropping to his chest again and aiming down the length of corridor, he decided to sit and wait.

And let the dogs sniff him out.

The silenced weapon felt heavy in Scott's hand as he and Amy slunk in the shadows, skirting the flood of headlights from the van. *Was he really about to shoot someone, a living being?* That question branded his mind and distracted him from the task at hand. Amy stopped once and glanced back at him, and he could feel her wondering what the hell was wrong. He thought about telling her, but it would take a good five minutes to explain why he wasn't certain he could pull a trigger and how killing dead things was pretty damn easy, comparatively speaking. The moral implications of shooting a living person bothered him, and if it was bothering him now, what would he be like if he actually did catch up to Tenner? The man who'd sliced up his friends and left them hanging from support beams in a basement?

Amy stopped behind a low drift, just under the van's passenger side window. Scott settled in beside her, watching the machine for any signs of life. He caught the unmistakable tang of blood and wondered if the dead would smell it as well. If so, they would have very little time.

"You ready?" Amy asked.

Scott blinked.

"Scott?" Amy asked, and he faced her.

"I don't know . . . I don't know if I can do this."

"What?"

A fine time to pussy out of shooting someone. *He winced and shook his head.*

"Give me the gun." Amy held out her hand and beckoned with gloved fingers. "I'll do it."

The sharpness in her voice surprised him. He did as he was told.

"I'm sorry."

"Just watch my back. Here." She handed him her tonfas.

"I'm sorry, Am—"

But she was already moving, on knees and elbows, approaching the van from the rear. Scott felt ashamed by his inability to act. He thought he could kill Tenner, knew he could put the murderer down, *swore* it, but those gears had slipped with the reality of the moment. The men in the van were savages, but he just couldn't do it. God above help him, he couldn't bring himself to kill another living, breathing person.

He held up one of the tonfas and briefly wondered if he could make it spin like Amy did. He settled on holding of it like any regular club.

Amy was at the back of the van and on her feet. She edged around the rear, holding the Ruger at shoulder height. Shouting came from the van, and Scott kept his eyes on the passenger side, occasionally glimpsing a hand coming up to the glass.

Amy disappeared around the side of the van.

His heart began to race. Scott wondered if he should go after her, but he decided against it. Amy could handle herself—had handled herself for a very long time. He could back her up, but—

The Ruger's hushed bark erupted from the other side of the van.

Amy didn't know why Scott couldn't pull the trigger, but she didn't force the issue. It took a lot to put down a living person. Lord above knew she'd crossed some dark line when her husband and daughter had become infected with the virus, clubbing them to death with a cast-iron frying pan of all things. They weren't her family anymore, of course. At the time, though, when wide-eyed Jordy came flying at her from the bathroom, he was *still* her husband of eight years. She'd flipped him over her hip and put him through the glass coffee table. He'd just kept coming, even when she broke his leg, then his arm, then his *other* arm, and finally his other leg, just to immobilize the twisting frothing thing that only that morning had held her in his loving arms.

She remembered going to the kitchen afterward and hearing the pounding on Joanne's door. Amy had gone to her daughter's room, placed her face to the door, and simultaneously felt and heard Jo beating the wood. She wouldn't answer her mother. Worse, the screeching had intensified at the sound of Amy's voice. Since then, she'd had nightmares of Jo clawing her way through the door and coming for her.

When Amy had turned around, she discovered Jordy slinking along the floor, bunching up a rug under his dripping mouth, eyeing her as he moved like some hellish slug.

She jumped over him in the hallway, his teeth snapping at her feet as she went over and found the only weapon in the house besides the knives. She'd completely forgotten about the golf clubs in the bedroom.

Amy clubbed Jordy's skull with the edge of the frying pan until he stopped moving, until the bone crumpled and grated under his scalp like the broken pieces of a plate.

When she regained control, she found out Jo was on the floor in her bedroom, her head mashed in as well. Somehow, Amy had forgotten the details, but she'd killed her own daughter. And that was that. The zombie apocalypse had baptized her in the harshest way possible.

She approached the driver's door. Something had smashed the side mirror, so she wasn't worried about being spotted, but there was a chance the driver might get out. She gripped the door handle with her right and brought up the Ruger with her left.

Amy had killed the two people who had meant the most to her. She still struggled with the psychological damage of those acts, even though they'd been necessary. Vick had tried to help her, but his forte was hand-to-hand combat; they both knew he wasn't cut out to be a grief counselor. He'd tried, though, eventually becoming her new family.

And these fuckers dressed for Halloween had cut him up. Probably even killed him. Outside the van's door, Amy adjusted her grip on the handle and took a short, clarifying breath.

Living or dead, it didn't mean too much to her. If someone fucked with her family, Amy would not hesitate.

She yanked the van door open and fired a salvo into the two men inside, making them jump and jolt in their seats. The driver came off the worst; his arm burst in a swell of blood, and his face became a spurting wreck of meat and bone. Blood spattered the dash. The guy on the passenger side took rounds to his armored chest. Amy fired high, but his head was encased in a battle helmet of some sort, and the air sizzled with the sound of bullets ricocheting off metal. Another lacy white hole appeared almost magically in the windshield. Rushing her shots, she put a round into the passenger's meaty thigh, his kidney, and blew off the pinky of his left hand as he tumbled out of his door and out of sight.

She stepped back from the driver's side, intent on going around and finishing the task, but she glimpsed the glazed eye of the driver swivel in her direction.

Amy stuck the barrel of the gun under his chin and squeezed the trigger, popping off the top of his skull.

Amid the blustery firing of the Ruger, a big man flung open the passenger door and fell from the van. He rose and pulled what looked to be a sawed-off, doubled-barreled shotgun from a thigh holster. Scott got up and charged, feeling his boots punch through the depths of snow, faintly aware of the final shots coming from within the van.

The survivor's head lurched up and homed in on Scott. The shotgun came around, and Scott realized he'd made a mistake. He lurched to the left, toward the back of the van. The brute in the military helmet fired, and Scott felt the hot storm of pellets rip by his shoulder.

Missed.

The shooter shouted in frustration and struggled to reload the weapon. Scott charged along the side of the van. The man's head flicked up, eyes going wide behind the visor.

Amy reached him first, snapping a kick into the warrior's midsection, buckling him over and mashing him against the side of the van. She grabbed the back of his head and pulled it down as her padded knee came up and crashed into the visor. There was a crack, and the shotgun dropped from his hand. Amy didn't stop. She kneed his head repeatedly and, when her victim slumped to the ground, she stomped, grunting with each impact.

"Amy."

She stopped and regarded Scott.

"He's done."

The man at her feet wasn't moving. The amount of blood leaving him told them both he wouldn't be going anywhere ever again. Scott scooped up the shotgun and threw it into the van. He turned the battered form at his feet onto its side, looked for more weapons, and saw none.

Amy went back around the van and hopped in the driver's seat.

"You coming?" she asked.

Scott stood outside the vehicle. The dormitory stood gloomy underneath the night sky, wisps of smoke lingering as if something burned.

"I can't," Scott said. "I have to . . ." *stop Tenner* he wanted to say, but couldn't.

"You think you can kill him?"

Scott didn't answer.

"Well?"

"I'm going to try," he said. "Gun, please."

"It's empty."

"You emptied it?" Scott was incredulous. "That's a little much, ain't it?"

"Hey . . ." Amy said, looking ahead. Perhaps she was going to say something sarcastic, but instead she hesitated, leaning forward into the steering wheel.

"Scott," Amy started. "Get in the van."

He was about to protest, but the sounds stopped him—that soft, unmistakable rustling that he'd already encountered too many times. He stared ahead and saw them scurry up over the white road, a writhing, knobby carpet. The rats had finally caught up with them. The blood and the recent dead all over the area had brought the seemingly unending wave of undead vermin.

An uneasy Scott got into the van. "Drop me off over there."

Amy gaped at him. "I'm not going anywhere near there. That's driving into them."

"Amy, drive me over there right fucking now and you can be on your way."

"No." She put the machine into gear.

"Goddammit." Scott gnashed his teeth and jumped out as she put the van into reverse. He never looked back. He got out his bat and climbed the nearby slope, getting out of the immediate path of the rats. There was no way he was going to let Tenner escape. If he did, the killer would only keep on killing innocent people. He doubted he could convince Amy he could stop him, not with Buckle and Vick probably dying somewhere. He didn't blame her.

But he had to see this through, had to steel himself to do what needed to be done.

Facing that familiar river of undead, Scott plunged forward toward the dormitory. Rats streamed by him, zeroing in on the meat, both old and fresh, lying in the street. He stepped on a few that got in his way, glancing back to see the van's headlights still on, Amy behind the wheel, rats teeming around the two motionless bodies the two of them had thrown into the street.

He was focused on the dark mass of the building ahead when he heard the angry exchange of gunfire.

40

The other two survivors of the grenade blast weaved around the opposite side of the dormitory until they came to the main entrance. High overhead, not visible from the road, was a pedway that connected the top floor with the adjacent building. Shards of glass from broken windows littered the ground as the two men walked up to the dormitory's closed door. White paint, still in relatively good condition, glowed with moonlight. Armed with shotguns and axes, the ready-to-kill pair opened the door and barged inside.

Cray had been something of a leatherworker back in the real world, and he'd seen right away the protective qualities of tire rubber, which he fashioned into armor for himself and the others. He'd also been a member of the local Society for Creative Anachronism, so he knew how to construct a Roman cuirass. Once he and the others went back west and got home, he intended to get to work making more tire cuirasses, improving on his initial design. The one thing he wanted to find on this trip were ancient weapons, and he cursed himself for not insisting on ravaging the big museum they'd passed in Toronto.

Nolan spoke mostly in grunts, growls, and barks of harsh laughter. Quick to anger, Nolan had already killed two men on this expedition over jokes at his expense. While he wasn't the best conversationalist in the world, he had other talents, like being able to kill people with little hesitation and swinging a murderous axe. No other man beside Fist instilled fear like Nolan, and some wondered if the crazy man would eventually make an attempt at the leader's position. Such a move would only incite a bloody breakdown in the party, as several of the Norsemen didn't want Nolan in charge. Fist was scary, but Nolan was unstable. Of all the people to be paired with as they went into a potential nest, Nolan was the best and perhaps the worst companion Cray could have asked for.

"This way," Cray said, pointing toward one of two corridors. An archway opened into some type of common area, its features nearly invisible under a blue-black canopy of darkness.

Not totally unexpected, Nolan ignored Cray and went the other way. Swearing to himself, Cray was half-tempted to shoot the bastard in the back. He turned around and followed the man's meaty frame. Nolan was the only one in the group who didn't wear any protection. His clothing consisted of a couple of sweaters, a leather jacket, and a thick winter coat that bulked him up even further. He did wear an old riot helmet missing its visor, but he didn't seem to care. Nolan was baiting the dead to fight him, but none had yet taken him.

They made their way to the end of the hall, pausing at open doorways and making certain the rooms were empty. When they located the stairwell, Nolan opened the door with one hand while holding on to his axe with the other.

Empty.

"Hrrm," Nolan growled, in a rattling voice, as if his throat was coated in smoker's phlegm.

Cray thought the killer might have said more, but he didn't dare reply.

"Meh," Nolan grunted, arching his head back and studying the stairs. He moved up. When Cray entered the stairwell, he couldn't see up or down. The darkness swallowed Nolan and, for a moment, Cray hesitated. The dark would be a perfect place for Nolan to kill him. He didn't have any reason to, but one simply couldn't tell what the brute might do.

"Mmhrrr," Nolan growled.

"Right," Cray muttered, holding his shotgun before him and carefully placing a shoulder against the wall for guidance. He started up the stairs.

He caught up to Nolan just as the man opened the door to the second floor. Pale light gave the corridor shape, and the corpses filling it turned at the clicking of the door. Over Nolan's shoulder, Cray could see the dead shuffle toward the unpredictable grunt, their dark faces moaning.

"Mehhehe," Nolan chortled, in what Cray thought was pure Orcish glee. Nolan hefted his axe and went to meet them, much to the other man's dismay. Cray hesitated to follow.

The corridor was dark and many doors had been left open, leaving the dead occupying them to slink forth as if escaping tombs. Nolan took ten steps and chopped downward—the ceiling just high enough for such a strike—cleaving one dead thing's head open with a crack. Nolan pushed the corpse back with his boot and wrenched his axe free. He drew in a breath and nearly decapitated another zombie with one mighty swipe. Nolan raised his axe again and split open another face, driving the thing to its knees. The dead filled the corridor beyond the slaughter, struggling to get into the melee. Nolan met them head on, wading into a fray that was potentially beyond even his vicious capabilities.

Ghoulish forms slinked forth from the open doorways in frightening silence, freezing Cray where he stood. They reached for Nolan, clawed at his back, and the warrior turned on them with a puzzled grunt. He grabbed the throat of one dead man and savagely put its head and torso through a nearby window. The blow might've killed a living man, but the dead thing's limbs only fluttered in annoyance. More dead closed in on Nolan, crowding him and his axe, and the killer soon found himself immersed in zombies. He released his weapon with one of his trademark grunts, not sounding panicked in the least.

The fool was trying the same thing Fist had done back when the van had crashed. Trouble was, as destructive as Nolan was, he was still no Fist. Cray dropped back to the stairwell, poised to bolt, unwilling to risk himself to save the brute's life. The corpses swarmed Nolan, and for a moment, he appeared as a great black lumberjack, methodically tearing at flesh as pale as maggots and grunting as he punched undead faces. He slammed one body into the wall. Another he hugged to his chest and crushed. The zombies latched onto him in a mesh of limbs, and Nolan disappeared from sight. Then a hammer rose into the air, and the killer began splitting the heads around him with surgical precision. With a roar, he lifted one zombie well above his head and threw it forward, where it tumbled out of sight with a fleshy rattle. He killed three zombies as they tried unsuccessfully to bite into his layered belly. Nolan got his back against a wall and, with one hand, grabbed a face, lined it up, and smashed it with his hammer. More zombies joined the fray with chilling eagerness. Nolan's strikes became slower, requiring more effort to pull the hammer free from a skull, until one zombie reached out with both hands and grasped Nolan's arm. Another did the same, homing in on Nolan's wrist, where the sleeve drooped down just enough to reveal skin.

One of the corpses sank its teeth into that meaty morsel. Nolan's grunt became a wheezy scream, as if something once fun had suddenly become quite serious. He jerked his wrist back and, in the sparse light, ripped out a chunk of his own flesh. Blood flowed down his arm like oil. Another zombie stretched over its brethren, and Nolan bashed its face away. But there were too many covering him. He actually head-butted a corpse, crunching its nose, but that didn't stop it from wrapping its white arms around Nolan's tiring form, its open mouth seeking his throat. Zombies grabbed his gushing wrist, siphoning off veins and chewing deeper.

Nolan slowly sank under the dead tide, finally disappearing with a muted whimper.

Cray almost wanted to help the man, but it was better this way. And it was better for him to get the hell away from the zombies. He'd made the mistake of standing about and watching Nolan fall.

Then he heard the hissing above him in the stairwell.

Cray looked up and just barely saw shapes squirming in the inky blackness, moving toward him. He brought up his shotgun and fired, briefly lighting the stairs and glimpsing a mass of torsos and limbs oozing downward. Cray backed up and figured it was time to beat a strategic retreat.

Something crashed into his legs from behind and staggered him. A corpse moved at his feet. Cray turned on the landing, heard the briefest rush of air, and didn't have time to look up. A weight slammed into his back, stunning him and driving him to his knees. A moment later, the tide of flesh on the stairs overran him, bending him backward until his knees popped painfully, all the while slowly wrenching the hockey helmet from his head, the chin strap finally snapping. Cray thrust his arms against the bodies, yelling for help, yelling for them to stop, and finally screaming, but they just continued to pile onto him, reaching, reaching . . .

He still had enough time to shriek when fingers clawed out his eyes, and mouths fastened onto his cheeks like toothy leeches.

That bloodcurdling scream ripped through all levels of the dormitory, making the few living things nearby stop and listen. The sound hung hauntingly on the air, ebbing away until it was abruptly cut off.

In another stairwell on the far side of the building, Fist stopped in his tracks and listened to the scream until it ended. He turned to Shipp and muttered, "That one hurt."

Hearing the same lingering scream, Tenner shifted on his belly and waited, listening to the sound until it stopped. When silence established itself once more, he set his attention on the dark corridor ahead and whoever or whatever might fill it. He hoped they came soon. He was getting bored, despite the intriguing sounds from elsewhere in building.

Then he heard something, faint, but coming from the end of the corridor. Almost gracefully, he placed an eye to his scope and studied the darkness, settling into a more comfortable position. A shard of light touched the lower part of the door, gashing it, and Tenner was just able to make out a widening crack. He waited. The question of who it might be would soon be answered. He hoped it was alive. The dead usually had trouble opening doors.

The crack widened.

Tenner *tsked* to himself. But then, there was no real way for his visitors to know what lay ahead of them.

Two shadows edged carefully into the corridor, one ahead of the other.

Tenner waited until they filled his sights, then he squeezed the trigger.

At the last possible moment, one shadow split from the other, the wall seemingly swallowing the dusky outline. It was at that moment that the AR-20 went full rock show and lit up the corridor, hammering vicious rounds into the remaining shadow and throwing it back into the stairwell. The weapon rattled slightly against Tenner's shoulder, stitching up the outline with tracers that cut the gloom like lasers. He stopped firing a few seconds later, smelling the cordite, and studied the results through the scope. The second shadow had disappeared, split from the other, while Tenner discerned boots pointing to the ceiling where his first kill had fallen on his back.

"Missed, you little prick," a voice called.

Tenner smiled wanly. "I'd say you were just lucky."

"Lucky?" A pause. "I'll show you lucky, when I'm ripping your balls out instead of your throat."

Tenner's expression slackened at that.

"Gonna cut you up. Eat your heart."

Another interesting threat. "Really? Well, I'll give you five seconds to make your move."

Through the scope, Tenner watched as an arm reached out and grabbed the leg of his first victim. It violently hauled the dead body into the nearby room, disappearing before Tenner could draw a bead on it.

Then he heard laughter. The man was laughing?

That made Tenner smile. He liked a victim with a sense of humor.

The noise of wood being shattered made him cock his brow.

Fist hauled Shipp's bleeding carcass into the room and grunted as he inspected the weapon's handiwork—an automatic of some sort, and a prize if he could get his hands on it. That was something he was going to work on, and his old buddy Shipp was going to help him. Fist stood, flung his maul to the floor, and inspected the room. There was a closet with open doors and these he attacked savagely, slamming them shut and putting a boot through one. He kicked one door down, ripped at the shards, and pulled them from the frame with furious energy. There was one man at the end of the hall, one very confident man, but he was about to find out what it was like to fuck around with Fist. He got his hands on Shipp's sawed-off shotgun, so common amongst the Norsemen, and rooted through the dead man's pockets, searching for extra shells.

Shoot at me, Fist fumed, baring his teeth. *No one shoots at me.*

He manhandled Shipp's corpse to its feet and pushed him against the wall, smelling his blood. Ol' Shipp was going to help him out once more. Ol' Shipp was going to help him get his paws on Confident Man with the gun and wring his goddamn neck.

"You ready, man?" Fist bellowed, struggling with Shipp's body.

"Ready, fucktard," the voice floated back.

Fucktard. Fist fumed and snarled. He was going to enjoy flaying this man.

He lifted Shipp so that his still-armored corpse faced away from him, the side with the bleeding holes facing out. He noted the plates on Shipp's back were fine. Fist counted on his own body armor to stop anything getting by the fleshy barrier. It seemed like a good idea—it worked in the movies.

Whirling around the corner, Fist and his human shield emerged into the corridor and thundered down its length.

A howl of fury and murderous intent accompanied by the pounding of heavy boots and a flopping shape charged Tenner's position. The rushing apparition startled him for all of two seconds, before he shook his head and fired. Tracers lashed into the thing coming at him, some audibly pinging off armor plates, but still it charged. Tenner kept firing, his forehead knotting in concerned concentration, hitting the torso dead center. The roar grew louder. The heavy stomping made the floor tremble. Tenner shifted targets and shot at the thing's legs, sending tracers into shins and hearing the crack of hard plastic. The mass faltered, stumbling, but still it came.

Tenner rose to one knee and unleashed the full fury of the weapon into the multi-limbed berserker barreling down on him. The tracers blasted into the mass until the magazine clicked dry.

Then it was on him.

Fist felt the bullets rip into his lower legs. One or two might've shattered a few ribs as well. Whatever the bastard was firing pelted him good and lit him up like a night of fireworks. He felt stings on his forearms where bullets blew through the twisted wreck of Shipp's body and grazed him. Fist went down. Before Shipp's legs struck the floor, Fist heaved him ahead and yelled. The body fell on what looked to be a soldier, who struggled to his knees in the doorway, but Shipp landed heavily and tangled up his assault rifle. Fist fell forward, the pain of his lower legs momentarily overridden by the furious eagerness of finally getting his hands on his foe.

The soldier tried to aim the rifle, but Fist slammed his mallet of a hand into the man's face, knocking him backward. The Norseman yanked his foe's helmet down, blinding him. The soldier punched, hitting Fist's cheek with substantial force, but rage diluted the blow. Fist clawed his way over Shipp's frame and jabbed an elbow into his foe's head, then another, which heralded a relentless flurry of heavy strikes. Fist snarled as he drummed punishing elbows into his target. Some shots hit flesh and bone; some connected with the helmet. The soldier released the rifle and a hand snaked to his side. Fist paid it no heed, quite happy to pummel the man's head, seeking to break it open.

Then something plunged into his guts twice, fast and hard. It retracted and went into him again, this time sawing upward. Fist felt his guts sizzle in agony. He slammed his elbow into the helmet again, bouncing the head off the floor, *but the knife was still in his midsection.* His strength waned. Fist felt that hot lick of steel disemboweling him, and he pushed the soldier away in reflex as he tried to back off the man like a fat crab.

But the soldier reached out and held on to him.

"Oh, no," seethed a hard voice. "You said you were gonna cut me up. Said you were gonna eat my heart."

The knife punched into Fist again, and the room spun. He needed to get off the soldier, but his armored foe reached out with his arms, one of which ended in a knife, and embraced him.

"Gonna eat my heart, huh? Gonna eat *my* heart?" Fist glimpsed a white smile, then cruel eyes that flashed red. The knife plunged into him once more, a length of searing light that cut into his arms to the bone.

Fist's breath left him.

The soldier punched his face cage and, with a mighty effort, heaved him off and got out from under the Norseman. Fist flailed an arm at his opponent's head, but it was caught and bent backward. It snapped with a crack, like hard candy.

More cuts with the knife, taking more of Fist's strength. Hands pulled off his armor plating. The soldier on him was no longer a man, but a spider. Fist bucked one last time and threw it off balance, sat up, and threw a punch to the creature's midsection. His knuckles slammed into armor plates. He twisted, throwing the other off-balance.

Fist got to his knees, bleeding, adrenaline surging. The spider screamed. Fist roared back and cracked a knee into its head, whipping the skull back and flinging the body against a wall. Fist thundered forward, bloody spittle spewing from his lips. He stomped, laying a boot into the wood where the spider's face had been only a split second earlier.

Then it was on him again in a scurry, punching and slicing into his guts and Fist didn't have the energy to fight it. It bore him backward, and they both fell to the floor. A quick scramble, then a pair of knees pinned the Norseman's shoulders. Fingers ripped away his face cage. A long knife appeared above him and descended slowly. The meager light in the room made the steel appear very cold.

"Gonna cut me, hm?" the spider croaked. Its eyes, like that of man, looked crazier than Fist's.

The Norseman felt the knife prick the soft part of his throat, right underneath his chin.

Then the heavy thrust, straight to the brain, and the sound of his own dying gurgle echoing in his ears.

41

Scott headed for the door in the parking lot underneath the dormitory building and stopped in his tracks. Memories of that ghost thing went through his head. He decided to enter the building through the hole in the foundation he'd seen seconds earlier. He started climbing the mass of debris and brick toward the gap.

A blinding wash of headlights made him lift a hand to shield his eyes. Amy drove up in the van. She stopped the machine and jumped out, a shotgun in her hand.

"You forgot this," she said and held out the weapon. It was his own.

"I had this," he said, indicating the bat. "But I'll take that. You heading out, then?"

"No. I'll hold off on searching for the boys a few minutes more. Bringing you along would be smarter. Extra manpower."

"Oh. Well." Scott looked at the jagged hole granting access to the lower room. "Better get going, then. Here, put this in my backpack," he said, handing her the bat.

When he turned, rats flooded the road beyond, still flowing toward the smell of blood and sending shivers through him. If Tenner was in there, they'd have to be fast.

He got moving over the crinkling pile of bricks and wood. Amy followed him, bumping into more debris and causing it to tumble.

"I heard gunfire earlier," Scott said, lifting the shotgun to his shoulder and peering ahead. "Inside."

Amy said nothing, so he continued on, glancing back at times to see if she was still behind him. She had her tonfas out and crouched, waiting for him to keep walking. Having her there was a huge relief. Time and time again she had proved herself to be an unflinching rock.

They shuffled over the debris and found a hallway and nearby stairwell. Scott started up the stairs, holding his shotgun before him even though he couldn't see a thing. He kept his shoulder to the wall, and his Nomex rasped as he rounded corners and proceeded up the stairs. Amy placed her hand on his back and followed. They went up three floors, passing two closed doors and coming to one that was wide open. It wasn't the door that caught his attention at first, although he saw the lump of something wedged underneath it to keep it in place. Pale light illuminated white and black tiling.

It also revealed a head. And boots.

Then the smell hit him.

Sticking out of the room were two bodies. Scott placed his back to the wall and took a breath. He whirled into the opening and discovered the dead men stretched far into the room. Suddenly fearful of his back, he turned around and looked down the hallway. Sensing the coast was clear and not hearing or seeing anything, he turned back to the corpse. Amy knelt beside them both, studying in silence. She looked at him in the limited light and held a spiked tonfa near her throat. She swished the weapon grimly underneath it, and Scott got the meaning. One man had been cut up and left with a knife in his head. A pool of blood as black as tar surrounded him, while the other was shredded by gunfire. Both were van warriors.

"Christ almighty," Scott muttered. The black tiling was really blood, and he realized he'd been stepping in it. He didn't like the idea of leaving bloody tracks. Memories of Teddy and Lea flashed through his head, and he knew then that if he ever had to kill a person, it was going to be the psycho he was after.

He eased around Amy and studied the floor, and his heart raced.

There, heading into the stairwell, were a set of boot tracks.

"Amy," he whispered.

"What?"

"Look."

They studied the blood, seeing where it hit the stairs and went up, fading into black. Scott took the lead, shotgun first, and Amy followed. They kept in contact with the wall as they climbed the stairs. At the top, a wide ray of moonlight split the darkness like a silver beacon. They paused at a wide landing. Scott pointed to the heavy metal door, which stood wide open.

"Pedway," Scott whispered, gesturing ahead with his shotgun. Fresh air hit their faces. A long stretch of tiling, concrete, and steel beams connected the dormitory with another building almost thirty meters away. Amy stepped onto the pedway, tonfas at her side, and stared up at the moon sitting low in the night sky. The glass had been smashed out in places, leaving shards of broken panes or entire sections missing, from the base of the pedway all the way to its roof. Vertical bars ran the length of the crossing, like a ladder whose rungs were spaced too far apart. Amy walked forward, gazing at a closed door, and Scott moved behind her. It was a four-story drop, but what really caught his attention were the rats milling about below, a thick knobby carpet surging through the buildings.

"Shit," Amy whispered, studying the mass.

"We can still get back. Or even wait them out. That door is metal."

"I'm not thinking about that," Amy informed him. "I'm thinking about Vick and Donny."

That made Scott peer at the shifting surface below with growing worry. A second later, he studied the floor and moved toward the other building.

"Where are you going?" Amy asked.

"Tracks go that way," Scott answered and started following them.

42

Wrestling with the dead bastard underneath him had been like wrangling with an angry elephant, but Tenner gutted him all the same. He got up from the wreck of a man at his feet and gazed around the room. He couldn't see his rifle. The van man had slapped it from his grip. A quick search revealed nothing and, with amazed horror, Tenner looked at the window. It couldn't have gone out there, could it? Tenner leaned out studied the ground. The rats were massed below, and the rifle was nowhere to be seen. Worse, the van was also missing. With a groan, Tenner pulled the helmet from his head, as well as the mask underneath, and tossed both onto the floor. There was no way he was going to try and get them back on. With his good hand, he felt the rubble of his broken nose and grimaced. His cheeks blared out in pain as well, shifting like shattered clay. Every breath felt like red embers flaring in his chest. Feeling the inside of his mouth with his tongue, he realized the savage had destroyed his teeth. His front ones were broken, leaving only shards of enamel. Others were gone completely, and more shifted loosely in his gums. That was on top of what felt like most of his facial bones being smashed. Blood seeped into his right eye, blinding him until he wiped it away.

He knew he looked like shit.

"But I look better than you, shit-fucker," Tenner whispered to the dead man at his feet, and even *that* hurt.

He growled in pain and frustration. He had to get out of here, but where? The screams from below suggested the Philistines were nearby. Tenner looked at the door and stepped into the corridor. The stairwell on the left beckoned, and he felt pulled in that direction for reasons unknown. Cradling his broken wrist, he allowed it to simply drop and hang at his side. For a moment, dizziness gripped his senses, as well as an overbearing feeling of unwellness. He leaned against the wall, breathing deeply, suffering, then grinning.

Gods didn't die. Reality would wink out the very instant he did.

But he grudgingly admitted they sometimes got seriously fucked up.

Using the wall as support, he climbed the stairway to a landing and an open portal that led to a bridge. Not a bridge, he realized, but a pedway, and with enough bars on it to make him think of cages in a zoo. Fresh air slapped his face and cleared his mind a little. He wiped at his eye and forehead, astonished by the amount of blood. Cringing at every painful breath, he crossed to the midway point of the pedway and gazed down.

Rats.

Tenner chuckled darkly and allowed a few plops of blood to fall from his face to the foragers on the street. Their reaction was quite interesting. The closest rats homed in on the blood the very second it blotted the snow. When the world had still functioned and he'd been forced to hide his true self, people had kept rats as pets. He thought that was a wonderful idea. When he was feeling better, he'd capture some of the furry little undead fucks, maybe use a small aquarium as a holding pen. He might even use them on future victims.

This on his mind, he reached the far door and opened it—another stairwell and another open door leading to a series of rooms. Another dormitory. One of the rooms would have a bed, and a bed sounded just fine to Tenner. With that firmly in mind, he closed the door behind him.

Then, through the square window, he saw Amy and the mystery man emerging from the building on the far side of the pedway.

Tenner blinked and made an agonized sound. The pair dawdled, being cautious, but then the man who knew him straightened up, shotgun ready, and walked toward him, oblivious that Tenner hid behind the door and watched from the darkness.

His left hand gripped his Glock and lifted it from its holster. Tenner placed it just behind the glass, keeping it in the shadows, and aimed. One burst would finish him. Mortals hunting gods, *wounding* gods, wasn't something to be taken lightly. He'd have to explain it to these lesser beings.

The mystery man got closer to the door, hand reaching for the handle.

And Tenner, despite his pain, smiled once more.

"Scott, wait," Amy called, and he did.

"What?" His hand was on the door handle.

"Don't get too far ahead of me."

Good point. Scott waited, trying to look beyond the window's safety glass. Another void, but there was faint light from a hallway to the left.

"All right," Amy said, just behind him.

"You ready?"

"All set."

Scott opened the door. He stepped across the threshold and a gun snaked out from the dark and pressed against his helmet. Amy froze.

"Don't move," Tenner warned. "One move, Amy, and I ventilate him."

Scott felt the click against his helmet, and his heart and stomach plummeted.

"Hello, Amy," Tenner said. Then to Scott he said, "Shithead."

Scott lowered his shotgun to his pelvis and Tenner leaned forward. "You lift that thing and I'll shoot your knees off. Might do it anyway."

The rats rippled beneath the pedway, sensing the living, but unable to locate them.

"Careful now. Drop the shotgun," Tenner instructed.

Scott set his jaw and did as he was told.

"Back up, Amy, and toss the sticks over the ledge."

She hesitated, just a moment, but complied.

"A little more, a little more. All right. Stop there. Excellent. Now, then." Tenner smiled, half-squinting in the pedway's shade. "There's been something puzzling the hell out of me for the past few hours, and I get to find out what it is, right now."

He paused and squinted in discomfort.

"Who the hell are you, anyway?" Tenner asked Scott.

"Huh?"

"Who are you?"

"You don't know?"

Tenner shook his head and grimaced. "Nope. Time to 'fess up."

Scott wavered. "A few months ago. You were down in Annapolis. You killed two friends of mine. Shot me in the back. Left me for dead."

Tenner's lips pursed in thought. "Woman and a guy? In the basement?"

"Yeah."

"I remember you. I shot you dead," Tenner hissed.

"You should've checked more carefully."

"Why? Would've found out you were still breathing. I'd have put a bullet into you for certain if I'd known. Or worse. Probably worse. Holy shit," he seethed with evil mirth. "That *was* you. Man, you owe me a thank you for not checking closer. You wouldn't be here today."

Scott held back a reply.

"So you healed up," Tenner continued. "Got all better. Locked, loaded, and looking for revenge. Hm? Looking to even things up. Get some cutting time in. Took you a while. I've been here for a month or so."

"Still found you," Scott said through clenched teeth.

"Yeah, you did. Tough shit, ain't it? I almost feel bad here."

He smiled again, pale and sinister, and Scott knew he only had another second to live. He turned just a little toward his captor.

Right then, sounds drifted up from the stairwell. Tenner's head flicked just enough to dislodge a large bead of blood welling up on his busted forehead and it slipped down into his eye, causing him to squint.

Scott ducked.

Tenner fired, the bullet grazing the top of Scott's helmet with a frightening *pop* and whizzing off into the dark.

Scott tackled the man and drove him into the wall just to the right of the open doorway. Cackling, Tenner drove a knee into his gut and spiked an elbow to the back of his neck. Even with his Nomex gear and hockey vest, the blows made Scott gasp. Tenner pushed him back and snapped out a front kick that pistoned Scott backward. He hit the wall off-balanced and put his foot down, except there was nothing underneath him.

With the sharp sensation of tipping, Scott fell into the darkness of the stairwell.

Tenner came forward, paused in the doorway, and turned just as Amy gripped his vest and rolled backward, flipping him over her and landing him flat on his back. The impact stunned him and he lost his Glock, but his indignity at being manhandled in such a way galvanized him to roll over and get to his knees. He grabbed for his remaining gun. Awkwardly, his left hand pulled the weapon from his right hip. Amy walked toward him as he fumbled with the gun, correcting his grip.

Tenner almost got it a second before Amy spun and kicked it from his hand, sending the weapon spinning off into the sea of vermin.

"Ohh you—"

Bitch, Tenner wanted to say, but Amy front-kicked him, sending him flying backward before scuttling to a stop on his ass. Once again he got to his knees, then his feet. His left hand found the hilt of his knife, and he jerked it free.

Amy came forward, her face dark and drawn, her hands in a fighter's guard.

Tenner giggled. He was going to *so* enjoy impregnating her.

He lunged.

The knife never reached her. She caught the blow with both arms and twisted his wrist in a direction it was never meant to go, eliciting a half-scream, half-grunt from Tenner. He dropped the knife and she spun into him, whipping the point of her elbow across his jaw with wrecking-ball force. Tenner barely felt the thunderous barrage of fists from the woman after that, which backed him along the pedway. He thrust out his wrecked right arm, almost *shooing* her away, but she swatted it to one side before stepping into his guard and lacing her fingers behind his head.

"For Tickle," he heard her say, before his head was pulled down to her upcoming knee, mashing them together like an egg hitting the floor. The impact unhinged his jaw and crumbled whatever facial bones were intact from his previous fight. She kneed him three more times—fast, punishing blows in devastating Muai Thai style—before finally releasing him.

Tenner collapsed in a heap, gasping, hurting, almost drunkenly bewildered.

Amy wasn't finished.

Not by a long shot.

"For Sammy and Schaffer." She stomped on the killer's midsection, buckling him like a broken plank, before unloading a hammer of a fist straight to his jaw. Tenner's eyes unfocused with the connection, and he trembled on the tiles. She soccer-kicked his ribs, and he didn't react. On a whim, she took interest in his right ankle and crushed it under a boot heel. That caused him to shiver and whimper.

"That one's for Vick," she panted, looking around for a gun. She could've choked him to death, but she didn't want to touch the killer anymore. Amy backed away from the human wreck on the pedway, with the intent of finding Scott's shotgun and blowing Tenner's head off.

"Amy," Scott said, standing in the doorway with his shotgun and still wearing his ruined helmet. "The hell you doing?"

She stopped. "Sorry."

"S'okay."

"Just that," she shrugged, "he murdered three people I knew. That other poor person we found in the street there. And maybe even Vick. I know you wanted to finish him off, but . . . I guess I wanted him more."

Scott didn't reply right away. "I guess you did. Don't worry. I'm not upset."

"Then give me that."

"This?" He held up the weapon. "Why?"

"You know why."

A current of blackness, deep and sparkling, whorled Tenner's senses about like a rag doll held up to the sky. Voices came from beyond, the sounds elongated and without meaning. The sky, black and empty, reminded him that he was a god, a fucking *god*, and with that thought, summoned whatever power he had remaining in lifting his left hand to his chest. Tenner rolled onto his side and fumbled at his vest. He was a monstrous deity, death on two legs, and so much more than the physical pain laying fiery siege to his mind. He was . . . a *sun* god . . . and his power and death for the world lay clenched in his fist.

With a feeble breath, Tenner cocked back his good arm, not bothering to take aim at the mortal shit standing at the end of the pedway.

Willpower *alone* would direct his wrath.

Finding the strength to smile, Tenner rolled the grenade toward Amy and Scott.

In the pause of Amy's last words, understanding what she wanted to do, Scott heard the wobbling rattle and saw the black thing rolling toward them, guided by the sloped edge of the pedway. Amy turned as Scott bolted by her. He didn't know what it was, only that it came from Tenner's spectral shape in the middle of the pedway.

And he kicked it back.

Too hard. The bauble flew across the gap between the two buildings and, for a split second, Scott lost sight of the thing. He heard it rattle off something solid, then glimpsed it drop to the floor in front of the open doorway on the opposite end of the pedway.

Before it exploded like a black sun.

Steel and concrete gave way like wet paper, and the pedway fell away from its moorings with a resounding shriek of metal and dust, before it slammed into the ground four levels below. The ceiling collapsed, pinching the ends of the structure into a V. The impact made the three figures still on the walkway tremble, fall, and finally slide down the sharply angled ramp.

Straight toward the rats.

Scott felt the ground go out from under him and he turned and flailed, letting go of the shotgun. He latched onto Amy's leg and held her as they both slid toward the bottom. He screamed. Amy screamed and grabbed at a bent metal bar. Her outspread fingers slapped off the first one.

She hooked a second, before Scott's weight pulled her down.

She missed the third entirely.

And snagged the fourth with both hands, halting their slide. Scott's weight dragged on her for a few seconds before he grabbed at another bar and released her legs. He gazed up, meeting her wide eyes, and clung to the bar as if it were life itself.

Then they both looked down.

They'd stopped perhaps ten feet from the bottom.

Far enough away to watch.

Tenner's side slammed into the base of the opposite building, where the roof and the floor squished together. Unfortunately it was his left side, and his own body weight pinned his arm beneath him. Dust coated his body and made him cough, and an awful ringing filled his ears. Disoriented, he twisted left then right, before realizing his arm was underneath him, feeling his fingers wriggle just past his ass. He lifted his chest off the shattered slab of concrete and looked up.

The first rat chomped into his nose with such ferocity that Tenner screamed as if his heart had been gouged from his chest. Two fastened onto his cheeks while another got a chunk of his ear. He twisted away with his free right arm, and the pain from ramming his useless hand into the ground turned it to fire. Rats swarmed up and over the rubble and foamed about his limbs. He pushed himself backward in an attempt to free his pinned left arm, just as a rush of rats dug into his destroyed ankle. *That* lit up his senses like a row of wailing klaxons. Flailing his pained white arm, he knocked the rats away from his face. Still in a deadly awkward position, he attempted to roll over and only partially succeeded. Rats piled on his body, enveloping him, biting *everywhere*, bypassing his body armor, and burrowing through to his flesh. *Seconds!* Tenner's mind shrieked the word.

"Help me!" he screeched, as a rat's jaws snapped onto his lower lip. More went for his throat. He swiped them away with his right hand and scooted his butt into the air, driving his shoulder into the furry wave overpowering him.

Teeth were gnashing down on his flesh all over.

"Help . . ." he managed to get out, the cry dying in his throat.

Then he remembered the grenades.

His death vest, and the one-yank pull system that would set them all off.

Rats bit at his ears, cheeks, and neck—he swiped those away quickly—and pushed himself back. He fumbled at his vest and looked down.

Tenner's jaw dropped.

His left hand had almost been stripped to the bone. Even as he watched, rats clung and chewed on the tatters of remaining meat.

By force of will alone, Tenner pushed away from the mass flowing over his legs, until his back pressed up against the stone slab behind him. The rats rose up over his legs, crowding his crotch, then his midsection. Their teeth gnawed at him in a frenzy. He slammed his head back one last time and glared in wild agony at the two survivors dangling just above him.

"HEEELLLL—"

A rat, perhaps the size of a well-fed puppy, with half of the flesh covering its skull sheared away as if it had been scraped off with a rock, rushed up Tenner's chest and bit down hard on the fat guitar string that was his jugular. Several more rats lashed into his face.

Tenner's world went red.

Scott and Amy saw the rats swallow Tenner's form, his throat exploding in red ink which showered the backs of the undead, making their hair gleam. Tenner's struggling weakened, but his body continued to shiver, jig, and jerk. He slipped downward, the sea of vermin claiming him, and disappeared into the undulating depths. The last thing Scott saw of Tenner was the top of his head.

And the rat burrowing under a flap of scalp.

Then he was gone, lost under that ravenous tide.

"Scott!"

He looked up.

"Climb!"

He blinked and started doing just that. Using the vertical bars of the pedway like a ladder, both of them climbed, well away from the gruesome display. They reached the open doorway and climbed inside, collapsing when they did.

Scott placed his shoulder to the doorframe and looked back down, but there was nothing to see besides the dead. They continued watching in silence, the sound of the feast below in their ears.

Amy laid a hand on his shoulder and pulled him away.

43

Sometime during the night, when the rats finished feeding and moved off in search of more prey, Scott and Amy got up and retreated inside the dormitory. They entered a room three doors down, went inside, and closed the door. Vick was either alive or dead, and finding him would take time and push them beyond their physical limits, having exhausted themselves in their confrontation with Tenner and the rats. As much as she hated to do it, Amy decided to sleep on it. Maybe, just maybe, things would take care of themselves in the morning.

They placed their packs to one side. There was a bare, single-person mattress in the room, but neither had any problem sharing it, and both were secretly grateful to do so. Amy took off her padded vest and helmet, and Scott removed his ruined motorcycle helmet, running his fingers over the lightning bolts. They lay down in their remaining protective wear and got comfortable. Sleep found them lying innocently next to each other.

Scott woke once, listening and imagining that something was scratching at the door. There wasn't, however, and he eventually went back to sleep, if only for a short time. He woke twice more in the dark. Once because the grinning, bleeding face of Tenner had found him in his dreams, just before the rats swelled up around the killer's face and sucked him down, chewing out the man's eyes before he disappeared under their teeming, hairy bodies.

The other time he woke when he felt an arm wrap around him and discovered Amy's sleeping, drooling face tucked into his shoulder.

That time he settled back and simply studied her features. Her face was the last thing he saw before he eventually closed his eyes and fell asleep.

And in sleep, as in life, she protected him from nightmares.

*

Morning found them in a sleepy tangle of limbs.

"Morning, pumpkin," Scott said as Amy opened her eyes and regarded him sleepily for a moment.

"Morning, squash," she replied. And they smiled.

They got up and sat next to each other on the bed.

"We better get moving," Amy said.

"Let's go, then."

They pulled on their headgear and outerwear. Moments later, they made their way through the corridor and down the nearest stairwell. They eventually emerged from the dormitory without incident and saw the skyline, pink with morning light. They wandered around to the edge of the building. Scott paused and peered around the corner, making certain the coast was clear.

"Nothing."

"They're all gone," Amy said, peeking out at the trampled snow.

"With the daylight," Scott said. "We better get moving."

But he hesitated.

"What is it?" she asked.

"I have to check on something."

He walked to the fallen pedway, stopping for a moment to marvel at the devastation Tenner's grenade had wrought. Amy came up behind him.

"I want to find my tonfas," Amy said softly, and Scott nodded. They searched the area, finding, of all things, Tenner's Glocks, several untouched spare magazines, as well as a tattered vest filled with six eggs that they both realized were grenades.

No Moe. No rats. Certainly no Tenner.

"I keep thinking the fucker's alive," Scott muttered and inspected the V of the crumpled pedway. Not much remained. They found his shotgun, as well as shreds of cloth and white armor plating surrounded by tatters of material—but no body. Scott hadn't expected one.

Amy found her tonfas in the snow, and they both located the tattered remains of what looked to be a vest of body armor, the bare, cream-colored plates exposed, and a few spare magazines for a larger, undiscovered gun.

"These will come in handy," Amy said, gathering up the extra munitions.

Scott looked at her for a moment, then took half of what she'd grabbed. His thoughts were reflective, relaxed. Tenner was gone. What else was there to do? Return to Gus? He looked at Amy. She felt his eyes and returned the look.

"What?"

"Nothing," Scott said. "Let's get looking for Vick and Buckle."

"Been thinking about that," she said. "Let's go."

They set out for the van. Along the way, resting atop of a pile of debris, was a ferocious assault rifle that matched the spare magazines they had just found.

This welcomed find was darkened by a much grimmer discovery in the rear of the parked van, something they hadn't taken the time to search during the night. Seats filled the rear, as well as meat hooks. Scott figured they'd be from a butcher's shop. A rack of cleavers and axes lined one section. An open milk crate of loose red shotgun shells was jammed behind the driver's seat.

"Thing looks like a battle wagon," Amy remarked.

"Gives me the creeps."

"I'm starting to think anything gives you the creeps."

"Well . . ." Scott said, but didn't protest. He was too glad to have her around. They got settled in the van and drove onto the street. Amy drove, watching the road through the bullet-battered windshield. The bodies that had been left in the road were gone, but neither of them said anything about it. The rats were almost all-consuming, it seemed. Along Oxford Street, nothing moved.

Sometime later Amy steered onto Robie, and they finally spotted Moe. The dead prowled streets in a half-frozen malaise. Only a few dozen of the creatures, however, and they looked wretched. The van drove through them slowly, knocking them aside or running over them. Some of the corpses turned around, as if they were surprised to see the big machine pushing through, but they didn't attack. Scott noticed that they didn't pursue them, either. He settled back into his seat and quietly appreciated the rumble of the van as it motored forward. The snow banks had been trampled, and they rumbled through it all with few problems.

It wasn't until they reached the 102 that they started hitting heavier drifts.

At one point, Amy stopped the van and got out. As always, the dead lingered nearby, but not in the immediate area. She returned to the van seconds later, paying greater attention to the road.

"Anything up?" Scott asked.

Amy regarded him. "Tire tracks."

Scott was glad Amy was at the wheel. Halifax was her city, and she drove around for the next couple of hours, searching for where the tracks might lead. Eventually she lost the trail, and Scott could tell it bothered her. She finally resolved to get them both to Scott's safe house, abandoning the search for her companions.

The roads were in better condition than what Scott remembered, and he attributed it to Amy. This was her city. She got them by clumps of deadheads and evaded larger clusters altogether. When one road was impassable, she got the van moving down another, getting as close to the house on School Avenue as possible. Zombies lurked all around, but any road or side street with large numbers were bypassed entirely. They stuck to the 102 and headed over deserted overpasses, but they were about to abandon the van when the snow became too deep for even the chained tires.

Scott was looking out the window when he spotted another black cargo van in the opposite lane. It appeared like a black beacon amongst the other half-stranded cars covered in snow.

"Amy?"

"I see it."

They drove over the snow slowly and got as close to the stopped van as they could. The front of the vehicle was squished inward, as if the thing had been driven into a tree or pole.

"Better check it out."

Amy was already out the door. Scott hauled up his shotgun and loaded it with the loose shells from the milk crate. He left the assault rifle, preferring the familiarity of the twelve gauge. He exited from the rear; Amy was already at the other vehicle. She had her tonfas out and ready.

Without asking, she rapped on one of the rear doors.

"Anyone in there?" she called. When there was no response, she rapped on the rear door once more. "Hey. You in there, Vick? Buckle?"

Something inside moved.

Amy regarded Scott, who had just arrived at her side, his shotgun ready.

"Amy?" a muffled voice asked from within.

The doors opened.

And Amy hugged the one-armed Vick, who was beaming weakly at her.

The house was a thirty-minute march away. Scott returned to the house, located a sled, and brought it back to the van. When he got back to Amy and the others, it was quarter to four. They talked about it for a minute, and none of them wanted to stay with the vans overnight. They loaded Buckle onto the sled, and Scott pulled it behind him. Vick marched with slow, deliberate steps, his one arm wrapped around Amy's shoulders for support.

They walked in the dark for about an hour until they found the house.

Six Months later

The trees along the highway blushed vibrant green, declaring that all was right with the world. All manner of vehicles dotted the shoulders and sometimes the road itself, and Scott had to take care driving around them all. Anything could jump out in front of the SUV. It hadn't happened yet, but one never knew in the real world. He drove the Durango along the highway, making the final approach to Gus's manor. The last month had been the hardest, he thought. Ever since he'd gotten up in the morning, emerging from the white house with satin green shutters that needed a new coat of paint, every hour was a challenge to control himself from stomping on the gas pedal.

"We there yet?" Buckle asked from the passenger seat.

"Almost."

"That why you're stomping on the gas?"

Scott felt an embarrassed heat creep into his face. "Sorry, man."

Buckle didn't answer. He pulled up the AR-20, locked, loaded, and ready to split undead hairs if need be. His ankle hadn't healed completely right, and he walked with an aching limp. "But," he would remark with a thankful expression every once in a while, "I still got everything."

"Look for a gate on your side," Scott told him.

"A gate?"

"Yeah, with leaves on . . ." Scott trailed off and shut his mouth, remembering how Gus had camouflaged the thing. "Don't worry. I'll see it."

"Nice area, the Valley. Always liked it," Buckle commented, becoming reflective.

Of the group, he was the only one who'd volunteered to come here with Scott, and for that, the New Brunswick native was thankful. Six months ago, they had taken what they could from the downtown and historical section of the city, transferring the MREs from the van that Tenner had booby-trapped to the SUV and the remaining van. These they drove down the highway, to the little town of Blandford, which would serve as a push-off point to Big Tancook. They linked up with the rest of the waiting group, a little more than a dozen men, women, and children. It took longer to transport everything, included the wounded, to the little island off the coast. Gas was spared for motorboats and, if the weather wasn't fair, they waited until the next day.

In the end, it was worth it.

Big Tancook was the undead-free refuge they had hunted for and, over the next few months, Scott actually felt much better about the survivors' chances. But despite the food, and the planting of Amy's seeds, Scott would look through the kitchen window of the deserted house he and Amy had taken as their own and stare out at the dark, shifting waters of the Atlantic and wonder.

Gus was still out there.

And he'd vowed, when he had the chance, he would return to the mainland and retrieve his friend.

"Hey, that it?" Buckle said and pointed, pulling Scott out of his thoughts. He slowed the SUV and felt his heart go cold.

The gate was flung wide open.

That wasn't like Gus—unless the man was shitfaced. Still, it wasn't like Gus to leave it open like that.

"Yeah," Scott muttered. "That's it."

"Something wrong?" Buckle said, fixing on the scattered cars and trucks littering the highway.

"Don't know."

The SUV turned off the highway and climbed the slope, passing under a full green canopy where sunlight dappled the crushed stone of the road. The machine bounced in places, and at one point Buckle had to place his hand against the dashboard. Scott drove on, forcing the vehicle to climb.

They went up the last bit of slope, and the stone walls came into view.

Scott's heart sank.

Cars and trucks lay before the gate. Some were burnt out, but others appeared fine—lifeless, but fine. Beyond the vehicles, the gate had been destroyed, its timbers burnt to black cinders. What was worse, the usual heights of the house, seen so easily from this point, simply did not exist anymore. Scott braked and brought the SUV to a rumbling stop. He stared, and not even Buckle dared to break that somber silence.

After a while, he drove closer to the gates, stopped the vehicle, and got out. Buckle limped after him. The air was fresh and a light breeze blew, making the treetops rustle softly.

"Well . . . shit." Scott exhaled, standing at the ruined mouth of the gate and taking in the black wreck of the house. Structural beams, black in the summer sun, rose up only halfway. The rest of the charred woodwork had collapsed on itself, but several pieces of wood lay all over the property, as if sprayed from the house.

Or exploded.

There were a lot of little black forms around the ground as well, scattered all over the place and cooked by the sun, looking like streaks of black leather. Scott stooped to inspect the stains, grimacing when he identified little bones and claws. Scott straightened up and lifted his twelve gauge. He studied the tree line for a moment, then the cars, marveling at the sheer number of rat stains there around the property. Buckle did the same, his face slowly hitching up in distaste.

Scott in the lead, they walked through the gate and approached the house. Every step made Scott's heart break a little more. The place had been devastated by fire. Even the garage was little more than a black stain ringed by an equally charred concrete foundation. He saw what he knew to be the shredded husk of the Beast, the roof of the van blown off, as if it had been caught in a blast of incinerating heat. Another vehicle was beside it, twisted and burnt, and Scott had to think for a moment. Gus must've found a second truck or van. He wouldn't have left his dear old Beast if he could help it. He loved that machine.

Scott walked right up to the front of the house and peered down into what had been the rec room, where he and Gus had sat in drunken stupors and watched horror movies from the '70s and '80s. The area was a murky pit filled with chunks and pieces of debris and covered in dried slivers of tar—an unearthed grave. Scott's shoulders slumped.

"You okay?" Buckle asked.

"Let's go around," Scott finally said, his throat tight, not okay in the least.

The pool was filled with burnt pieces of wood that bobbled idly. The deck appeared as if something had shelled it from above, and Scott figured whatever had destroyed the house had flung fire far enough to ignite it. The furniture Gus had kept out there was also gone. The lawn chairs had burnt down to the metal bones.

He stopped at the edge of the cliff and stared at the expanse of Annapolis, stretched out toward a mountain range like a sleeve of mottled skin. The city was just as black as the house in places, ravaged as if by some great fire.

"Jesus, Jesus," Buckle said, taking it all in.

Scott looked over the edge and spotted the charred bones far below, piled up right at the base of the cliff.

"And Jesus," Buckle muttered.

Scott swallowed and hunkered down. Skulls grinned back up at him, keeping their secrets.

What happened here? Perhaps the rats were here as well and they had somehow made it to the house. Perhaps Gus had burned the house down or accidentally started a fire. It was clear that a small war had happened on the property, and that losses were heavy on both sides. He wondered who the people were at the base of the cliff and if Gus was amongst them. Looking back out over the city, a feeling of despair and loss burned in Scott's chest.

Annapolis was gutted. The house was razed to the ground. And Gus was gone, probably dead.

"Well, Christ," Scott muttered.

"Sorry, man," Buckle offered.

"Yeah."

"You want to stick around?"

Scott thought about it. He gazed at the property, remembering the many times Gus and he had survived the city below and gotten epically wasted. Somehow, no matter how sad he felt, if Gus had indeed died on the side of this rock . . .

He'd probably taken an army with him.

"Nah. Let's . . . let's go on back."

Scott turned around, feeling his throat constrict and his eyes moisten, and quietly made his way back to the waiting SUV. As he passed the black crater of the house, he tried very hard not to look at it. Very hard, but he sneaked a peek anyway. Just as he turned his back on the now-dead sanctuary from an undead world, he heard, in the deep places of his mind, a mountain man's haunting laughter, distant and merry and probably drunk, tinged with a touch of madness.

Even though it was only a memory, Scott smiled feebly all the same.

And was ever so grateful for it.

44

They'd parked the Durango in a garage, along with some other vehicles that were still operational. The day was almost at an end, so they camped out in one of the deserted houses near the water, locked the doors—even though they believed the area was safe from Moe—and went to bed early. In the morning, they'd make the crossing.

Just after dawn, with the sun making the water shine, they got into one of the boats, started up the little outboard motor, and puttered away from shore. Seagulls sang as they glided over the boat, looking for handouts the two men didn't have.

They cut across the dead calm of the sea, approaching Big Tancook and its government-built wharf. Buckle steered, humming a maritime song about privateers. Newfoundlanders, he informed Scott in between verses and without a shred of arrogance, were born on the water and were the best when it came to boating and working the sea. The man from Saint John didn't dispute it. Over the past six months, Buckle and Vick both had grown fond of the young man, and they considered him an integral part of the group. Buckle liked him not because of his skills or his considerable work ethic, but because of his level head. In the new world, a calm head and common sense were gold. He could be withdrawn at times, like now, but given the circumstances, it was understandable. Vick liked the man for other reasons.

The Newfoundlander's arms and shoulders ached, and he knew he'd feel an arthritic burn well into the day and night, but he hummed away as he steered. The little outboard motor puttered away in the morning stillness, pushing the bow of the boat across the sunny turquoise glass of the water. It took a little over an hour to reach the grey shores of the island, and in time, its rocky shape slowly solidified, no longer indistinct on the horizon.

Buckle kept on humming tunes of the sea, filling the silence. Scott hadn't spoken much since Annapolis, and Buckle left the man to mourning his friend. He didn't have the entire story, but he'd heard enough about Gus and how the two men had taken turns saving the other's life. The thought that he might have succumbed to rats was a terrible one, but Scott didn't want to sign off on the man just yet. Perhaps Gus had survived the terrible blaze on his mountain. Maybe he still lived somewhere. And if he did, perhaps their paths would cross once more. In time, the little community might leave the island to live on the mainland again, after the virus that had taken so many lives finally burned itself out.

Looking over his shoulder, Buckle steered the boat to the wharf. There was a forty-foot yacht there, a home in itself, but far too harsh on fuel. The tall masts of sailboats were on the opposite side, as well as three smaller rowboats. Whoever had drawn watch to keep vigil over the deep waters had spotted them already, and a small crowd had gathered on the wharf under a bright sun.

When he caught a glimpse of Scott's profile, Buckle saw that the sadness the bearded man carried on his shoulders seemed to have sloughed off. On a whim, Buckle aimed the boat past the wharf, before cutting the motor and allowing them to drift to shore.

The figures on the wharf followed them in. One smaller figure, carrying a little bit more in the midsection these days, broke into a small run, leaving the others behind.

That made Buckle smile like a privateer. If only he had some rum—Captain Morgan, perhaps.

The salty smell of brine perfumed the air and made it smell good. A rock struck the bottom of their small craft, and Scott grunted a warning. Buckle just kept on humming, until the boat ran aground on a sandy beach.

"Home again, home again, jiggity jig," the Newfoundlander said in a weary voice. He checked the outboard motor and heard a splash. Scott plodded ashore, leaving wet tracks in the sand.

Wearing cargo shorts, a T-shirt, and a thankful smile, Amy met him halfway. They hugged as if they'd been separated for years instead of days. Buckle didn't overly care for public displays of affection, but there was something *right* about seeing those two embrace. He wouldn't pass that thought on to Vick. Buckle glimpsed him walking up the shore, his one arm swinging, a smile on his face. The six other people from the wharf approached the couple from behind.

Buckle decided to take his time hauling the boat ashore. He stole peeks at the pair every now and again and felt his own stony heart soften, if only just a bit.

On the beach, like a picturesque scene for a painter, Scott held Amy for a long time, kissing her forehead and lips. Just before the others joined them, he reached down and placed a careful hand on Amy's belly.

And felt the new life there.

About the Author

Keith C. Blackmore is the author of the Mountain Man, 131 Days, and Breeds series, among other horror, heroic fantasy, and crime novels. He lives on the island of Newfoundland in Canada. Visit his website at.

DISCOVER
STORIES UNBOUND

PodiumAudio.com

Printed in the USA
CPSIA information can be obtained
at www.ICGtesting.com
JSHW082151140824
68134JS00014B/183